They Lived in Devastating Intimacy

in a new development, Sunrise Hills. And they learned that the primitive human passions—sex, ambition, possession, hate and fear—are neither concealed nor tamed by this new kind of packaged community.

Troy[1] and Leola Noon[2] were originally hillbillies, she dreaming of a baby, he coveting his neighbor's wife.

Herman[3] and Betty Kreitzer[4] were a little older, a little steadier, anxious to help.

Jerry[5] and Isbel Flagg[6] were wild ones, for Jerry drank too much and chased other women and Isbel knew it, but not what to do about it.

David[7] and Jean Martin[8] were better educated than the rest, more sophisticated. But Jean was to face a moment of terror and uncontrolled passion and David would be called upon to forgive the unforgivable.

Their powerful and provocative story is told in this modern novel, originally published by Simon and Schuster, Inc., from which 20th Century-Fox made the CinemaScope picture produced by Jerry Wald and starring

1 CAMERON MITCHELL   **5** TONY RANDALL

2 JOANNE WOODWARD   **6** SHEREE NORTH

3 PAT HINGLE   **7** JEFFREY HUNTER

4 BARBARA RUSH   **8** PATRICIA OWENS

NO
DOWN
PAYMENT

BY JOHN McPARTLAND

POCKET BOOKS, INC. • NEW YORK

NO DOWN PAYMENT

Simon and Schuster edition published September, 1957

CARDINAL edition published December, 1957
4th printing .... December, 1957

L

To

Celia Kirschner

and for

Philip Yordan

1

THE TIME was this time, these years; the place was twenty miles or so south of San Francisco along the Bayshore Road. Five thousand homes of redwood, glass, steel and concrete had been built within six months, sold within a few weeks. Five thousand families had moved in and begun to be the new sort of persons, with sun, air and space, comfort and pleasure.

Among the five thousand homes of Sunrise Hills were four set so their patios and *lanais* adjoined: the homes of David and Jean Martin; of Herman and Betty Kreitzer with their two children; of Jerry and Isbel Flagg and their little boy; of Troy and Leola Noon.

This was a barbecue evening with three of the families together in the soft, cool darkness. There was floodlight from big bulbs hidden above the *lanai*, a warm glow from the barbecue gadget.

Jerry Flagg watched Jean Martin as her sandaled feet crossed the little square of flagstones from the open *lanai* window of the house. He tried to search out the body beneath the white cotton shirt, open two buttons down, and the white shorts rolled above her long, tanned thighs. Jerry Flagg's eyes were half-lidded, his lower lip thrusting out as he watched.

"How soon the steaks, David?" she asked as she stood by the three men, peering into the smoke winding upward from the red coals of the hickory under the iron grill of the barbecue.

"Dave doesn't know anything about barbecuing, Jean. I've taken over," said Jerry Flagg. He was a red-haired young man with pale-blue eyes, not so tall as David Martin.

Herman Kreitzer was standing close to the red-gray bricks of the barbecue pit, holding a long fork in his thick fingers.

"Getting awful hard to buy the right kind of charcoal for a real good barbecue," he said, not turning his head.

1

"No surprise," said David. "There's five thousand houses in Sunrise Hills, five thousand barbecue pits all pretty much alike, and every Saturday night most of them are broiling steaks."

"I like the wood smoke in the air," Jean Martin said, turning her head, the fine line of her profile showing. "Old-fashioned, sort of a village in the autumn—"

"They burned cordwood in kitchen stoves and they weren't broiling steaks in those old-fashioned villages. I was raised in one of 'em." Kreitzer used his long fork to turn a steak. "Stew mostly. What I like about this is it ain't like an old-fashioned village. Not at all."

"Ten more minutes? Time for me to kick up another Martini inside?" asked Jean. She spoke with expert use of her face; her lips would round, curly, never quite closed, and her eyes were always bright for the man looking at her.

"No more for Isbel," Jerry Flagg said. "After two she gets a little dingee." He was looking toward the open shirt at the high curve of Jean Martin's breast. He knew she noticed; he wanted her to notice.

"I'll make hers weak." Jean smiled, a smile given out individually to each of the three men, each for a moment. Wife-lover-and-our-team to David, friend-and-I-like-you to Herman Kreitzer, I-know-what-you-want-and-thanks-for-the-interest to Jerry Flagg. Like all of Jean Martin's living it was done with smooth competence.

She turned and walked toward the glass-walled living room of the Martin house beyond the twenty feet of flagstoned patio. David watched her, feeling the pride of possession he had known for four years. Jean was taller than most girls, with black hair worn short in the right year, long in the right year. She handled her legs like a showgirl, and yet there was a reserve, a dignity, even when she was in shorts and a half-opened shirt.

Jerry Flagg watched her buttocks until she was gone beyond the sliding glass door.

"Got a nice even heat now," said Herman. "That's what you need for a real good barbecue. A nice even heat."

2

"This is really wonderful," said David Martin, turning to Kreitzer. "A really good life."

"For you. Not for me," said Jerry Flagg.

"You're doing okay, Jerry."

"Me—I got no complaints that money won't cure." Jerry shook his head a little. "Nothing that money won't get well."

"Even without money—none of us have any stack of money —we're doing well, really well." Martin turned his head so that he could look beyond the green roofs of the houses in Sunrise Hills toward the hills, still golden in the last hour of the day.

"You were just born happy. And lucky. I was just born." Jerry Flagg was smiling. His red hair and blue eyes gave him a Huckleberry Finn look when he twisted his face into a smile. It looked boyish, innocent, mischievous. It was false; he never smiled deeper than his face.

"We were born at the right time. We were all lucky," said David.

"Maybe," Herman said. "When I finished grammar school the farm went broke, the family was on relief in Chicago, my old man was in a ditch for the WPA, and I worked nights to get through Lane Tech." He looked up from the grill. "I got a job at Chicago Tool and I got drafted the next year."

"But you're here now. Doing great."

"Now he's getting fatter than a pig." Jerry Flagg was looking toward the glass wall. "You should have been in Korea like Dave and me. That was a rough go—and those guys weren't any cousins of mine."

"At least we won the war I was in." Herman set his mouth in a square grin, then put his face right back into wood-block seriousness.

"Can't you guys enjoy the day you're living? Today? Today is fine."

Jerry Flagg slapped David on the shoulder. "Sure, if it's so fine, buy that station wagon from me. Jean wants it so bad she goes down to the showroom and nibbles on it."

"I can't afford a station wagon now. Next year, maybe."

This time Herman Kreitzer laughed. "You sure ain't like my customers, Dave. They'd say 'Can't afford a station wagon. Let's buy it now and pay for it next year, maybe.'"

3

"Good thing they do," Jerry Flagg said. "You couldn't sell any of that crud for cash. How's business anyway, Herm?"

Kreitzer shrugged. "Last year they were all buying those electric rotisseries, this year it's electric frying pans and electric knife-sharpeners. Two years ago it was deep-freezes. Always something. I'm selling some color TV sets, too. Five hundred bucks—eighty bucks down."

"I'll talk to you about that station wagon later—" Jerry began but David cut him off.

"How's for some more beer? Or do you want another Martini, Jerry?"

"Martini."

"Beer for me," said Kreitzer. "Those Martinis send guys to the booby hatch."

"Okay. I'll be right back." David turned toward his house.

Like his wife, he was taller than average. He was a quiet man, the kind of man who wasn't noticed at first except as broad-shouldered, slim-bodied and quiet. After a time he would begin to stand out, with people turning to listen to him. Still later he would be the leader, quiet, with a quick natural smile, unconsciously shy.

He knew almost exactly what he wanted from life. Nothing big, nothing dramatic. He wanted to be the kind of man his father and mother respected. He knew the elements of it— courage, kindness, patience, tolerance. Very important things to David Martin. As a boy they had been set up as guides for him, and as best he could he lived by these guides. As for money, success, his future—for these things he believed in work.

David Martin did not think of himself as a good—in the moral sense—man. He did believe that bad—again in the moral sense—was the result of malfunctioning, a poorly made or poorly maintained human being, even more—a person who wanted pleasure rather than contentment.

Lusting after women, drinking in slow self-poisoning, being lazy, being envious of the good fortune of others, risking what he had earned and what was needed in the hope of gaining something not earned and not necessary—all these were stupid actions to Martin.

4

Courage, patience, kindness, tolerance were the signs of a healthy human animal. God to David Martin was beyond human understanding, but the law of God was simple. Work for the rewards of living, live to avoid the penalties of malfunction.

He was a simple man and the possibilities for greatness were before him. At Verdun Laboratories, where he was assistant chief of methods, the top men watched him as tribal chiefs once watched the first years of a young warrior. "Showing a lot of promise. Keep bringing him along and in three or four years he might be important to us." So the research vice-president had written the chief of methods, David Martin's superior.

Verdun Laboratories itself was important, one of the unbelievable growths which began in the war years only fifteen years back. First a shop in the back of an Oakland garage where two young men hand-built high-energy-emission measurement devices. A year later the garage was the guarded warehouse of a block-long sprawl of metal shacks and cinder-block laboratories behind a twelve-foot woven-wire fence.

A thousand men and women were working at Verdun now, more than half of them having at least a B.Sc. degree, more than fifty of them with Ph.D. degrees. It was among these strange people of a new kind of human creative society that David Martin was marked as a man showing promise.

Jerry Flagg and Herman Kreitzer, with the other neighbors and friends of Sunrise Hills who knew the Martins, were aware that David was something unusual, more than merely a nice guy with a fair job. But with them he was at ease, talking of things which interested them, and so they were at ease with him, forgetting or even not realizing that this young man belonged to a different time, a different world, as they belonged to the old times.

Jean Martin knew only that her sure intuition, her near-perfect sense of what was right for her, had responded to this man. This would be an important man, a winner, a success. He did not know it, but she did and was content. Content at least in that area of marriage, the area of the tournament of

5

husbands, where a part of a woman's pride derives from the proved abilities of the man.

Had she been a young woman of the 1920s, she would not have married a David Martin, a scientist. It would not have been the time for scientists, and her sure intuition would have brought her a businessman, whose marks of strength and success would not yet have been apparent to anyone but her.

A century back her intuition might have led her to some thick-muscled young fellow who would have talked of steel, and coking coal, and the new kinds of furnaces being built in the old forge villages of western Pennsylvania.

But this was well past the midpoint of the twentieth century and it was a gift of God that she—as well—loved David with a woman's full passion.

David could not talk much of his work to her or to her friends in Sunrise Hills. They would not be able to understand. This was a difference which produced a break, a deep fracture far below the surfaces of marriage and of companionship with other men. The businessmen of the 20s might have talked a jargon of ventures, split-rights, yields and the rest, but it was money in the end, and money could be understood. Even the young ironmaster of the 1850s could be understood in broad terms: he took red ore, limestone, coal and made iron and steel.

David Martin's work was far different from anything Jean would have understood, or Herman and Jerry Flagg. It was not something he did by himself; he was only an important part of a complex team of men and women, and what they achieved were cavitrons, magnetrons, transistors linked in three-dimensional circuits to guide calculating machines, missiles, manufacturing processes.

Once David had pointed to a new portable radio, barely larger than a box of two decks of cards, which Isbel Flagg had just bought, and said, "This uses transistors something like a design I'm working on."

There had been a little talk about the radio, David's work, and so on, among them as they sat on the redwood chairs of the patio in the cool brightness, but it died out.

"Not exactly like the transistors in this radio," David had

6

said. "The same principles, of course—a crystal of germanium and the electron replacement within the crystal—" But he saw their faces, fixed smiles, the heads cocked like listening birds, and lost, thinking of other things, letting his words drop off the dark edges of their minds.

"It's kind of complicated. Anyhow it's a nice radio, Isbel," he had ended. Only in Jerry Flagg's eyes was there a shadow of resentment. Jerry had felt that Martin was showing off, trying to be impressive, yet even with the shadow in his pale-blue eyes his mouth was twisted into the Huckleberry Finn grin.

David walked into the bright pattern of color and shape which was the Martin living room. Jean was pouring the clear liquid of the Martinis into the stemmed glasses, clouded with thin frost, and talking to Isbel Flagg and Betty Kreitzer.

She looked up and saw David in the rectangle of light against the greens and grays and dull reds of the patio behind him.

"Came in for some beer," he said. "The steaks are almost ready. Jerry wants a Martini."

Betty Kreitzer was looking at him with the complete approval she had for the husband of Jean Martin. It was more than approval, because that would mean she had a choice of approving or disapproving. This was not so. To Betty Kreitzer the young Martins were the ideal couple, and individually the ideal young matron, the ideal man. She saw them this way without the least taint of envy or desire, content entirely in knowing them, being accepted by them, earning self-esteem by her very appreciation of them.

Isbel Flagg glanced at David, looked back at the thin-stemmed cloudy glass. She hated David Martin, hated Jean Martin, hated Betty Kreitzer. There was no one Isbel Flagg knew without hating. If she had seen a man or woman dying in utter screaming pain, helpless and damned, she would hate them for mirroring what might happen to her.

This acid fire of hate she concealed as best she could with quick thin words, with quick thin smiles, and it was revealed beyond her power to conceal by the lizardlike movements of her hands and by the shape of her mouth. To Jean Martin,

7

having Isbel Flagg as a friend was a new experience, her first real view of lives, still young, twisting and deforming. Isbel's hatred was harmless to Jean, as if she were some vicious, poisonous creature too small for its fangs to be dangerous.

Only in one area did Isbel Flagg face Jean Martin as a sorry victor, with a maimed and useless triumph. She had a son, Michael, who was seven. Jean Martin, living in a time when much of the expression of a successful woman was through her children, was as yet barren.

Both Jean and Isbel were aware of the nervous, uncertain movement of the boy's small hands, of the twisting of his thin lips. At night and often in the day he screamed in rage and pain and fear and loneliness.

Herman and Betty Kreitzer had two children—Sandra, who was eight, and Harmon, four. They were much like the children Jean hungered to have, only hers would be more beautiful, stronger, brighter children than Sandra and Harmon.

For Betty Kreitzer there was the secret knowledge where she was supreme and perfect, a mother goddess, fertile-loined and full-breasted in deification of the three aspects of sex: lust, comfort, motherhood. It was so important that she hid this from Jean, from Herman, from Sandra and Harmon, almost from herself.

"I'll pour Jerry's Martini," said Jean. "You can get the beer. I left one of those six-packs of cans on the workshelf so they wouldn't be too cold."

"Don't give Jerry any more Martinis—you know how he gets," Isbel said, reaching for the filled glass on the copper-edged wooden tray.

"Too bad Leola and Troy couldn't come over," said David from the kitchen.

The three women looked at each other, waited for Jean to answer.

Jean was Leola's friend and enemy. She had a woman's kindness for Leola Noon and received, in return, though not wanting it, a girl's eager admiration. To Jean, Leola seemed a blowzy child, and to Leola Mrs. Martin was mature, experienced, wonderful.

The young girl, not really ready to be a wife and married

8

to a man who belonged to another time, another kind of life than that of Sunrise Hills, was careless, eager and awkward.

Betty Kreitzer was gentle with Leola, but her own mother-taught disciplines of the home made her uncomfortable with a girl who had no discipline for her home, no discipline for herself. Most of the time Leola made no effort to dress up; when she did it was a disaster of color and costume jewelry; not bad taste but rather no taste at all. Like Jean, Betty was kind to her neighbor, but it was a kindness of condescension. The good mother, the good wife, being neighborly to the girl who didn't fit into the neighborhood.

Isbel was cruel to Leola; a special cruelty that was only half masked by a thin, oversweet pretense of friendship; the friendship serving to give Isbel the opportunity to say cruel things to Leola with a smile.

Jean liked Leola and hated her. She admitted the hate only to herself because it made no sense. Jean did not hate people; there was no room in her clear, searching mind for hate. There was no need in her ordered life, with each year better than the last, for the usual basic of hate—envy or self-pity. Jean knew that these self-destructive drives were themselves based in the most deadly hate of all—hatred for one's self.

Then why hate a puppy of a girl? Why hate a girl barely out of her teens, married to a hard, bitter man who had no friends and wanted no friends, a man whose dark, fierce eyes held always the flicker of rage?

She liked Leola. Liked Leola as she had liked and befriended the lost girls at college, the homely ones, the timid ones whose shyness was a sheath of pain to them, the stammerers and the nail-biters, the girls whose problems had been pushed so deep within themselves that they were beyond reach. These girls at college had come to Jean for friendship and for help; she had given both with a simple, open graciousness as she now gave these things to Leola Noon.

But within her was a flame of hate for Leola Noon and she did not know why.

She had not pressed the invitation for tonight's barbecue on Leola. It had been done in a woman's way she understood

9

and despised, contemptuous of herself for having done what she thought of as a "female trick."

"Is Troy working tomorrow night?" she had asked Leola. Leola was wearing what Isbel called her uniform—a sweater that needed cleaning, a skirt with stains, bobby sox that showed dirt, scuffed slip-on shoes. "We're having a barbecue," Jean had continued, finding it hard to look into the girl's eyes because she wanted to respond to the childlike friendship and admiration candidly exposed. Wanting to respond, and finding the strange hate flaring up within her.

"He's on the evening shift," Leola had said hopefully, waiting.

"Oh, I'm sorry. We'll try the next time for some evening when you both can come."

It had been a female trick and she despised herself for it. But Jean had a clean, healthy honesty with herself—there was something she had against Leola; something beyond dislike, beyond a gentle contempt for the girl's adolescent sloppiness and formless mind. She was ashamed of herself, and she intended to search out the corners of darkness within herself to find the reasons.

Jean smiled at David. "Troy couldn't come so Leola didn't want to."

"I like her, she's a lot of fun." David walked through the room.

"Like a puppy," said Betty Kreitzer.

"You know what female puppies grow up to be." Isbel Flagg caressed the glass with her lizard hands.

As David went outside Betty leaned toward Isbel. "There's no reason to be mean to her. She just wants to be friendly without knowing quite how."

"She's terribly lonely," said Jean.

"She doesn't fit in with the rest of us," Isbel said.

"None of us knew each other," Jean said. "Now we're neighbors, and we're more than neighbors. We're all the family most of us have out here."

"It is kind of strange," said Betty. "I was always used to knowing everybody in our block back home, and there were

10

cousins, uncles, aunts—and of course my own family, brothers, a sister, Momma—"

"That's the point," said Jean, walking to the glass wall by the patio and turning to look at Betty and Isbel. "You couldn't pick your family back home and your neighbors—well, they're all kinds. But here—in any of these new communities like Sunrise Hills—it's different."

"We're all pretty much the same age. We've all got nice homes."

"Thanks to the GI Bill and no money down," said Betty.

"That isn't it. These are nice homes. They have a touch of elegance, of good living. All of us—most of us—are on our way up. What we do now is important, it's going to determine the rest of our lives."

Screams like those of a hurt animal tore through the quiet.

"Damn! Michael woke up," said Isbel. She stubbed out her cigarette. "Now what do I do with him? You've got the Baker girl with Sandra and Harmon, Betty?"

Betty looked up, her face too open to hide her thoughts. "Yes, but they'll be going to bed soon—"

"Michael can watch television with them for a while. Otherwise he'll be here raising hell."

The screams, inhuman, ululating, ripped loudly. Outside Jerry Flagg was calling for Isbel.

"I'll take him to your place. He'll be quiet if he's watching television with Harmon and Sandra." Isbel Flagg pushed back the glass door, walked angrily across the patio to the gate in the wood-stick wall.

Betty shook her head. "I simply dread having him with Harmon and Sandra. That poor little guy's so mixed up he's like a loaded bomb."

Jean didn't answer. She was thinking of David, of the children she wanted.

2

THE WAXED-PAPER PLATES burned brightly for a minute or
two. David carried the tray of nearly empty cocktail glasses to
the kitchen and came back with a carton to hold the drained
beer cans. Jean put the picnic set of knives and forks in a compartment of the dishwasher and turned on the switch.

David swept off the patio, checked the fireguard in the barbecue pit to make sure there would be no sparks from the em-
bers of the plates or the still-glowing char. Jean had waited
for him in the kitchen and as he came in with the carton of
empty beer cans she switched off the floodlight which had
kept the patio bright after darkness had come over Sunrise
Hills.

"Nice party," said David. "Aren't you cold in those things?"

Jean looked down at her legs. "A little. It was a nice party
—sort of surprising."

David poured a glass of milk. "For you, Jean. Okay?"

She shook her head. "You take it. Milk just before bed puts
pounds on. Pound after pound."

He took a long drink of milk. "You don't have to worry
about pounds."

"That's why I do now—when I don't need to yet."

"What was so surprising about our party?"

Jean smiled. "A lot of things. Herman Kreitzer, of all people, talking about how he felt—really felt—about things. That
man has a lot of insight, a lot of awareness."

David rinsed out the glass. "He's a fine guy. I like him a lot.
What else?"

"Oh, Isbel singing. I've never heard her sing before."

"A low-down voice, a four-o'clock-in-the-morning smoky
night-club voice. It kind of fits Isbel, in a way."

Jean was looking at her kitchen. She found a sensual pleasure in its natural wood, the grain soft under the thin gloss of
wax, the warm-looking red bricks which made a wall for the

built-in broiler, the lemon-yellow enamel on the neatly hanging row of cast-iron utensils.

"You don't like Isbel much, do you, David?"

"She always seems so damned wound-up."

"Is that why you do like Leola? She's so relaxed she's sloppy."

David looked up quickly but Jean went on speaking before he could answer.

"And those stories Jerry told tonight! Wonderful! That one about—but the guests loved it!" Jean laughed a little, then stretched her beautifully tapered arms.

"I always want to remember Jerry's stories so I can tell them at the lab—but they don't come off for me. He's got a way—"

Jean looked over her kitchen for the last time of this night. "Jerry has lots of ways."

"He leches for you," David said it lightly but his voice lost its usual deep confidence on the last word.

She laughed a little and came close to him. "But naturally. Probably Herman does too, only he doesn't let himself know it the way Jerry Flagg does. And the butcher, the baker, and oh—just every man."

"Well, you proud witch."

Her laugh was high and happy. "A woman loves it, David, let's not pretend they don't. But you know what the real pleasure is?"

"What?"

"Don't you know?" She was laughing softly.

He realized the pressure of her fingers, of her other arm around the small of his back, and he grinned, but knowing that his grin was self-conscious, not quite natural.

"Is that the real pleasure?" he asked, partly to get rid of that schoolboy-telling-a-dirty-joke grin.

"Just the beginning, Davie." It was the love name she used for him. "The real pleasure is having a pretty fair body and just one wonderful man."

The start of love play was always a little disturbing to David if Jean began it. His physical response was immediate, but he seemed awkward to himself. It was almost as if he

13

were a very nice boy, and a very bad girl was too bold toward him. He swung her up in his arms, glad of his strength, letting his fingers spread wide against the smooth warm skin of her thigh and the ripe-fruit swell of her bra under the crisp cotton of the shirt.

"That's what I like about you," she whispered into his ear. "A man of action." He felt her tongue try to follow her warm breath into his ear as he carried her from the kitchen through the hall and into the big bedroom, dimly gray and white from a single lamp.

David lowered her to the bed, bent over and kissed her. He had to push himself up to free his neck from her arms and he walked to the wide window, pulling the transverse yellow cloth across it.

"But the neighbors loved it!" Jean said, giggling.

She stretched her arms and raised one knee. He knew she wanted him to take off her clothes. It was a gesture-symbol she liked and sometimes she would fight him a little as he did it.

He stood near the sliding doors of scored plywood which covered the wall closet and unbuttoned his shirt.

"You were something like Herman," she said.

"What?"

Jean laughed. "You leched when I first met you and you didn't even know it."

"But I damn soon found out." David stepped out of his slacks. These were curious times for him. He felt somewhat like two persons, and one of them might not be real, might not be any true part of David Martin.

The person who joked with Jean about love and sex, who could say, "But I damn soon found out," seemed to David like pretense, an act, as if the very nice boy pretended to be tough and experienced with the very bad, bold girl so she wouldn't find him out.

"The first, the last, the only," Jean said, her voice low and strong.

"What was that about Leola Noon this evening, Jean?" He stood, still in shorts, putting his trousers on a hanger when he

14

said it. As the words left him he damned himself for a fool, nor did he know why he had asked the question.

Jean did not answer for many seconds. Her knee went down and she swung herself up from the wide bed. She looked at David, letting her teeth slide over her lower lip, then she spoke. "Leola is sweet and good-natured but I have to tell you this, David. I don't really like her."

She saw the surprise lift his eyebrows slightly and she felt a compulsion to go on, to say more, much more.

"She's too damned female."

"You're pretty damned female yourself, darling." He was smiling, she was not.

"Moist and warm and I think there's always a beginning of a rut smell to her. Every time I see her I almost know about some boy, and the back seat of a car parked near some juke-joint. Maybe she's not like that, but, David, that's how she affects me."

"I'm sorry." His smile was gone and she knew he was disturbed; worse, she knew that she had been wrong. Whatever it was about young Leola Noon it had not been the thing she'd talked about.

"I'm sorry, too, David. I've said it and now I think I'm wrong. You could use an eraser, if you please."

They both smiled.

She stepped out of her shorts, pushing the tight rolls to get them down over her long thighs. He came up to her and she stepped away from him and then let him finish undressing her.

Their love-making was not brief, rather so continuing that it surprised him, but it was different. Different simply in that for once he did not feel a little frightened of her, uncertain of himself in the twisting inward tornado of her demands and her shaking, wide-eyed, gasping fulfillment. He felt completely the master of her, and knew that in feeling so he was deceived.

This was intuitive, a vague chill understanding that this was not complete for her, that it had been pretense which made him feel the illusion of mastery.

She turned to look at him. His fingers were intertwined beneath his head and he was looking upward. Their eyes met and she smiled at him. It was a smile that was strange to him, a little curving of her lips that he had not seen before.

There were no words. She stood up and went to the door of the bathroom, standing for a moment before she put the light on and closed the door behind her.

He thought of the stupid question. Stupid, stupid, stupid. Leola Noon meant nothing—a neighbor, a young girl who seemed maybe a little too eager to have people like her. Pleasant enough, certainly not interesting, even more certainly not important to David Martin and his wife, Jean.

But she had come—almost as if she had been really there, smiling like a laughing child, a little loud, talking a little too fast, in her gay, bright clothes—into this room tonight, into those most important seconds before the complete sharing and fusing that was love for David and his Jean.

He thought for a moment, hearing the soft sounds of the shower, about that "Complete sharing and fusing." Was that right, being fully honest? For Jean, yes. Wild, wanton, laughing, sobbing, and then like a child, content, smiling, eyes closing.

For him? Complete, wonderful, without a fragment of unsatisfied desire, but he felt a hidden inadequacy. For him there was something less than the complete abandonment of self into a fusion beyond selves. He was still a person; in violent love, but still a separate person. He did not give completely, as she did, and yet he did not know what was withheld, or how or why withheld. But he did not give her the fullness of self that she gave him.

Leola Noon. Breaking into his thoughts. Only it wasn't Leola. What he had been asking Jean when he stood by the closet, naked except for his shorts, was a question having nothing to do with any other woman. It was the question of a man in love, asking the woman he had loved for four years what this hidden thing was that she had revealed by casual chance, this cold edge of hatred for another woman.

That was why he had asked, in unconscious searching,

about Leola Noon before he made love to the woman he loved.

David sat up, reached to the low table beside the bed for a cigarette. It had not been stupid, it had come from deeper levels than he realized. Women had innate cruelty; he had talked about that with other young men as far back as his first years in college. Men in Korea would say it in bunker bull sessions like a pronouncement, "Women are a hell of a lot crueler than men." There were always men who disagreed, even seemed shocked at the idea.

He lit the cigarette from a match, watched the paper matchstick flare, die down, curling.

One of the things he respected in Jean, apart from loving her, was the unvarying kindness she had, the open generosity, her gracefulness with people. She was tender with people, as she was to Isbel tonight, to Michael at his besmeared-tantrum worst, or to Herman and Betty in those first days, months back, when they had come, days apart, to the still-damply-new emptiness of the houses in Sunrise Hills on Paso Robles Way.

Kind, generous, tender. Things he respected, and that he searched out before accepting another as a friend.

Jean was always this way.

Then why had she spoken that brief contemptuous sentence about the girl? Leola Noon wasn't that important, merely a younger woman with a scanty background who had not yet learned the right ways of doing things among the kind of people—the special, new-model, moving-upward kind of people—who lived in Sunrise Hills.

He could hear the splash of water in the shower beyond the bathroom door, beyond, farther, its own door of etched glass in a chromium frame.

The special, new-model kind of people in Sunrise Hills. What was so damn special about them anyway?

They were all rather young, for one thing. Thirty was the average, he guessed. Thirty-five was well along.

They didn't have much money in hand. The houses of Sunrise Hills for all of their patios, sliding glass walls, garbage

17

disposals, automatic washers and dryers, and the rest of the fancy gadgets, could be had in possession for a few hundred dollars in cash, and the payments were less than a dark-windowed flat in San Francisco cost in rent.

They had good incomes, even if they didn't have much money in hand. The cars were bright in contrasting colors, there seemed to be a winter-naked sapling forest of television aerials over the flat, sloping roofs of the five thousand homes of Sunrise Hills. Well-dressed, well-fed from deep-freezers, with barbecues, beer and Martinis almost every Saturday or Sunday night. They complained about income taxes, but never knew the price of anything big they bought—only the size of the monthly payments.

They had children. Two, three, more. Most of the homes in Sunrise Hills were three- and four-bedroom places.

They had children. Jean wanted children, and he felt a deep loss in living these best of the fine young-man years without sharing them first with a baby, then a little boy and a baby girl, as he did share them with Jean.

They had children and they were veterans—the men, and often their wives—the strange new world-travelers, cosmopolites of the dependents' housing and the Ginza PX, multilingual familiars of Frankfurt and the Air Force villages of England. Many of these family men of Sunrise Hills had been combat men who knew the ultimates of kill or be killed, the boredom, the fatigue, the fear, the simple naked facts of life and death. They had bedded, carelessly or with love, or both, the women of half the world.

These were the people of Sunrise Hills, and there were ten million more like them from Levittown to Lakewood Village. New, new, new. Like no other people who had ever lived.

The sound of the shower ceased and there was quiet. He saw the bright angle of the opening door widen and she stood there, naked and proud, for an instant before she darkened the room behind her.

She put on pajama tops and bottoms and came to bed.

"About Leola Noon," she said. "You asked, remember?"

"Yes," he said, and waited.

"She's perfectly all right. Fine. But I don't want her as a close friend."

"Why, Jean?"

"I feel sorry for her."

He felt Jean's body slacken, as if she were tired.

3

SUNDAY MORNING on Paso Robles Way in Sunrise Hills began with the screaming of Michael Flagg a few minutes after eight o'clock. He had wet his bed and upon wakening had gone to the bedroom of his parents.

As Jerry Flagg awoke the first sensation was of chill dampness along his left leg. He put his hand on the pajama leg and felt the thin body of his son squeezed between his father and mother.

"God damn!" he yelled, sitting up and throwing the sheet back. Michael woke up and began screaming.

Isbel opened her eyes; another day was upon her.

The screaming boy, almost a hundred feet away in another house, awakened David Martin. Jean was already in the kitchen, the little radio there tuned to KEAR, the music station. Sunday morning breakfast music.

Herman Kreitzer was in his garage. He was wearing a T-shirt, slacks, and standing barefoot, going over the sleek metal top of the Olds sedan with a pipe gadget, both mop and spray, washing off the dust. After breakfast he would begin his Sunday polishing, using a silicone wax.

His children were eating their breakfast in the patio, while Betty kept walking from their redwood table and benches to the electric stove in her kitchen. She had started them with tall plastic glasses of orange juice, mixed from the cans of frozen concentrate. Next had been bright yellow plastic bowls of Wheaties and cut fresh peaches; this was a period in which the box-top premiums of Wheaties—24-inch plastic bows and sets of vacuum-cup tipped arrows—were what the children wanted. Next week it might be another cereal whose television commercials offered some more desirable toy for a box top and a quarter. After the cereal there would be buckwheat cakes and sausages, the sausages from the Kreitzer deep-freeze, and milk. After breakfast Betty would drive the children to the Lutheran Sunday school in Redwood City, several miles from Sunrise Hills.

Michael's screams, reaching a climax of shrillness, broke into a chatter of sobs, still loud enough to be heard by Sandra and Harmon. They looked at each other, giggling a little.

"I bet his daddy's whipping him now," said Harmon, hunching up his shoulder. "Mikey's daddy whips him every Sunday morning. You know why?"

"Because they don't believe in God," said Sandra.

"How do you know? Put, put, put, put. Whee!"

"They don't go to church."

"Daddy doesn't go to church."

"We do. Mama does."

"Daddy doesn't. He'll go to hell when he dies."

"No he won't!" Sandra glared at Harmon, her lips pushing into a pout.

"He'll go to hell and burn up. Hell's hotter than a rocket ship blast. Hell's hotter than anything."

"Daddy will go to heaven."

Betty was at the table, carrying two plates of buckwheat cakes and sausages.

"Mama, Daddy's going to go to hell, isn't he?" Harmon looked up at her, his face serene and confident.

Betty put the plates on the redwood picnic table. "You haven't finished your cereal yet," she said. She didn't want to answer her little boy because she never lied to her children and he had touched deeply into her secret worry. Even her pastor had not found a satisfactory answer for the question, basically the same question Harmon had asked.

As a little girl on the North Side of Chicago, Betty had gone to a Lutheran school and the tenets of the Missouri Synod were as immutable laws of the universe to her as they had been to her parents. In all the Sundays of her life, from the time she was a swaddle of pink on her mother's lap in the square, hard pews of Bethlehem Church until now, she had missed fewer than a dozen Sundays at Lutheran services.

She could drink Martinis and smoke, there had been a time when she and Herman had gone to night clubs every Sat-

21

urday night for dancing, and she was maturely aware of the slight pleasure she found in wearing shorts as she shopped on a very warm day, with the men glancing at her nice legs; but these deviations from the truly good Lutheran life did not bother her.

"Times change," she thought, remembering her family: father, mother, two sisters and a brother around the kitchen table of the flat on Augustana Street in Chicago, drinking beer and eating liverwurst sandwiches. Those things didn't matter too much—drinking a little, dancing, wearing shorts —but there were things that did matter.

There was a word her pastor used about people like Herman—"the unchurched." People who had drifted away from the House of God.

If she thought about it she became confused. Men didn't come better than Herman: strong, kind, a good worker and a good father. Yet he had lost interest in the church, though his parents had been as good Lutherans as her own.

Hell? It was hard to believe in real hell, with fire and endless pain, but there was a life after death. She was sure of that as she was of today. In that life there would be rewards for those who had lived by faith, so there must be punishment for those who had not. Punishment for the unchurched, the lost, wayward ones. For Herman.

And he was a good man. She felt confused.

"Finish your cereal before your wheatcakes get cold," she said.

In the garage Herman Kreitzer was wiping the smooth metal of the car. An off-white with a brilliant blue, good colors. He felt that it was kind of crazy, but in a way he was in love with this car. Almost the kind of love he had for Betty. It was beautiful. He found a pleasure, sensual and emotional, in bathing his car. He remembered—like on the honeymoon when they had gone to Tahoe. Laughing together in the shower of the little motel room as he and Betty had washed each other, letting their fingers press into the smooth firmness of their young bodies.

Not so long ago. He felt a small shock of shame at himself that he had compared washing his car to those first days and nights of honeymoon in the motel on the road above Lake Tahoe. He put the specially-impregnated flannel wiping cloth away and walked out of the garage, going around his house to the patio.

"You're going to take us to the zoo today! You promised!" Harmon and Sandra were shouting almost the same words because the thought was complete and visual for both of them: Daddy, the car, the color and sound and smell of Fleischhacker Zoo in San Francisco, crackerjack and peanuts, the eyes of animals—bears, tigers, elephants—looking out at them, the sense of the small tyranny children can enjoy over the responsible giants who are their parents.

Herman laughed. "Sure, sure. After you come back from church. We'll take hot dogs and stuff along. Okay?"

His children were loud now in their excitement and he liked the sound of their voices. Better than that poor Mikey Flagg kid, the difference between Isbel and Betty, the difference between himself and Jerry Flagg.

Funny thing about Sunrise Hills—or Rancho Rinconada or Fairview Terraces or any of the scores of other developments that had crawled southward from San Francisco across the flatlands and hills along the Bayshore Freeway toward San Jose—you had neighbors, more than neighbors, friends that chance picked out for you. More than friends, something like a family.

In his case he hadn't much to say about it. Maybe they could have picked a house on Paraiso Way rather than Paso Robles Way, or they could have waited another few months before buying, but that was about all the choice he had.

He could see it like a series of photographs. Eight months ago, Betty and he and the kids in the rented house on Nineteenth Street. Not enough yard and the rooms were kind of small. He was still driving the '53 Chevvie and parking it on the street at night. One bath, and Betty didn't like the kitchen.

"Herman—have you read anything about that Sunrise Hills development? Down off the Bayshore?" the area supervisor had asked him one morning. It was about eight months

23

ago, more or less, and he sure hadn't realized how much his life would change. A lucky morning.

"Not particularly," he had said. Assistant manager of the appliance department of the Stonestown store; not a bad job and he'd made a good record. The area supervisor liked him; sometimes they had lunch together.

"Several thousand houses and a shopping center. We're putting a branch in the shopping center—the whole appliance line, tires, car accessories. We're figuring you for manager, Herm."

That was the way it had been.

"Of course, Herm, there are some other details. We like our managers to take part in civic activities—join Kiwanis or Lions, maybe even Rotary. You'd just about have to live in Sunrise Hills, buy a place."

Herman had looked the area supervisor straight in the eyes. "We haven't saved much money. Of course the car is paid for, and I've got quite a bit of insurance—"

"This Sunrise Hills thing is pretty good," the area supervisor had said. "I'm familiar with the specs and plans and so on. Not bad houses, all of them with two baths, flagstone patio, automatic garbage disposal—"

"How much down?"

"On a GI-FHA deal, nothing. Closing costs, maybe a couple hundred. Payments would run less than a hundred a month on a thirty-year deal."

"I'm paying more rent than that now."

"Why don't you run down there this weekend, Herm. Then I'll see you Monday on the manager thing."

On a Sunday morning he had taken Betty and the kids down U.S. 101 Bypass, the Bayshore Freeway, to the turnoff for Sunrise Hills. By that afternoon they'd closed the deal for a three-bedroom, two-bath house on Paso Robles Way, part of a little group of four houses, part of a larger group called Sunrise Hills West, part of the vast group of five thousand new houses which was the development of Sunrise Hills and which represented more than fifty million dollars of bank and insurance company money, part of the fifty thousand and

24

more of development homes which had exploded outward from San Francisco.

A month after moving in he had traded the Chevvie as down payment for the new Olds; the new furniture was a separate deal through the store.

Seventy-five hundred a year, base salary. Bonuses on his sales gross, participation in the profit-sharing and retirement fund of the company, plenty of life insurance, the company health plan which covered hospital and doctor bills for the whole family, some money in the joint checking account, nearly two thousand dollars worth of Series E bonds. Security.

Security and a damned fine life. A long way from the farmhouse in Wisconsin where his old man had gone broke, taking the family to Chicago and the relief rolls, the WPA. Cold water, beans or macaroni, cockroaches and rats. Dirty, dark, sour. Now it was security and a damned fine life and he was still a young man with a young wife and two fine kids.

"Herman, why don't you come to church with us today?"

Sandra and Harmon bobbed their heads up to look at him. His answer would be important to them. Every Sunday they went to the Lutheran school in the little building adjoining the Redwood City Church. Every morning they began the day with the prayers Betty had taught them, they said grace for each meal, and they ended the day with their going-to-sleep prayers. He thought it was a fine thing for kids, the right way to bring them up.

But not for him. Somewhere along the line he'd lost it and he wasn't quite sure how or why, only too honest with himself to sit in the pews of the church, singing the old hymns from the Lutheran Hymnal, listening to the earnest young man who was pastor give his sermon. He couldn't do it any more.

The church people meant well. He respected them for believing the things they did. He never had argued with Betty about religion or going to church. Funny, during the army years he'd believed in all of it, and he had carried his Bible from the induction center to basic, from the POE to

25

the long-ago battles of the European Theater of Operations—the ETO, and how much these letters had meant once, so far away in time.

Maybe it was because he was interested in science. First it had been *Popular Mechanics,* magazines like that. Then books, and a subscription to *Scientific American.* A lot of it was over his head, but he had been a kind of explorer, walking outward to the planets, to the yellow-white star which was the sun, to the stars beyond, the galaxies, the super-galaxies.

"A billion stars, a lot of them like our sun in our galaxy, a billion galaxies like our Milky Way—and what is beyond them?" He'd say things like that aloud to himself sometimes, feeling an awe, a reverence, much like that which he had felt the first time his parents had taken him to the grown people's church back in the Wisconsin town.

He had walked, an explorer, backward in time, looking at the pictures of fossil reptiles, huge and strange, at the diagrams of the hundreds of millions of years, at the maps of the spreading glaciers of the ice ages. With paper and pencil one night he had figured out what man's history represented in the long tapestry of the history of the planet. Two billion years, they said, was the age of the earth. Life on the earth for a billion years; some kind of manlike animal for maybe a million years, our kind of human being for a hundred thousand years, human history for five thousand years, less than one-thousandth part even for the ape-beasts that would some day change into man.

God. Certainly a God, but the understanding of that inconceivable God could not come from an earnest young man in a small church in Redwood City. And still, as he looked at Betty, at his children waiting for his answer, he felt that he had lost something and that he had not found something better to replace that which was lost.

"No," he said. "Not this Sunday. I want to finish waxing the car before you take it, and then I'll read the *Chronicle* until you get back."

Harmon bent his head to whisper in Sandra's ear. He was giggling and after she listened, she punched her brother.

"He will not!" she said.

Betty began taking the breakfast dishes into the kitchen. The sun had cut through the morning fog, and the morning was bright, beautiful.

4

HERMAN WAVED to Troy Noon across the wood-stick fence. "Hi, Troy!"

Troy waited a moment before turning his head. His movements were always deliberate, slow until he snapped into violence. He was not a man who smiled when he said hello and he did not like to shake hands with strangers.

"Morning, Herman," he said, his voice carrying well without being loud. Troy Noon was tall and he carried himself with top-sergeant smartness, his broad, square shoulders back, his body lean and straight. He liked to wear shirts and trousers cut tight to the supple muscles of his flat belly and hard buttocks, the way he'd worn his uniform when he had been a soldier.

He had been a soldier all the way. At fifteen, tall then and with man-hard muscles, he had hitchhiked from his home in the western Tennessee hills to Memphis where he'd enlisted, claiming he was eighteen. That had been in 1940, the early months of 1940.

Staff-Sergeant Noon won a battlefield commission in New Guinea in the bad time of the Pacific War, when the Japs had everything and the 32nd had nothing but sick men and hot guns on the steamy slopes of the Owen Stanley mountains.

Captain Noon won his Silver Star, a cluster for the Star. "One goddamned fine fighting man," said the division commander of Noon.

After the fighting was over he didn't win anything.

The worst day in his life had been the day he put on civilian clothes in 1946. They didn't look right on him, he didn't feel a real man in these clothes. Men didn't snap to as he passed them, and the gray-faced men of the streets of San Francisco couldn't tell by glancing at him, as soldiers could when he had been in uniform, what manner of man

28

he was. An infantry company commander, and one goddamned fine fighting man.

He had asked for active duty two days after the Korean
War began and the medics found the ulcer, the high blood
pressure.

He hadn't won a single fight since he'd taken off his uniform in 1946. Yes, he'd won something—Leola, and she was
all that he had, so completely important to him that he could
not let her know it, could not let her guess that without her
he was dead, the dead shell of a man around an empty core.

"What's doin', Troy?" Herman said, walking toward the
wood-stick fence.

"Not much."

Herman smiled. He liked the looks of this Troy Noon. The
man looked like a man, might even have some Indian blood in
him the way his face was, with the high cheekbones, the
sharp nose and flat, hard planes of bone and muscle.

"Sure a beautiful morning. You ever go fishing, Troy?"

Noon waited. He nodded after a second or so. "When I was
a kid I did a lot of fishing. Hunting, too."

"I'd like to go up in the Sierras sometime," said Herman.
"Supposed to be real good fishing."

Troy Noon was silent, then he shook his head. "Too damn
crowded." He walked back to his house and Herman turned
away. Herman felt a patience for the tall, bitter-eyed man.
He had seen good NCOs, good company officers in the long-
ago battles, and he knew the breed. When he thought of
his neighbor, Troy Noon, he did not think of the phrase,
but of the idea, "combat man."

As he stood by the glass wall of his house Troy Noon
waited before sliding the door open. He was thinking of fishing. Going fishing with Jeff and Chadwick in the cool, silent,
west Tennessee hills. Nobody talking much; getting into
hot-headed fights right soon after there was much talking.

That had been good. The Sierras wouldn't be any good.
Too many city people, all fancied up, with city-soft muscles
and chattering city talk.

It would be just like Sunrise Hills. Nothing real about it.
This house wasn't real, a make-believe shack all fancied up

with glass and gadgets, not a solid timber in it. It wouldn't last, it would fall down, warped and termite-ravaged. Cheap pretense. A man didn't have to work to have a house like this. Nothing down, anybody could have a fancied-up house in Sunrise Hills. Having one didn't mean anything; you couldn't hold up your head in pride over having a house in Sunrise Hills.

He was Troy Noon and what was he? Kids had grown into men since he had been Captain Troy Noon of Able Company. A dozen years of kicking around. One bad marriage, one good one.

Hildy. Met her Monday, married her Friday. A bitch, a tramp, a floozy. He'd almost killed her. He could still hear Hildy as he hit her in the face, slammed her against a wall, hit her again. The police had to break in the door and pull him from her. Another minute or two and they'd have broken into the apartment to find him standing over a dead woman.

She'd been a tramp and a bitch and she'd taken what money he'd saved in five years of service. All of it.

Now there was Leola and she was all that life had for him. Everything. Mother and wife, daughter and wife.

He pushed open the door.

"Hi, honey," she said, turning from the stove toward him, smiling.

"I wish you'd clean up this damn kitchen," said Troy Noon. "Place is a filthy mess."

"I'm sorry, honey. It just seems to get away from me every time I cook a meal."

He looked at his wife. Young and pretty and fresh, like a happy child. His dark eyes seemed hot and fierce. "I'm sick of having the place a mess," he said and walked past the brick fireplace-and-barbecue into the cluttered living room.

The Sunday *Chronicle* was scattered over the big chair, the low table, and the floor. Troy looked over the room, stretched his arms, pushed out his chest and held his breath until the beat of his heart was a violent hammer. He did this often, usually without thinking about it; when he found himself holding his breath he thought of it as a test, something a man could do to show himself that he was still young, still strong, still able.

"What time you goin' to the station, honey?" Leola was standing in the kitchen way, holding a bowl from the Mixmaster. The batter was splashed over the side, dripping to the floor.

"Watch that damn batter—it's all over the floor." He walked toward her, wishing there was some way he could discipline her, punish her. Got to keep the place policed up, apple-pie order, smart. You can always tell a smart, on-the-ball outfit with one look. Clean, policed-up.

A home is the same way.

Leola was looking down, surprised to see the little yellow mountainous island of batter on the floor.

"I'm sorry, honey. I'll clean it up right away. Just wanted to know when you were goin' to the station."

"Early. Right away." He was looking down at her. It would seem silly to take her in his arms now; there were times for loving, other times when it was silly nonsense no matter if you felt like doing it.

A blaze of rage stormed up suddenly behind his eyes. Besides—besides it was a trick she'd been trying to get away with for months now. Get him excited and loving her, so hot he'd forget everything else, too eager to have her in the fierce excitement so that he would not stop, go to the bathroom and make everything safe.

She tried it, knowing what she was doing, he thought. A cheap, low trick. Trying to have a baby. She didn't talk much about it these days, but he knew the wanting was inside her all the time.

She wanted to have a baby. For a moment, with a kind of shame, he remembered the first time. He was rolling the condom on and she saw him. Her face had changed.

"You don't need nothin' like that, Troy honey," she had said. "We're married. We can have all the babies we want—"

"I don't want any," he had said.

Later he tried to explain to her. These were not times for children. No times for men to weaken themselves with

31

responsibilities of children. War. Maybe a war that would last twenty years, the cities burned, the children dead.

"Nobody else feels like that, Troy. Children never had as good a chance as they have now, honey. You're doing fine, makin' good money—"

He hated her, almost blindly, when she talked like that. All she wanted was a big doll that would smile at her and make noises. He could see it—Leola and her baby. She'd break them buying things for it, fancy stuff, and yet it would always have a snotty nose and a dirty behind.

She had her duties right now, without bothering with any kids. Keeping the house in good order, things where they belonged and everything clean. Taking care of him.

Yet he loved her as he had never loved anyone before in his life. *Love* had been a word like *soul* to him before Leola, some word people used that didn't have any real meaning.

Hildy, she'd just been a woman. You married one, set up a house, and you both had your duties, your responsibilities. The man got loving out of it, and that was better than catting around. Saying "I love you" to the woman was like being polite, a friendly gesture of respect.

Hildy had shamed him. People probably laughed at him.

Leola had brought him understanding of what the word *love* meant. It was a real thing; when you were awake at night it was with you in the darkness, and even in the sunlight on the pavement of the station, with a car in front of you and you talking to the driver about the weather or a grease job, suddenly you would think of Leola and know about love.

"Nothin' wrong at the station, is there, Troy?" she asked, looking up at him. The batter was still dripping on the floor.

"I don't know. That's why I'm going early today. I want to see if my men are on the ball when I'm not there."

"Okay, honey. I'll have everything ready right away."

His men at the station. They were a pretty good outfit at that. They'd have to be a pretty good outfit to stay with him. He went to the sliding door of the front closet and opened it. Mahogany veneer; looking like something that it wasn't.

32

Paper-thin mahogany pressed down on some kind of plastic glue on cheap wood.

The real-estate salesman, when they were making the deal on the place, told him that it was better than solid mahogany. Just as pretty, would gloss up under a coat of wax, wouldn't warp or crack like solid wood might because it was a plywood veneer. Actually stronger than solid wood.

He'd just looked at the man. How in hell could an imitation be better than the real thing? It had made him so damn angry and disgusted that he didn't want to take the house. But Leola had wanted it so bad he could see her eyes getting wet and she could have anything in the world she wanted. Except a baby.

Not in this kind of a world with a war staring them in the face. A man couldn't have responsibilities, not outside his duty.

Troy Noon took his uniform jacket and cap from the closet. The jacket was starched and white, cut like the Ike jackets that had come out at the end of the war. The cap was cut like any garrison cap, and it was white, too.

He had a rule that none of the men from the station, including himself, could be there, even off duty, except wearing the jacket and cap.

Where he'd worn the captain's bars on the front of his old suntan khaki garrison cap there was the company trademark. He didn't love the company, but he had plenty of respect for it. Big outfit, well run and smart. He had been with them for three years now, starting as a grease-monkey. He'd worked hard and taken his share of hard times from customers, station managers, supervisors, but mostly they liked him. Three years from grease-monkey to managing a station that pumped thirty thousand gallons of gas a month.

What was the right phrase? "Command decision" like in the movie about the air corps? He'd reached that point. He had to make a command decision.

He had told his supervisor last week that he'd applied for the new job. The supervisor had come right back with an offer. A promotion in the company, moving up from managing

33

a station to a brains job, assistant supervisor in District 473 with forty-two stations under him.

Troy thought of the letter he had sent to the city manager's office. "Dear Sir:" He'd tried about fifteen different starts before he was satisfied with "This is a formal application for the new post of Chief of Police of Sunrise Hills. I am a former Army officer and served—"

Chief of Police was a big title for the job. The way it was going to be set up, now that Sunrise Hills had voted for incorporation as a city of the sixth class, was for an independent police department consisting of chief, an assistant chief, and three patrolmen. Sunrise Hills would buy two patrol cars and they planned to use the California Highway Patrol and the Redwood City police radio transmitters for their calls. It could be a hell of a smart little outfit. He'd like it.

It would be good wearing a uniform again that meant something, that had authority behind it. People respected a Chief of Police, and there'd be plenty of work to do. Trouble; there was lots of trouble behind these civilian faces in Sunrise Hills. People trying to get away with things, fooling around with women, drinking, sex perverts. Always a chance of some punks with guns coming in to knock over the supermarket or the drive-in theater boxoffice. There'd be plenty of work to do.

And he'd learn a lot. It would be just like the Army, especially in the early days when he was learning the new things, the new weapons, the rules. Working with the FBI, going to FBI school. Going up to San Francisco on cases. The police up there would show a lot of respect to a Chief of Police, even from a small town.

That was one thing about wearing a uniform that a civilian never could understand. Men in uniforms could read each other, as if they were wearing their personal history. The police, the state patrolmen, the other law officers would glance at his uniform, the way soldiers do, noticing the words on the gold badge, checking the uniform for the way it fitted, its condition, knowing the kind of man he was from his uniform.

34

Only there wouldn't be much money in the job. A little under five hundred dollars a month. The assistant district supervisor job would pay over six hundred.

It was a command decision on company level. He had to figure the other factors, the tough ones. Like figuring where the Japs had their land mines, their snipers, where they were zeroed in with their damn mortars. The rough side of the picture where you had to assume you'd take a beating.

Both jobs had too damn much paper work. Hell, he'd practically learned to read and write when he was taking his basic training; he didn't have much schooling. Most of the paper work was silly. You didn't run a police force with paper any more than you ran an infantry company with paper; you didn't pump gas, change oil, and grease a car properly with paper.

Back in Able Company he'd had some damn good clerks. He could almost see old skinny Ballinger hunched over the field desk, banging on his typewriter, keeping the pay records, the morning report and all the rest of the damned paper work.

Good exec officers, too. They'd taken care of that end of it and let him handle the man's work, the stuff that only a man could do by understanding men, by command, by leadership. Paper never made a leader.

Paper had probably ruined a lot of good leaders. Tangled them up and ruined them.

Troy Noon put the white jacket and white cap on the hanger, ready to wear as soon as he finished breakfast. He walked back to the kitchen, noticing that the splatters of batter were still on the floor.

5

MICHAEL WAS STILL screaming and Isbel was trying the only two things she knew.

"Please, Mikey boy," she said, kneeling in front of him. He was on the couch, twisting, sitting up and throwing himself back. His face was white, flushing into purple as he held his breath between screams.

"Please, Mikey, please. Mama will get you some orange juice. You want orange juice? Sweet and cold?"

The boy held his breath, his thin body rigid, legs stiff and straight. He flung his arms out and screamed.

"I'll get you ice cream. Please stop yelling, Mikey, please, please. I'll get you strawberry ice cream and I'll put fudge syrup on it. You come with Mama to the freezer and I'll get the ice cream out and I'll open a can of fudge syrup. Please, Mikey, please. Be a nice boy."

He jerked his body, twisting away from her.

"All right, you goddamned little monster." She slapped his head, and as he tried to cover himself with his hands she pulled them away and slapped him again.

"I'll call the police and have you put in jail," she shouted. "The police will come and grab you and put you in jail and I'll never have to see you again!"

Jerry Flagg opened the bathroom door and came into the living room. "Goddamn! Can't you do anything with the little bastard? Stick something in his mouth, gag the little son-of-a-bitch, will you?"

Isbel turned, pushed herself up from the couch.

"Just because you're all hung-over is no excuse for talking like that. Michael's got a bad pain in his stomach and if you were a real father you'd be calling the doctor instead of cursing at him and calling his mother a bitch!"

"I didn't mean you. Besides you've got just as bad a hang-

36

over as I do. You drank enough Martinis last night to float a cattle boat."

"But I didn't come back here and sit in a chair soaking up liquor all by myself like you did."

Michael tried to regain their attention. He sat up on the couch and began to bang his head against the wall. Jerry reached out and pulled him away. The boy pounded his fists against his father's head and Jerry slapped him.

"I don't have enough worries without this kid yelling night and day." He held the boy's hands.

Isbel's face changed; the hard mouth softened and the tension lines were gone. Even her eyes lost the glitter which made them seem almost those of an intent, watching, predatory animal.

"I know, darling," she said. "It's terribly hard for you." She put her hands on the boy, lifting him away from his father. Michael stopped screaming and began to sob against his mother's small breasts.

"God, when you want to you can handle him perfectly," said Jerry.

"He knows we love him. Your mama and daddy love you, Mikey. You're the most wonderful boy in the whole world."

Jerry Flagg went to the chair near the patio window-wall and sat down. "I'll bet he woke up the whole neighborhood."

"Your mother and daddy love you, Mikey. You can wake up the whole city if you want to—"

"I felt like killing him when he started this morning."

"Mama will take you into the kitchen and we'll have ice cream, Mikey."

"Not for breakfast. Don't give that damned kid ice cream for breakfast. No wonder he's all nerves, giving a kid ice cream for breakfast."

Isbel put Michael on the floor and he stood close to her, watching his father.

"Darling, this is a perfectly horrible way for a nice family to start Sunday. We'll just pretend that none of it happened. Our Mikey didn't cry and Daddy didn't get angry, and we all love each other."

She went to Jerry, bent over and kissed him. Her small

mouth opened wide briefly and then closed with the last of the kiss almost like a child's kiss.

"Now you kiss Michael, Daddy, and we'll all be happy."

The boy's face was still pale, the eyes wet and swollen. He stood stiffly in front of his father.

"I'll get a gun and shoot you dead," he said. "I'll blow your head into pieces."

Jerry Flagg looked into his son's eyes and felt a deep unease. This was hate. Somehow this boy hated him.

He reached out and tried to take Michael's hand; the boy pulled it away. "Son—let's be friends, huh? Let's shake like men."

"Shake hands with Daddy, Michael." Isbel guided her boy's hand to his father's.

"That's a lot better." Jerry smiled at the boy.

"That was a big fake," said Michael. "You're a big fake."

"Get that little son-of-a-bitch out of here!" Jerry stood up. He wanted to hit the boy. Hit him until the boy screamed in real pain.

Isbel was on her knees beside Michael. "That wasn't nice, Mikey. You have a wonderful, handsome daddy."

"I hate him."

"You love him. All little boys are supposed to love their daddies. If they don't something terrible happens to them."

"What?"

"Something real terrible. You love your daddy, don't you?"

"What happens?"

"They turn into little girls. Do you want to turn into a little girl?"

"No. That isn't so terrible. What happens to little girls that don't love their daddies?"

Michael stood straight, his thin face serious and intent. He knew that his mother and father would do their best to confuse him. They told him never to lie to them and he knew they lied almost all the time to him. Maybe his mother liked him but he didn't think his father did. What worried him most was that he didn't think his father liked his mother, either. Sometimes he wished his father would die or go

38

away, but when his father was angry with his mother sometimes he said he would go away and then Michael would lie awake, tense with fear.

He was afraid to go to school, he was afraid when his father came home in the evening, and he was afraid in the dark.

Jerry Flagg looked at his boy. Something was going wrong with the kid, but he didn't know what it was. He had plenty of good food, a nice house, a good place to play, and plenty of toys. He could watch the kid's programs on television, and there was a whole slew of kids to play with in the block. Sunrise Hills was a damn fine place for a kid.

It wasn't that he didn't get attention. Isbel spent plenty of time with the kid. Maybe he ought to have a brother or sister, but Isbel couldn't do it, not for a while, if ever. Two damn miscarriages in the last three years.

"Go on, have your ice cream, Mikey. Then you can go out and play with the Kreitzer kids."

Michael walked away holding his mother's hand.

Jerry picked up the Sunday *Examiner* from the grass in front of the house. Isbel would make him a cup of coffee and he'd read the paper. Then he'd go back to bed and sleep off this damn hang-over.

If he could get back to sleep.

Probably he'd lie awake in bed and worry.

He felt like an acrobat high in the air hanging on to a trapeze bar with his teeth, his hands outstretched to catch the other bar, the one that was swinging. If he could get his hands on that one everything would be okay. Sometimes his fingers barely touched it, but that was all. He kept hanging by his teeth.

That was a hell of a way to feel. He'd been feeling that way for years. A couple of times he'd slipped, too, and fallen all the way down. He couldn't afford to fall any more. Now was the time to make the big money, to get up in the big-wheel class.

If only something didn't go wrong every time. Now he was stuck with a lousy dealer and he was sliding downhill. He'd have to make a change and fast. Get a sales manager's job, or at least assistant, with some hot GM dealer. No use bucking them. They were the big outfit and they were taking over. The independents were dead. Ford, maybe. He could do okay with a fast-moving Mercury dealer, maybe.

But he was stuck with an independent and it was like a weight around his neck. His customers, the names in the card file that was his farm, that he cultivated and harvested each year, even the good guys he'd sold three, four cars to, were buying Buicks or some other goddamned GM car.

In his mind, vaguely, he saw it as a gigantic squeeze. A whole bunch of guys were in a big vise and the vise was squeezing tight, squeezing the little guys. They were pushing back and yelling and pushing at the closing vise but you knew they weren't going to make it.

He was one of those guys unless he could find a hell of a good deal with some high-riding, free-swinging GM dealer.

Only there were a hell of a lot of good men with the independents who were getting frantic and panicky and trying to climb aboard GM or Ford or even Chrysler. Good men with better card files of customers than he had.

Meanwhile it was the old ratrace. Lie to them, take a beating on a new-car sale hoping you could make it up by giving some guy a good screwing on the used car trade-in. Cutting deals so damn thin you could see right through your commission check.

He was still getting by. Car salesmen had a union and a contract with the dealers. He was sure of getting-by money as long as the dealer could still get by himself.

But the big goddamn vise was still squeezing down, and the independents were going, one by one, pushing back with all the little strength they had and yelling that their cars were better, safer, cheaper, stronger, nicer and all the rest of that crap—and it might be true, too—but the vise kept coming down and they were going broke.

Get in with a hot GM dealer and sit on top of the vise, doing some of the squeezing yourself, before it was too late.

Well, he'd been trying. Pretty soon he'd make a connection. Catch that swinging bar, not hang by his teeth any more.

He'd have his coffee, read the *Examiner* and then he'd go back to bed and think about Jean Martin.

Jean Martin. Those legs, those long, strong, lovely, squeezing legs. God, he was going to have to make his play for her pretty damn soon or he'd blow his cork some night like last night when he was half-gassed and he'd probably grab her right in front of Isbel and Dave and everybody.

She'd look at him, sometimes, in that certain way. Hell, he knew enough about broads, he'd had enough broads to know about them. He knew that look.

That look said, "How'd you like to try something really fine, man? You got the nerve to try? I think I might go—if you make a real strong smart try."

Jean Martin with the long, strong, slim, beautiful legs gave him that kind of a look.

Isbel had told him that Jean wanted a baby and that no matter how much she and David tried they didn't have any luck.

By God, she'd have some luck with him.

And he'd get a connection with a live GM dealer. In a couple of years maybe he could swing a franchise of his own, move up in class, buy some larger house than this, send Michael to a good military school.

That would make a man of him.

"Isbel, coffee ready yet?" he called.

6

JEAN SLIPPED OUT of bed and glanced at David. It was the first look of the new day, the first chance to resolve the meanings of the night.

Both of them knew that the night had been a point of change. It was as if they had walked together for a long time, each content with their direction together. Their choice at each intersection or branch had been simple: which is the best direction for us? Several years in which they had walked together and their choices of direction had been easy.

Each day is full of small choices. The kind of food for dinner, the tie which looks best with a pale yellow shirt, the way the easy evening hours would be spent. Larger choices with the factors searched out and evaluated over weeks: the kind and model of car to buy, the colors of the car; whether to buy a house, and where. The style of furniture, and whether David should buy a really good jacket with slacks, or another suit.

There were decisions to be made with even deeper implications than the question of the house and the selection of Sunrise Hills.

Jean talking through the smoke of her cigarette one night and suggesting that they face the problem together.

"It might be some tiny little thing, David," she had said. "Maybe a change in our diet, more vitamin E, or soy oil or something. Maybe it's me—I've fouled up this business with the chart and the thermometer and the rest of it. But let's get some professional advice about it. What do you think of my making appointments for both of us this week?"

They had walked together through these first years and had made their decisions together. Last night had been a point of change.

The act of love last night had been an act of cold anger, an act of rebuke. Seconds after David Martin awakened he had remembered that, the memory coming in a heaviness of morning sorrow. Morning sorrow was not new to him but it was strange; his life had not been one in which remorse and regret were waiting for him each morning. A few times he had felt the heaviness, but most of the mornings of his life had been fine with a healthy welcome to the new day.

He looked up at Jean and she looked away. She walked to the kitchen and began the morning coffee. Weekdays the automatic radio clock awakened them and turned on the electric coffee maker at the same time; it was pleasant to have the first cup while still sleepy and with the sound of music. On Sunday mornings the routine they had chosen together was different. Jean would open the slim, frosted cans of orange juice, make thin toasts of rye bread, sometimes there would be a soft cheese on the toast, sometimes a special jam she would find in an imported foods store in Burlingame.

Sunday mornings were a particular kind of pleasure for them, a lazy enjoyment of being young, of living in a spacious house, of having love.

David tried to find the source of the wrongness in last night. There did not seem to be any real source; the barbecue had been the simple kind of fun it was intended to be, and when they were alone Jean had come to him with the teasing, soul-deep serious sex invitation he knew so well. Knew so well was like the bright flowers around an entrance to a cave whose entrance swelled almost at once into a vast nether-world of darkness alive with jungle animals, strange scents, and the deep warm breathing of a great mother. He knew that much of the life of his woman was in this nether-world, revealed only by the bright, teasing, intent invitation.

But last night there had been nothing. He had responded to the familiar invitation and had found nothing.

Because he had mentioned that girl's name at the wrong time? It wasn't that important, the girl was only a neighbor, and then he remembered his night thoughts of Jean and himself. The place of importance had nothing to do with Leola

43

Noon, but with the areas of self which both he and his wife had not explored together.

It was—he thought, trying to find something like a dream, a little like a chart, that would have meaning and be un-derstandable—as if Jean and David together were a vast continent, unexplored and wild, with a fringe of civilization along one coast. Something like North America had been in colonial times.

In that fringe of civilization on the continent of their lives was where they knew each other. But beyond it was the vastness of the unknown lands, some rich, some barren, with their own places of bright sunlight and of darkness, with forests, mountains, tremendous rivers, small brooks.

Each of them had some secret knowledge of the wild continent; each of them—alone, and without sharing—knew some of the splendor and the terror, some of the quiet peace, of the lands unexplored beyond the fringe.

In a good marriage, he thought, the man and woman would find the daring and strength to make the exploration of the continent of their lives together.

In a bad marriage—

But he and Jean had a good marriage. Until children came they would act like lovers, playmates, just beginning, part-ners. When the first child arrived they would start a whole new splendid period.

He got out of bed, stretched. There were the sounds of Jean in the kitchen, of Michael Flagg yowling, of the little Sunday noises—cars in the distance, faraway children shout-ing.

David walked into the kitchen and kissed Jean on the back of her neck.

She turned around, smiling.

It looked like the smile of yesterday morning, or of a week ago, or of any of the times, but he knew that it was not. He could sense, have a sharp quick awareness, that this smile masked the face of a person apart from him.

It surprised Jean. She had not intended anything except a smile, a return for the friendliness of the kiss. But as she smiled at her husband she realized the change.

44

Strange. This was the man, the only other person in the world, except her mother, who was important. More than important, it was as if the two of them shared the world, the whole universe together. Other people had places, meanings, roles to play, cores of vitality, but the world did not belong to them; it belonged to Jean and David Martin.

That was the way it had been.

Strange. He was standing beside her in the bright-warm kitchen, and he was the man whose maleness had been like the world exploding, the stars falling out of the sky for her. He was the man who could have stood on a mountain and called to her and she would have climbed that mountain because he wanted her. He was the man she had to possess, enfold, seize, and open herself to, giving all, showing all, frantic, enslaved, owned. There had been no other man, there would be no other man, but there had to be this man again and again as there must be breathing again and again through one's whole life.

She had been his completely and now she was not.

Jean had panic. It was as if she realized, without warning, that the floor of the kitchen was dissolving and there was nothing beneath it. She put a hand on the butter-yellow Formica counter top and looked at the electric coils of the range, at the shining chromium maw of the garbage disposal unit, at the pale gray door of the refrigerator, for something to do with her hands. She had to do something, pour coffee, butter the thin slices of rye bread, go out in the patio and sweep, run, scream, weep.

She had not realized last night, not even this morning when she stood beside the bed and glanced down at David. She had not realized until he had kissed her and she had smiled.

Her hands were using the butter-knife on the toast and David was back in their bedroom putting on his robe so that he could go outside and bring in the Sunday paper.

It was a small laugh, but honest. She remembered another time when she had felt much like this. Long ago, ten years ago, and she was walking up the broad, shallow steps at high school. She had seen Terry and he had been just another

45

boy; the realization that Terry was unimportant started a machinery in her mind, and it was as if she looked at a fuzzy movie scene of herself.

For about seven weeks Terry had been the morning, the day, the evening and the night to her. For seven weeks she had done nothing without first worrying how whatever it was she did would make her look to Terry.

It had been a remote romance, the self-contained tropical storm of young-girl love for a boy that is revealed only in awkwardness, and which often is not noticed by the boy. Probably Terry never knew that for seven weeks he had been Apollo.

He had been Apollo to her until the day her sky ripped apart and fell in pieces. Something about seeing him in a car with another girl, both of them laughing. She could not even remember the other girl, but Apollo had died in that moment, and at night she had wept for him until she thought such lonely utter pain could not be endured.

Then on the high school steps she had looked at him and beyond him before she realized that this boy, this ordinary boy, had caused her torment beyond understanding. It had been funny.

In a way this was the same feeling. Maturing, growing up. It meant—and this was frightening—being more alone. The schoolgirl dreams of love with long-ago and long-forgotten Terry had been dreams of two people totally together, with no one else existing. Maturing as a schoolgirl into a woman had, in time, brought her to David. With David she had thought of the two of them as a unit, with the world belonging to them, but a world with other people in it.

Now, maybe there was a new maturing. She would be more alone.

The smile and her controlled frigidity last night were the two things that had shaken her. You watch a stage and there is a backdrop which remains through scene after scene; you become accustomed to it, and in time it seems permanent, solid. What happens on the stage will happen in front of this backdrop. Then it lifts and is gone, hidden away above the stage, and you see that the stage is deeper with a new scene, a greater area for action.

The backdrop of her marriage had lifted as suddenly as if it had been pulled up and out of her life.

She poured the coffee into cups, feeling as if she should laugh.

Such a simple incident. The barbecue had gone off well, a rehearsal in a way for more elaborate and more subtle social rites that would come in the years ahead. It was Saturday night and the lazy promise of Sunday morning made it seem like a night in a palace.

She had begun her little play, almost as wanton as she wanted to be, almost too wanton for her shy husband. It was pure delight, those minutes of building up, watching his eyes change and his lips open a little, seeing David change into a lover. Pure delight as she felt her own body become rich and eager to spend its riches, feeling the slow, moist unfolding, the readiness.

Then he had said something stupid and it was as if she were empty.

The shock had not been in knowing that the delight was gone, but the realization that she would let him come to her when for the first time she did not want him. To find herself capable of this betrayal had been the shock.

Other women talked to her of their nights and she listened to them as a strong young girl might listen to an old woman tell of her weariness and her sickness.

There were girls who had the wrong men for themselves, girls who went into the act of love as they might go to a formal dance where they would be badly dressed and strangers, women who lived in panic fear of pregnancy, and women to whom it was all no more than a frenzy of the clitoris.

Until last night she had lived with the pleasant backdrop of easy passion, familiar yet always surprising in the excitement of its violence. In the four years of marriage there had been better times and poorer times, times of tiredness, and times of frenetic joy. Things had not always been managed

47

perfectly, yet there had never been a time when she had not accepted the backdrop of utter giving, utter taking.

Now she appreciated the depth of the stage.

Maturity was less dependency, maturity was the individual's discovery of ways to control his environment, maturity was finding greater strength in being alone.

David was bringing in the paper, looking at her with an intentness he tried to hide by smiling.

"I'll put our breakfast on trays and we can have it in the living room," she said.

"Fine. Jean—"

"Yes?"

"How do you feel?"

"Fine."

"Jean—"

"Yes, David?"

"I'm sorry about last night."

She had to choose, almost instantaneously, which action would be better: to look up at him brightly, her face showing bewilderment; or to do something with dishes or the tray, letting him say something else.

Jean turned, lifted the two etched glass trays from the cupboard, and said, "Sorry? Why, David? It was a lovely party."

He came up to her and put his arms around her waist.

"About afterwards. Bringing up Leola Noon at a time like that."

She moved slowly around, gently so as not to seem to be pulling out of his arms.

"You're building up Leola Noon to an importance she simply doesn't have, David."

"Not her, I mean not her as an individual. It was stupid to talk about something else—anybody—at just that moment."

"Why are you talking about it now, David?"

"I don't like to have things between us."

She looked at him with tenderness. He was a man, he would fumble with apologies so that he would not feel unease; what he was doing now was trying to find the emo-

48

tional security he ordinarily took for granted. Not mature, not finding his strength in being alone.

"We're all right, Davie."

It was the secret name. She had used it with sure deliberation, a test of herself. He would be uncertain, not knowing what this use of the love name meant; unsure as to whether he should wait for a further sign.

Then she stepped away from him and he stood there, his arms still out and high.

"Would you help me? You carry your tray and I'll put the things on it."

Jean turned away, began to reach for the saucers.

"Why did you call me Davie just now?"

"Sometimes I like to call you Davie."

"I thought it always had a sort of special meaning."

"Can't I think of you that way, David, even when we're doing other things?" She felt like a tower; at the top, with the windows open, she was talking to David. A few floors down, with the windows closed but still transparent, she was managing the incident, using David for his weakness as a man rather than for his strength. Still lower, in a place without windows, she was angry—he had come to her to make himself feel better, not to find how she felt. And somewhere, very deep in the base of the tower, was a blind sense of love for this man, need for him, a need to search out the mysteries with him and not alone.

"You're still trying to point out that I was clumsy and blundering— Okay, I was. I can't say any more."

"It wasn't necessary to say anything, David. Now let's have breakfast."

He took his tray and walked into the living room. It had a sense of spaciousness and comfort; it was an easy room to live in.

"You know, Jean," he said a little later after they had lit cigarettes for their second cup of coffee, "I'll bet people in Sunrise Hills get along with each other lots better than people used to do."

"Why, David?"

"They used to—a great many people still do, I suppose—

49

live in small rooms all bound up together, closed in. Rooms like boxes, cluttered with things. It's just too easy for people to bruise each other in a little room like a box. And then as far as the women are concerned—"

"The women here in Sunrise Hills?"

"Well, we don't have children—" he glanced at her but her face did not change nor did the moment she held her breath show—"but take Betty Kreitzer and her two youngsters. Even only a few years ago, why she'd be starting to show what it was taking out of her. Here she's got an automatic washer, a dryer, a dishwasher, this disposal gadget to handle garbage, and not only that, she can buy most of her food all fixed up for her. The cake is in a box, the gravy is in another box, the coffee is in a jar ready to go—"

"You're saying all this is good, David?"

"Why sure. She's got time for her children—to really play with them and teach them—and she doesn't reach the end of the day all bushed. She doesn't feel locked in the house all day because the house is open, like being half a garden."

"You make it sound wonderful, David."

"It is wonderful. She knows ten times as much as her mother did, maybe a hundred times as much as her grandmother. Magazines, movies, television. She's a citizen of the world. So are you. But that isn't the point I was making—"

"Oh?"

"It was about us."

"I have even more time than Betty. David, I want to get a job."

"What?"

"The only reason I haven't worked is because each month we hoped it would be the next time. For the moment, right now at least, I've sort of lost hope in the next time."

"Jean, I'm sorry."

"We can use the money in a hundred ways—"

"We don't really need it, Jean."

"You made the point yourself, David. Sunrise Hills, without children, doesn't require anything from me but shopping for those boxes, jars and frozen packages, turning on a few switches, and sitting in the patio."

50

"But you do so many other things, Jean. League of Women Voters, the Mental Health Society, that volunteer work you do at the Council of Social Agencies—"

"Do you mind my taking a job, David?"

"Not exactly. None of this 'It's a man's duty to support his wife' stuff. It just seems strange, that's all."

"If I'm a citizen of the world, as you said, I want to get out in it a little more."

"Jean—"

"Yes?"

"People often go along for several years before they have their first one. I hope you don't think—"

"Oh, I'll be optimistic again one of these days. Maybe I'll get just a wonderful job, all glamour and excitement and money and—bang—higher than a kite, as the boys say."

David stubbed out his cigarette.

"Do you have any ideas about a job, Jean?"

She looked at him with an open frankness. "As a matter of fact I didn't really decide to get one until you began talking about Sunrise Hills. The only place for a young woman in Sunrise Hills is with her children while they're little. God knows what she does after they grow up."

"That isn't fair, Jean. You make it sound as if somebody like Betty would be better off doing the washing in a tub, making her own bread—"

"No, David. I love this wonderful stuff of no bent back and no red hands and all the rest of it. Love is fine, but God, David, what am I really doing with my life?"

They looked at each other and there were no words.

He lit another cigarette and found himself saying, "About Leola Noon, Jean. You always seem to back away from her somehow."

Jean stood up. "Let's not talk about Leola."

"I can't touch the problem here," David said, "but I've got a feeling there is a problem."

"David, I don't ask you for much; and you give me a lot more than I ask for. This is something different. Right now, this house on Paso Robles Way is my home. My home is very important, important to both of us. If we live here twenty

51

years and Leola Noon is next door for twenty years we still won't understand each other."

The chimes of the front door sounded. David shrugged his shoulders and went to the door. As it opened Jean heard the high, thin voice of Leola.

"I didn't want to come round the back because I don't know how you folks run around on Sunday. Me, sometimes I don't have hardly anything on. But David, the reason I came over—our TV set broke. Could we watch Ed Sullivan on yours tonight?"

7

LEOLA NOON WORE shorts and a halter, there was a yellow smear of something on the not-quite-white shorts and the halter had been carelessly tied. As David looked down on her he could see the dark-red and pink swell of her right nipple.

"Are you folks going to be home tonight, David?"

She was like a child, a puppy, he thought. Careless, open, eager, foolish.

"I guess so. Sure." He looked over her head, embarrassed.

"It's sort of nice you know, watching TV with other people. Like being at a theater. You sure Jean won't mind?"

David wet his lips. Jean would mind. Coming like this she might make a major issue of it. Yet what could he say to this puppy, this child, this girl, barefoot in his doorway, one breast nearly bare, with her tangled hair and fresh prettiness? Tell her that she wasn't wanted?

"Is Jean up yet, David?" She hadn't waited for an answer. "I'm up."

David turned to his wife, standing behind him. Her eyes had seen the yellow smear on the grayish shorts, the tangled hair, the loosely open halter.

"I just came over to ask a big favor, Jeannie—"

No one called Jean Martin "Jeannie."

"You did?" The weapon of a woman, the coldly flat voice.

"Our set's busted and Troy loves to watch Ed Sullivan on Sunday nights—"

"I'm sorry. We're going to be away."

Disappoint a child. Speak with unexpected harshness to a child. Slap a child, thought David. Something perverse from the sexual clash of last night came to him and he moved closer to Leola, looked down at the tan-pink pear of her breast. Jean would notice.

Leola noticed first and her hand came up to push the halter tight against her body. Her eyes met David's and he was surprised at the sign of shock he saw in hers. He was surprised, feeling both annoyance and amusement. She had been standing in front of him with slim, naked legs, a naked flat belly, and a halter loose enough to fall away from her body, yet she pretended shock when she found him looking at her. Pretended? He wasn't sure.

"Oh, you won't be home?" She spoke as a child might who had been denied something expected.

There was a change in Jean. "What time's your program, Leola? Eight? That's all right, then. You and Troy come over. Don't dress up—we'll all just sit around and watch—"

The child was happy again, but her eyes glanced sideways once at David and her hand held the halter tight. "I'll bring sandwiches. How about beer or something? Troy could get—"

"You bring the sandwiches. We'll have the rest of the stuff." There was a special quality to Jean's voice and David tried to guess at what it meant. A catlike quality.

Leola smiled at Jean, looked at David. "We'll be here a little before eight. Don't mind if Troy is cross with me tonight —I can't help talking most of the time and he gets so sore—"

She turned away, looked back once and smiled.

"She does have a nice body, doesn't she, David?"

"Jean, she's like a kid—"

"A brat. A dirty little exhibitionist brat."

"Why did you change your mind, Jean?"

Jean seemed to soften. This was the aspect of his wife most loved by David. She would seem younger at these times, more like an easy companion, a warm, open friend. Once he had thought she was always like this, but in the last two years he had learned that there were many Jeans and this was only one, to him the nicest.

"Believe me, David, I'm not being irrational about this girl. It isn't one of those woman things that don't make sense."

She was close to him; her face was relaxed, almost boylike, her mouth soft.

"It's simply that Leola Noon is trouble, a nuisance. I'll even believe that she didn't know her breasts were all but

54

sticking out of that halter. Most women aren't careless about things like that—what they show they damn well know they're showing no matter what they pretend, but this Leola, well—"

"She's like a kid, Jean."

"You said that, David. But you can't expect a wife to want a messy twenty-two-year-old female kid to come bouncing into her house like that. There are places in Sunrise Hills where that would be accepted—we don't happen to live in one of those places."

They were still close and he felt the special liking, neither love nor need nor desire, toward her that was the most comfortable of all the kinds of relationships he had with his wife.

"I don't follow, Jean."

"Haven't you heard the various Sunrise Hills scandals?" she said, smiling. "I'll bring coffee in and tell you all the details."

He watched her walk toward the kitchen. In his work he used charts, graphs. No longer the simple affairs of neat squares with red and blue lines jigging across. The graphs now were twisting, complex affairs in several dimensions, and he thought, almost seeing the picture of the curling vectors, that a man and his wife might be graphed in some such way: lines approaching, paralleling, sheering off in complex rhythms, darkening, broadening, narrowing again. This suddenly was a place on their graph where the lines were close, parallel.

She was back with the tray of coffee. "We drink a terrible lot of coffee, David. Lots more than we did before we came here."

"It's pleasant, and it's something to do—like smoking."

"More cigarettes, more coffee." She poured for him.

"What's this about certain places in Sunrise Hills?" he asked.

She shook back her hair. "It's one of the funny things about a place like this, like Sunrise Hills and its five thousand young families. You get different kinds of tribal customs. Some parts of Sunrise Hills are getting nicknames—'Alcohol Alley,' 'the nudist camp,' 'Holy Hills'—"

55

"Sounds interesting. Tell me more."

"Just stuff we wives hear around. When the first families moved in, months ago, each group of houses would have kind of a wrestling match to see what the style of the group would be. I mean what would be the right things to do and so on."

"'Alcohol Alley'—a bunch of lushes?"

"Sunday morning brunches at each other's houses with buckets of Bloody Marys to ease the wounds from the Saturday night Martini storm. Alcohol Alley is over on Campos Way. Holy Hills is just the opposite—those are the families around the Del Rey Circle. No drinking, lots of church activities, Cub Scouts, stuff like that."

"I don't see why they should clot up like that, all the drunks in one group of houses and so on—"

Jean was quite serious in her explanation. "We've talked about it, Betty and I. I say there are two reasons. When Sunrise Hills was opened to buyers, people who were friends in San Francisco tended to look over the place together and buy near each other. In town they were scattered all over, but as you say, they sort of clotted up in Sunrise Hills. The other reason is more interesting."

David drank some coffee and lit a cigarette. "So?"

Jean leaned forward. "Remember how it was when we moved in? Meeting the other families around us? Sort of feeling them out, finding what they were like?"

He laughed. "The thing that amused me was the words."

"Words?"

"Sure. Those first few times we got together—the Flaggs, and Herman and Betty, us—how careful everybody was about what was okay to say and what would shock somebody. Like saying, 'Where's Betty?' and Herman saying, 'Oh, she's in the can,' and then everybody looking to see if anybody else minded being vulgar."

Jean nodded. "That's exactly it, David. There's apt to be one strong person, or one strong family, in each group of houses. They set the style, set the tribal customs for the whole place. Like the nudist camp—"

"That's the one I want to hear about."

"Sandy Barker—you've seen her around, tall, good-looking, blond. She just plain goes naked all day around the house. Doesn't give a damn who sees her. Well, after about three months that got to be the style in Alvarado Way. There's six houses, and five of the women and their husbands are so used to seeing each other in the raw that they don't give it a thought. The other woman is miserable; they're trying to sell their house. She won't even speak to the other five."

"Maybe Troy and Leola ought to buy that place and sell this one."

"Troy would kill her if he thought she'd do that. It's a damn good thing he didn't see her over here with you looking down her halter."

"You know, Jean, I don't know why in hell I did that."

Her eyes were gentle. "Whatever reason you figure out, David, isn't likely to be the right one."

"You never did say why you switched like that. Inviting her over tonight."

"Don't you know why, David?"

"I know you haven't changed your mind about her."

"I'm going to get her nice and drunk, let her make a mess of herself right here. Maybe that will do it."

David put his hand on hers, hard and tight. "I won't let you. It's a stupid idea and it's cruel."

Jean turned her hand and let her fingers curl over David's. As she looked at him he knew that this was still the simple, friendly companion aspect of his wife. She was being honest, open, hoping to be understood.

"Off and on, since last night, we've been bickering over this," she said. "Against our whole marriage, against everything we have or will have together, Leola is not important. But right now, here, she is damned important. You've had it easy, David, and you don't even realize it."

"I've had it easy? Maybe so, but how? Why bring that up?"

"You don't know about killing people—maybe that's too dramatic; let's say you don't know about making people walk the plank."

"That sounds a little dramatic, too. I'm not following you at all, Jean."

"At school, at Verdun Labs—have you ever pushed anybody down, got rid of them?"

"I'm sorry, Jean. You're way out beyond left field for me."

Both of her hands were on his. He could tell from her eyes, her mouth, that she was trying to be understood. She had something important she was trying to communicate.

"Supposing there was something you wanted, something you absolutely had to have, David. Supposing there was another man striving for the same thing. How far would you go to make sure that you got it and he didn't?"

David shifted in his chair and took his hand away from hers to light another cigarette.

"That's not a fair question. It depends—"

She interrupted him. "It's a perfectly fair question for a woman to ask a man. To ask her man."

"As far as the rules of the game permitted." David closed his mouth, blew smoke from his nostrils.

"The right answer is simple, David. Go as far as necessary, as far as you can."

He shook his head. "You're not even talking like yourself, Jean. You're no ruthless person, power-hungry or money-hungry or something. You know I'm not. And thank God I've got a job that doesn't need that kind of stuff." David picked up his cup, saw that it was empty, put it down again. "If I was in an advertising agency, or selling stuff, something like that—but not at Verdun. I'll get ahead by what I can do, not by any nonsense of cutting somebody else out."

"If you were a different kind of man, if you were the kind of man you think you are, I wouldn't say these things to you, David. But you haven't realized yet what kind of man you are."

He laughed, then looked at her eyes to see if there had been the quick tightening that meant she was angry or hurt. There was none; Jean seemed patient, a woman willing to take time.

"I know what kind of man I am. I'm a fairly good methods engineer in a damned good electronics firm. Next year I'll be better. I love you. That's about all the kind of man I am."

"No, David, no." Her hands sought his again.

Without waiting for her to say more he felt a kind of irritation flare out from him. "Jean—what goes today? We've never had a morning like this one. You tell me you want to get a job, you're first bitter about this poor kid next door and then you invite her here to get her drunk—you say—and now you try to explain that by some damned nonsense about me not knowing myself, and going all the way to get what I want—"

She was patient, waiting. The flare of irritation had not kindled any heat of resentment or annoyance in her.

David finished off. "I'm going to get behind the Sunday paper for a while, and then I'm going to watch television. You are not getting either one of the Noons drunk tonight, and I'm going to keep on being the same kind of guy I am. As to your getting a job—maybe you need to get out with people again!"

She was silent, waiting. Jean's face was still easy, relaxed; in time he would come back to this and she waited for him.

"Jean—" he said, not more than a minute later.

"Yes, David."

"What was all that about?"

"My saying you didn't know who you were, what you are, yet?"

"Yes."

"Do you think I know you? Love you?"

"Yes. You know me very well, Jean. Pretty damned near completely, I guess."

"There are two kinds of men, David. You think you are one kind. I know that you are the other kind."

"What kind do you think I am?"

"I'd better explain both kinds. One kind of man gets by, survives, maybe even does very well, by simply doing something. Run an elevator, paint a house, design a television set—"

"That elevator man had better watch out, Jean." David had a small half-smile.

She looked surprised at the interruption. She knew that

he was not listening with appreciation, but this was only the beginning. "Why should the elevator man watch out? Is that a joke—one that I haven't heard?"

The half-smile was gone. "I didn't mean to break in on you —but when you said elevator man I thought of one of our gadgets at Verdun. Otis, they build elevators, have something like it. It's a series of electronic controls for a bank of elevators—no men needed to run the cars, no starter downstairs either. Better, faster service, too."

"Could you get me a job at Verdun, David?"

"If I could, I wouldn't. If you worked there they might as well design an electronic pair of gadgets and call them David and Jean. There wouldn't be much point to being flesh and blood, driving from here to the plant every morning, driving back every evening. Just two more gadgets—David and Jean."

"That's what I'm trying to explain, David."

He stood up, stretched. He felt that he too was being patient.

"I guess I'm sort of dull on Sunday mornings, Jean. Sorry."

"There are men who could just as well be gadgets, no matter what they do. They get by doing something that sooner or later your Verdun people will design a machine to do better. You think you're that kind of a man, and I'm spending this lovely Sunday morning explaining to you that you goddamn well are not."

"I'll be damned," he said, his voice low and soft.

"What's the matter, David?"

"Last week Soke and I were fooling around with the schematics on some of the new IBM control systems and I pointed out that we could work out a projection that would damn near duplicate the work of a regular methods engineer. I'll be jolly well bloody damned. I'd forgotten about it."

He was still standing and he began to walk in the shadowed part of the long living room.

"Well, anyway, it'll be a long time before it's cheaper to build a methods engineer out of transistors and wire than to hire a live one." He laughed but his eyes had the expression

60

of a man trying to see through the mist of very early morning.

"You don't have to worry, David."

"I'm not worrying."

"You would have to if you were the kind of man you still think you are. The kind of man who'd hold his job only as long as he was cheaper than a machine built out of wire and transistors."

"There's more to it than that," David said, serious. "Memory drums, input relays, analog devices—"

"Don't tell me about them. There's more to you."

Suddenly he asked her, meaning the question, "What kind of a man am I?"

"The kind of man who competes with all other men. The kind of a man who must fight to be a leader."

"I don't give a whoop in billy hell for being a leader." He spun and began to walk away from her.

"No, you don't. But you want to do things, you want to challenge everything that's known and solid now, change it, make it new, better, different."

"That's partially true." He walked back slowly.

"You're still a schoolboy at Verdun, still learning."

He smiled, not in amusement but in the enjoyment of agreement. "That's completely true. Our field is going up and out wide, about as fast as we can keep up with it. If people only knew what's happening in electronics, what it's going to do to their lives—"

"You've told me. I know you're right, David. But if you were in some other field, totally different, what I'm saying would still be true. You are the kind of man who can survive only by forcing your will on other men. You want to lead, not to have other men follow you, but to find new things. But if you don't dominate the other men they won't let you move. Can't you understand?"

"Why all this this morning, Jean?"

She stood up, waited for him to come to her. "Because you're my husband, because you're still a schoolboy, because somehow I know that the time is here, the growing-up time. Up to here you've learned and worked; from here on you

61

have to fight. You have to get what you want, regardless of what you have to do to get it, before someone else does."

He shook his head. "No sale, Jean. I'm still just a good methods engineer. I don't have to outsmart or beat down anybody else."

They were together and he kissed her, smiling. "Now how about this other crazy Sunday morning idea of getting Leola drunk?"

Jean let her head fall back as David still held her. She didn't know what to say in answer. The truth was too simple: she had felt anger and jealousy when she had seen David make an open thing of looking at Leola. She had wanted to slap him, slap the girl; instead she thought of Leola drunk and stupid, Leola disgusting. With the thought had come the plan. It had been that simple.

The rest of the morning had been almost as simple, with the plain layer of simplicity covering unknown complexities. Getting a job, talking to David about the kind of man he was, and the rest of all that. She wanted a job because she needed something, and she was not sure what she needed, but she knew she would not find it in the empty, childless days at Sunrise Hills.

Not until she said these things aloud did she realize how strongly she believed them.

He would either fall back among the losers, among the elevator men waiting only for the machine to be installed which would do their job better, or he would take his place among the men who would lead their lives as they wished.

And for her? For Jean Martin? Three things mattered for her, and David was the foundation of all three.

Deepest, like an ocean, touching everything, the source for all her life, was the torment-pleasure-release of her body. Like an ocean, still, restless, hurricane-raked.

Above this was her need for children. She knew the depression of each barren month, the dark, involute dissatisfaction of her body.

And like a tower above everything: her pride. She did not need to search out the birth and strengthening of pride; it could be taken for granted. The need to satisfy the manifold, complex hungers of pride was as basic to her as the need for air to breathe, or food to eat.

She had said once, at school, as a young woman knowing clearly what she wanted, what she must have in the half-century or so of living that was ahead of her, to a friend who had accused her, as college juniors will, of being proud: "The quality of pride is the only thing that distinguishes a woman from any other female animal."

Remembering that, in the years since, she knew two things she believed of that statement now—it had been college-girl talk and it was true.

Without pride a woman was nothing. Let her have faith instead of pride and she achieved only a peculiar, blind kind of selfishness. The selfishness of the believing animal, which holds to some way of survival by believing that it will be protected. Protected as a reward for believing in its protector.

But pride had none of the sheep-run humiliation of faith. Faith was for the weak, pride was for the strong.

The women without pride, the women with only faith, had been the women of peasant men in mud huts, suckling dying children from empty breasts.

The women who lived by their pride, who lived to satisfy its demands in each small action of their lives, in each major function of their years of life, had brought about this whole time of pride, this America, this full-living generation rich with goods, which lived in a whole world as its grandparents had once lived locked in a village, this generation rich with promise of even finer generations to come. The hungers and demands of proud women had shaped this America.

Pride showed its need and its victory in her clothes, in the food she served, in the home in which she lived and in the garden by its walls, in the car, in the very plans they made for next year, for all the years to come, for their children.

Without the hungers of the strong pride that was the very texture of her as a woman, what would she be? An animal needing only food and comfort, and if without enough food

63

or comfort, maybe an animal turning to faith that something would take care of it.

She knew she had to walk carefully, be subtle in her use of her own pride with David. The rewards, the things success brought as tangible symbols, really did not matter, nor did the soft, masked envy of other women. She would wear the fine clothes, the furs; preside graciously over the serene, elegant home; take her place among the other women whose men were successful in the merciless tournament; but Jean understood that these were only the symbols of the single matter of importance. The single matter of importance would be that her man had done his part in shaping the world, a man with strength and ability urged on by a proud woman.

She knew the weakness in her man. He was willing to work with the patient brilliance his job required. He continued to learn as the frontiers of his work expanded so rapidly as to be terrifying. He had the manner and the appearance of a young man on his way upward. But he did not want to hurt other men for his own gain. He did not want to compete as fighters compete on their way to a championship. He was content to work with facts and theory rather than with men.

As a girl in college Jean had prepared a paper in history on the California gold rush of '49. She could compare David with the men who had come crashing across a continent, going over the great mountains to the goldfields. In a way the men at Verdun Laboratories, all the men in this incredible electronics business, were crashing through an unexplored continent toward a newer kind of goldfield. The men of '49 who had come through to found the great families, to live high on Nob Hill, were not the miners who could handle the tools of the miners' trade. They were the men who could handle men.

If David failed? If he did not have the strength, the drive, the masked ruthlessness—what then? In time still younger men would come, some of them hustling by him, using him, and her pride would hunger, wither away. You could look for another man, but you would not be so sure of yourself ever again.

It had to be David, because she loved him without needing to understand her love; David, because he was her first and only choice for all that she had to give: the completeness of her body, her understanding and gentleness, the fierce and righteous demands of her pride.

She looked up at him and smiled.

The telephone rang.

8

THAT SUNDAY MORNING the four men who usually met in Bill Verdun's office were there. The meetings had their beginning about the time the first American troops were hitting North Africa, back in 1942, and then they were Bill, Pat Twohig—since dead from a heart attack, Jimmy Pierson—long since a penniless drunk on Howard Street, and Turner Fry. Then they were four young men slopping up fast cups of coffee at the hot plate on Bill Verdun's desk in the corner of the shed, before they went back to work on the machines cutting out cavity resonators for ultra-secret radar components. Four young men in a war, four young men just beginning to realize how big the dragon could be that they were learning to harness in electronics.

That Sunday morning had been a long time ago.

Bill Verdun, at forty, was president, chief engineer and chairman of the board of Verdun Laboratories. Verdun Labs were incorporated in 1941, received a $488,000 loan from the government in 1943, another loan of $7,000,000 in 1944, and paid off all loans in 1951. The corporation was listed on the New York Stock Exchange and was quoted at around 114. Last year it had earned $6.22 per share and paid a regular dividend of $3.00 and an extra of $1.00. The first quarter earnings this year, after allowance for taxes, were $3.52 on the 130,000 shares of common outstanding.

Turner Fry, at forty-six, was executive vice-president. He had graduated from the University of California at Berkeley at twenty and for the next two years he had pumped gas at a service station in Vallejo. There were no jobs then for a very young man with a degree in mathematics and a background in electronic theory; in fact there were few employers who knew there was such a thing as electronic theory. Turner Fry's total income now included a fifty-thousand-dollar-a-year salary from Verdun Laboratories and more than sixty thousand dollars in dividends.

The year of 1951 had killed pudgy, red-faced Pat Twohig. Lean colonels of the Air Force had come to Verdun Labs with locked brief cases full of prints. All of them seemed merely variations on one type; hard-boiled old-young men, insistent and informed. They wanted fire-control systems for jet fighters, anti-aircraft gun computers, radar sweep analyzers, identification-friend-or-foe feedback circuits, and Pat Twohig had ruptured his heart trying to give them what they wanted.

Pat Twohig's place at Verdun had not been filled since. Not adequately. The plump beer-drinker with the bright bird's eyes in his swollen red face had been a dedicated man. There had been two Pat Twohigs: the outer husk of a fat man who got slowly and happily drunk on beer, loud-voiced, a great laugher and teller of stories; the man inside the husk of fat, driven by curiosity, an explorer in a universe of electrons, better informed and even more insistent upon his own output of work than the lanky, fierce-eyed colonels.

Bill Verdun and Pat Twohig had met when Pat ran a radio repair shop back in the late '30s. Pat's radio shop had a reputation for fine work and Bill had come to him for help in building the model tracking device for anti-aircraft guns he had designed and was submitting to the War Department. Pat had found in Bill something he had himself, and much that he did not have. Bill was a tinkerer, like Pat an explorer in that universe of electrons, but he was also an organizer.

While Pat would work, as he once did, for fifty-two consecutive sleepless hours on new circuits using transistors in place of the suddenly obsolete tubes, Bill would be busy in violent spurts of work locating sources of supply on transistor elements, scheduling orders and production of the new circuits, selling customers who were hearing for the first time of automation and electronic control.

Bill had the money and the wolflike hunting ability to find more money quickly—from the RFC—so that the Labs were incorporated as Verdun and not as Verdun and Twohig. But since the day Pat had straightened up, with a frightened,

67

surprised look on his face, and then had toppled over his desk, smashing a clutter of prints, vacuum tubes and circuits printed on thin sheets of plastic, Bill Verdun had looked for another dedicated man, much as a widow will search for a man like the man she has loved.

Jimmy Pierson, the fourth of those in the long-ago Sunday morning conferences at Bill's desk in the corner of the shed, had walked a different road. One which at the beginning seemed steeply upward and smooth but which had begun to wind slowly downward through Martinis to straight gin, and then inevitably to the 39-cent fifth of white port passed from slobbering lips to shaking hands in an alley off Howard Street.

Jimmy, whose thin red hair was already halfway back on his skull at thirty, had lost his life in World War II. Not by dying, but by losing it somewhere in the parties for the big men at the Mayfair in Washington, in the hard-drinking conferences in rooms at the Mark or the Fairmont or the Palace, with the party girls already in their cabs on the way over. Lost his life as a man will lose sand from his clenched hands without realizing how rapidly it is slipping away.

A divorce for Jimmy Pierson in late 1944, another wife somewhere around '46 and she was gone by '48, and the years whirling around him in hotel rooms, on planes headed for Washington, with the lights bright on the stars of generals and the eagles of young colonels, the soft talk of congressmen from Alabama and Kentucky, and a thousand places to have fun, a hundred bars that would cash a hundred-dollar check for Jimmy Pierson any time.

Now he was a wisp of a man in dirty khaki pants and shirt walking unsteadily along Howard toward Third, his body screaming for the wine, his eyes frightened. The eyes of a man who knows he has lost his life.

Bill had tried with Jimmy. The wives had tried. There had been psychiatrists and a few hopeful months with AA. In the end he was gone.

This Sunday morning conference had the four men of a different time. Bill Verdun and Turner Fry were both beginning to gray. They had the same kind of face, marked with the signs of success. The muscles of their faces were firm, the kind of muscles that held mouth and chin strong; they were both tanned, and the tan was the deep, permanent rich brown which comes not only from golf, but from deep-sea fishing, Sierra and Idaho hunting. They both wore finely tailored suits of soft and elegant materials but they did not need such clothes to impress other men into quick respect. Their faces—eyes, mouths, and the firm muscles—did that; the way they spoke confirmed the signs.

They looked like men who had earned power and knew how to handle it.

The other two were Robert "Soke" Sokolik, project vice-president, and Seaman Cowles. Cowles, who still looked like the oarsman from the Princeton shell he had been, was personnel vice-president. Both of them were men only on their way to earn power, with the final maturity problem of knowing how to handle it still not yet real for them. The differences between Soke and Cowles as against Bill Verdun and Turner Fry were evident; the two younger men had not yet learned, with full skill, to conceal their eagerness and unsureness. Each of them spoke a little faster, a little more often, than Verdun and Fry.

Cowles and Sokolik had won their way to vice-presidencies within the Verdun Labs. Cowles had come to Verdun as a twenty-six-year-old lieutenant-colonel just out of the Army in 1946, and his family—father, uncle, older brother and his wife—had acquired by purchase some twenty thousand shares of Verdun Labs stock since then. Their combined paper profits now totaled more than eight hundred thousand dollars.

Yet beneath the Princeton veneer, the lieutenant-colonel-at-twenty-six veneer, the personnel-vice-president veneer, and the thick money veneer, Seaman Cowles seemed to Bill Verdun, oddly and largely by intuition, sometimes as an uncertain and maybe even untrustworthy young man. Odd because the slim strong fingers of Seaman Cowles touched nothing but success, and the man had never failed a responsibility in his years at the Labs. He had married a Burlingame girl, who looked like an aristocratic and finely bred milkmaid, and they had two sons and a daughter. The sons would be bigger, stronger, richer and more assured than their father, like adding a few extra horsepower to an already powerful and smooth-running motor. The daughter would be beautiful.

Sokolik was different. Verdun paid him twenty-five thousand a year and he saved ten thousand of it, even after taxes. His money went into bank accounts, building and loan accounts and AT&T stock. He was not married and lived in a monk's-neat bachelor apartment high on Russian Hill.

Robert Sokolik knew that he had worked his way all the way, and by himself. In his four years at Cal he had averaged only four hours' sleep a night and could still smell the sour yeastiness of dishwater merely by closing his eyes and thinking of the counter restaurant on Telegraph where he had worked for the first two years of college.

Even after he had come to Verdun, Sokolik had gone to school at night, finally earning his master's. He had continued with ICS correspondence courses for years, a lonely, intent man bent over a desk in his room until most of the lights of San Francisco below him were dark.

He did not drink, he did not smoke, and though he was tortured by thoughts of lechery he entered each new relationship with a woman as a hunter with a single round in his gun will enter a jungle alive with dangerous beasts.

Robert "Soke" Sokolik was David Martin's boss at Verdun Laboratories. This Sunday morning one of the items on the list was David Martin.

"What's the present outside figure on this Coast Gas & Power installation, Bill?" asked Turner Fry. "If we covered their whole set-up? Ten, fifteen million?"

Bill Verdun looked at Sokolik. "Well, Soke?"

Sokolik put his hands together, looked toward the broad window which banded the executive conference room. "As of now, the whole C.G.&P. automation on billing and accounting would run just under fourteen million. But since they want to run this test first they won't make a decision for maybe three months. Costs may be higher."

Fry waited a moment, sipping coffee from a translucent cup. The executive conference room of Verdun Laboratories was paneled in silver-gray wood; the single band of clear glass overlooked the gardened patio and pool set between the two main wings of the plant. Like the coffee service the room had a discreet, quiet luxury. Behind one set of panels was a motion picture screen, which showed—in color—a choice of views throughout the entire laboratories. A third panel concealed a regular television screen, and the fourth was a series of visible electronic control screens which carried a continuous record of production activities shown in flowing lines on etched glass.

"As I see it," said Turner Fry, "we're making quite a gamble on this test. We all agree that Coast will have to go to automation in billing and accounting—if they don't do it in the next three months they'll certainly go within the next year. Right?"

Bill Verdun nodded. "Soke figures they're losing about three hundred thousand dollars a month using employees and standard equipment as against full automation. They'll go."

"And Soke thinks we should send David Martin as chief on this Los Angeles test? Does Martin have the stuff? We sour the test down in LA and Coast Gas & Power will still go full automation, but not Verdun automation. That's fourteen million dollars' worth of business, and we don't want to lose it."

"We won't lose it, Turner. I think Martin will do it fine." As Verdun spoke he was thinking, not of young, strong, slim David Martin, but of another man, dead these several years. A man who was twenty years older then than Martin, older then than Martin was now, red-faced and fat, wheezing; Pat Twohig. It was strange, he thought, that he felt Martin and Twohig were so much alike. Something about the way they went into a problem, tearing it apart and putting it together in a dozen different changes. He liked Martin.

Yet the two men, the fat man who had been his right hand and his good friend, the quiet young Martin, were different in many ways. There had been a quality of strength in Pat—you knew that no matter how rough they got with

71

Pat, no matter how they tried to slick him or bear down on him, he'd come through strong.

Sokolik continued to look at the window and at the bright flowers in the garden below. Specially blended coffee in a fine porcelain cup, he thought, and a flowered patio in the center of a factory. Everything was changing, and he had kept up with the change. He closed his eyes and remembered the two years of the nights of clattering, dirty dishes and sour dishwater.

"Martin's my best man. Maybe he won't work out in a tough situation—but if he won't we might as well know now." Sokolik turned to Verdun as he talked. Saying the words he was conscious of the truth, rather the truths, because there were more than one.

Martin was a good man. That was true. He liked this man, that was half-true. Liked him because there was nothing wrong about Martin; "one of the good guys of the world," Sokolik thought, his lip curling a little.

But Martin was also like an unexploded bomb to Sokolik. He had watched him develop as a man in the Labs and Robert Sokolik had decided that Martin might not stay tame. He was beginning to come up with his own ideas, and in some areas of automation methods he was ahead of his boss. He had an intuitive ability for cybernetic circuits and operations that years of plodding study had not given to the older man. In another year or two it was probable that Martin would be a problem. Too good, too alert, too creative, and wanting the power to do things his way.

When that time came—yet Sokolik did not want to lose David Martin. The man was good; he needed him. Caltech, Berkeley, a dozen schools were putting out young geniuses fresh with a complete knowledge of modern electronics that simply had not existed when Sokolik had gone to school. For all of his lonely nights studying the journals, the new textbooks, he knew that he wasn't keeping up. He needed a man like Martin just under him to keep him safe from the young men.

The goddamned young men who knew so goddamned much. He could have learned it—but it hadn't existed, none

72

of it, when he'd gone to Cal, washing those stacks of greasy dishes for seven hundred nights.

He needed David Martin but he had to break him, break him just enough so that Martin would know his place. Break him now so that Martin would be afraid to take on more responsibility, afraid to leave Verdun.

The place to break him was setting up the test in the Los Angeles offices of Coast Gas & Power.

"That's the reason I'd rather send Martin than go myself. If Martin can whip that situation he's going to be a big man for us." Sokolik said the words easily, but he was thinking that a man had to gamble. Stay away from cards, dice, horses, it didn't matter—you had to gamble for the big stakes anyway. Gamble now that Martin couldn't handle a tough human situation. If he did—

If he did then there would be only another year or so left for Sokolik here at Verdun. Not that Bill or Turner would put any pressure on him; he could stay on for life as project vice-president. But he had a thin, bitter pride: once everyone realized that David Martin was really the strong man in the project, Sokolik would have to go. And outside, at the other places, there were these bright, friendly young men who knew so goddamned much—

Turner Fry finished his coffee and leaned back. "Let's count the factors," he said, his voice quiet and easy, as always.

"We know about the possibility of fourteen million in business. We know the general importance of this test for C.G.&P. in Los Angeles. What are the specifics?

"First, we approached C.G.&P. some months ago on the idea of replacing their existing billing and accounting departments with full automation electronic installations. We've done it for smaller companies and we showed them that within three years the old-fashioned office full of employees working tabulating machines, typing bills, and the rest of it will be a thing of the past.

"They asked us to lay out a test installation in one of their West Los Angeles offices. The office has about a hundred employees, mostly women and girls.

"We put in a system that will do the job of figuring the bills, mailing them out, and running the full accounting on them with three employees. These three will be maintenance personnel on the automation installation. That is, we put in this system as a test if G. C. Wise approves after talking to our man.

"Wise is a vice-president and a director of Coast Gas & Power. He took the lead twenty years ago—when it was the new thing and the big thing—of working out good employee relationships. He believes C.G.&P. has two functions: one, to provide efficient service in supplying electricity and gas to its customers, the other, to provide a solid structure of employment for the 60,000 people who work for them. He says if these two functions are handled right the stockholders will have no worries."

"Wise has been one hell of a good man for C.G.&P.," said Bill Verdun.

"He's getting a touch old," said Seaman Cowles. "He must be over sixty. When's compulsory retirement at Coast?"

"Sixty-five," said Fry. "Sure he's a good man. Only he can't see the long-term benefits in replacing a hundred women with a single integrated automation. I've talked to him. You've talked to him, Bill. We all went marlin fishing together one weekend in his boat off Balboa. But the test is still up in the air. He wants to watch one of our men lay out the test installation and he doesn't want any of us there when it's done.

"He'd let you do it, Soke. Just an ordinary vice-president doesn't bother him; he just thinks Bill or I would be too full of fancy tricks."

Cowles lit his pipe. "I can't see that it matters. Martin or Soke or whoever goes there will set up the test department. The hundred women find jobs somewhere else. What can Wise do to foul us? Nothing."

Fry shook his head. "Not true. He can force our man to bastardize the installation. Wise is perfectly willing to use the machines—he's no fool, and he knows costs and efficiency as well as any executive on the Coast—but he's going to try

74

and keep most of the present staff along with the machines."

"That's stupid," said Sokolik.

Fry looked at him for a moment. "Stupid? Apart from sentiment he's damn well aware of two other factors. Almost two thirds of Coast's employees are also stockholders and they can raise particular hell at meetings. Second, they've got a watertight union. Fool around with Coast's employees and you're fooling with a nest of hornets. Wise knows that. So he wants to pay for his cake and not eat it. Put in the machines, keep the people."

"He's a fool," said Sokolik.

Fry swung around in his chair. "Soke, you know electronics. That's fine as long as you don't have to go beyond transistors, microwave guides and the rest of it. Wise knows people—particularly he knows people in relationship to his company. That's why Coast pays him a hundred thousand dollars a year and that's why this automation test isn't a simple matter of setting in the equipment." He swung his chair back to face Seaman Cowles.

"Sea—personnel is your end of this. How do you size up David Martin?"

Seaman used his pipe, pulling in smoke, letting it rise slowly from his open mouth. He didn't particularly want the responsibility of this.

Seaman Cowles had learned his own set of basic rules for living back at Princeton in the years ending with the war. For a man adept at following them they made life as simple as an ordinary tennis game is for a Davis Cup player. Essentially it was only one rule: play it safe, but don't let it look as if you're playing it safe. When you have to fight, fight with everything you've got but only when your opponent isn't expecting it or doesn't know it's happening. Never get in a corner. Do all this with an easy, casual good humor.

Above all—never let another living person into your confidence on anything.

The rules worked well. Seaman Cowles was still young, rich, good-looking. He'd been a success at Princeton, a success in the war, a success at Verdun. He knew that the rules worked only if you followed them in every circumstance, even one as small as advising Turner Fry on the qualifications of David Martin for this test job.

"He's a good lab man," Cowles said after the smoke was gone.

"You don't think he could solve this Coast problem then?"

"I don't see that there's a problem, Turner. Martin can work out the installation. Wise can't keep a hundred girls sitting around just looking at the automation units doing all the work. If Soke's got faith in Martin I think I'll take Soke's word on it."

Bill Verdun pushed himself back. "That's not it, Sea. Wise isn't the last word at Coast. If we let him bastardize the test installation it isn't going to show the right result money-wise. If they need only three employees after it's set up and they use even fifty instead of the hundred they've got now the Verdun equipment is going to look bad."

"Put the blame on their man, Wise, then," said Cowles.

"Martin's going to have to do three things," Bill Verdun continued. "First, set up a good automation installation to process around twenty thousand billings a day. He'll know how to do that. Second, he'll have to fight Wise without it looking like he's fighting him at all. That's a rough go. Third—"

"If he's done the first two, he's got it made," said Seaman Cowles.

Verdun shook his head. "No, because the third is even rougher. He's got to start where G. C. Wise left off with the human beings of Coast Gas & Power. Wise worked with them so they got a union, worked with the union so they have damn good wage levels, health insurance, retirement, a credit union, and now he wants to guarantee their jobs."

"All that is outside of Martin's work," said Fry. "His job is just to see that our automation equipment goes in and those hundred girls they don't need go out. Then in three months we've got a cost story to show Coast that'll be so damn strong they'll order the rest of the fifteen million dollars' worth of automation for the rest of their offices. That's Martin's job, if we send him—and I'm still not convinced he won't be way out of his depth on it."

76

"He won't be out of his depth, Turner, if he follows through on the third step. He's got to sell those hundred women into believing in what he's doing."

Cowles laughed. "That will be the day. Take some old hag that's been pounding an adding machine for twenty years. She doesn't know how to do anything else and nobody'd hire her if she did. At Coast, like Bill says, she's in clover. Easy job, good money, every kind of benefit the union can think of demanding. Martin comes in to lay out a machine that will end her job forever. He's going to be able to sell her that this is a good idea? Like I say, that will be the day."

Verdun spoke slowly. "And if he doesn't she'll go right to the union, she'll take her twenty shares of Coast stock and show up at the next stockholders' meeting—"

Fry broke in. "Bill, what is the answer for some old doll like Sea was describing? We're close enough to the business to know that automation isn't going to stop. Within three years there are going to be damn few jobs left in white-collar fields. What in hell is going to happen to all those people?"

Verdun looked at Turner Fry for several seconds before he answered, and then he did not answer Fry directly.

"Soke, what's your answer on that one?"

Sokolik shook his head. "Not in my field, Bill. I design the machines; what happens afterward is somebody else's job."

"You, Sea?"

"Retirement, I suppose. They all get some kind of money from some place—severance pay when they get the old ax, unemployment insurance until that runs out, and then they've got savings. Insurance, too. If they don't try to live it up they can survive, somehow. The young ones can get married."

Verdun waited and then said, "You've already asked the question, Turner, so I won't come back to you with it. It always kind of amazes me that the men who are changing the world are so damn interested in the process of changing it that they never look up to see what's happening."

He was silent again and the other three waited for him.

"Is there any reason people should be made to do drudgery if something else can do it for them?" he asked. "If you don't

77

think of this in terms of one woman who is willing to keep on pounding a billing machine's keys because she's been doing it for twenty years and think of what we're doing as making it unnecessary for any woman to sit at a machine for twenty years you've got your answer."

"We may have our answer, Bill," said Turner Fry, "we're on the right side of the situation. But does she have her answer?"

This time the four men were silent.

"Why not call Martin? If he's at home have him meet us at the club for lunch. We can make up our minds today on him." Cowles did not resent the custom of the four top Verdun executives spending their Sunday mornings working. He liked the feeling of intimacy it gave, and besides, the top Verdun men could take whole weeks off for fishing, golf or even trips to Europe and the Far East on company time and company expenses.

"Fine. Soke, would you call him now, please? I'd like to send him to Los Angeles tonight if we decide he can handle it."

Robert Sokolik picked up the pale green phone from the low table.

9

AT EIGHT O'CLOCK on Sunday evening David Martin was getting into a cab at International Airport in Los Angeles.

He had tried to explain, first after the phone call from Sokolik, and then after his return from the lunch conference when he had come home to pack, both the opportunity and the problem. Jean had seemed to understand without his telling her.

"You're like a fortune-teller," he'd said to her. "This is exactly the kind of stuff you were talking about—"

She acted a role, knowing that her smiles, her excitement, her tenderness were only the movements and the sounds of a skillful actress. It could not be real to her—these things a young wife did when her husband was sent suddenly into his big opportunity, the questions and hurried words, the packing and the little excited swings into his arms between words—because of the intensity of her feeling.

Jean Martin knew that if she dropped her mask David would see his wife in a way that might frighten him. Frighten him because men, almost all men, are unaware of the implacable sense of reality in women.

If she dropped her mask he would have seen a young woman whose face showed deep concern. In four years of marriage she had watched this man, this man who was everything, as he became ready for the time that would prove him out. And now the time was upon them.

He might have other chances later but this first big one would be the time of meaning. When he came back she would know in the first seconds she saw him.

If he won—if he won, the two of them could go forward into the years together as equals. They could plan together; she would meet the Verduns, the Frys, the society-section Cowles, socially, and she could help David in the women's end of the

79

polite, ruthless war in which their men fought for power and the rewards of success.

It wasn't fair, she thought bitterly, that the time should come so quickly, without warning. That it should be so nakedly a single answer, with David Martin sorted as a farmer might pick one bull calf to live strong and male, the other bull calf to be castrated and given his few months of fattening for death.

Let David miss out this time and she would know that she was married to a man who was a good, competent electronics engineer. Nothing more, not enough.

She had driven him to the airport below San Francisco, watched him walk up the stairs into the plane, watched the plane taxi away down the runway.

On the drive back to Sunrise Hills, with the car radio playing softly, she tried to find a different way of looking at her marriage.

"For better or for worse—"

A man and woman spending the years of living together, not judging each other against the values of other people, accepting each other until death because of the love-excitement of a few months of youth?

She had chosen David Martin over other men because she sensed that he was the kind of man she needed, the man who might need the special woman things she had to offer.

He was a man of the time. That was important. He belonged to this latter half of the twentieth century; he was a part of the exploding change.

And during four years she had realized that he was a gentle man, quiet, honest, competent.

Hell, she thought, there are plenty of gentle, quiet women; let them have the men like themselves.

She tried again. Men earned success for themselves, sometimes, by this quality of simple competence. David knew his field; might that not be enough?

Not any more, except by rare chance. She knew that. Electronics was a team science, there were no single jobs. David had explained that to her. The sciences and the technologies were impossibly complex now except to teams of highly trained specialists working together. If David could not show his ability to control men he would be lost in the anonymity of a team of specialists at Verdun.

David had told her—he liked to tell her about his job and Verdun and she wanted to listen to him—that his boss, Sokolik, would have a difficult time of it now if he was not already project vice-president of Verdun.

"Soke's competent enough, and he keeps up with things, but he's pretty much afraid to shoot ahead on his own. He'll wait for Bill Verdun or Turner Fry to point out the way on something new, then Soke'll set up a project on it. All he does is keep the project team on its toes—he doesn't lead—"

If David succeeded on this Los Angeles assignment, he might be in line for Sokolik's job. Sokolik wasn't married; he didn't have a wife fighting for him with Mrs. Verdun, Turner Fry's wife, or that elegant Mrs. Cowles.

David would be in Los Angeles all of the coming week, alone until Wednesday, and then four of the young men from the projects section would come down to work under his direction. On Saturday either Bill Verdun or Turner Fry would fly down for a check-up conference.

Again she tried to stand away from herself and look at Jean Martin, at Mrs. David Martin.

"You're building this thing up terribly," she said aloud, letting her voice ride above the music of the car radio. "A little sexual embarrassment last night and you're trying to get back at your husband because of it."

It was as if an older sister were talking to her. "A rather sluttish girl who happens to be a neighbor annoys you. She annoys you because there's simply nothing right about her. David doesn't understand this and he pops off with her name at exactly the wrong time.

"So it was a lousy one. Don't take it so big, they can't all be balls. Don't explode it into it's life or death how David makes out in Los Angeles. He's got a good job, he's a good man, he's going places. You know that—David's going places."

And then, her voice at a different pitch, as if she were answering that older sister, "That's the whole point. I don't know whether David is going places or not."

She waited for the light and made the right turn from Bay-shore toward Sunrise Hills.

The lights of five thousand homes were going on as the late Sunday afternoon darkened with the wall of clouds storming over the hills from the Pacific.

Five thousand here, she thought, and Lord knows how many tens of thousands more on the Peninsula south of San Francisco! All of them new, with redwood, fieldstone and glass, all of them with patios and shining kitchens, television sets, automatic washers and dryers, automatic mixers, coffee-makers, toasters, garbage disposal gadgets, clock radios, freezer cabinets, automatic lawn sprinkling systems, electric lawnmowers, dishwashing machines. Nothing down and not much a month, and everybody young, secure, with the healthiest children, all of them still little and fun, full of vitamins and whole wheat cereals, drinking endless quarts of extra-rich milk.

Mostly sunshine and never a real winter, never bone-hurting cold; never a real summer, with the bed sheets clinging wet at night. A kind of Islands of the Blest where nobody was old and everybody had as much pleasure and ease as the rich people.

Everybody anxious to belong, to join, to take part. The Parent-Teachers' Association—that was the big one, and Betty would come over the morning after each meeting with a long report, sometimes angry, sometimes pantomiming out the mannerisms and antics of other mothers as they had talked up from the floor. The PTA was the big one, all right, the impor-tant one.

But not for her. She had to be content with the Mental Health Society, the League of Women Voters, her day at the volunteer desk of the Council of Social Agencies.

For the men there were the Legion and the VFW, the Elks, the Sunrise Hills Civic Improvement Club, and if they worked nearby there was Rotary for the older, more important ones, Kiwanis, the Lions, the Optimists, the 20-30 Club, and the Jaycees.

For the church members there were all kinds of clubs and projects beginning with a Sunday nursery school for the smaller ones. In the few months since families had moved into Sunrise Hills a Garden Club had been established and Jean had heard of a Camera Club and some of the young couples had started a sports car club built around a dozen MGs, a TR2, and one elegant XK-140.

Join, take part, belong. She had talked to Betty about this part of life in the vast suburbs, all of them so much like Sunrise Hills.

"It's wonderful," Betty had said. "Back in San Francisco, I just wasted so much time, not really accomplishing anything. In the evening we'd go to the movies or watch television. Maybe one night a week Herman would take me out to Fisherman's Wharf or someplace like that for dinner.

"But since we've come to Sunrise Hills—my! I've found out I can speak in public, you know about the school program and everything; there's the evening art class once a week at the junior high, and Herman and I go to the meetings of the Improvement Club—I feel like I'm really doing some worthwhile things—"

Pride. Betty Kreitzer had pride, and Jean knew that it was good, solid, womanly pride in her man, her children, her home, and in herself. Yet it was a pride without teeth; she was satisfied if these objects of her pride had the normal values of the community, nothing less, nothing more.

She wondered for a moment, as she turned into the driveway of her house, why she could not be like Betty Kreitzer.

There were women like Betty who fitted in so well but who were really no more than honest, cheerful peasants in fieldstone-and-glass ranch-style houses; there were women like Leola Noon, who belonged in a dirty furnished room in San Francisco; and there were women with the strong, unsatisfied pride, like herself.

As Jean Martin parked her car and went into her home, Betty Kreitzer was fighting to keep from crying. What had been a good Sunday for her had gone bad. She had brought the children back from church and Sunday school; they had told her—as they did each Sunday morning—about the lesson. Today it had been Noah, the rain of forty days and forty nights, the great flood.

Sandra and Harmon had lots of questions for their mother as she drove the bright blue-and-white car in the Sunday flood of traffic. When they got home they found their father had taken apart the gasoline-engine powered lawnmower and while Betty Kreitzer prepared the picnic lunch, Sandra and Harmon helped their father put the mower together.

"I know how that works, Daddy," said Sandra reaching into the ordered row of parts Herman had put beside him.

"Don't touch—" His hand shot out to grab his daughter's.

"It's okay, Daddy. I know where it goes."

He heard Harmon running and turned to see his four-year-old taking off with a spark plug.

"Damn it. Bring that back. Right now!"

Betty walked outside from the kitchen in time to see her husband catch a boy doubled up with laughter. Back at the mower chassis Sandra was trying to set a part in place with a screw driver.

"I'll give them something to eat. You'll never be able to get that back together with the kids deviling you." Betty looked at the strewn parts. "What happened? Did it break down?"

Herman had the spark plug and his boy was jumping in the air, trying to reach it. "No. I just wanted to see how it was made. It's pretty simple."

"Who's the four-year-old? You or him?"

"Look, Daddy, I got it together!" Sandra's face was bright with pride.

"If we're going to the zoo we'd better take off. Traffic's going to be fierce." Herman wiped his face. Harmon had run over to his sister and she was showing him the part she had tightened into place.

"I wanta put one in, Daddy. Sandra put one in and I didn't!" The boy's face was shiny with eagerness.

"Okay. Can I help you, boy?"

Betty smiled at her family. This was the way things should be. A good house, a bright Sunday, the two kids healthy and happy, Herm working at things around the house and the family going to the zoo together.

She could hear Michael Flagg screaming next door. There was a crash of glass shattering and Isbel's voice. "You smashed that on purpose, you little devil! Jerry, come here and see what this little devil just did!"

Betty's wide, strongly formed mouth tightened. The Flagg boy was being ruined by his parents. He was still pretty helpless against them but day by day he'd learn the tricks an unhappy boy learns to use against his world. Michael will be all right as long as he still breaks dishes, she thought. The real trouble will start when he stops breaking things openly. He still hasn't learned to hide from them, but one of these days he'll learn how to do that. Then they'll have a bad boy. A real bad boy.

She made cold sandwiches for everybody before they left, and the picnic hamper was loaded as in the old days back home. German potato salad with hard-boiled eggs and little chunks of crisp bacon mixed with the pickled onion slices and the homemade mayonnaise. Sometimes Betty liked to do everything the way her mother had taught her: make her own pie and biscuit dough, stir up her own mix for cakes, blend her own salad dressing. It was fun, but it was a lot of work, even with the electric mixer. The main trouble was that the things didn't taste much better, sometimes not as good, as the prepared stuff she could pick up at the supermarket in the shopping center.

Betty Kreitzer was a woman who ran her home instinctively and as she had been taught by her mother. When she had been small it had been hard going for her family in the old flat near Milwaukee Avenue in Chicago. Her clearest memories of her mother were always of the kitchen, her mother stirring with a big spoon or cranking the handle of the egg-beater, her mother sitting in a kitchen chair working at something on the oilcloth-covered table.

Her mother had pride in her kitchen work and she had been a severe teacher with her daughter. Gone and useless now, all the little skills and tricks her mother had taught her so patiently. What good now to know her mother's secret of the right time and way to fold in the ingredients of cake batter?

She could remember the messy excitement of learning to clean a chicken, to gut and bone a fish. She hadn't cleaned a fowl since—longer than she could remember.

So many other things that her mother had taught her. Home remedies for coughs and colds, even using spider web on a deep cut.

What was left of all that careful teaching? Not much. German potato salad for a picnic, the special Christmas cookies. And all the rest of it had been taught, mother to daughter, for so long. Her mother had learned these same things from Betty's grandmother back before the First World War when the family still lived on the South Side near the stockyards. Betty's grandmother had learned them from her mother on the little farm in Württemberg.

They had so much pride, those women, Betty thought. They measured other women against themselves by the cleanliness of their houses, broom-swept and hand-scrubbed; by their cooking and baking; by their needle-sewing and knitting; by their old-wife wisdom on babies, sickness, morality. The other things, their men and the work their men did, their churchgoing, even their children, were taken for granted. The men worked, had their own fun sometimes; the whole family went to church and to church activities; the children minded.

A woman was measured by the things she did for her family, the things she knew how to do.

You had called a doctor when somebody had been hurt bad, or was very sick; you went to the hospital to die.

Betty knew about this only from her mother; by the time she was growing up it had changed quite a lot, and she had seen the rest of the change.

It had all changed so fast. Betty's Aunt Gracie, her mother's younger sister, had been something called a flapper about the time Betty was a baby, and she had guzzled gin in speakeasies before she eventually settled down. In Betty's mind, Gracie somehow marked the end of the old series of mother and daughter keeping to the same ways, knowing the same mother and woman secrets, having the same kind of woman pride that reached back across to Württemberg and the old times, the very old times.

All that was really left was her religion, the religion which had begun with Christ and Peter, that had been founded again in the reformation of Martin Luther.

She wondered sometimes about the neat packages of frozen foods, the ready-mixes, the brown-and-serve bakery goods, the canned orange juice, the instant coffee, the cellophane-wrapped cuts of meat, fowl, and fish. Sometimes the three of them, Jean, Isbel, and herself, had talked about it.

"Don't misunderstand me, Jean," she had said, "I wouldn't go back to the old days, but sometimes I wonder what's happening to women?"

"The same thing that's always happened to them," said Isbel. "We just dress it up fancier nowadays."

"Freedom from drudgery—the same thing that's happening to men in their work," said Jean.

"I know that," Betty had said. "I'm still amazed at how much easier it is to take care of this whole house than it was with that flat we had on Nineteenth in the city—about half the work. But that isn't what I meant."

"They haven't changed kids any. Maybe they have—they're more trouble than ever now," said Isbel. "When Mikey's home —well, I can't get anything done. If I'd been that much trouble when I was a kid—wham! But if I wham Mikey he just gets meaner."

"I think television has changed kids a lot. They know about ten times more about things than they used to—why when I was a little girl I might see a movie about once a month, sneaking out mostly because my parents thought movies were bad. Now Sandra and Harmon see a picture every Saturday, and about five hours of TV every day. They just see an awful lot."

Jean said, "We're something like the children. We've got more hours every day to do things, we understand so much more than our mothers did, we don't have to get fat or scrawny or tired-looking, we can talk to our husbands about something besides the house and the neighbors."

"Maybe you can," Isbel broke in. "All Jerry's interested in is sports and complaining about business."

"Herman's way ahead of me. He tries to read me things from the paper or some magazine, and it's way over my head. Sometimes I feel so ashamed— Sandra's eight years old and she can understand him sometimes when it's all Greek to me."

"I often wondered why you didn't get a job, Jean," Isbel said.

Jean smiled. "I keep hoping."

"But I still wonder sometimes what's happening," Betty said. "By the time Harmon goes to school I might as well get a job myself. Sandra could even make supper for the family. She knows how to heat up those TV dinners and brown the rolls and everything. When I was eight I was just learning how to make bread dough, and she can open a few packages, turn a few controls on the range, and serve up a good supper. It makes me feel a little bit unnecessary."

"We're getting more like men—that's all," said Jean. "And men are getting more like us. All this do-it-yourself stuff, that's like housework for men."

"Not when Herman can stop doing it any time he feels like it. He'll start something, get halfway through, and decide to read. Anyway, Jean, I don't think men are getting any less masculine."

"Sure they are. Look at their jobs—salesmen, clerks, accountants, desk jobs. A woman could do nine out of ten of them just as well."

"I'd like to switch with Jerry. I'd have a lot of fun selling cars, and I mean the same kind of fun he has."

"Men are trying to look better, wear bright colors, show off more. They go on diets as much as the women do. I think they're getting a lot more like women than they used to be."

"Not where it counts. At least Herman hasn't," said Betty.

"No, that's where women are getting more like men."

"Oh? I'm behind the times."

"Well, we all want children—that's one thing. But beyond that don't we all have more fun with you-know than men and women used to? I'm sure we do."

"Why? They haven't improved the equipment much."

"That's just it," said Jean. "We've learned a lot more about how to use it."

"We'll have to exchange notes sometime," said Betty. "Maybe there's a new sheet of instructions out. More fun in bed."

"I could stand a new sheet of instructions," Isbel said.

"Sometimes I think the whole thing is just one hell of a nuisance."

"So that's what I mean," Jean had said. "About the only real difference between how a man and his wife live now is that she has children. They do pretty much the same kind of work —she pushes buttons and runs machinery at home, he does it at work or he's being pleasant to somebody as a salesman. Mostly they drink about the same, go out about the same, have the same kind of fun in bed. The girls are even getting bigger—have you noticed those young girls at Redwood Junior High? A lot of them look as big as boys."

"What's it all coming to?" asked Betty. "I think mostly it's wonderful, but I can't believe things are headed the way it looks."

"What way is that?" asked Isbel.

"Well, Harmon goes off to school, so does Sandra. The gadgets—they'll have newer and greater ones. Herman's been telling me about some that are coming out—take care of the house, the dishes, the washing, the meals. I go off to the club, off to school myself, maybe run for office or something.

"Maybe you've got it, Jean. I don't see too much difference between myself and Herman once I've produced the children. As far as being parents there isn't any difference in the way we treat the kids. I can't spend much more time on church work than I do now."

"You've turned out a beautiful garden," said Jean.

"There's only so much time you can put into a garden. You know, my mother wouldn't understand the kind of life we lead at all. I think she'd go crazy."

"Everybody's going crazy, anyhow," said Isbel.

"Not as much as they used to. We had the statistics on that at a Mental Health meeting. More people who have mental illness are being put in hospitals for care, but people generally have never been in better mental health."

"I'll never believe that," said Isbel. "I only wish I could afford a psychiatrist myself."

As Betty Kreitzer packed away the jars of old-fashioned potato salad tidily sealed in the clear, transparent Saran, she remembered that conversation.

She could not imagine her mother ever having had a conversation like that. Nor any of the other proud, woman-wise, mother-wise females of her ancestral line. Their wisdom had been turned into dust after so many centuries of having been the way of life, of the good family life.

The good old family life had been a hard one from what she knew of it, Betty thought. Nobody knew much of the world around them; they were fearful and suspicious of all strangers, of anybody even a little bit different. They had worked hard and grown old fast, most of them getting bitter or whining as they grew old. Their children were apt to die as babies. All most of them had known was drudgery and worry.

She could still remember the flat on the North Side, near Milwaukee Avenue. Her mother had scrubbed endlessly to keep it clean, but it was always dark and dreary, smelling of cheap food, of the sewers and drains. There were five thousand families in Sunrise Hills; there were twenty thousand families in her ward in Chicago, and almost all of them lived in dark, dreary flats. Most of the city had been like that.

In her heart she was sure she knew the answers to some of the questions. It was the truth she had been taught from her childhood on. The prayers, the Christian goodness of people, the faith of good Christians had brought them into the light and comfort of today.

There had to be a reason and this was the only reason she could understand. This was a sign of the life that could come forever to those who followed the way of Jesus. The way of the Lord had carried her family through war and famine, through pestilence and torment since the time of Martin Luther. In this new day it could give her and her family strength in a time of change.

As Betty had prepared the picnic lunch, with the children in the house to watch television, Herman Kreitzer finished his work with the power lawnmower. In a way it was a joke to him, using a little gasoline engine to push a lawnmower. He had earned his school clothes one summer pushing a lawnmower and he could well remember the clatter of the blades, the green fountain of grass blades spouting up from the bright edges, the shove of the thick wood handle against his calloused young hands as he pushed uphill.

And now a power mower, practical for a lawn this size. He might not have bought it except for the employees' discount at his store, and for the memories of the summer he had earned enough money for his suit of clothes and his shoes to wear to high school.

High school—he wished that he could have finished, earned a diploma. His personnel form at the store said that he had a high school diploma because he felt that he'd earned the equivalent in other ways. Some of the employees under him thought he'd been a college man. Reading and learning had done that; now he was beginning to think about taking some extension courses from Cal.

A power lawnmower. He started to count, thinking of them, the motors in his house. One in the car, and a big one, 240 horses. Probably too big, but then gas was the smallest item of cost connected with running a car.

One in the vacuum cleaner, one here in the mower. One in the refrigerator and another in the deep-freezer. One in the washer, another in the dryer. One in the garbage disposal, another in the kitchen fan. Two tiny induction motors in the electric clocks, skip those but count the armature-wound motor in his electric shaver. Three in his workshop in the garage —power saw, power drill, and a utility eighth-horsepower motor. Thirteen of them.

Forgot one. Betty's mixer—and another in the high-speed blender. Fifteen. Fifteen motors working for him and his family, just to make things easy and pleasant for them.

It was sure the answer to that old "sweat of thy brow" thing in the Bible. A source of power and the tools to use it.

This whole life of Sunrise Hills was only the natural result of that simple factor: power sources and the tools to use them. The difference between Herman Kreitzer, peasant, breaking his back with a hoe while his youth and strength drained away from him, and Herman Kreitzer, manager of an appliance store, owner of a home in Sunrise Hills, working over his power mower for fun on a lazy Sunday morning was the vast power source of America—oil, coal, hydroelectricity—and the incredible complex of tools to use that power.

He had begun to see this simple truth back in the army in ETO. The American armed forces were rich beyond the understanding of even their allies, the British, beyond the imagination of the Italians, the Germans. Yet Herman Kreitzer had spent his adolescence in the empty poverty of the United States during the great depression.

The country was broke and on its back, he thought. The guys in the papers were telling us that the country was so far in debt our grandchildren would still be broke. Now, it's four years later and we're fat rich. Need another 100,000 planes? Roll 'em out. Men don't like the chow? Hell, get 'em the best —try 10-in-1 until we can find something better. Uniforms for soldiers? Hell, get the top-grade wool, nothing's too good for our boys and Uncle's rich.

But where had Uncle got all that money? Busted in 1940 and deep in debt. Stateside didn't have more than a little fraction of the land in the world, and there were a lot more people in western Europe alone. You can't just print money or Hitler would have done that. When they tried just printing it it went down just that fast in value. But not the buck.

Where had Uncle got that enormous stack of real spending money?

He had finally figured it out. The United States produced more oil and more coal than any other country, more electric power. They had tools to make tools—Herman knew about those because he'd worked at Chicago Tool and Die where they used electric power in automatic tools that made tools to use more power to make whatever anybody wanted.

Now as he put the power mower in the shed he smiled. Fifteen motors in his house in Sunrise Hills. How many had he in the flat on Nineteenth? Some, not as many. How many would he have in another ten years? God knew. More; maybe fifty of them all working away to make life easy and pleasant for Herman Kreitzer and his wife and kids.

Life easy and pleasant, he thought as he walked toward the house. That's like having a damn good breakfast to start the

92

day—it's fine, but it can't be the whole story. A man has to have more in life than ease and pleasure.

He had security. God, what his old man—lying awake back there in Chicago listening to his hungry kids cry because the relief check was two days late, back there when Herman had thought cold beans poured over stale bread was fine eating—would have given for all this! Security in his job, physician and hospital insurance, life insurance, government bonds—not a goddamned worry in the world. Good wife, good kids, good house, good car, good everything. And it all came from plenty of power available for plenty of tools.

Not many guys had to really sweat their cans off any more. Not in the States. In the rest of the world there was plenty goddamned sweat pouring off guys' cans. There was only one answer for those poor sons-of-bitches—plenty of power and plenty of tools to use the power. Then they could build places nicer than Sunrise Hills and have lots of ease and pleasure.

But that was only the start for living now. A man had to work against something, do something he was proud of. In the old days, just keeping his family going was enough for a guy to be proud of, but that was getting to be taken for granted. Just the good breakfast that started a man's day.

Just working on his job wasn't enough. Too easy and getting easier. It was like being part of a big, winning team with lots of specialists, damn smart specialists, on it.

He was manager of a branch store of a far-spread company. Their market analysis of his district told him what his quota would be for each major appliance, and gave him a series of charts, maps, and pictures of where his customers would be, how much money they'd have, what they needed, what they wanted to buy, what they could be sold, what they could pay for.

Their advertising poured out of television screens, billboards, magazines, radios, newspapers and his own show windows. It was damned good advertising; they thought the stuff up, tested it in a typical market, changed it, tested it again, and finally turned it on full blast. It found those people who needed things, or wanted to buy things, or could be sold things, and sold them.

He had people working for him. They'd been hired after their backgrounds measured up right for the jobs, not too smart, not too stupid, and after they'd taken aptitude and personality tests which spotted the losers among the people who had the right backgrounds, and then they'd been interviewed by specially trained young men and women who spotted the losers which the tests had missed. Those he got as employees were a good bunch. No losers.

That was only the start with his people in the branch store. Twice a week there were special films in sound and color to train them in doing their job better. There were courses for them to take, teaching them more about their jobs. And he, Herman, got his special training too. Special manager-training films he saw once a week downtown with the other managers; special courses for him.

All he had to do was do what the high-priced smart team told him to do, and beat his quotas. He'd do that by figuring out some things that the films didn't show. It was a damned good job, and an easy one. Call it lunch for a man's day.

Herman Kreitzer had seen enough of the old days in the years before he'd grown to manhood and had become young Private Kreitzer at Camp Forrest, Tennessee, to realize how different life was now for men like himself.

He'd been too frightened when he was in his teens. There had been an advertisement for some insurance company—a full-page ad—in a copy of the *Saturday Evening Post* that he was looking through in the reading room of the Englewood YMCA. All he remembered of that ad, all that he remembered of it even the next day, had been one statement: "Fifteen out of every sixteen men over 65 are dependent upon their children or upon charity."

It had frightened him, more possibly because he was so young. What he knew of living had been as a boy on the farm, which had been miserably hard work and which had failed, and as a youth in Chicago living with his family on relief. What he could look forward to was more of the same; year after year of hard work and worry until he was old and "dependent upon their children or upon charity."

The swaggering certainty of their own success which young

men are supposed to have did not come to Herman Kreitzer until years later when he was Tech. Sergeant Kreitzer, well-fed and hard-muscled, combat wise, and with a sense of leadership.

Herman Kreitzer who once had known only the dirty streets of Chicago, walking without knowing of any place to walk toward, with empty pockets, had by then walked the streets of London toward Rainbow Corner, the streets of Paris toward Pigalle, as a man rich and powerful. He'd been a five-striper and he knew the thick feel of a pocketful of pounds or francs; he'd learned enough French to have fun; he knew his way around London and around the Sussex village near his camp; and he was to talk the halting German he remembered from his boyhood to the white-faced people of the rubble of Frankfurt.

He had come back to life as a civilian, a balanced man and one whose sense of appreciation for his own country was strong and sharp.

The years after had gone well at first, then better. Now he had what had been an impossible dream for men until these years of the second half of the twentieth century. Men had dreamed of being rich, he figured, not because they wanted millions of dollars, but because it was possible only for rich men to be without worry, to have a healthy family in a pleasant, spacious house, to live without drudgery. He had these things.

And having them he now had several choices.

He could drift through the years, eating contentment as a fat hog in the sun eats swill. Let the fifteen motors—he'd forgotten the one in the rotisserie and the one in the barbecue pit, seventeen—let the seventeen motors become fifty, buy a better car every two years or so until it was common to buy helicopters or whatever, accumulate more things, let his cushion of security become even deeper. Drift, contented, and slowly ever more useless as the big team finally solved all the problems and all the work for the manager of any of their appliance branches.

He could become ambitious, get into the big game of "Who is going to the top?" In this district there were a lot of managers; some of them would move up the ladder to supervisor, and maybe still further. Just going along easy it was likely that he'd move up, step by step. But if he wanted to go fast he knew how it was done. Sell more than the quota figures for his branch, speak up to the right men at the district meetings, send memos up the chain of command, play politics with other managers and with supervisors. Move up among the big wheels.

But why? To be called "Mr. Kreitzer" rather than "Herm"? To have a $35,000 house in Hillsborough rather than a $15,-000 house in Sunrise Hills? To have two cars instead of one? Fifty motors in his house right now instead of years from now? Most of all, he knew he didn't get his kicks out of the ratrace.

He could go big for hobbies. He liked this do-it-yourself business; it gave a man's hands something to work with. There must be dozens of little muscles, big muscles, nerve complexes, the whole living machinery of a man's body all useless these days. The muscles and nerves that had been developed so that a man could feed his family, defend them, build a shelter for them, all useless except for those you used in driving a car. Even in a car, the quiet automatic slaves were taking over so that all you needed to do was turn the wheel, gently because power did the work.

The least a man could do for that splendid mechanism of nerves and muscles which had once meant life to him and now meant nothing was to give it something to do. But even in his do-it-yourself workshop in the garage the quiet automatic slaves were waiting for him: the power saw, the power drill, the multi-purpose eighth-horsepower motor.

Go bowling. He did that, rolling a good 158 average. Get other hobbies—move into the mountains with the red wave of hunters in the deer season, the cars bumper-to-bumper on the roads? Fish for trout or salmon with the fishermen like clouds of fat flies along the streams? All that would get worse, not better.

One thing he wanted to do was his share in seeing that no human being was stopped from trying his best at whatever he wanted to try. Mostly that meant, at this time and here, that Negroes and Orientals got as fair a shake as anybody else. No more than that; no arguments about prejudice or the rest of it, only that Herman Kreitzer would work at the job of pulling down barriers.

Sometimes Herman tried to imagine how he would do as a Negro. He figured there were only a few possible ways to do.

He would try to forget about it, as far as circumstances would let him. That was the cool way of playing it, maybe the best.

He'd fight the insane tangle of stupid unfairness until he'd torn at least a little of it down, even if it meant a lifetime of fighting. That was the man's way, the lonely man's way. It might be too rough on a man's family.

He'd go along, taking everything with a smile, his hatred hidden and boiling within him. Not such a good way, the hatred would eat out his insides in time.

He'd give up, go the lazy, drinking, gambling, stealing route. It might be the only answer for a man who didn't think there was a chance.

Of course a man's woman might change the way he did as a Negro. If he and Betty were Negroes, she'd want him to try the first way. Work, study, move up, forgetting or ignoring the unfairness until you had it beat. Jackie Robinson, Bunche, tens of thousands of others.

If they wouldn't let him work his life out that way, Betty would want him to go down fighting. There was her respect and young Harmon's to make it worthwhile.

But what Herman hated was the knowing that human beings were made to take one of these choices.

He'd thought about it for a long time, since coming to San Francisco after the war. He'd attempted to know the other side, and decided, some years later, that it was impossible for a white man to know the other side.

He believed now that the terrible enemy of the Negro was not the violent man of narrow prejudice but rather the majority of people, the majority of white people who were not interested. The dead weight of habit was the weapon they used against the Negro.

The more Herman learned and thought about unfairness by labeling a human being the more he knew that it had to end.

He wanted to help end it. That was something for a man to buck against that had human value to it.

Herman knew that he was a practical man. He'd learned that in combat. The men who lived, who were promoted, who took a part in accomplishing a mission, were practical men. You figured the odds in combat like you figured a poker hand. You made a big bet in combat or in poker only if the big bet was against a hell of a big pot with a fair chance, or if the big bet would buy a small pot.

The practical way of fighting unfairness was not to storm around. Some white men had been storming around for ninety years and more and most of the help Negroes got against unfairness had been their own help, not the white man's.

But he could help in a practical way. If there was a wall with Negroes on one side and whites on the other the wall was important, but if you could get enough Negroes on this side of the wall the wall wouldn't be so damned important any more. What he was doing was getting around the wall.

Sunrise Hills was all white; as a practical man he couldn't fight that. But there were Negro customers in the shopping center and Negro customers at his store. Kreitzer had hired a Negro to help him in the storeroom before the store was first opened. He'd hired Jim Kemp from the other applicants for the job as carefully as personnel hired his clerks.

After a month he'd used Jim in demonstrating appliances. A month later Herman had talked to the district supervisor about him. "He's a good man and I'd like to put him on as a salesman here in the store—"

"But policy—"

"You have Negro clerks in some stores."

"Those are in Negro neighborhoods."

"Kemp is a good salesman with white customers."

"Have you had any complaints from customers because he acted as a salesman?"

"A few. Are you going to line up with that kind?"

Herman steered Kemp through the traps in personnel and the young man now had the same kind of security for himself, his wife and their baby, as Herman had for his family.

Herman knew some of the men in one of the smaller luncheon clubs. They were Korean veterans and they understood what Herman was talking about. A week ago Jim Kemp had been initiated as a member in the luncheon club, representing the store Herman managed.

That was as far as he had gone here. He would not make a special effort to hire another Negro, but he had seen that reports on Kemp had gone up through personnel. He'd taken one man over the wall, others would follow.

This was something a man could take pride in doing. He would do more, but always in a practical way.

Herman Kreitzer had tried to understand why this business of fairness should be important to him. Maybe it was because he'd been on the wrong side of the wall when he was a kid, on the wrong side because his family was goddamned poor. Then during the war he'd found himself as a man. He didn't like a game where the rules weren't fair. That was about all the reason he could figure.

The other thing—the big thing was completely different. He'd gone to Lane Tech for as long as he could; he had wanted to be a scientist or an engineer. Somebody like David Martin.

He couldn't make that any more. Herman Kreitzer's chance of being a scientist was pretty well lost before Pearl Harbor and the war finished it. But the curiosity was there, the need to search out and understand. He had no math background, only a few months of high school chemistry and physics, but he had the scientist's ability to remain curious, to move forward in understanding by being willing to let old beliefs be pulled apart.

If he could not build betatrons or analyze the spectograms of stars beyond Andromeda because he had not been trained, at least he could work at a more practical problem: what is the purpose of man?

It was not something to be talked about, except sometimes to Betty. He was a practical man and he realized that the men at the bowling alleys would not be interested in what Herman Kreitzer thought might be the purpose of man.

Nor did he want recognition as any profound thinker. He felt that there was a certain dignity in being a human being;

in these times of enormity, of change beyond yesterday's imagination, each man should give thought—as befitted human dignity—to the purpose of man among the triad realities of time, space, and energy.

This had brought him to the only real problem of his marriage. Betty's faith in the religion of her family was a part of her entirety; if it was destroyed or taken from her Betty Kreitzer would be less than she had been. She had lived her childhood, her adolescence, her years as a young married woman and as a mother within a framework of rigid faith.

There was God, the Bible with His Word, and His Son Jesus had died to give mankind eternal life. The faith of the apostles had been brought anew by Martin Luther, and there could be no salvation for those who did not believe and worship God.

To Betty, it would be damning sin to allow Sandra and Harmon to grow up without exactly the same beliefs which had been given to her in her childhood.

If he weakened the growing faith and orthodoxy of his children Betty would see him as a mortal danger to her children. If he attempted to destroy his wife's own orthodoxy he would take something precious from her, leaving her nothing with which to replace it.

But Herman Kreitzer had a faith and understanding of his own. He believed wholeheartedly in a God beyond the gods of men. A God of Law, of precise and immediate punishment, of infinite power, and of eternal life.

It was not Betty's God, and in this was the possibility of tragedy.

10

Coming back on Camino Real from the zoo late Sunday afternoon Sandra had raised the question.

"Daddy—"

"Yes?"

"The lesson this morning was about Noah and the Ark."

"And the big rain," yelled Harmon. "It rained whoosh! whoosh! and everybody drowned—"

"Not everybody," Sandra corrected. "Noah and his family didn't. And that's what I wanted to ask about. Noah took two of all the animals there are on the Ark—"

"Elephants and lions and tigers and giraffes and monkeys and zebras—" Harmon chanted.

"How big was the Ark, Daddy?"

"I don't know. Ask your mother."

"She doesn't know anything about boats. How big do you think it was?"

"It must have been very big."

Sandra nodded firmly. "It sure must of. There'd have to be food for forty days, like hay for the elephants and meat for the lions and tigers—What about birds? Did he have birds besides those doves?"

"What did your lesson say?"

"I want you to tell me, Daddy; do you believe that was a true story?"

Herman was busy watching the Sunday drivers. The Camino Real ate through what had once been a string of quiet suburban towns south of San Francisco. It was a fast-flowing steel river with people for fish, and its narrow banks were a swampland of motels, drive-ins, bars and service stations.

"Is it all true about Noah and the Ark and all the animals?"

Herman hated these questions. He had a firm rule, which Betty shared, of not lying to the children. Not about big things, not about the most trivial things. It was a difficult rule

101

to follow because what is truth to adults is not always truth to children, but he tried as best he could.

"There have been big floods, Sandra, and farmers always try to rescue their animals."

"Lions and tigers, too?"

"Noah had to have cages," said Harmon, "or get et."

"What animal did you like best at the zoo today?" asked Betty Kreitzer.

"The bears," shouted Harmon. "How many different kinds of bears did Noah have on the Ark, Daddy?"

"All bears are related," said his mother. "Ordinary bears change into polar bears when they live near the North Pole."

"How about bugs? Did he take all the kinds of bugs there are?"

"Most bugs can live even when there's a big flood," said Herman.

"How about penguins?" asked Sandra.

"I don't know about them."

"You never told me—do you think Noah's Ark is a true story?"

Herman braked the car to leave a space for an MG cutting in ahead of him.

"Like I said, Sandra, there've been lots of big floods. This is the story of one of them—a real huge flood."

"Does God cause all the floods to punish people?"

"I don't know. What did your teacher tell you at Sunday school?"

"We all cut out cardboard animals and there was a tremendous big cardboard ship the teacher had—" said Harmon.

Herman Kreitzer had been impressed by the ingenuity and imagination of the materials used in their Sunday school. The Bible stories were given reality and substance by devices of paper and plastic, and often the lesson was supplemented by sound and color motion pictures, much like those his firm used for training salesmen except that the Biblical pictures seemed to be much more effective.

"I want to know if the Noah's Ark story is exactly true or not," said Sandra. "I don't think it's exactly true because Noah couldn't get all the animals in the zoo in just one boat. They just had little boats in those days."

Betty Kreitzer broke in. "Sometimes the Old Testament stories have to be understood, Sandra. They're really true, but they have to be understood because the truth is sometimes hidden."

"Why don't we ever have Sunday school lessons about dinosaurs and the Ice Age and about when people lived in caves and were half-ape? We see them on television but we never hear about them at Sunday school. Why is that, Daddy?"

"Like your mother says—you have to understand what the Bible means. When you grow older you'll understand it better."

"Was there really an Adam and Eve or were there really people like apes?"

"How do you know what Adam and Eve looked like, Sandra?"

"They looked like God. It says so in the Bible."

"It doesn't mean they looked exactly like God," said Betty. "It says 'in His image.'"

"I want some root beer, Daddy!" said Harmon.

Herman was glad to pull into a drive-in and get his family root-beer floats.

He was trying to make up his mind about the decision that he knew could not be avoided.

The ingenious toys and the elaborate motion pictures of Sunday school were fighting a losing action against the realities, he thought. Sandra and Harmon, as they grew into adolescence, would find some compromise between what they were taught by their mother and their church and what they would learn in the public schools and from motion pictures and television. The cardboard ark and paper animals would not survive geology as it must now be taught in high school.

Herman remembered Lieutenant Tyler from his old outfit. Tyler was an oil geologist in civilian life, a man accustomed to read the rock and clay cores which spanned hundreds of millions of years of geologic time. In his profession he would speak of Jurassic sands and Triassic rocks, yet Tyler had been a member of a Fundamentalist sect which believed the world had been created, wholly, in the year 4004 B.C.

He didn't want his kids to get in a mix-up like that. But even that kind of double-thinking would be better than what probably would happen. The kids would have doubts about some of the teachings of Sunday school, then gradually become skeptics, concealing this from their mother. A kind of dishonesty would separate them from Betty and it would be something that could not be healed.

Eventually they would realize that their father did not believe as their mother did, but they might have contempt for him because he had not been open and frank with them.

It was a hell of a situation, he thought. He had no bitterness toward Betty for her belief; possibly it was her faith which had formed her into the fine wife and mother she was. The church had little to do with her daily life; she had fun, she could be bawdy at times, she drank a little and liked to dance.

But she would be like a lost child without the certainties that religion gave her. She had tried, done a good job trying, to change a little. This business of Noah—she would talk to her children these days as if the Bible was not merely a simple factual story, but rather a mystical one in which truths were hidden in stories which did not need to be taken as exact fact.

She could not leave nor change the great basic story of her faith: He had lived as a man, had been crucified, and had died as a man, returning again as God, all to ensure an eternal life for those who believed in Him.

Herman knew many churchgoers who made their faith a kind of insubstantial dream world which they took for granted, neither questioning it nor using it. Even one of the regimental chaplains he had known was a man who had treated his religion as a special fraternity full of meaning and practicality in everyday affairs—a help socially and economically, but with no real connection to insubstantial things like eternal life, Mosaic morality, or God.

Betty was not like this. She believed in a time when her husband would join her in Heaven, a time that would not happen if either of them sinned or lost faith.

Sandra and Harmon. What would he do about them? He took a long drink of the sweet, milky root beer. He could pretend, he could evade, or he could be as frank with them as he hoped they would be with him in their years toward womanhood and manhood.

If he did it, guilt would bloom up like a great poisonous flower in Betty. The torturing certainty of personal, fatal, offense-against-God guilt. That sense of guilt which seemed like a great mainspring in so many people who clung to faith. What caused it? Was a feeling of guilt pounded deep into them when they were kids so that ever after—as men or women, as fathers or mothers, as lovers, even as workers—every damn thing in their living was related somewhere secretly inside them to this certainty of their own guilt. Guilt about what?

Some of them became faith drunkards, using their faith for excitement.

He wondered, putting down the empty glass, if maybe Betty was right. Right about everything. He did not understand the mystery of faith; he was like a Lucifer, proud and lonely. Betty's faith gave her a sense of greatness, of an importance linked to the importance of every other soul. But Herman's God made him feel ever smaller, ever less important against a staggering infinity of forces beyond understanding.

In a way belief in his God was a belief in death; belief in Betty's God was a belief in life.

Living must be a lot simpler for people like Betty, he thought.

"Everybody finished? Wipe your face, Harmon," he said. He swung the car back and moved into traffic again, headed south on Camino Real.

"Did Adam and Eve look like apes, Daddy, or did they look like us?" asked Sandra. With the subtle intuitions of the eight-year-old, she sensed that her questions were bothering her mother and father. The cat would sooner leave the frantic mouse than an eight-year-old girl relent in such a situation.

Herman knew he had made his decision.

"Depends on your question, Sandra. If by Adam and Eve

105

you mean the first animals that were more like we are now than they were like apes, why they'd still look pretty much the other way."

"Were Adam and Eve animals, Daddy?" she felt that she had him in her teeth now.

"We're animals," he said. "We're just animals with good communication, and we've learned to use power and tools."

"Herman—" He could tell by Betty's voice that she had been aware, as a good wife who has known her man for many years will be aware, of the problem he had faced. Her voice was calm, but like a good husband, he sensed the fear in it.

"Religion isn't about things like that, Sandra," he began.

The two children looked at each other, and then at their mother.

"Religion is believing there is a purpose—a bigger purpose than we can understand—"

"Daddy said Adam and Eve were animals, Mama." There was an obvious sound of shock in his daughter's voice, yet Herman Kreitzer knew that the sound was false, put on. Sandra knew that she should sound shocked and so she did.

"We won't talk about it now," said Betty Kreitzer.

"You never talk about anything that's important!" This time the sound of complaint was honest. Both parents understood; the complaint was only partly because the suddenly exciting talk about the truth of the Bible stories they had been taught was being shut off; mostly it was the frustration of an audience seeing the start of a good boxing match and having it stopped before the first solid blow had been struck, the first blood drawn.

"Betty, sometime we're going to have to face up to these things. The kids aren't going to keep on believing in those stories forever—"

"Why shouldn't they? They're true. They're the written word of God." Betty felt anger flooding over her worry.

A rottenness, a decay. The Word of God known, understood, believed in by her father and mother, by their fathers and mothers, back, back to almost the beginning. These modern times, *sanftleben* times, easy-living times without belief,

106

Babylon times, Sodom and Gomorrah times. Laughing, dancing, drunken people forsaking the Church, mocking the beliefs, maybe pretending—like Pharisees—to believe, but winking at the literal meaning of the Word of God.

A rottenness, a decay, and over the night-bright cities was the shadow of the manmade destruction of the world. Herman was right—it was time to face up to things; her children might die in the universal holocaust, but they would die as Christians, secure for eternity because of their faith in Christ, and in the Word of God.

This was the ancient pitfall, this sly changing of the literal meaning of the Bible. Even to saying as she had said herself, only a little while ago, that the "truth had to be understood." Here was the ancient pitfall, opening at the feet of her children, and if they fell into it they would die lost, unsaved, mortal wasters of the sacrifice Jesus made.

Herman was snared and seduced by the books and magazines he read, made into an unbeliever, and with the double curse of the unbeliever upon him he must now try to destroy the eternal life of her children. The double curse: the unbelievers had raised the shadow of destruction over the entire earth, the terrible shadow of destruction by science; and as they made this enormous erection of the machines of death they tried to destroy the faith of the Christians, taking them from their ancient belief in God and salvation into a belief in nothing.

The children were silent, waiting.

Herman swung the car to avoid a weaving driver. It was damn foolishness to drive on Sunday. The roads were clogged and stinking; every fool with a car was out today.

This was no time to argue with Betty, not with the kids here in the car listening, and not with a man driving and having his every-second, all-directions strain of alertness.

If it wasn't killing time on the highways, this late Sunday afternoon, it was smashing time. Killing time came after dark. They had passed one intersection with the sparkle of broken glass, the blinking red lights of the highway patrol, the two cars crumpled. There would be more along the Camino and

107

the Bayshore this fine Sunday evening, and this was no time to argue with Betty.

But they would have to work something out between them on this and damn soon. Otherwise Sandra and Harmon would get confused, not quite believing either one of them.

11

Jerry Flagg put two ice cubes into each glass, poured vodka until the cubes were covered.

"Isbel! Let's have one for the house. Come on." He took a long drink from one glass, poured in more vodka, and wiped his wet lips with his knuckles. Sunday afternoon. He felt like getting drunk.

It was kind of wonderful. There were only three ways of getting drunk that were really fun: with some guys in a comfortable, high-class bar where everybody was gambling for the drinks and telling stories and laughing; or with some new broad—drinking with her for the first time and watching the phony stuff, all the pretense and crap, melt away from her, until you could put your hand up her leg or an arm around her back so that your hand could feel the base of her breast and you could tell whether her flesh puffed up along the edge of her bra or if the bra was too big and stiff because it was holding up some floppy fat bag or if things were just right, just a light nylon web stretched firm by the goody inside it; or drinking like this at home on a Sunday afternoon, watching things blur and soften out and you didn't have a goddamn trouble in the world.

But you had to pay for them, like you had to pay for every goddamned thing that was halfway fun: too goddamned much. That's what you always had to pay.

In the bar with the other guys, hell, that could cost a lot of dough. Three, four hours and there you were—ten bucks shot or maybe more. The gang would break up and you'd be sitting there alone and maybe having to cash a check, if you hadn't cashed one already, and nothing much to show for it except some stories, and there were damned few new stories and some guys couldn't tell a story for sour owl shit. A man wasted a hell of a lot of time drinking with the guys. Money, too. Hell, it would be great if you were loaded with gold, really making it. Get the big treatment from the guys then, too. Everybody's nice to the guy who's got the money.

You had to pay for drinking with a broad, too. Half the time you'd both end up sloppy drunk and the broad would be changing in other ways than just dropping the mask and easing up, letting you feel her and telling her stories about dolls and what they could do for a man. They sure changed when they got gassed. You might be making out like crazy and without any warning the broad would freeze and you'd have pretty good reason to guess she was secretly a Les and it took the drinks to peel her down to what she really was, or it would be like breaking a faucet and the stuff—all goddamned personal troubles you didn't give a shit about—would come pouring out of her and you couldn't shut her up. Listen to a lot of crap about all the guys that laid her and what she said and how the guys all got killed or went off to the Army or some crap like that.

Even a Sunday afternoon had its price. It would always start out fine, and you'd work up one fine glow fast and easy. Isbel would be right along with you, laughing and drinking, and you'd be thinking of how much more fun it was getting gassed right at home buying vodka by the bottle, cheap, rather than paying half a buck a throw for it at some crummy bar.

Naturally, after a while, you'd get charged up and you'd start messing with Isbel and she'd lock up the house so the kid wouldn't come running in, and there'd be one of those sweet matinee pieces that are so goddamned good because you really want to.

That was the good part but then nine times out of ten the goddamned trouble would start.

Yeah, it always cost too damned much.

He poured his third drink and yelled for his wife again.

Isbel was in the patio putting black enamel on the thin legs of the wrought-iron furniture they'd bought when they moved to Sunrise Hills. Michael was watching her and she'd let him take the narrow brush from time to time. It made her furious, the way he'd slop the enamel around, getting it on the glass tabletop or on the flagstone of the patio, or mostly on himself. But what in hell could you do; the boy'd scream bloody murder if you didn't let him do some of the painting every little while.

She had her choice: either listen to Michael screaming and try to keep him from beating his head against the flagstones, or let him smear the whole place up with black enamel.

Jerry was yelling for her; he was probably set for one of his big Sunday afternoons, getting potted and getting her potted too, and then getting hot pants from the drinks.

Sober he had practically no interest in her, but if he came home stinking he'd try.

And these Sunday afternoons. They were kind of fun. They were nicer to each other on a Sunday afternoon when they were alone and Michael was at a movie or someplace; they'd drink and talk about things, and she'd come over to him and they'd fool around and she'd get excited, crazy excited. She would be proud, knowing what she could do to him, waiting for that instant when his mouth would open and his whole body would tremble and he'd be arching up his back—

But, God, how she felt afterward. Mixed-up. Unsatisfied, mostly; not sure whether she should be ashamed again, like she was that first time, and there had been hundreds of times since then—but she had never made up her mind if it was something to be ashamed of or not.

He would come home drunk, three or four in the morning, falling into things in the bedroom, and say the dirtiest things he knew to her.

"Mama, it's my turn to paint." Her boy's thin arm, streaked with black enamel, reached out for the brush in her hand.

"Michael, I'm almost finished—"

His narrow face pinched up and he began to jump up and down.

"Oh, all right but don't splash any of it— Look out! Oh, God damn!"

Michael had knocked over the can of enamel and some of it had splashed on her slacks, the rest of it spreading over the soft peach and gray flagstones.

He was crying and of course he had to step in the puddle

111

of black. She slapped him across the face and he bent forward, his eyes shut tight, his mouth open wide, the chords and arteries of his neck knotted out as he screamed.

"What in hell are you doing to the kid? Murdering him? Oh, Christ, who spilled the goddamned paint?"

"Don't talk like that in front of Michael!"

"He can't hear me, he's yelling too loud. Hell, they could hear him in San Francisco. Why does he have to yell every goddamned minute he's home?"

"If you'd help instead of shouting at him we could get this mess cleaned up before it dries on."

"Yeah, you make the mess and expect me to clean it up."

"You could have been out here helping me instead of slopping up that vodka all day—"

"Sunday is the only day I've got to enjoy myself—"

"Oh hell, forget it. I'll clean it up myself."

Jerry smiled, the twist of anger gone from his face. "I'm sorry, honey. I'll get the thinner and wipe it off. Then we'll have a few drinks together, and forget about it. Okay?"

She saw that his face was flushed. He'd had enough to be on his way. She felt a tensing of excitement, knowing that in an hour or less she'd have him in that horrible, incomplete, frantic, crazy, dirty way. Wanted it.

What kind of a love was this? She looked at her husband, helpless with the old mixed-up thoughts, mixed-up emotions she'd had since she first knew Jerry Flagg.

He was blind, selfish, careless, and yet she knew no other word for the way she felt toward him except love. Love a man who comes home with smears of lipstick from barroom tramps, mean-tempered and indifferent to her; but somewhere inside of Jerry there must be love for her, she had to believe that.

All these years of marriage, Michael, this new house, the bright-colored convertible—these things mattered, added up.

It was her fault. She was afraid of having another child—afraid of the thick-legged, belly-heavy, clumsy-bodied months; afraid of the days mounting toward the time when the pains would start; screamingly, crazily afraid of the pain.

Michael had been an accident, coming into life in spite of

the jelly and the diaphragm. They'd planned to have a few years of fun, young marrieds, before starting a family. Jerry was just back from the war, selling cars like mad, and every night a party.

What a crazy kid she had been, with her mother pecking and preaching at her before she'd even had her first period. She knew what it was all about when she was twelve, what with the girls at school and in the neighborhood always talking about it, giggling and playing with each other sometimes. Knew the words and what was supposed to happen, and scared into an icicle to let a boy put his arm around her. She got scared and stayed scared until Jerry said he wanted to marry her, and she was as scared while he was fooling with her the first time as she was when the labor pains started with Michael.

Damn her mother for all that. If she'd gone like the other girls did, having show-parties when they were just little kids, letting boys feel her, and then when she was sixteen letting one of the boys she had crushes on screw her, she'd probably have a hell of a lot better marriage than she had.

Of course it was Michael that did it. Having a kid when she was so damned sure she was safe, never letting Jerry do it until she'd gone into the bathroom and squeezed the jelly up inside her and pushed the diaphragm into place. Those had been wonderful months, those months of pregnancy— they'd be driving in Jerry's demonstrator and he'd put his hand up her leg and then she'd reach over and unzip his trousers, and sometimes they'd go to a drive-in movie, with thousands of people around them in the other cars in the darkness. God, what wonderful months, not worrying about anything with the jelly and the diaphragm, and just going crazy with Jerry.

But after Michael was born she'd turned into a lousy screw. Jerry said so and he was right, she knew she was. Scared.

Their marriage had gone to hell with that, and that's where it stayed.

If it was just giving Jerry pleasure, satisfying him, and if she could show how crazy it made her when she was doing it, they could get along all right that way. But there was more meanness in him than pleasure; she could tell by the way he looked at her. And then afterward he was edgy and jumpy, not easy and content the way he used to be after they'd fooled around and screwed and fooled around and screwed again the way it had been in those first months. He'd want her to do it, and she'd want to do it, but she couldn't let him know how much, and then when it was done neither one of them was happy.

There was guilt, too, and it didn't all come from her old witch of a mother.

That time that she found out, the very first time, that Jerry had cheated on her. She'd been so goddamned mixed up she didn't know what to do for a week, just pretending with Jerry every second of the time they were together, being sweet and loving, all the time inside she was churning over and over.

So they'd gone to that goddamned miserable party where everybody got sloppy drunk and that kid salesman who worked for the same dealer as Jerry began making passes at her.

Everybody was milling around and she and the kid salesman, Chick, went out to a car.

Oh God, that morning. Sick like a dog, and then having it come back to her, remembering. Scared—if Jerry found out he'd kill her, and that Chick would talk, he'd brag about it and every son-of-a-bitch in the whole sales organization would know about Isbel Flagg. Scared so bad that she started vomiting.

Disgusted, with remorse tearing at her, and that dirty, smirking satisfaction in having done that, getting even with Jerry, getting more than even.

But ever since that party she couldn't really let herself go doing it with Jerry.

And they didn't have a hell of a lot else between them.

A nice house in Sunrise Hills, a good car, TV and all that stuff, Michael, a paper mountain of bills. Not a hell of a lot else.

But they sure would have if they could just be two young

114

people in love the way they had been in those good months, laughing and loving damn near all the time.

She stood up and took Michael by the hand. "I'll clean up first."

Jerry picked up the paint can, put the brush into it, and went toward the kitchen.

"I want to go to the zoo, Mama," Michael said. "Sandra and Harmon went—"

"Not this afternoon—don't put your hands on your clothes! They're dripping with enamel. God, there you go!"

"I want to go to the zoo!" Michael began his jumping up and down.

The kid was right, Isbel thought. Betty and Herman took their kids around, the zoo, the airport, up to that wonderful park in Oakland. It was damn seldom that Jerry wanted to take Michael any place.

Before they got the house in Sunrise Hills, when they still lived in that dark, cramped little place in San Francisco, they had taken Michael to the zoo one Sunday. He'd gotten sick all over Jerry's suit and Jerry was angry enough to kill the kid.

It was lousy. Living here in a really nice place, with nice people like Jean and David, Herman and Betty for neighbors, and it was all pretense.

All pretense, even at the barbecue last night. It was fun, okay it was fun. But everybody could see Jerry's eyes eating up Jean Martin, trying to look up her shorts every time she sat down, getting his hands as near as he could to her rump.

Betty Kreitzer so smug and happy with her family and her life. Probably Herman gave Betty a good pounding every single night—Betty kind of said as much—and if she got caught again she'd probably be happy about it. God, it must be wonderful just making love to your man and having him make love to you and give him everything you had in passion and not give a solitary damn if you got caught or not.

And Jean with that absolutely perfect body of hers; it made her mad just to see Jean naked with those stunning breasts and legs and that round firm ass. She was satisfied. By God that was something you could tell in another woman—

whether she was getting enough and whether it was right or not.

Jean had that look, that goddamned kind of sleepy look that a satisfied woman always has. Betty had it, too, but not so much. Betty took that stuff for granted, just another part of her goddamned well-adjusted goddamned life. But Jean lived for it, the way she used to live for it in those first good months with Jerry.

It was the pretense that made her sick, and yet she had to pretend all the time. Pretend that she and Jerry and Michael were all lovely people, happy as hell to have their nice new house in Sunrise Hills, and with a wonderful life ahead of them.

Pretend to talk about all kinds of things with Jean and Betty; three women who were good friends, all modern and with the modern outlook on life. Talk about natural childbirth—when the very thought of those pains breaking your back almost made her scream—and clothes and house furnishings, going to the shopping center with them, and it was all pretense.

They knew exactly what they were doing in life, where they were and where they were going, and she didn't know a goddamned thing.

Michael was just as nice as the Kreitzer kids, smarter, but what the hell chance did he have? She didn't know the right things to do for him, and she knew that Jerry didn't care.

All he cared about was getting his loving and getting drunk. He didn't care who it was, or how it was done, and he didn't even get real pleasure out of it. Just get drunk, brag about what a Jesus-by-God salesman he was, brag about the women, talk about the 49ers and the UCLA teams in the fall, and some goddamned baseball teams in the summer, talk big about hunting deer, shooting ducks, fishing for trout, get drunk and get it in any way handy with anybody handy, even if it was his wife.

Owe everybody and fight for every miserable dollar she got from Jerry. Most Sundays end up getting drunk with Jerry, locking the kid out in the patio, and doing what Jerry wanted her to do while he looked at her with mean eyes.

116

Hell.

"We aren't taking you to the zoo today!" she yelled at Michael. "You come in with me right now and get cleaned up. After that I want you to go outside and play."

"You and Daddy will get drunk and then you'll fight!"

Seven years old, she thought, and he's got us pegged cold.

12

DAVID MARTIN registered in at the Hollywood-Roosevelt and went up to his room. The bellman put the suitcase in its rack and placed the thick brief case on the desk. After he left David went to the window and looked at the lights of Hollywood Boulevard eight floors below him.

It was a sick city, he thought, a dying monster of a city. Choking on its own excretions of gas and smoke, clogged by its own internal arteries of freeways, and its damnation was marked on the faces of its people.

He remembered how their faces looked, here on the Boulevard, downtown on Broadway, at the drive-ins on Ventura in the Valley. Not happy people; he tried to think of what it was about their faces that made them different from the faces of people in San Francisco or New York.

New York—its people were tired, resentful, frenetic, pugnacious. They had the faces of people who were pressed, the same kind of faces you'd probably find in any too-crowded city of any time. The yellow faces of Hong Kong or the gray ones of New York must show the same signs of being enclosed by people, pushed in on yourself by people, jostled by people, stacked above and below people, not fully realizing the discomfort of the muggy summer heat or the sleet-laced soggy winters because the prime discomfort was people. They had gamin faces, the New Yorkers he remembered; the faces of people who wiggled in excitement in a shallow, fast-moving stream of life, bruised by others, yet knowing some kind of a swarm satisfaction in the very discomforts of the swarm.

San Francisco people, David thought, were much like New Yorkers except not as tired, not as crowded. The men looked younger and healthier in San Francisco, and the mouths of San Francisco women were softer than the tight lines of the mouths of the women of New York. For San Francisco there was Marin County across the Golden Gate, and no Bronx; for San Francisco there was Contra Costa and no Brooklyn. No brutal summers, no merciless winters, and less than one-tenth as many people. San Francisco was a town where it was still possible to be individually human, not mass human as in New York.

But Los Angeles—David shut the blind and turned away from the window. All these people had come here looking for the attributes of youth. Even if they were ninety years old they'd hoped to find part of being young again in Southern California. And the young people who had come here from the Midwest and the East, they had expected that their youth would find full flower in Los Angeles. The money and the sun, the beautiful girls and the convertibles, the big success —or even if it was no big success it would be more fun, more like being young forever, in Los Angeles.

So their faces were different from the faces of people in New York or San Francisco, or from the faces of the small towns, the cities of the rest of the continent. These people looked as if they were being cheated, as if they sat in a game that they now believed to be a crooked game but they couldn't leave it now because there was no other place to go. Cheated, to be cheated more, and yet sitting in; and they had the bitter faces of people in a crooked game.

What the hell did people want? David asked himself. They wanted drive-ins where the food was quick, they wanted freeways so they wouldn't have to stop on the way to wherever it was they were going, they wanted television and shopping centers, they wanted cars. Their lives were built around their cars, they reshaped their city to accommodate their cars, and they declared the co-ordinates of their particular personalities and their status of income by their choice of cars.

Dinosaur cars, evolving on the lines of vast power and immense size to satisfy the little people within them, and now the little people had bounded themselves within the confines of highways, parking places, drive-ins, the vehicle code, and the impersonal, inhuman currents of traffic.

And, David knew as an engineer, four million exhausts pouring thousands of tons of carbon residues into the air each day. It was death air.

He washed and went downstairs to the Cinegrill bar. It was Sunday evening and the ritual sex dance was on, the bar crowded with men and women who came to this place to drink, dance, maybe find someone who could have meaning to them.

David ordered a bourbon and water, sensing the glances of the men—casual evaluation of another buck, another competitor—and the more careful evaluations of the women—a man, fairly young, good-looking, maybe from out of town.

The girl at his right spoke to him. "Stranger?"

David turned. "Yes, I'm from San Francisco."

"Oh, I like that town!" She was blond, her hair metal-yellow and lacquered; she wore a formal gown of light blue, with petals coming up and out over her breasts, giving the impression that behind the petals her breasts might be bare.

He remembered the young-girl breast of Leola Noon, carelessly shown. This blond woman was meticulously careful with her sex display—the lacquered hair, the promise-of-revealment petals, the musky perfume, the red lips.

Without resentment, without criticism, he thought of her as having a kind of whore's display, the advertising of something more than being female because this was an advertising of competition for the enjoyment of pleasure so that the naked woman body behind and beneath the blue gown, the cloth petals, the arranged and colored hair, the perfume, the scarlet lipstick, the eye shadow, the engineered structures of bra and girdle, would be something much less than promised, something too human to be glamorous.

David thought of all this without emotion. He could guess that this girl was not a whore, she might not even be casually promiscuous, but she sat alone at a bar at night looking for something and her initial offer of herself as a person was to wrap whatever person she was in the display a smart whore might make.

There was no bad in this, and there might not even be evil, but he thought of her as having a baroque pathetic quality: think of me as a woman, I hint that I am wanton, and you know that I am lonely.

"It's a fine town," he said.

"I hate Los Angeles." She took a cigarette from her purse and he lit it for her.

"Why?" He was not interested in this woman, along the Cinegrill bar there were a dozen more much like her, a few years older, about her age, slightly prettier, not as pretty, but with the sameness you might find in a squad of soldiers. At the tables around the small dance floor there were more.

"The smog for one thing. The people, mostly, I suppose."

"The people?"

She looked toward the bottles on the shelf behind the white-jacketed barman.

"This town squeezes the niceness out of people. Maybe they were okay back home, wherever they came from, but after they've been out here a couple of years they get to be sons-of-bitches like everybody else."

She turned her head, holding her chin high, her eyes frankly on his. Her face was good, finely structured with pleasant eyes, and her lipstick was not daubed beyond her natural lips.

"Are you a salesman?" she asked.

"No, an engineer."

"Oh? Good, I hate salesmen."

David took a drink of his bourbon highball.

"I was married to one once. It was pitiful—watching him become more of a son-of-a-bitch every year."

"Maybe I'm a kind of a salesman," said David. "At least I've got to do some selling this week."

"What do you think of the people you sell to?"

"I don't do it as a regular thing. Like I said, I'm really an engineer."

"Why did you come to this bar? Do you mind if I ask?" Her eyes were still looking into his.

"Not at all. I'm staying here in the hotel—just got in. I came here for a drink, no particular reason."

"Why do you suppose I'm here?"

"To dance? It seems like the sort of place a girl might come to dance."

She waited, smiling a little with her lips parted.

"I don't know. Why did you?"

"I work five days a week as a legal stenographer. Saturday nights I go out if I have a date, if not I baby-sit with my sister's kids. I live with my sister and her husband. Sunday nights I usually come here. Like you said, to dance. Are you married?"

"Yes." The girl's Martini was finished. David wondered about buying her another one; he didn't want to get involved with her, didn't want to dance with her, but he didn't mind having her talk to him. "Another Martini?"

"Thanks. Happily married?"

"Very." He motioned to the barman. "Another Martini, please."

"I find myself in a very curious situation," the girl said.

"Oh?" He wondered how many Martinis she'd had before he had come to the bar.

"I made some calculations and I find that my chances of ever being happily married are very slight."

"Why?"

"I'm nearly thirty. I was married for six years and I have a little girl. More than anything else in the world I want to be married again. This time not to a man who'll turn into a son-of-a-bitch."

"You probably will marry again."

"I probably won't. In my office—we have about twenty men there—every man over twenty-five is married. Zero chances there. When Harry and I were married we used to go around with a crowd, and I hardly ever see any of them any more since I got divorced. There weren't any single men in the crowd anyway."

"There must be a lot of unmarried men in Los Angeles. Thousands of them."

"Not so many. Even less if you cross out all of them under thirty. Cross out the queers, the lushes, the uncatchable wolves, and what have you got left?"

"Probably still a lot."

"Not by my calculations, mister. Take a man who's thirty or more, unmarried, not a drunk or a homo, and what have you got?"

"I don't know. What?"

"Either he's divorced—and either way that's a black mark against him, maybe he's impossible to get along with, or not a very good man in the man department, or anyway probably something wrong, or he's a widower—and believe me I'm hunting for a good solid widower—or he's got some quirk that's kept him from getting married up till now. Very likely a son-of-a-bitch in one way or another. See?"

"I still think you'll get married again—soon."

"Supposing you and your wife split up—not that you will, but just supposing you did. What would she do? Get a job? Do you have any children?"

"No."

"That gives her a big advantage. I've got to find a man who'll be willing to be a daddy to Barbie. But your wife—how do you suppose she'd find another husband?"

"I hope she'll never have to."

"Do you know the first thing that would happen to her?"

"As you said, she'd try and get a job," David motioned for another bourbon and water. He had decided that the woman was not drunk, that she was deeply serious but talking about herself to a stranger because she did not know what else to do.

"The first thing is that about half of your friends—yours, the men, would try to get into bed with her. The wives of all your friends would treat her like a walking case of the plague. Maybe rightly so."

"I've heard that that's the way it is."

"She'd feel like the biggest flop in the world. The sensation of being divorced, no matter how much you might want the divorce, is like having the floor fall out from under you. You feel like a big failure. And then you find all Harry's good friends—forget the ones that have been making passes at you all these years, them you know about—but the others, the nice guys, let you know that they'd like to take you out for dinner and a few drinks. The first thing you know they're talking about motels, and how all these years they've had a secret lech for you but they respected Harry too much and now—shit!"

David didn't say anything. Jerry Flagg—sure. Not Herman.

He couldn't imagine Jean as a divorced woman, yet if they didn't have a child she might become more and more restless.

"I don't want to bore you—?"

"Not at all."

"My sister's heard all this and anyway she's more anxious for me to be married than I am—get me and Barbie out of her house. Not that I blame her. But anyway after you've gone through that phase, and getting a job to have enough to live on, then you start looking for a good man. Like they say, they're hard to find."

"Expect to find one here?"

She smiled, looking away. She was pretty, although there were small lines around her eyes.

"Older men, divorced, widowed. They come here along with the wolf pack. Besides, I'm crazy about dancing and it's fun to dance here. I'll tell you something, though, I've never gone to bed with a man I've met here. Never, not once."

She looked down at her glass. "Sometimes, when I can't stand it any more I go to the beach and get picked up. Never see the guy again—just a dose of salts, that's all."

A man with a face ballooned out by soft, fat foods and liquor came up behind the woman. "Pardon me, but maybe a dance?"

She looked at him; at the Cinegrill there were dozens more like him, as there were so many other women like her. "All right, sure," she said. Turning to David, "I'm sorry I talked so much about myself but you were easy to talk to, and thanks."

After she was gone David finished his second drink and left the bar. He hadn't belonged there, and the woman had been a pathetic figure to him. More than pathetic in her own troubles, she was also disturbing.

Disturbing because she had used Jean as an example. He had never thought of divorce in connection with Jean and himself, it made no sense, and yet he could realize—suddenly, shockingly—that it was possible.

Not because of what the woman had said; he could guess at those years with "the son-of-a-bitch." An apartment somewhere in Los Angeles, a baby and this woman a young mother fussing with her child, the salesman finding his home something other than what he had expected, what he wanted. Complaints, quarrels, the man away with other, less bothersome women, drunk, complaining about the money his home cost because he wanted to spend that money on liquor and fun.

David walked out of the hotel, and the Boulevard was in front of him. On his left was the tangle of neon across the front of Grauman's Chinese, ahead of him was the tawdry street, choked with cars. Sunday night—what would be open would be the eating places, the bars, the picture houses. Maybe best to buy a book or magazine and go up to the room.

But he walked on. Jean and David Martin, divorced. It made no sense, and yet what held them together was, on analysis, only pleasure and convenience. What might pull them apart would be discomfort and inconvenience. That, nine chances out of ten, was what had pulled the woman and her husband apart.

Love. I love you, Jean. David, I love you.

Sex, that might be the big part of love. This is the woman who excites me; this is the man who excites me. It had been —was still—like that. After the first times, the first weeks, there was more: this is the woman who excites me and brings me to fulfillment; after her I am content, feeling totally and sensually alive, yet content. After years, still the excitement, the contentment. Gone only these few days, he would hunger for her, and he wanted no other woman.

Sex and all the pattern of large and small excitements, the needs and the fulfilling, was major in love. But why only Jean for David, only David for Jean? Something special and unique for each of them so that they sought each other before they had ever met? Some unique fulfillment that no other person could ever offer?

It could not be so. If they had not met—and the meeting of any boy and girl in this mobile, fluid, changing nation must be random chance—they would have found others to love, to marry.

He tried to figure the probabilities: there must be something on the order of a half million other men who might be more exciting to Jean than he was; a smaller number of women to excite him because he was fairly ordinary and she was beautiful.

Beyond sex, what else did they have? They wanted children. Why didn't they succeed at least once in all of these hundreds of nights?

Maybe the secret of their barrenness was in that failure he sensed in himself, that not quite meeting and conquering this strong-thighed complete woman whose hard, full breasts and erect nipples pressed so tight to him, her mouth open wide, her fingers clenched into the muscle ridges of his buttocks. Maybe her need was greater; maybe for some hairy bull of a man who would make her scream until she was exhausted and finally content as she had never known contentment with David.

It was a hell of a way to think. He put the picture away from his mind, the picture of the thick-legged hairy man and the slim, strong, smooth legs of Jean, his red, wet mouth with yellow stumps of teeth and the throaty screams of Jean—

God, what a man's mind could dredge up. Yet he might as well face it—the only time he had ever felt he was the sexual master of Jean was last night, when she was cold and angry, and she had let him master her.

But there was much more to love between a man and his woman. They didn't live all day for that half hour or so of loving at night. If Jean needed—wanted—that hairy bull-monster she would not have married him, stayed through these years.

Why did she? What did she want? God knows she wanted those half hours at night. It was as if she ripped off a cool, doll-like outer covering and showed herself to him more than naked.

Two women then. The night woman and she was faithful to him, maybe waiting for some strengthening in him, some new violence, some new skill and understanding, and then she would be utterly content, the night woman. The day woman, what of her?

Somehow he had been what she wanted as a husband. Love, too, perhaps in this? In these next few days he would

126

be lonely for her as a person, apart from lust and need. He liked her, found her an art gallery of little pleasures—the way the small muscles of her face and mouth moved, the way she walked and handled things, her minor clumsiness at some tasks, her jokes, her ideas and opinions. Jean gave him pleasure in being with her. Love? Nonsexual or only partly sexual, companionship.

There were formal satisfactions. The way she looked and dressed, giving him pride in his wife as she conformed to the values of their society, their culture. Knowing that he was respected for his wife as well as for himself. Love here too? A special kind of respect and admiration, which she had for him as well.

More; the fierce drive toward accomplishment she had shown to him this morning. The need and want for him to be a leader, to give her the firm, rich red meat upon which to feed her pride. This also was a component of love: the woman demanding of her man, demanding more than the mounting wildness of hands and mouth upon her mouth, tongue against her tongue, hard body thrusting and pounding; demanding more than the good, pleasant friend and companion; demanding more than that he conform to the values of their kind and their times; demanding that he must be a fighter, a competitor, and more—that he win.

The shape of love, he thought. He was walking on the human-cluttered sidewalk of Hollywood Boulevard, not caring to notice the visual clatter of the glowing signs nor the faces of the people he passed.

This was the shape of love between them, Jean and David. Where were the weaknesses?

What did Jean want? She wanted to escape out into the challenge of strangers, finding a new way of life for the days in some job in San Francisco. Tired of companionship?

She might find a new system of values, a new grouping of people as friends, and in this group he might be out of place.

And he might fail in this Los Angeles assignment. He was an engineer; he did not have the ruthless ego-drive of the big men, the leaders. They had to believe, completely, that the only thing that mattered was what they wanted.

127

He didn't have that shark's hunger drive. A man had to feel himself the only person who was important; he had to hate anyone who competed with him, hate any person who served as an obstacle. He knew that he was not like that.

It was a simple balance: would he rather do without something than hurt someone; or would he rather hurt someone than do without something?

Utter selfishness and the unceasing need to control the lives of others.

Could he be the man Jean wanted without having these two qualities?

He was being extreme, he thought, making it black and white. A man can compete and win without being driven by power-lust, or being totally selfish.

But this was the shape of failure for David and Jean. Each element of their life together which was a component of love could also turn sour, defeat them.

He wanted to get off the Boulevard, have another drink in some bar that was quiet, peaceful. Then he'd buy a magazine and go back to the hotel. Tomorrow began something new and important, and he didn't want to think about it tonight.

There was a sign for a bar, Jack O'Brien's. He went in and was pleased to see that it was a quiet place. A young man and a girl were together in the half-round of a booth, a slender, older man sat at the bar. There was no one else except the barman, a man who was enormous without being fat.

"Bourbon and water." David sat on a stool. He had searched out some of the meaning of his marriage and he was scientist enough, rigorous enough in his thinking, to know that this was only some of the meaning of his marriage as he saw it on this particular night, at this point of progress in his life, at a time of loneliness when he was in a city too loud, too bright, choked and poisoned, and when he had listened to a lonely, bitter woman who was finding emptiness when she had hoped to find all of the good in life.

As he put down his glass after the first swallow he turned a little and saw the profile of the other man at the bar. He recognized it; this recognition gave him a little shake of excitement and pleasure such as a boy might feel upon recognizing a sports hero close to him.

The other man at the bar was Paul Wood Lesser.

Nobel Prize winners in the physical sciences are not rare in the faculties of the great California universities. The Berkeley campus of the University of California, the University of Los Angeles, Southern California, and the California Institute of Technology all have men who have traveled to Stockholm and received their Nobel awards.

Among these great ones Paul Wood Lesser was himself a giant. A mathematician of the stature of Dirac and Einstein, a physicist of the stature of Ernest Lawrence and Felix Bloch, a scientist philosopher of the stature of Oppenheimer, Lesser stood almost alone in eminence.

As David Martin continued to stare at Paul Wood Lesser, fascinated to see the face he knew from photos in *Time* and *Life*, the newspapers and television, as the face of a living man close to him, Lesser turned toward Martin and smiled.

"I'm sorry," said David. "It's that I recognized you—"

Lesser was slim, handsome. He was in his fifties, David knew, but his face was that of a young man, a disciplined man.

"Oh? Thank you." Lesser's voice was soft, each word spoken as if it was carved, but without arrogance or remoteness.

"Dr. Lesser? You are Dr. Lesser?"

"Why yes. I don't believe we've met." Paul Wood Lesser held out his hand.

This was something to tell the men back at Verdun, that he had shaken hands with Paul Wood Lesser.

"My name's David Martin. I work at the Verdun Labs, near San Francisco."

"Pleasant to meet you, David. Verdun? Oh, I know of them. Bill Verdun, and there was Pat Twohig, too. You're doing some very nice work at Verdun. Very interesting."

"Thank you, sir." David sounded reverent; he felt privileged and humble in talking to Paul Wood Lesser. And at a bar in Hollywood—fantastic!

"You're an engineer, David?" Soft, friendly voice, carefully carved words, the young face, the gray-silver hair, and the eyes—David had never realized the impact and power that a man's eyes could have.

"Just in methods—" David was stammering.

"This is a pleasant bar," said Lesser. "I like to come here sometimes and get quietly drunk."

David felt a sense of shock, and then a warm feeling of friendliness. This was something like a god, and this man's name would be remembered in history a thousand years in the future, and yet the god was friendly, the god said he liked to get quietly drunk.

"You don't live here?" asked Lesser.

"No, I'm down to work with Coast Gas & Power on a project—"

"Automation?"

"Why yes, in their accounting and billing departments. Have you—?"

"Only a guess. It seemed likely."

David was thinking: this man near him at this little barroom was Dr. Lesser, Lesser who had advised three Presidents, who knew Los Alamos, Hanford, Argonne and Brookhaven laboratories, the hydrogen-tritium plant spread over the Carolina hills; a man who was revered by Seaborg and Rabi and McMillan.

"Would you have another drink, sir?" he asked.

"I'd like one very much. Really, I'm planning on getting quietly drunk tonight. Move over—or better, I'll slide over."

The enormous barman looked at them, waiting. David wondered if he knew who Paul Wood Lesser was, if he realized that he was serving drinks to one of the great men of the world.

A half hour later they were talking as friends, even arguing. They drank slowly because they talked a great deal, but the barman knew—from knowing the ways of men who meet as strangers and find something of desperate interest to talk about as they drink—that these two would be here until he closed.

"But I don't see why you say you're drinking to the end of the human race, Paul?" The first name was at Dr. Lesser's request, and the barter of thoughts on a basis of equality was because of a kind of drunkenness in David Martin. Not from whiskey, he'd had only four drinks thus far in the evening, but from a young man's excitement. "You said you don't think there will be a hydrogen war—"

"Only paranoiacs would fight a hydrogen war, David. If men compelled to self-destruction obtain political power, it's possible. No different from a suicide blowing up an apartment house to kill himself, except of course this would be a planet. That would be a misfortune, but a minor one."

"The end of mankind a minor misfortune, Paul?"

"A misfortune only because we're achieving the Purpose so well at present. I wonder how many others are as far along?"

"I'm not with you, Paul. What Purpose, what others?"

"Surely you believe in some kind of Purpose, David? This tournament of living things, you believe there is some Purpose to it?"

"Yes, of course. It isn't all just chance. There is God."

"And His Purpose, David?"

"Well, I'm not sure a human being could understand it. We have to take it for granted."

"The time for taking God's Purpose for granted is almost over, David."

"But we have some idea of how to achieve it. We're getting there."

"We're getting there, I agree. But I doubt if you—even though you, David, are one of those who might understand— are willing to guess at where we are getting."

"Somehow I didn't think you'd be one of those who say we're all going to hell these days, Dr. Lesser. I don't think we're going to hell at all—Lord, when you compare the way an ordinary American family lives, how they think, the tolerance and communication they have today, compared to what it was like even twenty years ago, why it's incredible.

"I'm sorry, but I get angry when the doom prophets talk about the good old days when everybody was happy because they weren't rushed and hurried, and everybody lived in a neat little cottage, believing in God and their church, content and happy. That's a lot of crap, Paul."

David took a long drink, and continued. "Take this place where I live—one of those big GI developments south of San Francisco. Compare the kind of life those people live with what it was like before.

"Damn it, Paul, we're all descended from long lines of peasants. Our people didn't live in neat little cottages, they lived in filthy hovels, half-starved all their lives. That's why they got the hell out of Europe.

"They were diseased, their kids died like flies, and most of the men and women were old, sick and beaten at forty. They feared almost everything, and they hated every stranger. They'd hang and burn women and children just for belonging to a different church.

"And in the United States they weren't much better, not until our times. They lived in crawling slums in the cities or in farmhouses that didn't even have privies in back. They were just as cruel and ignorant as they were when they were peasants in the old country, and don't think we all didn't come from peasant families, dirty, ignorant, cruel, diseased, drudging damned peasants with pig-shit on their hands, because we did. Ninety-five out of every hundred people in Europe—our people—were peasants who'd beat you to death with clubs just because you were a stranger or a Catholic or a Jew or a Protestant."

"I don't disagree, David. I do have some sense of cultural history."

Martin flushed and looked down at his empty glass. "I'm sorry, Dr. Lesser. It's just that I'm sick of the Toynbees—"

"What do you think of Arnold Toynbee, David?"

"I think he's probably a nice old scholar, pretentious as hell, without any understanding of history at all. Here we are in the time of the most significant change that's ever happened to the human race and that old bird turns out millions of words about why civilizations failed and how we're going to fail the same way—"

"Do you think his theories are wrong, David?"

"Ready for another drink? Fine. Two more, please." David

132

turned back to Paul Wood Lesser. "I think I know. It was a choice between eating and having a society, something more than a tribe or a village. If people wanted to have a nation and a religion the costs were too high—up until our time."

"The costs were too high in what way, David?"

"If they were to have enough food about eight out of every ten persons had to work at getting that food, farmers and fishermen. But if they were to have a fancy national government with rulers, soldiers, teachers and the rest of it, not to mention a religion with priests and churches—those things needed three or four people out of every ten. It added up to more than ten out of ten. You know, Paul, that until our time no civilization could exist without three things being true—naturally protected boundaries, good luck with the food supply, and a high infant death rate."

"Naturally protected boundaries? Like England, or maybe the Pacific Islands, I suppose?"

"The Pacific Islands are a good example. They didn't have to take men away from the work of producing food in order to keep an enemy away. They had good luck with their food supply—unless a hurricane knocked down their breadfruit and palm trees, and the fish disappeared from the sea around them. But they had to have a high infant death rate, or rather, a damn low birth rate. That's why the system of taboos—to keep the screwing down, and they regarded those taboos as a matter of life and death, which they were. Of course they were expert abortionists too, they had to be.

"Look at what happened in Java when the Dutch cut the infant death rate and smashed the taboo systems—there were five million people on the island two generations ago and there are forty million today, on the same amount of land.

"So you had to have all three—natural protection, good luck with the food, and either few babies or a hell of a high infant death rate. Our tourists go to Europe and look at all the ruined monasteries and nunneries and if they think about them at all they think of how nice and religious people were in those days. How easy it is to forget the laws of life and death. Those nuns and monks were our taboo system. A

133

way to keep a major part of their populations celibate, keep them from having children. And when the taboos were broken by the Reformation the population of Europe skyrocketed."

"Why all this interest in history, David?"

"Toynbee's *Study of History* started me. I read it when I was at school and I thought it was a lot of pedantic knowledge squeezed around into nonsense. He had no idea of the forces of history here in America at all—"

"What do you think were the forces, David?"

"The kind of people that came here, and the simple fact that there was enough land for draft animals here, enough fuel for lights and heat in a farmhouse after sundown."

"It was rough people who came here, David."

"Yes, rough people. Dissatisfied people, brawlers, thieves, whores, drunkards, paupers. Our founding forefathers were the worst people in Europe—either their governments shipped them here to get rid of them or they came here because they were having such a bad time of it that they figured they couldn't be worse off coming to America.

"The bigoted gin-drinking Puritans, the greedy piratical Dutch, the rum-swilling scum of Liverpool and London, the Indian-slaughtering Scots—and thank God for every one of them, whores, thieves and pirates that they were."

"How about the Quakers, David? There must have been plenty of good people, and why thank God for those that weren't?"

"Because they were rebels against the kind of society Europe had. Not because of any good reasons—all bad reasons, but they still were rebels. And over here there was enough pasture to feed work animals, horses and oxen. The women and children didn't have to pull the plows here; we could afford to feed horses. They didn't have to all crawl into bed together at sunset, each of them wearing one outfit of clothes night and day all winter—stinking, crawling with lice. Over here they could afford firewood because it was there to be chopped down, and they could stay up at night talking to each other. The man stopped being a peasant and became a farmer—the difference was he had animals to do the heavy work, and before long Americans invented the reaper and a hell of a lot of farm equipment all pulled by horses.

"He was a farmer, not a peasant. He had time to read the Bible at night and maybe a weekly newspaper. His wife was a woman, somewhat, instead of being the human one of the farm animals. She was a woman and not a peasant's woman.

"Then we found coal and iron in Pennsylvania and we stopped being a poor nation. But the farmer wasn't out of the woods until our time—almost every damned farm in America has been foreclosed upon for taxes, some of them twenty times. A man, even with working animals and pretty good land, couldn't make it enough years to save his farm. Taxes—those three or four people out of every ten who were in the government, teachers, soldiers, road-builders, clerks, and the people necessary for him to sell his crops, the railroads, millers, merchants, all lived off him and would always bust him in time. A couple of years of bad luck with the crops and he was tenant-farming or off to the city to work for a factory.

"But we've changed all that in our time, in the last twenty years. What changed it? Power farm equipment. The farmer has energy to use, and the energy comes in gas tanks, diesel fuel tanks, and electric wires.

"We're getting to know enough about soil biology to take the luck out of producing food.

"Here's the point, Paul. Two hundred years ago he was an animal in dirty clothes, ignorant of everything except his own little village; bigoted, dying of smallpox or typhoid, watching most of his children die before they were even a year old, toothless by the time he was thirty, old and sick at forty.

"Fifty years ago he was a changed human being. He wasn't as sickly and he was a lot cleaner. His wife was better-looking and lasted longer, most of his children lived. He worked animals, he had pride, he was an individual. He was still ignorant, his children found out about sex by incest —and incest was the most common sexual crime in America

135

until the Model T Ford let the kids screw the kids in some other family beside their own, but at least he could read.

"Twenty years ago he was just beginning to hope the war might help pay off the mortgage. And now he's a complete person—he drives his car all over the North American continent, he's a part of the mass audience of television and radio, his children go to college, and his wife is well-dressed, well-informed. He's not so apt to be a bigot, and he's got faith in the world he lives in."

David looked away from Paul Wood Lesser. "Energy sources like coal, oil and hydropower. Tools, big automatic tools, to use that power. Communication—television, telephones, motion pictures, publications, highways. And that poor Toynbee doesn't understand that these things have changed human beings into something different from what they ever were before."

"And do you understand that, David?" Dr. Lesser's voice had a peculiar quality of sadness to it.

"Why, I think so." David finished his drink, motioned for another for each of them. "I'm sorry about my speech—of course none of it was new to you." He felt embarrassed, suddenly, like a schoolboy who realizes he has talked foolishly and too much.

"Not exactly new. But you say it well, David. Very few histories ever tell the real story of people; their story is always their energy supplies—food, animals, slaves—balanced against their energy expenditures—government, communication, war, construction.

"None of the classic philosophers ever paid any attention to these things; they were worried about setting up ideal human societies without knowing anything of what society is based upon, the energy balance. Nor for that matter did any of them mention that little matter of births—that either you stop people from procreating freely or the time will come when you must kill children. The situation is ruthless and inexorable."

"I'm not worried about that any more, Dr. Lesser. We're able to increase our food supply as rapidly as we produce children. The ocean—yeasts, photosynthesis in protein manufacture. We'll make out."

"And you never did tell me the Purpose behind all this, David?"

"I said it's God's Purpose. We wouldn't be able to understand it."

"What do you think human living will be like in another thousand years, David?"

David Martin didn't answer at once. It was strange, talking of the Purpose of God in a little barroom off Hollywood Boulevard with the vast, light-spattered, choked and sickened city of Los Angeles around them. Ironic—to have talked his fine theories of human progress, of the growing individuality and dignity of Man, in this city. Talking to one of the great intellects of the century, much as he had listened to the lonely woman an hour ago.

"Not a fair question, Dr. Lesser. No one in the year 957 A.D. could have projected our time. The best I could do would be to extend the lines of progress I know at present and throw in a few wild guesses. Sorry, Paul, I won't even try."

"How about fifty years, David? Say the year 2000—you're almost certain to live to see it."

"The year 2000? No more disease, probably one world government, maybe we'll have reached the moon, Mars, Venus. The world should be pretty much one great garden, with the cities made obsolete by vast suburban belts with no crowded downtown areas. Automation doing almost all productive work, taking care of transportation and communication. The big problem will be utilizing free time—maybe a twenty- or even a ten-hour work week. Almost everybody will be a specialist—we'll all probably go to school until we're thirty-five or forty, keep going part-time after that as long as we live.

"No wars or fears of war—communication will take care of that. I know that war is caused by communication difference, nothing else. If government means exactly the same thing to a Russian as it does to an American, if all the other

137

communication channels have high-order feedback—no conflict.

"I think it will be a pretty damn fine life, Paul. Human beings will be healthy, strong, well-fed, free of drudgery and worry. A Garden of Eden, Paul, and we're moving toward it every second. We should have it by then, we've come a longer way in the last fifty years than we have in the whole rest of human history. How does my guess sound to you?"

"On the surface I'm inclined to agree, David."

"On the surface?"

"Will this Garden of Eden we're going to make the world into satisfy God's Purpose?"

"I've got rather an odd point of view on that, Paul. A point of view about Heaven and Hell, about rewards and punishment."

"I am very much interested."

"God is ruthless, just, and merciful—exactly as we were taught He was when we were kids. He has a system of rewards and equally of penalties. You follow His rules and you're rewarded immediately and in exact proportion to what you've earned. Break them and the punishment is equally exact and immediate."

"But you said 'merciful.'"

"We have so many chances."

"And the rules, David?"

"He wants people—well, it's going to sound kind of crazy—"

"Go on."

"To establish ever better communication. I'm using that word in the modern sense, Dr. Lesser. You know what I mean—communication is the organized use of energy. Reverse entropy."

"I understand very well what you mean, David. But most people don't. How do they follow His rules when they don't know what entropy is?"

"Rewards and punishments, like guiding a horse by its reins and bit. The more you work with other people, the more clearly you understand them and help them to understand you, the more you search out the physical laws of the universe, and—most important—the more you use the energy of the universe in this communication, the greater your rewards. Move away from this direction and you are punished by drudgery, disease, death—and the terrible punishment of not understanding, of not being understood."

"But all the rites, the orthodoxies, the beliefs of the churches, David?"

"They have had their importance, Paul. We've come a long way. To have an organization among barbarians we had to have orthodoxy, conformity.

"When we found out how to use solar energy locked away and stored in enormous quantities in coal and oil we were rewarded by God for our learning how to use these energies and we were freed from drudgery.

"Each time we follow His rules, improve our communication, our use of energy, we're rewarded. We're working our way toward that Garden of Eden, Dr. Lesser."

"And that's all of it, David? We reverse entropy—instead of letting the energies of the universe run down, diffuse into cold molecular dust—and we serve the Purpose of God?"

"Remember all that stuff I said about peasants and farmers, Paul. Where did their rewards come from—and why?"

Paul Wood Lesser nodded. "It's not that I disagree with you, David. I'm waiting for you to go further—go beyond this Garden of Eden."

The younger man shook his head, took a sip of his highball.

"To the planets, to the stars maybe."

"And why Man, David?"

"Life's always followed these rules of God, Dr. Lesser. The proteins used sun energy to bind them together, then a primitive cell serving its purpose by hunting food, turning the energy into its larger organization, and then the big organizations of specialized cells—and that includes us—all trying to serve God's Purpose by greater communication, greater organization of energy.

"We were the first and maybe thereby the only one of the animals to use fire. In each step toward this Garden of

139

Eden it has been our use of energy—organizing it into communication—that has pleased God, and permitted Him to reward us. And we've only begun—we're free now, Paul—we have begun to master the energy beyond the Sun—"

David realized again that he was talking to one of the half-dozen men in the entire world who was mastering that energy beyond the Sun.

"I've been waiting for you to say the one thing, David—"

"The one thing? I don't understand, Dr. Lesser."

"The human race is not the terminal. We're being rewarded—our pleasure senses satisfied—as you say. These rewards, all of them, do come from our communication, our organizing of energy. It doesn't matter whether it's a farm tractor, a Cadillac, an electron microscope to search out a virus, a betatron, or an air-conditioning unit in a church—the rules apply, just as you said.

"But David, you outlined the ladder: Maybe the protein molecule, and the first primitive cell a step upward from it, then the organization of specialized cells into the first primitive animal life, and the two billion years of trial and failure until one species of animal with billions of cells, and the most highly specialized cells of all, the human brain, was able to cross the great threshold to the use of nuclear energy.

"The next step, David? What would it be?"

David looked at the older man. "It would be the organization of those creatures—us—into some unit still greater."

"Look at the monster forming," said Paul Wood Lesser. "In our generation the monster has begun to live. A vast digestive system—and we don't think of the packaged and processed foods in our supermarkets as being part of the digestive system of a monster of which we are the cells, nor our electronic communications as being its neural network, its nervous system, nor have we yet realized that this monster will have movement and purpose of its own as far beyond human understanding as our purposes—our foolish, casual purposes, getting drunk, making love, working, hating, fearing, wondering—are beyond the understanding of our body cells.

"The monster is just beginning to form, David. We live in the time of the embryo of the vast monster, but remember —it is beloved by God.

"Whatever His Purpose, we have been His good and faithful servants. We have gone far enough so that there can be another step up His ladder."

David nodded. "That's the logic of it, but I'm too much of a human being to accept that logic. I can think of Man going forward, out to the stars, but I can't think in your terms of some superorganism of which we are only a part."

Paul Wood Lesser swung around to David.

"That's one of the reasons I drink in lonely bars, David. But can you see what's happening to men like myself? Some of the lucky ones are too intent on the trail in front of them— they can go to church on Sunday, believing vaguely in the little sliver of the understanding of God that is any human religion.

"And some of us are outside. Two billion stars in this little galaxy of ours, a million other galaxies like it already visible to the cameras of Palomar. An immensity—and time itself splinters in our labs now, David. Four separate kinds of time which we work with, and now our math has led us into reverse time. Wherever I look, David, an immensity.

"I'm like one of the Polynesians who left his known, safe home island to search out, to adventure, and now I am alone on the surface of a greater sea than my mind can comprehend."

David stood up. He was unsteady. He said, "Thank you for your mind, Paul."

He walked out on Wilcox Avenue, turned toward the Boulevard. He got a taxi and went back to his hotel.

13

THEIR FACES WERE sullen when he left them. Troy Noon held his car door open and looked at Smith and Rothrock across the station driveway. Rothrock was looking back at him, a chunky man, a hell of a good worker—up until today.

Troy Noon knew what it was. That lanky, lazy, long drink-of-water of a Smith. Lazy, no-good bum.

He had driven in to the station on the far side; not that he suspected his men, but a good CO makes a point of quick drop-ins. No point to an inspection if you come in like a circus parade and they have a chance to snap to. If you're going to have a sharp outfit you never give an enlisted man a chance to goof off because about three quarters of the sons-of-bitches will take it.

So he'd come in on this fine Sunday and found his two men playing cards on top of the safe—Smith and Rothrock, their heads turning and their mouths popping open as they saw him in his whites, inspection-white and stiff, looking through the glass at them.

Troy Noon knew men. It was the lanky bum's fault, but they'd both have to go. Goddamn shame to lose Rothrock; the man was a good worker, kept the station clean and sharp. Had one weakness, and he'd admitted it to Troy. Gambling. Couldn't stay away from cards, dice, pool. He was a good gambler; Troy knew the type. Made good senior NCOs, played cool and hard, to win. Talked easy, the talk Troy remembered from the western Tennessee hills. Easy talk with meat in every word.

Rothrock had a good hill kind of funning, too. The time Smith rubbed his hand over the top of Rocky's head, mussing the hair, and said, "By God, Rocky, your head feels just like my wife's pussy." And old Rocky, he rubbed his hand on his head and said, real slow, "Damn if it don't." That skinny bum Smith sure turned red on that one.

Smith. He'd been a lieutenant in the infantry. That had started· him aces up with Troy. Came from up Southern California way, had worked at all kinds of jobs since coming back from Korea, finally hit the company for a job as a grease-monkey.

He was pretty smart; too smart as a matter of cold fact. Troy could have put up with the smartness if Smith had cut it. But the bum sure didn't cut it, damn near didn't try.

They'd stood up and the cards fell to the floor. Smith had bent over, picking them up, but Rothrock he'd just stood there, damn near at attention, and looked Troy straight in the eye.

Troy had walked around the station. What you could expect when the men are playing cards instead of keeping it policed smart. Dust and dirt on the gas pump islands; somebody had pissed on the floor in the crapper and there it was, a puddle of piss on the floor.

The whole station was a filthy, screwed-up mess.

Of course he fired them both and he caught his hand moving up like he was going to rip the stripes off some sergeant he was busting.

What he wanted to do was hit them each in their teeth, splatting their lips all over their faces, the way he'd done to Mellicker back in Guinea. Mellicker thought he could goof off just because he'd buddied up with Troy when they'd been holding the Huggins perimeter. The buddy business had its limits, and Mellicker sucked C-ration soup for a month after that.

He'd told them they could get their pay at the office the next day. He was coming back at the end of their shift and the station had Jesus Christ best be clean and in good order when he came back or he'd take them one by one and—

Rothrock was pretty solid; he might have to take a jack handle to beat old Rocky down, but he knew he wouldn't have to. Rocky was a man—outside of his gambling weakness—and he'd have the station clean and shining. Even if it was his last day.

Troy Noon looked at the two men, slid behind the wheel, pulled the door shut, and backed out of the station. He had called the supervisor at home and told him to get two new men out tomorrow to take over Smith and Rothrock's shifts.

He drove off, white-mad, his lips edged with blue as he held them tight. The whole country was soft and rotten. He knew what was going to happen. The Russians would cut through like a double-blade ax going through rotten yellow pine.

Nothing soft in Russia. You goddamned well snapped to or your ass had had it. No back talk, no worrying about what the voters would say, or the congressmen. No medical discharges for a phony pain in the back. You just cut it, or you went to a work camp where they didn't care which choice you made—work or starve.

Korea. The first war in its history that the United States didn't win. Crawled to the peace table and gave the stinking Reds every son-of-a-bitching thing they asked for. We found we couldn't whip them and we quit.

Soft talk all you want to—that was it cold; we couldn't whip them and so we quit fighting before they whipped the hot living crap out of us.

Men like those two back there; couldn't even cut it at running a gas station. That wasn't fair to Rocky, but you don't take excuses for one of your men. Take excuses and your outfit is dead men.

So he hadn't been good enough for Korea. Not good enough for the Army any more. Not even good enough for an Army that couldn't win. It had been six years ago and it was a live pain through his belly for every day of those six years.

He had known what was going to happen to those garrison soldiers from the First Cav and the Twenty-fourth when they had pulled them out of their rack-outs with their Jap coosies, pulled them away from their desks in steam-heated buildings in Tokyo, pulled them out of the Jap ginmills and slapped M1's in their hands and sent them to Korea to meet knot-gut fighting men. They got the shit shot out of them.

Not that the old First Cav hadn't cut it; they cut it goddamned fine eleven—twelve years ago, Jesus God how time goes! The old Cav was men.

144

The car in front of him turned slightly to the left and he moved his wheel to pass it when it slowed for the left turn, and then the car cut sharply right.

"Goddamned sons-of-bitches!" he shouted aloud. "Why do you living fart-sacks always have to turn left before you turn right?"

He was aware that he was cursing more than he usually did.

Running that station was authority and responsibility. The company gave him the authority and they sure as Christ gave him the responsibility that it had to be right. A right station was clean and neat, shining, with the crappers fit to eat off the floor, and if the men weren't pumping gas or greasing or washing a customer's car they goddamned well better be polishing the pumps or sweeping the driveways or mopping up that puddle of piss in the latrine.

Playing cards on a Sunday shift. Like those garrison soldiers in Japan when the Korean war broke, these sons-of-bitches would look mighty sorry if the Reds hit us tonight. They'd be ready to soldier—in a pig's fat pink ass.

Troy was a good driver, but impatient with the clumsiness of others. He cut past a Ford and timed himself toward the red-glowing stoplight at the next street, slowing enough to be able to gun it as the light changed.

A '57 Cad was in the left-hand lane on the other side, headed opposite his direction. As the crosswise lights turned to amber Troy reached the street.

The Cad was already inching forward, its wheels turned left. A woman at the wheel, a man next to her. Troy knew she was planning to beat the oncoming traffic, make her left turn first, and to hell with everybody else.

Well, screw her. He gunned his car and she saw that if he made it she'd be blocked off from the left turn for all of the long string of cars behind Troy.

The Cad swung like a big yellow rabbit moving fast and low to the ground. Troy wanted her to jam the damn brake pedal and let those big power brakes chew into the linings; he kept going, swinging to the right at the moment he realized she hadn't bluffed.

Metal clanged into a crunching sound, and the fall of shattered glass to the pavement.

Troy Noon's hands were white from pressure on his wheel and he yelled, "God damn your whore's ass, you dirty bitch!" through the open window at his left. Then he turned off the ignition, set the hand brake and swung open the door.

She was out, too, and she'd heard him. Half a dozen drivers stopped, had heard him.

This was a tall woman, thirty-something, wearing a gray suit of some soft material that looked like the breast feathers of a dove, with a long stole of reddish-dark long-haired fur. Rich bitch, '57 Cad, bulling her way into a left turn.

She didn't even look at Troy; the man—her age, big, well-tanned face and expensive-looking clothes—was out standing next to her, and they were looking at the folded-in fender of the Cad. The thick fender guard was jammed back against the tire and the inset headlamp was shattered. Part of the rectangular patterned grill was smashed.

Neither the man nor the woman turned toward Troy as he came up to them. His own car was busted up in much the same way as theirs. Crumpled fender, broken headlamp. For him, maybe fifty bucks; for them, maybe two, three hundred.

"You tried to sneak a left turn," he said to the woman.

She did not look at him. "See if you can call the police, Hal. I'll wait here."

The man turned his head, looked Troy in the eyes. "Do you think this fellow might give you any trouble?" He stared at Troy while he spoke. "He won't." Even the contempt and scorn in her voice were remote, as if Troy was not entitled even to much of those.

"It was your fault—" Troy began, but the man had walked away.

People were crowding along the curb, and several had edged their way through the tangle of cars to group around the V formed by the Cad and Troy's car.

Troy stepped in front of the woman. "You were trying to—"

She looked through and beyond him.

"You're not so goddamned high and mighty—"

"Shut it off, fella." A college-man kind of young man shouldered his way up to Troy. "Just wait until the cops get here; meanwhile don't bother this lady."

Troy could feel his blood, and then he let his arm drop back. Get into a brawl with somebody else here and he'd end up in the can. Somehow he had to cool down, not let the icy rich bitch get him hot, not get into a beef with the college boy.

Hal was back. "They'll be here in a minute, Virginia. Any trouble?"

"I think the man's drunk," she said.

Troy began to pull his fender back from the tire, letting the metal take his anger, scraping skin from his fingers. He could hear the siren of the cops' car.

When they came they were polite and attentive to the woman; cold and businesslike with him. He was in the right, and they knew it, but they checked him out carefully, opening his glove compartment, asking questions about his driver's license, standing close enough so that they could smell his breath for liquor. They wanted to find some way to put him in the wrong and he knew it.

He heard the woman refer to him once, "—this gas station attendant—" and when it was over the man, Hal, came up to him.

"I know the men in your firm quite well," he said, his eyes in the massaged, well-tanned face coldly on Troy's. "I have your name and you can be sure that I will get in touch with them tomorrow."

"Go ahead," said Troy. He wanted to hit this man but the highway patrolmen were there. "It was her fault. You know that."

"If you'd had the courtesy—the decency to wait a second before speeding up there would have been no accident. You know that." The anger in Hal's voice was remote, as the contempt in the woman's voice had been. "You better start looking for another job, because I'll see to it that you need one. That's all."

The man turned his finely tailored back on Troy. The men from the patrol were pushing the heavy Cad fender out.

147

Troy got in his car and drove home. He was too enraged to have thoughts; he was thinking in red.

He left the car in the driveway. "Let the screwing neighbors see that I've piled up my car. Maybe they'll think I was drunk, too. Goddamn everything to hell!"

Leola was asleep on the wine-purple couch, one slim naked leg was drawn up and the cloth of her shorts fell away from her crotch, showing a line of copperish curly hair against the smooth tan of her thigh. The halter was loose, pushed up from her right breast which stood out firm as a small apple.

Troy reached down, took her by the wrist and pulled her up from the couch. She awakened, startled.

"Oh, oh, Troy, it's you. You scared me."

"You been going around like this all day?"

"Like what, Troy? I was sleeping—"

"Not wearing any pants, your tit sticking out—"

Leola pulled the halter down over her breasts, reached back to retie it. Troy yanked it away from her and she covered her nipples with her hands.

"Troy! Honey!"

He knew what he wanted to do. He wanted to push her shorts down, throw her back on the couch and ride the living hell out of her until she yelled like that gook girl had, back in Manila.

Yeah, and knock her up higher than a cloud. That's what she wanted.

"It's Sunday, Troy. Nobody comes around. I could walk around the house stark naked—"

"But you don't stay in the house, you bare-assed little tramp. You go around showing your stuff, maybe wanting to get some guy hot enough so that you'll get knocked up. That's all you want—a kid, and you don't give a damn who gives it to you!"

"Troy!"

"No pants, no bra. Go all over the neighborhood on Sunday when the guys are home."

"I didn't go anywhere, Troy. Nobody saw me." Leola felt

the little shock of guilt, of lying to Troy, of remembering how David Martin had looked down inside her halter. She was lying to Troy.

"You ought to wear pants no matter what. Only whores go around without pants."

"All right, Troy. I'm sorry. You want something to eat, honey? Can I open you a can of beer or something?"

"No." He went to the television set, flipped on the switch.

"Troy—it's busted. You know, I called the man to fix it. He'll be here tomorrow."

"Goddamn."

"But you can see the Ed Sullivan show. I asked David Martin."

He was at her like a cougar springing. "When did you ask Martin?"

"While you were gone—Jean was there. She said—"

"You were showing your little tits to Martin? Lying to me about not going any place bare-assed like you are? You little bitch tramp."

"Troy—you're hurting me!"

"I ought to hurt you." He pushed her away.

As he walked away from her he looked down and saw the splash of batter, dried and yellow-gray, still on the floor.

The telephone birred and he picked up the receiver. Leola waited; their telephone seldom rang and when it did it caused a small excitement for her.

"Hello." Maybe it was about that goddamned accident.

"Hello? Mr. Noon, Troy Noon?" Man's voice.

"Yeah."

"Mr. Noon, this is John Shephard. City manager—you wrote me—"

"The job as chief of police?" Troy's stomach muscles tightened.

"That's what I'm calling you about, Mr. Noon. Your letter of application."

"Yes?" God, the lousy day would be great after all. Chief of police.

"I thought it might be better if I called you instead of processing it."

"What do you mean, Mr. Shephard?"

"Well, this way it's informal. Nothing on the records. This way you won't have an official refusal—"

"Refusal?"

"Mr. Noon, your background is splendid. I'm sure you might make an excellent man—"

"But?"

"That's why I'm calling you. I didn't want to embarrass you. After I received your letter I called the personnel office of your present employer and, well, I found out that you have only a grammar school education. Eight years of schooling. Is that correct, Mr. Noon?"

"Well, yes, Mr. Shephard. But while I was in the Army I took courses—USAFE courses. Like a high school education—"

"Yes, the personnel office told me that, too. But you see, Mr. Noon, when we set up the qualification background for applicants for the position of chief of police of Sunrise Hills we put in the requirement that the man must have a college degree—"

"To be chief of police? What the hell does college have to do with what kind of a man I'd make as chief—"

"I'm sorry, Mr. Noon. Maybe you're right, but that's the way we set it up. I'm returning your letter, but I wanted you to know that we appreciate—"

Troy hung up the phone.

14

Betty had taken Harmon and Sandra to the movies and Herman stayed home to read. He had a new copy of *Scientific American* and he felt a sensuous pleasure in stretching out in his big chair, a good light over his shoulder, three cool cans of beer and an opener on the table beside him, his pipe and tobacco next to the beer.

This was living. Other people could watch Allen or Ed Sullivan, Herman Kreitzer would spend his Sunday evening taking a little walk through the universe.

The magazine's cover was beautiful, as always. This time it was a magnification of a six-sided crystal shading through deep pinks and lavender. He turned the pages. Inside front cover was an advertisement of Union Carbide, but not for its products. The ad described a scholarship fund of the company which had provided, to date, some 400 scholarships to 45 colleges and technical institutes. There was an ad, pages on, for Ampex and its magnetic tape recording, describing radio telemetering from a plane to the permanent record of the tape at a rate of 67 items of information from the plane—eight miles up—every second.

Remington Rand, with a picture of a jet engine in the stars above a UNIVAC computing system, advertised, "Because of its ability to reduce large volumes of data at tremendous speeds, the UNIVAC Scientific System easily handles even the most difficult research problems . . ."

Armstrong Industrial advertised, over two pages "How a new method of ion control is opening up amazing industrial uses for paper." Bell Telephone Laboratories—mightiest and most esoteric of all the industrial adventurers into the unknown—showed in its ad the perforated steel cards which give directions to the long-distance dial telephone system.

Boeing Aviation, on its page, "offers a real creative challenge to engineers . . . supersonic planes . . . guided missiles

. . . nuclear propulsion . . . employs twice as many engineers as at the peak of World War II . . ."

Sigma Instruments advertised an electrically driven counter with a rate of 8,000 counts per minute. Ramo-Woolridge, ". . . through its computer systems division, offers to business and industry the consulting services of a team of scientists, engineers and business methods and procedure analysts experienced in the application of modern analytical and machine methods. With no equipment of their own to sell to nonmilitary customers—"

In the back of the magazine Lockheed advertised in a full page for "Physicists and engineers with broad analytical ability"; Raytheon offered jobs in "microwave tubes, guided missiles, transistors, radar, sonar, computers, ultrasonics, servomechanisms, solid state physics . . ."

The High Voltage Engineering Corporation headed its page "Advances in Applied Radiation." Westinghouse asked for engineers for "unlimited opportunities in atomic power." RCA in a page asked for engineers in the fields of color TV tubes, aviation electronics, computers, missile guidance.

God, thought Herman. If I'd only had the right breaks— If I'd been able to go on to the university, working my way, getting a degree in science, working on to my master's, my Ph.D. So satisfying, so exciting, so wonderful to be a man like Seaborg, or Lawrence, or Oppenheimer, or Lesser.

Instead of managing an appliance store where the products were a kind of afterthought of the corporations which were moving outward in time and space. Washers, dryers, rotisseries, electric frying pans—stuff to keep the people happy and let them pay the freight, along with Uncle Sugar, on the research that really mattered.

The door chimes sounded. Herman pulled himself up from the chair and went to answer.

Jim Kemp stood outside the door, his white hat in his dark hand.

"Well, Jim, I'll be darned. Come on in."

Kemp followed him to the long, wide living room. The tall Negro looked around and waited until Herman asked him to sit down.

"Have a beer, Jim?"

"No, thanks. Why, yes, I believe I will. Thank you, Mr. Kreitzer."

Herman bit through the top of the can with the opener, handed it to Kemp and opened another for himself.

"Good to see you, Jim. Betty and the kids are out to a movie." Herman waited for Jim to talk. Kemp had never come to the house before, and Herman remembered now that he had never invited his salesman.

Kemp was a handsome man in his late twenties. His skin was dark brown, and his face was well-proportioned, with good, clean-lined bone structure. He was about six-foot-three, slender at around 180 pounds. He was wearing a dark-blue suit, white shirt, dark tie, and he put his silver-white soft hat on a chair as he took the beer can. He seemed embarrassed, hesitant.

"You've got to bring the family over sometime, Jim. You've got two, haven't you?"

"That's right, Mr. Kreitzer. A boy, two, and a little baby girl."

"Mine are older."

Kemp took a long drink of beer, offered a cigarette to Herman, lit one for himself.

"They're kind of the reason I came over tonight, Mr. Kreitzer."

"I wish you'd call me Herm."

"Well, I regard you as a real friend. Maybe you don't know it, but that word 'friend' has a special meaning for us. You know, for people of my race."

"Oh?"

"It means white people who don't let race bother them. Real friends."

Herman waited; Kemp took another drink of beer and spoke again. "I know how you worked it around for me to have a man's job at the store, instead of being a porter. And you sure surprised me about the luncheon club. I was scared. Did you know how scared I was?"

"Scared? Why scared, Jim?"

"The first time you took me there."

"They're all nice guys, Jim. In business, or working for somebody, same as we are. Why were you scared?"

"Well—" Kemp looked around, took another drink of beer, and then looked away as he talked. "I've been around white people a good deal. The high school I went to was mostly white. I played football, about eight of us on the squad, about twenty white boys. Most of them real good friends.

"Then in the Army. Well, I was with the 25th—an all-Negro regiment in Korea. That wasn't so good. I don't suppose you know it, but in an outfit like that we divide up almost the way a mixed outfit divides up. Different groups.

"After that was busted up and we were integrated into mixed outfits I got along fine. Not that I objected to the other men like me, not at all, but it gives you a kind of different feeling to be in an outfit supposed to be all one color. Most of us didn't like it much; of course there were some as said they wouldn't be in an outfit with white men. Sore-headed guys, mostly, or mixed-up, or kind of hurt."

"I understand, Jim. Ready for more beer? I've got a case in the kitchen."

"No, Mr. Kreitzer. Herm. Well, that's what I came to see you about. Like at that luncheon club the first day—these men weren't soldiers, and it was at a restaurant that I'd never been in or even thought much of going in. I was scared."

"I don't see what you were scared about, Jim."

"Several things. I wanted to do the right things and I don't know if you do things exactly the same way we do. Everybody was making jokes and I'd laugh and then I'd think I was laughing too loud, or at the wrong time. Your jokes aren't always exactly the same as our jokes."

Kemp stood up. "And I was afraid somebody might say a wrong thing. I don't know what I'd say if somebody said a wrong thing. Say or do. I was like a guest there, and you were responsible for me, and if a man said a wrong thing I supposed I'd have to pay no attention to it, but I get hot-headed, Mr. Kreitzer, and I knew I couldn't guarantee what I might do if somebody said a wrong thing. I was all tense and nervous."

"It worked out fine," said Herman.

"It sure did. Been fine ever since. Now I know about those men, and how to take them. I'm at ease with them, I look forward to going to that lunch every Thursday."

"I'm glad, Jim. They think a lot of you, there."

"They do, really, Mr. Kreitzer?"

"Sure."

"I owe a lot to you, Mr. Kreitzer. And now I'm going to ask for more."

"Go right ahead, Jim. If I can."

"I want to buy a house here in Sunrise Hills."

Herman looked away. "Oh."

"I know they don't sell except to white families."

"I think that's right, Jim."

"But maybe you could help change them. You live here, you're manager of the store—"

"I don't carry any weight, Jim."

"Maybe you could, Mr. Kreitzer."

"Why do you want to live in Sunrise Hills?"

"Because of my two kids."

"There are other nice places, Jim."

Kemp shook his head slowly. "Lots of nice places, Mr. Kreitzer, but I don't know of any I could get in—except the housing projects in San Francisco."

"They're pretty good."

"My wife's been after me, Mr. Kreitzer. I think maybe she's got the picture a little mixed up. Me being a salesman in a white store, now, and belonging to the luncheon club. She's been reading the real-estate ads, you know, like in the Sunday paper today. Three-bedroom house, two baths; we could handle the down payment, handle the monthly payments. And since I work in the Sunrise Hills shopping center, and belong to the Sunrise Hills service club—"

"I'd like to have you for a neighbor, Jim."

"Way I figured it, if you stand up for me, take the lead, sort of, then I could ask some of the men I meet on Thursday—"

"What's wrong with where you live, Jim?"

"It's all my people. Don't misunderstand me, Mr. Kreitzer,

I like my people. Matter of fact I like them better than white people, mostly. Not that I've got anything against white people, it's just that I understand my own a little bit better. But an all-colored neighborhood isn't a good place to raise little children."

"I don't see why it shouldn't be."

"Lots of reasons, Mr. Kreitzer. A Negro man or a Negro woman, by the time they're thirty, forty years old have been bruised around considerable. It doesn't always show, and sometimes the troubles make them even better people, but mostly not. A lot of them are so filled up with frustration and resentment that inside they're pretty mean. It isn't natural for our kind of people—we have a good deal of pride and dignity, Mr. Kreitzer."

"I know that, Jim."

"Things are changing for the better fast, Mr. Kreitzer, like they have for me. It's like getting out into the world after you've been shut up in a kind of open-air prison all your life. In a prison, and you haven't committed any crime."

"We'll see it change completely in our lifetime, Jim. I'm sure of that. And damn it, stop that Mister Kreitzer business. Please. Herm. Or I'll start calling you Mr. Kemp."

"But still, mostly, in a neighborhood like the one I live in there's only certain kinds of people. There's those who still have the old-time kind of jobs like portering, shoe shining, different kinds of servant jobs. An awful lot of them.

"Then there's the men in the open unions. They make good money, keep their families good. Carpenters, stevedores, railroad men, steel workers, packinghouse men. They make good money but there still aren't enough of us making that kind of money.

"Some of us work with our own people, like insurance men, or bartenders, or store clerks. Mostly they're all right, do okay.

"A lot of us kind of resent the other old-timers in jobs—like in the post office and different kinds of civil service. There used to be talk around that they didn't want things to change none because they were on top of the social heap so long as the rest of us were porters and shoe-shine boys. People are funny about that stuff.

"Since the war, why we have lots of Army and Navy people. Officers and noncoms. They do fine, and man, they've sure changed the South fast. Faster'n you'd think—because they make good money, and good money'll even change a Southerner."

"Want some more beer, Jim?"

"I believe I will, Mr.—Herm."

"I'll be right back, Jim."

While Herman was in the kitchen getting cans of beer, Jim looked around at the room. What he saw most was that it was big. A big room, and there was room outside around the house. Just for one family, and you could have a wall around it if you wanted one. Big rooms and lots of space.

It was one of the few times in his whole life, Jim Kemp thought, that he had been in a big room, a good-sized house, with space around it outside, for just one family. He'd come from a good family and they had lived pretty good, but they'd always lived either in old houses that were crowded, or new places that were awfully small.

"Here you are, Jim," said Herman, coming back and handing him a beer.

"So that's the way our neighborhood is, except for one bad thing. You take young people and when they start finding out that there's lots of things they can't do because of their skins they are likely to act up."

"I don't blame them," said Kreitzer. "I'd be ashamed of them if they didn't."

"Yeah, but they get into trouble. Boy gangs, even with little tiny kids in them. Girl gangs, and man they can be double rough. Lots of drinking—wine and beer mostly. There's always some gauge—that's marijuana, Mr. Kreitzer—floating around, and goofballs, and red devils, dope like that. There's heroin around in my neighborhood, Mr. Kreitzer. There's some cutting, boys and girls even at school using knives. And a lot of girls start messing with boys pretty early."

"They do in white neighborhoods, too, Jim."

"But there usually isn't a whole gang of boys waiting to

pounce on a little thirteen-year-old girl and pull her into a car or a building. Don't misunderstand me—most of our folks do all right, mostly the young folks work it out all right. But it's a lot worse place to raise kids than a white neighborhood.

"I'm earning the money, Mr. Kreitzer, Herm, and I've got a right to live in a nice place that I can afford. That's why I'm asking you to help me."

"Things are changing, Jim. In another few years—"

"I don't have another few years. In another few years my little kids will be big kids. I want them to have the good things now, when they'll help them."

"Aren't there some good GI developments for your people, Jim?"

"If there were, Mr. Kreitzer, my wife wouldn't let us move into one of them. I don't suppose you understand about the women of our people. If there's any real hate for what white people have done, it's our women that have the hate.

"Like my own mother. She put on real good; she was a good church lady, she was an officer in social organizations, she worked hard and raised her family nice. But every time my father, or one of us boys, every time we had a humiliation or got hurt or lost something good because of our skin, I could tell in her eyes. She never said much, but I know the hate is there. My wife's young—she don't want it to happen to her.

"She's not going to raise our children in an all-colored neighborhood and that's it. She told me. I earn good money. I work in a white store, I belong to a white luncheon club. I've got a right to raise my children the same way you raise yours, give them the same opportunity.

"And I can't wait much—because right now is the years for my kids. Right now is when they need it."

"Jim, you know I agree with you."

"Are you going to help me?"

"What can I do?"

"I was hoping you might go to the people selling these houses in Sunrise Hills, or maybe you could talk it around with some of the men at the shopping center. They're all real friendly to me."

"You know what the problem is, Jim."

"People here would say that my family would hurt property values. They wouldn't say that they didn't want us living next to them, they'd just say it would hurt property values. Is that right, Mr. Kreitzer?"

"That's right, Jim."

"Saying it isn't fair doesn't help my children. When I go home my wife isn't going to be satisfied if I just tell her it isn't fair. I've got to do something and you've been a friend, Mr. Kreitzer, a real good friend. The best I've ever had."

"Let me think about it, Jim."

"Can I tell my wife you might help?"

Herman Kreitzer did not answer. He looked across the room to the fieldstone fireplace, to the glass wall, blue-dark now, the moonlight on the patio showing faintly. It was a good house, a long way from the crowded flat in the old, dirty building in Chicago.

He wondered if Jim Kemp knew about the risk he had taken in getting just one Negro across the wall, getting him classified as a salesman instead of porter help, engineering and politicking around until the four or five bigots in the service club had to back down, were afraid to blackball Jim Kemp.

There was no chance of getting a Negro family into Sunrise Hills. He was a practical man and he knew what would happen if he tried to force an issue on it. Betty and the children would suffer. He would be transferred out of the Sunrise Hills store, maybe lose his manager's rating. Jim Kemp would be transferred to the store in the Fillmore district in the city, the one with all-Negro personnel from the manager down. All he had to do to start all that happening was to say one word at the Sunrise Hills development sales office, or say one word to the men at the shopping center, the men Jim Kemp considered as friends.

That was the way it was.

"No, Jim. You can't tell your wife that I might help. I can't."

"You won't even try, Mr. Kreitzer?"

"No, Jim. I won't even try."

"You want to be a tolerant man, Mr. Kreitzer, but you want to keep the price you pay to be tolerant pretty low, is that it?" Jim Kemp spoke slowly, there was no anger, only a cold and remote dignity.

"I can't pay a very high price, Jim."

Kemp lit a cigarette. "That's all right, Mr. Kreitzer. We'll just forget all about it. I understand, and you're the best friend I have."

Jim smiled. Herman Kreitzer knew why Jim Kemp was smiling—he had his own job at the store to worry about. He had to protect that, just as Herman had to protect himself.

15

JEAN MARTIN curled her legs under her as she sat down on the broad orange-gray couch. She had changed into tight-fitting trousers which clung to her buttocks and thighs with a pleasant sense of contact, shaped to her legs and ending four inches below her knees. Her jacket was a wrap-around of cashmere, long-sleeved, open at a V between her breasts. Her feet were in black satin low slippers.

After she had come home she showered again, made herself tea and a sandwich. Later, before she went to bed, she intended to have a tall drink of Scotch.

Tomorrow she would go into San Francisco and get a job.

She swung up from the couch and walked across the room. Restless, feeling that she must do something. Not only a job, much more.

Day by day by day, and nothing. Like a sleek cat on a soft pillow. She wanted to change the house around; it was good, she could glance over it and see the good subtle things she had done with it—elements of design, the thin slabs of gold-veined white marble on slender tapered tulip shapes of polished gray wood, which were her two low tables; the faint, precise color prints of roosters; the flower troughs on the floor at the far wall, almost crazy with bright color. She wanted to change it all, not that it wasn't good, but simply that it was there.

A job.

Two things about a job, three if you thought of the money. The money would be for clothes, some actually elegant things for the house; but the two important things about a job would be the sense of doing something, of using her mind to accomplish something, that was one. The other was people. New people, people with desires, wanting something, working to get what they wanted.

A home in Sunrise Hills was not enough for a woman

without children. Fine for Betty, good for Isbel, maybe even good enough for Isbel to free her from the tensions and worries which locked whatever real person she was deep within the thin, nervous woman she was on the surface.

But not enough for Jean Martin.

David would come back from Los Angeles changed, matured. He would be working with important people, managing a small staff of men from Verdun, representing Verdun himself. She'd sense the change in him when he came back; it would be all the difference: until now he had been a young man who worked with things, with his mind searching out circuits and units of electronic equipment, showing some brilliance, much ability. When he came back from Los Angeles he would know about the greater things, working with people, his mind searching out relationships, strengths and weaknesses of important people; and his brilliance and ability would then have real meaning.

If it had not been for Mamie her husband might have ended as a retired colonel, playing lazy golf at Pebble Beach, maybe. But she had never left him, beginning with him when he was a young second lieutenant, seeing that he worked upward as the other men from the class of '15 reached their dead ends, or lost out against him in the tight social game where decisions were made in Washington. And when the war came she had stayed in that arena of decisions at Washington, and the colonel became supreme commander in two years as the other generals, without shrewd, determined, knowing wives, slipped into obscurity. Jean knew the story from a cousin married to one of the men passed over.

Of course, Mamie had the full life; she had raised a family, and she had seen her man accomplish what she had intended him to do. Without Mamie, a colonel retired and playing golf. Because of his wife, a man of history.

It was the men without strong women who became the colossal failures no matter how far upward they soared before the collapse; the Napoleons and Hitlers.

Have a good man, with some brilliance and much ability; see that he strives, work with him on the big decisions, don't let him get lazy or go off on the wild erratic enthusiasms men

162

find for themselves; smooth him and polish him; finally your man is a man of power, and your pride in him is at last completely satisfying.

If you are a woman with these abilities and you do not use them, if you let your man work through the years with things, laying out his circuits and his gadgets, until the younger men come along—then you are a failure as a woman. If you have this driving hunger for pride in yourself reflected in pride for your man, it must be satisfied and it is right that it should be satisfied, just as the hungers for sex and children are right hungers.

David would come back and they would have to start on the next phase of their lives. Jean at a job in San Francisco, not just a job for money or to ease off boredom at Sunrise Hills, but a job with meaning, with responsibility, with rewards. David more than just a good technical man at Verdun Labs, David on his way up.

Maybe then something about the biology of her body would change, or of David's sperm, and she would know—after these scores of months of waiting—the special and unique pride of the pregnant woman.

Her hands reached up under the cashmere wrap-around, and fingers curved, palms up, pushed her breasts high.

This must be what frustrated women felt, she thought. Restlessness and a need, a crazy stream of thoughts about success and other women who drove their men upward.

God, last night had been too bad, so bad, so wasted. Having let him take her, without response, as a whore would earn her fee, had been a damning thing.

Maybe she was mixed up, a little bit out of her mind. It was a time of restlessness for women without children, these last years of their twenties. Dissatisfied with her house, thought out and done with such care when they moved here such a few months back; thinking of some improbable and uncertain job in San Francisco; comparing herself with that woman who had achieved everything; and now standing here with her hands on her naked breasts, thinking of David.

She put her hands down, pulled the cashmere wrap-around into place, and went to the flower trough on the floor, her expert fingers working with the violent-bright flowers.

Kneeling she could feel the cool, tight smoothness of the satin trousers against her hips and thighs.

Get a job or she would go crazy here; no house, no experiments in menus for herself and David, no garden, no Mental Health Society or Civic League would be enough. She was a woman at her finest time and she was letting her days slip away, meaningless.

Love David. But love has to have more vitality than only the nights, the rich nights that were always, in the end, barren; more vitality than clever meals and a house with something, at least, of elegant charm. Love David, and she had not yet found enough in that.

A woman was never complete in herself, a woman was only complete as a triad—her children, her man, herself as a woman.

If she was some female like Leola, without awareness of self, good for nothing more than a few years, pretty enough to have men want her as they'd want any young pretty woman, and after those few years—nothing. . . . Then incomplete as she had been incomplete all her life.

She knew what she had been waiting for, fearful. Leola's slimness, almost little-girl slimness beginning to swell.

From the time, moving into the Sunrise Hills house, Leola had first met her and she had seen the young girl, farm girl, peasant girl, dairymaid, already so many years, six or more, younger than herself, with good young-girl, peasant-girl breasts, good legs, strong thighs and good solid bottom; met her lean, angry animal of a husband, she had waited—fearful but unaware—for that girl to be pregnant. Hated her because it might happen.

Jean had not wanted a dog or cat, no proxy baby to fondle and slowly drain out the pressure of her need; no fussing over Harmon and Sandra, or poor Michael; she did not want to fool her desires by satisfying them with something less than her own child, living, fused out of David and herself.

So she must have watched, through these months of seem-

164

ingly irrational dislike, for that young girl to have what she had not. Might never have.

It was as simple as that: basic, womb-deep jealousy of a younger woman because of the day-to-day chance she might be pregnant. There was no jealousy of Betty, fully contented by her husband, already with two fine children; nor of thin, nervous Isbel with her boy; they were her age or older, and they had their children. She was jealous only of the young girl.

Silly, irrational, powerful. What difference would it make to her if Leola Noon had a litter of babies? Why be jealous of her? Pretty but unkempt, knowing nothing, given a little treasure of a pretty face, good small breasts, good legs, for a little time.

A man who belonged back in whatever wild hills he had come from. A man lost and desperate in these times.

A girl with nothing more than ripeness.

And for that she had hated her, probably—below awareness—still hated her.

Now she understood the mixture of feeling she'd had this morning when Leola stood there in the loose halter, her breasts—smaller, less fine than her own—carelessly shown; and David had peeked at them.

A mixture: a kind of twisted pride in her man seeing and able to compare Leola's with hers; a kind of enjoyment in that this rival, this girl who might become pregnant first, was displaying herself to Jean's man, as if her own man was not man enough; no jealousy nor fear of losing David to Leola, she knew too well the power her loins had to lock David, satiated, exhausted, content, to her. She would almost be content to let David try this country girl, to find no woman like his wife, only a thinly pretty body.

Jean shook her head; at least she was understanding herself; becoming aware of the blindly savage female, the female within her, and how that female of the unconscious exercised her fears and hates, blind fears and blind hates, through the pleasant, educated, polite young woman who was Jean Martin.

Maybe with realization this irrational dislike of Leola

165

would disappear. In actuality the girl was rather nice, puppy-friendly, anxious to please, paying Jean the nuisance compliment of imitating her as well as she could.

The door chimes sounded, and as they sounded Jean remembered that she had invited Leola and Troy over to watch the Ed Sullivan show. As she remembered she realized what she was wearing—the cashmere, the tight trousers, slippers, nothing else.

Oh, Lord!

She held the cashmere closed with her left hand as she went to the door.

Troy Noon was standing there, alone.

"Oh—hello, Mr. Noon," she said. "Won't you come in? Where's Leola?"

He didn't answer her until he had walked past her into the center of the big room. He was looking around, and she realized that this was the first time he had ever been in her house.

"I came over to explain that we weren't coming, Mrs. Martin."

"I'm sorry." Jean had a feeling of pity for this man; he did not belong and he knew that he did not.

"You're not sorry." His voice was flat, but there was a pounding sound to it, as if he were angry.

"I don't understand."

"I'd rather talk to your husband. Just to tell him how we stand."

"He's away. He went to Los Angeles on business. Whatever it is about how we stand—you can tell me about it."

"We've been living next door to you for months. As far as Leola is concerned, she might as well be a nigger—you treat her like one."

"I've never been unfriendly to your wife. After all I did invite the two of you over tonight. Besides, I don't much care to have you come here alone and criticize me."

"I said I wanted to talk to your husband. She came over here and asked to be invited. I suppose I ought to apologize for that. And apologize because she showed herself off like a tramp to your husband. All right, I apologize. From now

166

on, leave us be. We'll leave you be. She won't come here again, and she won't go around the neighborhood showing her ass."

This woman was like the one in the Cadillac, Troy thought. Cold, remote, not interested in whether Troy Noon was alive or dead.

Interested enough to see that he lost his job. He was a manager, he couldn't even ask help from the goddamned union. Not that he would.

"Thank you for telling me all this, Mr. Noon."

She was waiting for him to leave. Cold, faraway, not even bothering to despise him because he was ignorant, a hillbilly.

When the war came they'd forget about hillbilly, forget about ignorance. When they needed men, these soft Cadillac-riding sons-of-bitches, they'd come to Troy Noon. Crawl to him.

But they wouldn't. Even the Army didn't want him any more.

She was standing there, probably not wearing a goddamned thing except that soft thing around her body and those skin-tight pants. Waiting for the hillbilly, the stupid ignorant son-of-a-bitch, to leave her fine house.

Well, he had one just as fine—and he was just as good as her smart-assed husband. He was a college man, he could be any screwing thing he wanted because he'd sat on his skinny ass in some college for four years.

He didn't think about it, know that he was going to do it. It was maybe her eyes, her mouth, that soft thing around her, or the tight trousers.

He hooked his left arm around behind her, grabbing her right arm from the back, bringing his face down on hers, his lips closed tight, rubbing his mouth across hers hard and close, bruising her, hurting her. His right hand pulled the soft thing away from her, closed hard on her big, firm breast.

She was tearing at him with her left hand, trying to pull her right arm free and he let his iron-hard fingers bite into it; her mouth was open but he kept his own pressed against it, feeling her teeth as she tried to bite him.

He ran his right hand, fingers together and straight, pressing against the flat smooth stomach, crossing her navel and pressing it, reaching the trousers, hooking the fingers back of the cloth, pulling it until it tore free and the trousers fell down and back, dragging from her thighs.

He bore down on her and they fell to the floor. This time she screamed and he hit her on the side of the head with his left hand after pulling it free from beneath her. The scream stopped and she looked up at him with wide eyes.

She said, "Don't. Please, please—"

He pulled up from her, looking down at her. She was naked except for the torn trousers around her legs. She tried to squirm away and he slapped her, hard, thick-handed. For a few seconds he was still, on his knees above her, just looking at her. She was a fine woman, rich-bodied.

At first she was rigid, not fighting him, but flat on the floor, her head back, her eyes staring at him.

And then she was a crazy woman, around him, pulling him in as no woman had ever pulled him before; a living, moving, frenzied smooth-skinned animal, biting at him, wilder than any woman had ever been, magnificently strong in back and thighs, her legs arched, then locking him.

It was a long time before these two were done, minutes after that before he stood up and looked down at her.

"You are a dirty, filthy son-of-a-bitch," she said slowly.

There wasn't anything for him to say. What they had been to each other on the floor they both knew. Now that was over; no matter how full it had been for each of them it was over.

He knew there would not be another time like that one. There could not be. He'd been crazy angry; he'd wanted to hurt her more than it was lust for her in the start; after she had let herself go it was something else, there had never been a woman like that. She wouldn't be like that for him again, it had been the way he'd taken her, angry, crazy, that had made her crazy.

He wanted to smoke a cigarette, have a drink of something ice-cold.

What do you say to a woman after you've raped her? The gook girl outside Manila—she didn't have any English, besides he gave her money, and she had been very young. Not like this animal of a woman.

She was still on the floor, spread-eagled, her arms straight out, her legs apart. As if she were waiting for him to come back to her, to bring her the anger and violence and body storm again.

But she said, "Get out of here, you filthy, dirty son-of-a-bitch. Get out before I kill you."

He walked to the door, turned before opening it.

"Get out."

Troy Noon closed the door behind him. He did not go home, but got in his car and drove toward Camino Real. He was going to get drunk. Blind drunk.

After the door closed Jean Martin got up, pulled off the rags of the satin trousers and walked to her bathroom. She stood before the long mirror and looked at herself.

"Mess." She said the word aloud, and again. "Mess."

She was looking into her eyes, reflected close and clear in the mirror as if she were looking into the eyes of another woman, someone known and familiar, but not herself. She could almost expect that mirror-woman to change, to act on her own with her own life, speaking back to Jean. How would she be: Contemptuous? Kind? Cruel? Helping?

But only the reflection was there; as Jean curled her bruised, swelling lips back from her teeth, the mirror-woman did the same, no more. Poor mirror-woman, she looked hurt— What was the old phrase David used? "Beat-up."

Beat-up. Her fingers moved slowly over her face, over the lips that had been pressed back against her teeth hard, over the side of her face where he had slapped her, over the side of her head where he had hit her.

Her fingers went slowly over her breast, as if to ease the soreness his fingers had made; followed, in sharp tactile memory, the road of those fingers as they had moved downward, stopping at her navel as if surprised, curious, then faster down, hooking, talons, intruding, invading, taking.

"Mess."

Without closing her eyes she could see his eyes as they had looked.

169

Changed; he had changed her, moved her from all women, the class of all women who had not known this, to the smaller class of women who had been raped. Women talked about this; sometimes made small claims of having been brought close to rape in the back seat of some car by some boy, some man, they knew; talked, and smiled—or were apparently angry—about a kind of rape their husbands might do to them. There was, too, a shadowland of rape—not fully the darkness and violence of force, not fully the excitement of opening and giving: the talk at school among girls was sometimes about this shadowland.

Time of being drunk, sleepy; and they had asked, "How about when he tells you a lot of lies and you let him, because of the lies he's told?"

Girl-talk years ago. "When he's real experienced and skillful and you don't want to but you can't help yourself?"

But this was no shadowland. He had come to her home. He had been angry. He had looked at her, torn her clothes away, slapped her, pushed her knees apart, and then they had shared something.

Why had she been ready? Why the soft unfolding, the deep fluttering?

She looked into the eyes of the mirror-woman.

"Why did you forget he was coming here tonight—with his woman?" Her fingers rested on the porcelain of the lavatory and she leaned forward.

"Why nothing more than those pants and the cashmere?" She had to know about herself and she understood that the bright insect flight of conscious thoughts across the deep pond of her mind showed nothing of the truths beneath. To continue to be Jean Martin she would have to understand.

All the years of learning, of rules, of near disaster and careful success in the only important part of living.

At eleven, still skinny, still a little girl. The girls who had crossed over the tremendous line and who now talked knowingly of Kotex and Tampax, already with the proud small swellings of breasts. Jean listening, curious, learning much from her mother. At eleven she watched the foolish ones, the boy-crazy girls, living in a ragged hysteria of giggles, dirty jokes, and the fumbling of boys.

She had known instinctively that they were foolish, stupid. Not bad—but clumsy.

Before she had reached the all-changing dividing line at twelve she was prepared to be a girl who would handle boys with understanding and skill.

Even then, at eleven, much of the whole shape of these things was beginning to show. She guessed, as a skinny, unformed child, that the boy-crazy girls were that way for other reasons than boys. She had looked speculatively at their mothers, wondered about their fathers.

But the boys were after her, too. The games at parties, in the park across from school. She could remember her mother talking to her, yet she could not remember what her mother had said. The talks with other girls, not the foolish ones, and things she read or guessed, or knew somehow by instinct, mixed together to give her—as she passed, in the spring of her thirteenth year, into the privileged, exciting, dangerous, changed group—a code of rules and the start of a bag of tricks whereby she might enforce those rules without separating herself, still popular, still sought, but not foolish.

And that was a little aristocracy of young girls, freshmen now at high school. The aristocracy had special, seldom eased standards of admission. At least two of these conditions must exist: either the girl was pretty, wore the right clothes and had some rights of decision in choosing her clothes, or came from a family with some importance. She must have some social ability—be fun, know the bop music of the time and the corn-sweet dance stuff, be smart in classes or a good talker, aggressive enough to compete and hold a place in the pecking order of all girls in the freshman class; and, at least openly, have a code of rules on boys. On sex.

There was another—parallel but separate—girl aristocracy in the freshman class of those who were already sexually aggressive. At times the two would mix, or a girl would move from Jean's group to the other, but Jean maintained her position, her popularity, her carefulness.

And then, swiftly, you moved into the mainstream of

being young. Boys were all-important, boys and your best girl-friend or girl-friends.

You wanted the most dangerous boys, the most exciting boys, but you wanted to swing fast and careless into almost going over the edge and then swinging back again.

Boys. The few of them that had a kind of magnificence, lean and hard-bodied, with their cruelness displayed like their strength, but laughing and sure of themselves. Trouble boys, but exciting and fine.

The other boys who had some importance—the smart ones, or the ones with good families or money, the boys who were good at something and you could think of them as heroes. The boys—of all these qualifications, or of none of them—who had some special charm, maybe the way their eyes looked, or their mouths, or some fresh kind of crazy fun, or something you could not even understand.

Then a wasted mob of boys who had none of these things, but who still were boys who soon would be men.

And you walked through these years like a princess walking through a bright cave with sudden darknesses, sudden turnings, where the good things were sometimes poisonous.

There were girls, and this was the more subtle danger. Sometimes the good friend, the girl you locked arms with as you walked, the girl who laughed with you, throwing her head back, the crimson mouth open and white teeth apart as she laughed, would be someone of a hot mouth suddenly tight on yours and hands like a boy's hands on you; changed and never to be the same again, even though you both might pretend.

You wondered about it, and in honesty to yourself you knew that here too you had played close to it at times.

For all the years of youth playing close to violence. Dating the young buck males, the football players, the hard-muscle boys. Dating the smoothies, the smiling talkers with hands like soft spiders. Dating the boys with dark minds, lit with strange ideas like summer lightning or sometimes thunderbolts of brilliance, boys whose interest—and it could be close to fascination—was in their own enormous interest in themselves, their explosive enthusiasm for themselves and

172

for no one else. The poet kind of boy, the actor kind of boy, the music kind of boy.

She could remember, as a parade running past her eyes, all of them, from the first who had any importance as a boy, as a desiring, curious, compelling predator to the last of them, already unimportant, background voices to her love for David. The Lesbian girls were in this hurrying parade of faces, the older men who had moved cautiously or foolishly toward her with their words like lumps of rancid butter, and all the boys, all the young men who had desired her.

Then, shaking her, came the remembrances of David. His hands, his eyes and mouth above her, the words he used, and the way he looked, asleep, after.

Jean shook her head. "Fantasies—trying to smother the mess with fantasy. You're no princess in a castle—you're a woman and you've been beaten up and raped. Where in hell are you now? What are you going to do about it?"

She thought of the police, stepping over the thought as if it were a small heap of dirt, and faced up to the real decisions. Decisions which could not be avoided.

He, a word of two letters, a pronoun with infinite meanings: "the butcher—he," "my husband—he," "our doctor—he," had only one meaning for her now. Not his name; you did not think of that lean male savage, that final complete maleness, by his name. He could only be "he" now, the one special "he" of all the men alive.

He would be living beside her. She would see him mornings, afternoons. She would see his wife.

He and David would see each other, men's eyes meeting briefly, one knowing, the other not knowing.

He might come back and what would she do if he came back?

What would she say to him when she saw him again? Pretend there was nothing? Act a part, and he would know that it was a role, a pretense?

One thing they both knew, because it had been shared between them: the utter violence, love and hate, pleasure and pain, giving and release, complete and terrible, as it should be.

173

Every time she saw him they would both remember that.

What had that man-crazy girl at school said as a catch-word? "I'm available." Would she be available to him now?

She despised him.

She did not know how she would act or talk when she met him again. What she did would be determined by unknown drives deep within her. She knew that she might stammer, be uncomfortable, close to hysteria; or she might be cold with rage and hatred; or she might look at him so that he would know he could come to her again.

And she did not know, could not know until she saw him what way it would be.

Tell David? Stupid to do. The honest, right thing would be stupid. Not to tell him would permit him to think of—of this man—as his neighbor, maybe even as a friend. Not to tell David, more importantly, would be not to let him know his wife, not to let him know that his woman was changed, different, would be different for the rest of her life. Not to tell David would be unfair in every way.

To tell him would be stupid.

Jean walked across the floor of her cool, elegant house, and wondered what her new life would be like.

The castle opened to the rabble, the drawbridge crazily down and littered with the filth of the enemy who had entered the castle; reveled within it, drunken and gluttonous. And the princess had been with them, dancing naked for their pleasure.

She was alone now in her dishonored castle, without faith in its moats and walls and watchtowers.

Hell, thought Jean. Her life wasn't wrecked; she had no need for fantasies. Men had tried to force her before. Maybe this time she'd been ready to be forced.

16

Troy Noon pulled his car into the parking lot behind the Horseshoe Cafe. The sound of the jukebox in the barroom was loud and he walked into the sound, the muted lights.

This was what he wanted, a joint. A joint for the steady drinkers, the ones who never went home until the joints were closed, and who hated their homes.

A dozen men and women along the bar, talking and laughing. Bums, Troy thought. Men whiskey-soft and women that weren't worth a damn. He found a stool midway along the bar, slid on it.

"Double shot, water back." He put a dollar bill on the damp wood.

The bartender was carrying on some talk with a man and woman, breaking it only to pour Troy's drink, push a glass of water behind it and ring up the dollar.

What in hell was he in now? Troy drank half the whiskey, letting it work down his throat in a hot trickle.

Bad trouble. Would she call the cops? He must be going crazy, pushing over a woman like he did tonight. Not even drunk when he did it.

But angry. Angry at the whole goddamned smug world of sons-of-bitches. Hating like he'd never even hated during the war. He'd killed men he didn't hate as much as he hated these people around him.

Not like if he'd always had hot pants for her. He'd never even thought about her much. Maybe wished Leola was more like her.

God knows Leola tried to be like her. Leola thought she was perfect.

Well, he knew something about women now. It had taken him a goddamned long time to learn but he knew them now. None of them were any good.

His first wife, the dirty floozie. Leola walking around

the neighborhood damn near bare-assed. And this Mrs. David Martin, so cool and fancy.

He was trying to keep angry, he knew, so that the fear within him wouldn't reach out into his arms and legs and head. It was like a belly-deep fear now, the way even some good officers and noncoms got on night patrol or under mortar fire. Keep it down there in your belly and you could still make out.

Let that fear explode into your head and arms and legs— the way it happened to green kids sometimes under their first fire—and you were a dead son-of-a-bitch.

He was afraid of the cops. Afraid of having them, so goddamned sure of themselves and right, like Jack Webb on "Dragnet," taking him to their cold concrete jail. They'd call him Troy, not like a friend but like you call a nigger by his first name.

He'd always been on their side, on the side of the guys wearing the uniform and following the book, with all the right behind them, and all they had to know was what the book said and do it exactly like that. It was the fuck-ups and the eight-balls, the bolos and the wise guys that he was against. And that's what he'd be to them. That's what he was.

Not about what he'd done to her. She'd asked for it in those pants with nothing under them and tight to her butt like paint.

A teaser. Her old man was out of town and she'd have sat around if Leola had come over with him showing herself off and laughing at him, polite and cold as if she'd never said "shit" in her life.

"Another." He didn't need much talk with this barkeep and he sure didn't want any talk from him. He wanted whiskey until he'd figured things out and then he'd figure what to do next.

She wouldn't call the cops. Not unless she changed the story about how things had happened. She wouldn't want anybody to know that she'd been flopped over on her can.

What about her husband? What about that college son-of-a-bitch without a worry in the goddamned world, except that things would get better for him all the time, and he'd worry

176

about his goddamned income tax and which country club he ought to join. What about him?

Would she tell him that this jerk Troy Noon, this hillbilly that didn't even belong in Sunrise Hills, this poor stupid bastard that was fired from his job as gas flunky, this guy that couldn't even ask for a job with the police force because he was too dumb and uneducated, this guy had raped her?

Would this wise bastard of a husband of hers come looking for him with a gun? He hoped to Jesus Christ he would because he'd blow the guy's guts out from him. Maybe Troy Noon wasn't worth a fart in a windstorm for anything else but that was one goddamned thing he could do better than the next boy. He could kill a guy.

He'd killed them with an Mı and a carbine and a greasegun—that ripped a man apart like he'd been cut open with a mill saw—and he'd killed them with his hands, too.

Let that soft, educated son-of-a-bitch come looking for him and he'd kill him.

All he'd asked was to fit in. Have a decent wife and a decent home. A job where people would respect him. That was all he'd asked in the whole goddamned world. And he was willing to work his butt off in return.

But all the smart sons-of-bitches had got together against men like himself. Why? Because they were afraid of him. They wouldn't follow the book—they were too goddamned lazy or soft to follow the book. He knew—he'd had them come through his outfit by the scores. Trying to figure angles so they wouldn't have to follow the book—get out of duty, duck off details, let their barracks and equipment get gook filthy, and then when the time came to go to combat these weak, soft, smart sons-of-bitches would try every trick there was to keep from facing up to it. And they called themselves Americans, the cowardly, filthy, yellow, smart, soft, angle-figuring sons-of-dirty-whore-bitches.

We'd all be speaking Nazi or Jap by now if we'd left it up to those smart bastards. And they'd be speaking the best Jap there was and having the best soft jobs the Japs or Nazis would give them.

And when we lost the next war they'd suck up to the Reds

and live high on the hog—only the Reds were too smart for those angle-working bastards. The Reds would line them up and gun them down and let them rot.

She wouldn't tell the cops. She wouldn't tell her husband. And she sure wouldn't tell Leola.

She'd just keep it to herself. Say nothing. Look cool and elegant and smiling, sitting high on the tree. She'd know and he'd know and nobody else'd know.

She'd expect him to come back regular now. She'd gone like a goddamned skyrocket, wild and crazy, and she'd loved it. All the stuff that came after was fancy cover-up. The kind of thing a man could expect from the kind of woman that was married to one of those soft, goof-off, college educated, successful bastards.

Well, he had a laugh for her. He didn't want her. The only reason he'd gone so good was because he hated her.

A man you didn't like you fought, or if the book said you could, like in a war, you killed him. A woman—if she was worth it—you took.

Like all the words for giving somebody a bad time. When some guy got really taken, you said he got screwed. Or when you hated somebody you'd say you were going to screw that son-of-a-bitch. The words about screwing weren't love words, they were hate words.

And everybody used them the same way.

And what did you call some dirty no-good son-of-a-bitch? A prick. Nothing to be proud of, or clean, or something you'd say this is the love tool and it's the finest part of a guy's body. Hell, no. It was the word you used to describe somebody dirty and no good.

A dog-eat-dog dirty son-of-a-bitching world.

He could forget that fear. She wouldn't do anything except give him the eye the next time she saw him.

And he'd tell her to go screw herself.

That was a kind of joke. He never much went for jokes. The wise guys who were always cracking off and making jokes usually weren't much good in combat, or in garrison duty.

Not always. Some pretty good men made jokes sometimes

178

but they were man jokes. Like McQueen with his flame thrower, burning out the caves with the Japs still in them. "I'm going to get my MOS changed," he'd said. "I ought to be carried as a cook. A short-order cook." That was a good joke.

What was he going to do now?

Tomorrow he'd be fired from his job. What could he do? Look for another job as grease-monkey at a service station? Not even being manager, just starting at the bottom, pumping gas?

Try to get a job at some defense plant as a security guard?

What ate him out was going to the personnel office, sitting in a chair, filling out forms, waiting until some smooth, soft son-of-a-bitch would talk to him.

Troy Noon, who could freeze to a hillside and wait hour after hour, not moving and his nerves like cool steel wires, until he could move forward, with mortar shells blooming out like big, hot dust devils close to him. Troy Noon, who got as jittery as a tomcat caught on a bob-wire fence when he had to sit in a chair waiting for some smooth son-of-a-bitch to start smiling at him.

The fear had him now. He wouldn't even go to the station, maybe, tomorrow. That prick had meant what he'd said about getting him fired.

Not even go to the office for his check.

But what would he do? Look for a job?

He didn't feel the liquor at all. Two double shots and nothing had happened except he could taste the cheap bar bourbon in his mouth.

Christ, why had the war ever ended? Why couldn't he just go on, fighting, moving forward, keeping his men whipped into shape, fit and hard and knowing he was a goddamned good company commander?

Or even with no fighting, he could have stayed in. Follow the book, and make sure that every man under you followed the book. There was no place for an eight-ball or a screw-up in his outfit. Book soldiers.

What was he going to do tomorrow?

He'd had enough of this sour, stinking swill that couldn't

even get a man drunk. He got up and went out of the chatter of voices, the sweet fog of perfume and smoke and the smell of liquor, the clanging blare of the jukebox, into the dark chill.

He got into his car and drove home.

There was her house. Dark.

Well, he knew and she knew.

Like if he'd been a Red soldier coming through, seeing her, knocking her off hard and fast, not even smiling at her, and then moving on, just so she'd know her soft, angle-figuring, duty-ducking sons-of-bitches had lost a war at last.

His house was dark, too, but Leola was awake.

"Troy—I was worried about you—I called Mrs. Martin—"

"Yeah? What did she say?"

"She said you'd just stopped in for a moment—"

"Yeah? Well, in that just stoppin' in I gave her a damned good screw. That's what I did to your fancy Jean Martin. I gave her a damned good screw."

17

BETTY KREITZER, used to listening for sounds from the children at night, heard it first.

She held her breath, suddenly and completely awake. A sound at night, but not from the children. Her ears were immeasurably sharp for any noise from their rooms, a cough, the rustling pats of bare feet on the floor, or—rarely—a child crying in the night.

This was not from the children. She knew the house sounds, the little clicks of the refrigerator or the deep-freeze going into phase, the metal moans of the floor heater cooling, the noise the house itself sometimes made as it stretched and pulled on its not-too-well-kilned timbers. What she had heard was none of these.

It was at the door. The front door. A kind of knocking. But there was a phosphorescent button and door chimes, no need for anyone to knock. What time was it? She let her eyes focus on the pale dial of the automatic clock radio, at first finding only one hand, then seeing it was nearly ten minutes past two.

She heard the faint knock again. Her body tightened into rigidity.

"Herman—" she whispered. "Herman—"

He turned a little in bed and his breathing became hoarse.

"Herman." She put her fingers on his forehead. He turned again, and was awake.

"Betty?"

"There's somebody at the front door."

He too held his breath, and she could sense the tightening of his muscles. Then he pushed back the covers and swung out of bed.

"Be careful—"

He must still be half-asleep, she thought. She got out of bed, switched on one of the small lamps. She could hear

181

Herman's bare feet padding on the floor, going toward the door.

Then his voice, unnaturally loud and heavy, a putting on of nighttime fierceness. "Who's there?"

Her ears could not catch the answer, if any, but she heard Herman slide the latch open and she felt the faint stir of air as the front door swung wide. There was a quick terror in her—bad news? An accident?

A woman's voice, very low, and the sound of Herman coming back to the bedroom. She met him at the doorway, pulling her robe on.

"What—?"

He shook a sleep-thickened face. "Leola Noon. Says she has to see you. I don't know why—"

Betty was already on her way to the living room. Herman waited a moment, then moved toward the bed. If Betty needed him she could wake him again.

Leola wore a light coat wrapped over pajamas. Betty could see that the girl was in trouble, her mouth half-open, her eyes staring, her small hands clenched white.

"Leola—honey, what in the world—?"

Surprisingly, the girl did not come to her, but backed away a little as Betty approached her.

"Is somebody sick?"

Leola's eyes were strange, as if she were badly frightened.

"Troy. He came home, awful drunk—"

"Oh, you poor darling. Let me make you a glass of warm milk and you just don't worry about a thing—"

Leola held out a hand as if to ward her away.

"It's not that. Not being drunk. He told me—I thought it was just mean talk like a drunk man will make—"

"Leola, a man will say all kinds of things he doesn't mean when—"

"No, no. Not like that. I had to come here, I don't know what to do, I just couldn't wait until it got morning, not just sitting there thinking about it—"

Betty reached her, put an arm around the girl. The thin shoulders were shaking.

"He—he—he raped Jean tonight!"

"What!" Betty's arm fell away.

The words came almost too fast to be understood. "He came home, terrible drunk, the mean drunk when his lips get blue and his eyes real little, and the first thing he said was that—that—you know, that he'd done it to Jean Martin. Then he talked terrible about her and said he had to take it away from her but that she was glad to do it when they were doing it. He said she was just standing there with hardly anything on and talking mean to him to make him angry and he got mad and grabbed her and she wasn't wearing almost nothing and he did it to her. Right on the floor. And then he walked out and got drunk. And he wasn't lying. I never known Troy Noon to tell any kind of lie, drunk or not. Betty—he did it. What'll I do? Betty, what'll I do?"

Betty's arm had gone around Leola as the girl had talked. The first shock was over.

She had a decision to make. If this story was true—and it could be true—Jean might be hurt. She could be alone in her house, maybe hurt bad.

She tried to remember; when she and the children had come home from the movie had the Martin house been dark? She thought it had been. Yes, she was sure of it.

"Leola—did he say he hurt her?"

"Yes. Yes. He said he slapped her around first, to knock the bitchiness out of her, he said—"

"Oh, Lord." It would be terrible if Jean was lying in the dark house, alone and hurt. She had to go there—or maybe call her—

"Leola, you just sit down here. I'll put some water on for coffee or tea—or would you think a glass of brandy maybe? I don't know if we have any in the house—"

The girl, looking like a lost child in the coat wrapped over her pajamas, sat down in Herman's big chair. She shook her head and found it hard to say the word, "Nothing."

Go over or call? Maybe it would be better to try the telephone first, then if there wasn't any answer she and Herman could go over.

"What is—what's your, what's he doing now?" she asked Leola.

The girl looked up, tiny and frail in the big chair. She shook her head. "I waited till he fell asleep and then I came here. What'll I do?"

Betty put both hands on the girl's cheeks. "It sounds like a terrible thing but after all you say he was drunk when he was talking and maybe—"

"No. Troy don't lie or brag up or nothing like that. He said he did it. He did it all right. But what am I going to do?"

"I've got to see if Jean's all right—" Betty went to the phone, dialed the Martin number.

A long ring, another, a third. She'd get Herman dressed and they'd go right over—

"Hello?" Jean's voice.

"Jean—are you all right?"

There was a long wait—and Betty realized that something irrevocable had been done, something that might have happened, probably would have happened anyway because of Troy's talking to Leola, but that it was her, Betty Kreitzer's, doing now, and that it might have been better if she had not phoned, but how could she have waited, knowing what Leola told her? Irrevocable and awful—before Jean spoke again.

"You know about it?" Betty had heard this kind of tone in Jean Martin's voice before, at meetings, when Jean was pinning somebody's ears back coolly and smoothly.

"Leola's here." Maybe that would help Jean understand that the phone call had not been meddling. Or, oh, good Lord, it might make it seem worse meddling than ever.

"And what is Mrs. Noon saying?"

"She says her husband came home drunk, said all kinds of wild things—"

"About me?"

"Well, I don't understand what it's all about, but I guess— Leola's all upset—"

"But, Betty, why did you phone me?"

For a moment Betty felt a wild relief, and a quick anger at Leola for causing a lot of trouble, and then she realized that Jean's voice was still different. Not the way it should

184

have been if Betty had called her after two o'clock in the morning and all the rest of it hadn't happened.

With complete insight she could see it as Jean Martin did. Something terrible had happened tonight, but it had been a secret, known only to two people. Then, tearing the night apart, had come this phone call. Jean had been caught off balance and her first thought had been to pretend, to withdraw, to act as if there had been no terrible thing tonight which could change her life.

"I guess I was foolish, Jean," Betty said. "It was just that I was asleep and Leola came here and I started imagining all kinds of wild things—"

"Is there anything I can do to help?" Jean asked.

"No—maybe Leola'd better stay here until morning. I'm sure everything'll be all right—"

"Yes," said Jean. "I'm sure. Good night, Betty."

Betty put the phone in its cradle and went to Leola. The girl was crying, her hands covering her face.

"I talked to Jean," said Betty. "She's fine." The word sounded odd to her as she said it. Leola didn't answer.

In their bedroom Herman was twisting, restless and unable to go back to sleep. As he became more awake he began to wonder about the kind of trouble that had brought Mrs. Noon seeking Betty out after two in the morning. Maybe her husband was drunk, something like that. He might as well get up.

Leola had her face against Betty's breast, sobbing, when Herman came into the living room. He looked at his wife. Her lips were pursed tight; he knew her face, she was angry and shocked.

"Anything I can do?" he asked.

"Leola's going to stay here tonight. Help me make up the studio couch."

"I just don't know what to do," said Leola, looking up.

Herman did not ask any questions, but after three, when they were in their bed again, Betty told him what had happened.

"You sure he really did it? A young girl like her can get pretty crazy ideas—"

185

"He did it. I could tell from talking to Jean. She was as cold as ice—because I knew. Oh, Herm—it's terrible, terrible—"

"What's Jean going to do about it?"

"I don't know. Nothing maybe—"

"Nothing?"

"If she was going to call the police she'd have called them right away, as soon as he left. I can understand how she'd feel—you know, the shame and everything."

"But he can't just be allowed to get away with it—"

"I know. But what can we do? It's up to Jean."

"David's away, isn't he?"

"He went to Los Angeles this afternoon. She drove him to the airport."

"Do you suppose she's going to tell him?"

"I don't know. It's an awful thing to tell your husband."

"But we can't just let that man stay around here. In the Army men were hung for that. He deserves to be hung."

"He was probably drunk."

"There's no excuse. He told Leola he'd beat Jean too, you say?"

"Slapped her. He'd have to use force, I'm sure of that."

"If Jean won't do something, we'll have to."

"How can we?"

"You mean you're willing to live in the next house to a man who'd do that? He might do it again. And just driving him out of the neighborhood won't be enough. It would be like driving a mad dog into somebody else's neighborhood."

"But Herman, if it comes out—what will it do to Jean?"

"What's his wife going to do?"

"She doesn't know. The poor kid's just sick with shock. She loves him—it's easy to see that."

"By tomorrow she'll probably be ready to forgive him."

"Herm, she's such a young girl. I feel so sorry for her."

"Damn," he said. "It sure is a mess, isn't it?"

"We don't have to do anything about it tonight, Herman."

"I suppose not."

She held him tightly in her arms and kissed him. And then, her eyes closed, she prayed. The comfort of prayer came to her, and she asked her God for the power of understanding. Without prayer she would have been uncertain and frightened.

Herman did not pray; he lay awake.

Rape. A man he knew, a woman who was a friend and a neighbor. He could believe it of the man. There was an animal fierceness to Troy Noon, he was a man who could be violent.

But rape. In a way it was even worse than murder. Everything a family lived by could be destroyed by sexual violence. Why would a man do it? Drunk? But then the liquor would have only peeled away the restraints which kept him—sober —from doing what he always wanted to do.

Herman thought of Jean Martin as he had seen her at the barbecue last night. She had a fine body and she carried herself like a woman who wanted to be desirable, to be desired. Jerry—that Jerry certainly ate her up with his eyes. But she was always ladylike, not an exhibitionist or a teaser. But why the shorts last night then? Because she liked to show those smooth, strong, tapered thighs? Why else?

Troy's wife was pretty enough, almost like a teen-ager. Why would he want another woman? Even some girl that was willing?

What did a man feel like when he was doing that? Not just being with a woman, but with a woman who was fighting and scratching at him.

Men must have all been that way once. Dr. Margaret Mead —or was it her? some anthropologist anyway—had written of what it had been like for tens of thousands of human generations, reaching back half a million years.

Like a hunting party of Australian bushmen; find a woman from another clan, rape her, kill her. Each of the men in the hunting party would have the woman, then they would smash her head with their hunting clubs. Why kill her?

The soldiers of the Red Army coming into Germany in World War II; they had raped like savages.

And we had raped with chocolate bars and cigarettes and soap, thought Herman. Italy, France, Germany. And in the Philippines and Japan. A difference maybe, possibly even

187

a moral difference. Which is the more moral: to pull a woman's skirt over her arms and head, have her, and move on, leaving her still with whatever code of belief she'd had for herself, or to buy a woman who had not been a whore, have her, and move on, leaving her with no code of belief?

In one case the woman had no choice, in the other she'd had choice, but Herman remembered that the women who had sold themselves were not always the ones you would have figured to do so.

And in a way those German and Japanese women had raped the conquerors, demanding to be taken. Why? To show hatred for their own beaten men? A basic drive for survival, needing to lock their bodies in submission to the strong and the powerful, the gangling kids the draft boards had sent overseas?

Rape. Herman wondered how many times in his own blood lines, connecting back into the millions of copulations which had produced the men and women whose own sperm and eggs had joined through the thousands of generations to produce—at this time and at this place—Herman Kreitzer as one male unit of the life fabric, how many times those copulations had been rape. Go back far enough and it had all been something like rape.

The women had worked and talked and used soft fingers and pretended passions to change the ways in which men could have them. Smaller-boned and with softer muscles, they had found ways to protect the entrance to their bodies, inventing modesty and pride of fatherhood—who was it that said there had been no pride of fatherhood in men until there was personal property to be passed on to sons?—and the sanctity of marriage. And out of that the wild hunters had been tamed and become husbands and fathers, protectors of their women.

Rape, the crime which destroys a woman's dignity by taking away her right of choice as to who will father her children.

But there were women who wanted to be raped, who invited a kind of rape in their sexual teasing. Women who

188

searched out the ugly, brutal men. Sick women? Twisted women? Herman did not know.

And the vast complex in each human body of blood and muscle and glands and nerves which served to open the female to the rigid, insistent male was deeply and darkly more than the conscious mind could understand. The woman, ecstatic, biting and scratching at her lover at the moment of love while he hoped that his hardness would hurt her, strangely cruel and hating while loving the most.

Herman felt alone in the darkness, awake. Betty was beside him, asleep. What did he know of Betty as a woman? What did Betty know of herself, how much could she ever admit to herself?

And he? Could there be a moment with a woman when he would take her with his strength as she fought him?

He'd have to go to sleep. Tomorrow there'd be appliances to sell, customers to serve. The eyes of Jim Kemp looking at him.

The first thing tomorrow: do something about Troy Noon. The rapist.

In the quiet room he could hear the sound of Leola Noon sobbing in the converted daybed in the living room.

18

HER FACE HURT from crying. But she couldn't stop.

Fear mostly, thought Leola. Afraid of tomorrow as if it were the day they would come with knives and cut her into pieces.

Afraid because now she had no place to go. Get a waitress job somewhere, find a cheap room, move her clothes out.

No more house in Sunrise Hills, and she'd never been as proud of anything in her life as she had been of the house. It was like belonging.

She didn't belong anywhere any more.

Hate Troy? Maybe she'd hate him by tomorrow. She hadn't got to that point yet. All she could be now was afraid.

Afraid and hurt. Like if Troy had beat her inside where she was soft; beat her for no reason except to hurt her. Beat her so bad her insides ached.

Maybe she ought to stick by him. He was different than most men, he had to be understood and she hadn't learned to really understand him yet. Maybe it hadn't been his fault, not entirely, tonight.

It was her fault, some. He was so particular about her keeping covered up. It seemed awful important to him that no other man look at her; especially not her breasts and her middle. So when he came home tonight he saw right away that she didn't have pants on under her shorts or any bra under her halter. And then she had lied to him and got caught in the lie and for all he knew every man in Sunrise Hills could have seen her all bare today.

David Martin had. Maybe Troy was pretty sure about it, but she knew that David had peeked at her. He didn't have to do much peeking because she'd gone over there with not enough on.

That's probably what set Troy off. And her—the woman—

she must have done something. There isn't any man who'll go in a neighbor's house and just pull her clothes off her and rape her on the floor.

God, if he'd only done it to her. She waited day after day, doing everything she could to get him hot, and she could tell sometimes that he would be getting excited, he'd breathe different, and move jerkily, and she'd move her knees a little ways apart and pull her shoulders back, and her mouth would be open a little bit, and she'd be ready.

What she wanted was that he'd come to her and kiss her real hard, pushing her head back, and his hands would hurt her a little bit, and he'd hurt her a lot because he'd be crazy excited, and she'd go crazy too like she always wanted to do, and she'd feel that he'd put a baby in her.

That's the way it was really supposed to be. And she'd tried everything she knew to get him to do it to her just that way.

But he'd done it to that woman.

God, why? Why? Why not to her?

What had that woman done to get Troy excited that way when she never could?

What would they do to Troy?

Mrs. Kreitzer had acted kind of funny after she called that woman. She said she was fine.

How could she be fine if she hadn't wanted Troy to do it?

It didn't sound as if she were going to call the police. Maybe she wouldn't even tell her husband.

Maybe it hadn't been Troy's fault at all.

Maybe Troy put a baby into her.

Maybe that's what she wanted. Maybe her own husband couldn't do it. She'd always acted kind of strained when there was talk about having kids. Just like she herself acted strange.

Maybe that's why she got Troy hot tonight.

She'd kill her if that was true.

But God, why couldn't she ever do it? She couldn't ever really reach him, not like he should be.

But Troy said it had been different. He said he just did it to show the whole dirty world what he thought of it. He said she fought him at first and scratched at him and he used his strength to make her do it.

He says it wasn't her fault at all and I've never known Troy Noon to tell a lie. But maybe he just didn't see the tricks she was using.

What would she do now?

She couldn't go back to Troy.

Even if he'd come to her now and pull her clothes off and do it just like she'd always dreamed of him doing it, she wouldn't be able to stand it because he'd done it that way to Jean.

She was lying to herself. If he came into this room right now like that she'd show him she was a better woman than that other woman ever could be even with her long legs and big bust.

But she couldn't go back to Troy. She wouldn't have any pride left if she went back to Troy Noon now.

That was the one thing she couldn't do.

Get a job as a waitress, find a room tomorrow, move her things out.

If he tried to stop her she'd call the cops.

Tell them what he did tonight.

That would be the best thing. Punish them both. Call the cops and let the cops take care of him. That would fix her, too.

Jean. Jean Martin. Mrs. David Martin.

She'd been the perfect woman as far as she was concerned. Lovely, refined, elegant. A dreamboat of a nice guy for a husband, and her house was just wonderful, perfect. The way she wore clothes, and the way she talked. Everything about her.

She'd never been friendly but that didn't matter. She'd never been mean or nasty; just kind of standoffish.

Her husband was awful nice. Just a real sweet guy. They always acted as if they were in love and got along swell. This would break him up when he heard about it.

When he heard about it what would he do to Troy? Try and kill him? That's what Troy would do if somebody raped her. Or just call the cops and have Troy sent to the peniten-

192

tiary? That would kill Troy just as sure as any bullet in his heart. Maybe he wouldn't do anything, just leave her, go away. Or maybe they'd both go away.

Why had Troy done it? If she could only understand why Troy had done it she'd know what to do.

She might stick by him through anything if she just understood why he'd done it.

But it had been so horrible tonight. He woke her up and sat on the bed and told her about it like if he was describing a show he'd seen on TV. Everything he did and everything she did. What she wore and what she looked like after she was naked.

She'd listened to him like if he was a crazy man. But he was telling the truth. She knew that all right.

And then he'd fallen asleep, drunk and slobbering in his whites, all mussed up. And she'd come here. She had to talk to somebody about it before morning and Betty was the only person she could think of.

Why had he done it?

And what was she going to do tomorrow?

What would she do when she saw Troy again?

She loved him.

19

THERE WAS NO alarm clock in Troy Noon's bedroom; at a
quarter of six each morning he awoke. In the spring, at the
switch to Daylight Saving Time, he could tell himself that
it had to be an hour earlier and the clock within him changed
accordingly.

He was awake. All over and all at once, which was his way.

First was the taste, the crud in his mouth, a hang-over
mouth. He remembered the double shots; not much to drink,
but they must have hit him hard.

He had told Leola. This memory came hard, like a slap,
before he could remember what he had told her.

Jean Martin.

He felt his palms go cold and wet.

After more than a minute he turned his head. Leola was
gone. She never awakened before he did, which meant she
must have left last night after he'd fallen asleep.

Poor kid. What else could she do? And what was he
going to do?

Pushed too far, that's what had happened to him yesterday.
Went psycho from just a lot of little things. Rocky and Smith
goofing off at the station, the way Leola let the house go
sloppy, the pile-up with the Cad—knowing it was his fault—
and the way the Cad people had treated him. Going to get
him fired. Then Leola lying to him, that was the worst—
catching Leola in a lie. If she'd lie about anything, no matter how unimportant, she could lie about everything.

And then Jean Martin, so cool, so sure of herself. So the
guy went psycho and now his ass had had it.

What was he going to do now? He knew what to do first,
the book answer for what to do first. He was out of bed and
finished with the shave, the shower, the dozen push-ups on
the floor before he tried to think out ahead.

The rasp of the cold water on his body in the shower had
made him feel clean again; he still shaved with the plastic

194

razor the Army had issued him, and he used salt, wet on a brush, for his teeth.

Even during the push-ups, precise and as easy as if a machine were doing them for him, he did not try to think five minutes ahead.

Reality met him after he'd put on his shorts, T-shirt, and socks. What about the white uniform today? Even if he had a job that part of his life was over.

Over like when a psycho kid in combat disregards a direct order from an officer, tries to slug the officer. Maybe ten seconds, that's all the time it takes for the goof-off, but the kid's life—if he isn't shot down right there—is changed forever. Busted all to pieces that don't glue together again.

Hard to guess where Leola went. She had a few bucks. Maybe up to San Francisco. He went to the window and looked out. The car was still there. It must have been around midnight or so when he'd come back. No way for her to get very far unless she tried hitching rides, and she was too smart to take that kind of chance.

Well, she was on her own now. He wouldn't mess her up in this. Leola was some of the broken pieces.

He took a pair of slacks and a white shirt from his closet. If the police came for him this morning it would be the best kind of outfit for jail. No tie, no coat.

She wouldn't call the police, and he didn't think Leola would call them either.

He had been an officer on a general court martial once which found a sergeant guilty of rape. The sergeant had been hanged.

But there had been that little gook girl. If she'd talked they might have hanged Capt. Troy Noon, Inf., AUS.

It was different with civilians. Everything was different with civilians. They wouldn't hang him even if Jean Martin blew the whistle on him.

He could still see that sergeant's face when the board of officers found him guilty of rape. Not a muscle moving on the boy's face; he could have been standing inspection instead of hearing that he'd never know anything about being twenty-four years old.

195

Troy went into the kitchen. The kitchen told more about Leola, he thought, than anything else could. She tried hard to keep it clean and it never was. He made his coffee strong and hot, drank it black.

Only one thing to do first. There wasn't any book rule covering this particular situation, but there was a damn big book rule that covered all situations: face up.

Before he walked out of the house he turned and looked at the big room. Leola was sure crazy about this house. If the people in the other houses had been more friendly she'd have been a real happy kid here.

Kid. Supposing he'd let her have a kid, like she wanted so bad. It sure would be a bitched-up deal for that kid now.

Kids. They were having them by the millions; girls just out of high school couldn't wait to get married and start getting knocked up. They thought kids were cute. They got a charge out of having two or three kids in the house, spoiling them rotten, treating them like some kind of wind-up dolls.

He wouldn't bring a kid into this world. To get fouled-up like that Michael in this block, or to die yelling when the big one everybody was waiting for hit, or just to have a bitched-up out-of-work old man like Troy Noon.

The door closed softly behind him and he squared his shoulders, sucked in his hard, flat belly, and walked to the Martin house.

Nothing to say. The Army had it cold and right; when you've goofed you best face up, but keep your mouth shut. You've got nothing to say, soldier, you're here to be told.

This was the door he'd come to last night, mean and hot to go. If her husband had been there it was a lock he'd have tangled asses with him. But the ball had bounced the other way.

He pressed the button and heard the chimes inside. Nothing to do now but wait.

The door opened and she was standing there looking at him.

Nothing to do but wait; his eyes were on hers, and his mouth was closed in a straight line.

"What do you want?" she said.

He shook his head. "Nothing."

"Then get out of here," she said. Somehow her face reminded him of that sergeant when he'd heard the GCM verdict, a carved face, nothing moving, nothing alive in it.

He waited another ten seconds, turned and walked away.

"Wait." Her voice was like her face had been.

Troy turned, looked back at her. She was waiting for him to return, standing in the doorway, one hand high up on the edge of the half-opened door.

When he came up to her again her tongue slipped out, wet her lips.

"Why? It's important to know why."

"Why I'm here?"

"No. Last night."

Jean Martin did not know what answer would be possible to her, possible for her to use in living. Maybe it would be better if he did not answer. Her eyes, almost unmoving, were in reality searching out his face, scanning it, remembering it, trying to find significance in the edge of muscle, the shape of cheekbone and mouth, in his eyes.

Again he shook his head. "I don't know."

"Mrs. Kreitzer phoned me at two this morning. She knew about it. How?"

He started to shake his head again, paused. "My wife must have gone to her."

Jean's voice was low, almost hoarse. "You told your wife?"

He couldn't answer. He nodded.

God, she thought. Betty Kreitzer is right, there is a God like a great Father and He watches each one of us. I despised that girl, for no reason that I could understand, and for no good reason, and now what has been done to me? To both of us? It was a strange thought for her and was gone quickly. She could hear Michael screaming and Isbel's voice shouting at him. The air had morning coolness and the edge of the hills was bright. She knew that it was not yet seven o'clock. It had been the first night since her college days in which she had not slept at all.

Until there had been the shock of the telephone ringing,

and Betty's voice, she had sat reading and smoking. After Betty's call she had gone into her kitchen and cleaned it; finishing that at about five, she had started on her closets.

She had the kind of tiredness that made her feel empty, as if she were a porcelain shell. In a little while she would go to her bed and sleep.

Too tired to curse this man, or to scratch at his eyes. Too tired to do more than explain, as to a dirty child, "There was a chance—now there isn't. I don't know what to do now."

He knew what she would do. She had one right way of doing—if it wasn't already too late. Call the police and tell them that Troy Noon had taken her by force.

If she didn't do that there'd be another house in this block of Sunrise Hills going back to the land company. It was very clear to him.

Jean Martin did not think it was possible to hate a human being as she hated this man.

Still slowly, carefully, she said, "If you get away from here now, far enough away so that I'll never see you again or know that you exist—" She did not finish.

"I'm going away. There's nothing here for me," he said. After a dozen steps he turned, looked back at her. "There never was."

She watched him go to his car and drive away. As she closed the door, his fierce, lean, dark hill-man's face was as clear to her as if it had been last night, or a few minutes ago.

Leaning against the wall she thought, "What is he? Is that the man, that kind of a man, that's right for me? Don't I have any choice? Doesn't a woman have a choice?"

Her hands pressed against her sides. Everything else could be solved, even now, even after in whatever way he'd done it—remorse, fear (no, not fear in that man), drunkenness, bragging, vengefulness—he'd told that girl. Even after that disaster there could be a solution, some balancing of her personal ethics, some way of honesty that would still permit her to be Jean Martin, the wife of David Martin; some use of intelligence and the civilized understandings that would have been an honest solution.

Everything could be solved but her memory, nerve-deep, deeper than that, of the way she had loved this man for a few minutes last night. It had been everything, love and hate, and ferocity, unbearably complete.

As she walked to the low lounge, noticing that some of her flowers had lost their freshness, she thought of Lillian Rockwell. Maybe there was some understanding of how she felt today in what had happened to Lil.

The great American love story, simple and beautiful, that had been Lillian and Mark. It had blown to pieces, as if Lil had suddenly gone crazy and had destroyed it herself.

They'd gone steady in high school, arm in arm and eyes only for each other. Mark was big, over six feet, good-looking and well-built. A pleasant boy as Jean remembered him.

It had been a big church wedding and there must have been more than a hundred relatives of the two families at the reception. Mark was already in business for himself, a contractor, and he built their home himself. The girls who knew the couple thought of Mark as a standard for husbands —fun, strong, good to Lil, no chaser and no drinker. A big, nice guy.

Somehow Lil had met a bartender in some place along Camino Real. Jean had seen him, months later, and her feeling in seeing the man who had wrecked Lil and Mark's marriage was intense curiosity, nothing more.

A man nearly forty, skinny, with a skull-like face. An evil-tempered drunk, three times divorced, with a record of arrests for street fights and drunken driving. Worthless.

For this man Lil had thrown away her marriage, ending up as a cocktail waitress in Reno.

One time, meeting Mark by chance on Post Street, Jean had heard part of his story. His story was simple: he could not understand it at all.

He had even tried a reconciliation when he had found where Lil was working in Reno. She had been cruel and bitter to him, wanting money, the household goods, title to their home. During the divorce she'd got most of these things.

"But he's no good to her, Jean," Mark had said. "He's never

been any good to her. If she'd run off with a better man—some guy that had something—"

Maybe some urge to self-destruction? Some feeling of inadequacy against Mark, to be overbalanced by a deep contempt for her new lover?

This had to be understood because Jean was finding that logic did not give her an answer this morning. Last night had not been pleasure, it had been horrible. Troy Noon was not a man to be loved; what little she had seen of him in these past few months was of a man always on the verge of anger, seemingly ill-at-ease as if he were among a kind of people different from himself. And yet she had noticed him.

He had no abilities, no future. He was married to the kind of girl you would expect him to have.

And this was the man, the male, with the wild, selfish violence, that had taken her when all the handsome boys, the merchants, the poets, and the schemers had failed.

Selfish. Maybe that was the key. Instinctively she knew that Troy Noon's world had no other people in it. He was completely alone.

Was there some magic in a completely selfish man? Lil's bartender had been such a man, must have been.

Too much of the man-woman thing was below the surface of understanding, thought Jean. Forces powerful enough to wreck your life within you, and you could understand nothing of them. A few guesses by Freud, a few theories by others, a kind of a shaky science built on the theories and guesses, and where was help for her in that?

That block last night. All of her fancy thinking in her bathroom, but not thinking of living sperm within her. Not thinking of that until suddenly the block broke and she was in frantic panic using water almost scalding hot, over and over again.

What battle of forces within her had first produced that block against thinking of the sperm, Troy Noon's sperm, and then had shattered the block, forcing her into the near-agony of the scalding water?

Why had she called him back this morning? A stupid

question— "What were your reasons for raping me last night, Mr. Troy Noon?"

Like one of those Tobacco Road novels with a tussle under the chinaberry tree. Funny as hell. She began to laugh, doubled over on herself laughing as if she were being torn apart.

20

Jerry Flagg leaned against the four-door hardtop near the front of the showroom. Another lousy Monday morning, he thought, the start of another lousy week.

He watched old Bill Markham come toward him from his office, cigar ashes falling on his rumpled, pin-stripe suit.

"Got anything lined up for this week, Jerry?"

Jerry looked at Markham's face. By God, the strain was starting to show on the old thief. A lot full of new cars gathering dust, the vice-president of the bank calling first thing every morning, only two guys—both of them old—left in the garage. Bill Markham was about to end forty years in the new car business by going broke.

Not the first time for old Bill, Jerry knew, but it would be the last time.

"Yeah, I got a few."

"Close 'em, Jerry. Do anything you got to do—but close them." Markham relit the stump of cigar and Jerry noticed the tremor in the white, puffy hand.

Markham blew out smoke and tapped Flagg on the shoulder. "I'm not worried, Jerry," he said. "Not worried at all. You know why?"

"Why?" Jerry looked out the window, at the cars passing on the street. Plenty bright-colored new ones, and almost all of the new ones were GM jobs or Fords. Yeah, he'd have to make a move, and quick. Get out of the independents and under a roof, maybe with a hot, fast-trading Chevvie dealer.

"Because we're salesmen, Jerry. You and me—we're salesmen. We know how to sell cars."

Yeah, thought Jerry, you old goat, you knew how to sell Reos and Auburns and Grahams and Hupmobiles or whatever they were. You knew how to sell them until the outfit folded. Like this one is going to do.

"That's what my first boss told me," Markham went on. "I

was just out of the Army, the first week of 1919. Walking down Michigan Boulevard in Chicago—I happened to look in at the cars they had in the Moon agency and got to talking with the sales manager. You know, by three o'clock that afternoon I'd sold a deluxe touring car to a couple from Evanston? My first sale—a Moon deluxe touring car."

What the hell was a touring car, Jerry wondered. Moon, well that was another; he hadn't even been born when Moon went out of business. Old Markham must have been a regular undertaker for cars.

"I learned something that afternoon, Jerry, that I've never forgotten. It takes a salesman to sell cars."

Yeah, thought Jerry, and what does it take to buck GM and Ford? You work for an independent, maybe you're handling a fair little car. Dollar for dollar maybe you're matching even with the GM car or Ford and Plymouth. But the big page ads in the papers—you don't have them, or the color pages in the magazines, or the dozen big-name TV shows. And most of all they've got the money club over you—making people think they can't get good money trade-in on an independent. So when you get a chance at a buyer you've got to bid up for whatever old heap he's trying to unload, bid it up and chisel on price until when you've got the deal you don't make a buck.

"The independents are going to come back this year, Jerry," said Markham. "Yes sir, this is going to be a big year for us. But we have to go out and sell. Sell them on the car—not the price. A real salesman doesn't give a good gollywoggle about price."

The old bird had seen it all, Jerry thought. A 1919 Moon, that must have been a dilly. Hand crank and carbide lamps, probably. Touring car—he remembered what they were. A canvas top on wooden struts, isinglass side panels to put up when it rained. The big boom years when ordinary working people first started getting cars—Model Ts and Model As, those old boxlike Chevvies with the mohair upholstery and the little glass vases for flowers on the doorposts.

And during the war—War II and for a few years after—

this old burglar of a Markham must have robbed the peasants blind. Salesmanship he talked about—in a pig's eye.

But they'd caught up with him. This must have been a pretty nice little dealership once but it was a sinking ship now.

"I can take over the floor, Jerry, if you want to go out and see some prospects—"

"I'm expecting some people in. Maybe after lunch."

The phone in the office rang and Markham went back to answer it. "For you, Jerry," he called. "Your wife."

Jerry picked up the phone angrily. Isbel had no need to bother him here at the salesroom.

"Yeah?" he said.

"Jerry? Jerry—listen. Brother, have I got the scandal for you."

"You call me up just to give me some gossip?"

"Wait till you hear it! You know what happened last night?"

"No, and I don't give a goddamn."

"Troy Noon raped Jean Martin."

"What!"

"Betty Kreitzer told me about it. She's all upset and she had that Leola Noon staying at her house last night and after Michael went to school I dropped by Betty's and I could see she was upset. But I don't think she'd have told me except for that girl Leola still being there and that Betty was so upset about having called Jean last night—real late, after two, when she heard about it, just to see if she was all right and Jean acted as if nothing had happened. Betty didn't mean to tell me but it was all bottled up in her and it just came out—"

"Yeah, but what exactly happened?"

"Troy Noon went over to Jean's house and she was alone. He must have been drunk or something—anyway he came home drunk and told Leola all about it. Another thing that upset Betty was Herman. Right after breakfast he went over looking for Troy to tell him to get out of the neighborhood but he couldn't find him."

"You sure this isn't just a big story?"

"I'm sure. That's exactly what happened. He raped her last night."

Jerry Flagg let himself breathe, forcing the air out of his lungs in a soft gasp. He had looked much like he did now not long ago at a bar in Redwood City, watching a fighter—with twenty dollars of Flagg's money riding on him in a bet—get knocked out. It had not been a fast or clean knock-out; his man had been doing fine until the round in which the other man suddenly battered him, hitting him with com-binations, hooks, straight rights to the face until the man's knees bent, his face fell slowly forward and he went down, bloody and broken. Jerry had looked then, watched his man smashed, his twenty dollars lost, much the way he did now holding the telephone and hearing Isbel tell him of Jean Martin and Troy Noon.

"What's she going to do about it?"

"I don't know. Maybe nothing. You'd think she'd call the cops—"

"You really think he did it?" His fighter, the look of a man gone from his face, the mouth open and twisted, the mouth-piece knocked flying away, blood on the hurt animal face, stupid and empty and hurt. Twenty bucks shot.

"You know what that fellow's like—mean-looking, a regular hillbilly—"

"You mean she's just going to let him walk away whistling 'Yankee Doodle'?" He'd had twenty-three bucks in his pocket. Well, that had blown the night for him; he'd had two more Martinis and gone home, broke. They had to pick his man up, arms hanging, head lolling. Smashed real good, the yellow son-of-a-bitch, the dirty bum.

"Well, something will have to be done. Like Betty said, we can't just let a sex maniac run around the neighborhood—"

"Why don't you call the cops yourself?" Long legs, the full, straight lines of muscle, the smooth knees and the swell of calves, the hard, round, tight, small buttocks under the white shorts. Long, strong, demanding legs. Bitch.

"Oh, I couldn't do that. Butting in—"

"Yeah, but we can't let the bastard get away with it. He ought to be strung up by his—"

"What do you think we ought to do?"

"Well, playing around is one thing, but just taking it away

205

from a broad is something else—" Over his shoulder he could see a couple outside the agency, looking through the big show window at the four-door hardtop up in front. "Look —I've got to get back on the floor. Call me if anything happens, will you?"

"I just don't know what to do—"

"Okay, call me." Man, just rip those shorts off her, maybe hit her in the face, she wouldn't mind, she'd love it, the bitch. Damn Troy Noon! Damn his soul to hell. He put the phone in the cradle and walked out on the floor just as the couple came through the double doors from the street.

As he smiled he sized them up: a skinny guy in his midthirties wearing cheap slacks and a sports shirt, a fattening woman also in slacks with a grayish-tan imitation camel-hair short coat. Jerry's eyes picked out their shoes in a quick glance. The man wore brown ones, scuffed and unpolished, the heels worn down. She had dirty white-and-tan saddle shoes.

Maybe he could sneak over and see her tonight. He had the pitch— Got to do something about that son-of-a-bitch, honey. Boy—what a deal, be there alone with her and you could start right in talking about it. And then if she didn't warm up—just push her over and tear off a good one. What the hell could she do about it now? Go to the cops and say, "My goddamned neighbors are raping me every night?"

"Hello," he said to the two lookers. "She sure is a beauty, isn't she?" he continued, walking toward the hardtop. They followed him, as he knew they would, and as he reached the car he swung open the front door by the driver's seat and half bowed to the woman so that she hesitated only a moment before getting in behind the wheel. He closed the door gently and looked at her in admiration. As he stepped away from the car a little he said, "I just wish you could see yourself now. Doesn't she look great in a sporty car like this?"

The man didn't answer; Jerry prompted him, "Doesn't she?"

"Why, yeah. Sure."

"That's the only style car for you, ma'am," said Jerry to her. "No matter what make of motorcar you buy, be sure it's

206

got the sport lines like this one. Young and bold." He chuckled a little, looking her in the eyes. She giggled once, and he leaned over the door. "Put your hands on that wheel—notice everything's automatic, and notice the class. Inside it's just like the outside—classiest car on the road. Can't you just see your neighbors looking bug-eyed at you—"

"It's sure a nice-looking car," she said.

He couldn't let Isbel know he was going over there. Wait until it got dark. Start off nice and sympathetic, maybe? Try and talk her into it first and then if she still tried to play hard to get—she was strong, a well-built broad, looked more like one of those college girl swimming champs, big, firm jugs and those wonderful goddamned legs—better take a bottle with him, vodka maybe—

"We're just looking," said the man.

"I understand. I'll be glad to show you the motor. Most powerful car on the road. Nothing'll pass you in this baby. A real bomb, a beautiful bomb."

"They're making all the cars pretty powerful," the man said.

"My name's Jerry Flagg. I'm sales manager here." Jerry held out his hand. The man hesitated, held his hand for Jerry to shake.

Let her slop up the vodka, going easy himself. Get her to talking about that son-of-a-dirty-bitch, Noon, and how it happened, how it felt. Would he want her to talk about that? Maybe yes, maybe no. He wasn't sure.

"And what's your name, sir?" he asked the man, tightening his grip.

"Burnett. J. H. Burnett."

Jerry turned to the woman behind the wheel. "Pleased to meet you, Mrs. Burnett. I'm Jerry Flagg."

"How much does a job like this run?" asked the man.

"What are you trading in, Mr. Burnett?"

"Well, we've got a 1950 Hudson—"

Yeah, thought Jerry, it figures, a dog. A real dog, and it's probably fallen apart and they don't have a dime to get it fixed and so they've decided to trade it in. He doesn't want to buy a new car, has no damn intention in the world of buying anything but another dog, and they probably don't have credit enough to buy a can of beer with ninety per cent down.

But I've got to sell them. I've got to sell them to get the money and I need to sell them to wipe away this dirty, drag-ass Monday morning. I've got to take them good and then I'll feel better.

Tonight. Ring her doorbell, smile at her, sell her. He'd go nuts if he couldn't get her tonight. Knowing that Troy Noon had had her and got away with it. Damn Troy Noon's soul to hell.

"That's funny," he said to Burnett. "It wouldn't happen to be a sedan, would it? A 1950 Hudson sedan?"

"Yeah, it's a sedan." Burnett looked at him, curious.

"Did you happen to hear about us? Is that why you came, Mr. Burnett?"

"We were just going by, and she wanted to take a look. I was just kind of wondering how much a car like this would run—"

"You'll shop around today, Mr. Burnett. I want you to shop around. Go to all of our competitors and go to the used car lots—but I don't think you want a used car. You want a brand-new one with lots of power and guts and—" he turned to the woman, leaning against the door and smiling down at her— "your wife certainly deserves the classiest car on the road. Now look—I'm going to write something down for you, but I want you to keep it a secret."

Jerry's face was serious and intent as he wrote a few figures on the back of his business card.

"You were very lucky, coming in here this morning, Mr. Burnett. We're getting a big shipment of new cars in—business has been terrific with us—and the boss has ordered me to clear out the floor today. Not tomorrow—today. So look—" He bent over the card, his head close to Burnett's, then he looked at the woman and said, "Mrs. Burnett, you appreciate the value of a dollar—I want you to see these hard figures, too." He let her get out of the car, holding the door open for her, and then, dropping his voice, he talked, letting his right forefinger tap the car as he spoke.

"Your sedan, that 1950 Hudson, Bluebooks at a hundred dollars. List price on this car is $3278.26. That's a big jump, an awful big jump."

They both nodded, the man wetting his lips, and they began to edge away from him.

"But you can drive this big, fine car out of here today without another dime down—and no payments for sixty days. Then your payments will be only $62.11 a month. That's the deal I'll make you—see it right here on my card? Nothing down, no payments for two full months, and only $62.11 after that. You can pay $62.11, can't you?"

"Why sure," said the man and the woman nodded. "But we can't afford more than three thousand dollars for a car—"

"And you won't have to pay it," said Jerry. "I'll make you a real deal—but it has to be quick."

He backed away from them, frowning at his card. Then he handed it to Burnett.

"Check these," he said. "You go to any place you want, new or used car dealers. Get their best deal for any model or year you like or think you can afford. But do one thing to protect yourself—protect your best interests. Will you?"

"Sure, but—"

"A four-door hardtop convertible, brand new, in rich red and white. Check that. Nearly three hundred horsepower —fastest car on the road. Air-conditioning heater and ten-tube radio, white wall tires, power steering and power brakes, and Easy-go fully automatic transmission. Check these things. And then when somebody offers you a deal for an old car, or for some cheap car without any style or power, remember my personal deal to you—your present car as full down payment, sixty days until your first payment, and then only $62.11 a month—"

"We certainly could afford that," said the woman, looking back at the car.

Jerry began to edge them toward the door. "For your own protection I want you to shop around. Just remember you'll have to be back here this afternoon, if you want to drive this car home today." He held the door open for them.

They walked away slowly, talking to each other. Jerry

ran his fingers through his hair. They'd be back. They'd never find a deal like the one he'd offered them. There were no such deals—least of all, here.

He'd called his house twice before they came back. Isbel was away, he'd let the phone ring a full minute each time. It was going to be hard to wait for tonight.

When the Burnetts walked in they were just the way he expected them to be; anxious and eager to close the deal. No dealer along the street would have touched the terms he'd offered them and for the last hour they'd probably been living in a dream world, Burnett racing along 101, passing Cadillacs, his wife looking contemptuously at the bug-eyes of the neighbors as she got into her classy car. Now they were going to face reality and Jerry's only job now would be to keep them from seeing it.

"Well," said Burnett, "we figured we'd come back and talk business with you—"

"That's fine," said Jerry. "I've just closed some deals and I have to make out the papers. Why don't you and Mrs. Burnett look over your new car for a few minutes?"

He went into the office and tried to call Isbel again. There was no answer. He looked over the price sheets on cars for a few minutes and penciled out the screwing he was going to give the Burnetts. When he went out to the floor the Burnetts were in the front seat of the car. Jerry waited for them to get out and walk over to him.

"Let's see," he said, frowning. "I quoted you a price of $3428.26, didn't I?"

"I don't remember the price," Burnett said, wetting his lips, "but you said it would be about $62 a month, and no down payment—"

"Where is your car? The old Hudson?" Jerry said sharply.

"Down the block aways—"

"Let's go down and look at it."

Jerry walked briskly, making the Burnetts hurry a little to keep up with him. As they passed the Plymouth Agency Jerry saw Hank Michaels looking out. Hank smiled as he looked at Jerry and the Burnetts; it was a picture with a story to him.

The salesman going out to look at the trade-in, the shark circling in the lagoon.

It was a dog, no better and no worse than he expected it to be. The body had a few bangs, one rear window was cracked, the interior was filthy.

Jerry spent five minutes looking at it. In a straight deal there would have been no point to bothering to look at it at all. An old car with no resale value except for cash at maybe a hundred dollars or less. But in this one he had to give the Burnetts plenty of time to see what a junk they had.

"Okay," he said at last. "Okay. I think I can allow you nine hundred and fifty dollars on it."

The Burnetts looked at each other, trying to keep the elation out of their faces. Flagg led them, again hurrying, to the showroom, gave them one more loving glance at the hardtop, and then took them into the small, glassed-in office.

"What kind of work do you do, Mr. Burnett?" he asked after the couple had seated themselves next to the desk.

"I'm a bartender—on Geary Street—"

"How long have you had your present job?"

"About eight months—"

The credit form on the desk was another problem to be solved, nothing more, to Jerry Flagg. In the blank for "Length of present employment" he put in "Three years."

"What's your average weekly income?" he asked.

Burnett shifted in his chair. Flagg knew that Burnett would lie, up the amount ten dollars or so.

"About a hundred a week. And the missus earns over sixty."

Jerry nodded. Their actual take-home pay was probably one hundred and ten a week, total. He filled in the blanks with $105 for the man, $72.50 for the woman. During the next fifteen minutes he put in the rest of the information required. They rented a flat, had been there six months. He made it an unfurnished house, listed them as having lived there three years.

"What's the name of the boss where you work?"

"Pete Palumbo—"

"If the bank calls him up will you have him say that you've been there three years?"

211

Burnett shook his head while his wife began to recolor her lips, the lipstick darkly orange. "Naw, Palumbo didn't do no favors for anybody—"

"Anybody there that would?"

"Yeah, the other bartender, Smitty."

"He on days?"

"Yeah."

Jerry made a note on the credit form, "Ask for Mr. Smith, day manager."

When he finished the form he gave it to the Burnetts to sign. If there was any kickback on the lies and misinformation—they'd signed it.

The credit application gave a picture of a hard-working couple with an income of nearly ten thousand dollars a year, two children, a long occupancy in a nice home where they owned their furniture, steady employment. The application would also show a trade-in and a large cash down payment. It looked good.

But he knew them, had known them on sight, and their clumsy lies to him—compared to his own smooth, careful, larger lies on the application—had confirmed what he knew of them.

Like a couple of pieces of driftwood. Both of them would be drinkers, spending maybe a third of their income across the wet, scarred bars of neighborhood joints. They hadn't told him but he knew each of them would have one or two or three divorces behind them. They probably owed everybody in their home section, but these would be debts not reported to the central credit rating bureau.

A couple of children. Living in some dirty flat, the building forty or fifty years old, the old man and the old lady working nights, sleeping days, quarreling, filthy, bitter, vicious. The smell of hatred around them always.

But they earned enough dough to make a few payments. He'd get his commission and he'd have left this dying agency before the bank bounced the car back on them. As it would.

Now he had to get the money out of them. Money—they'd come out to Motor Row looking for a no-money-down deal and he'd hooked them on the promise of one. In Burnett's slacks pocket and his wife's grease-stained purse there might be a total of thirty bucks. To make this sale hold up Jerry needed at least three hundred in cash.

"Boy," he said, pulling at the neck of his shirt, "I sure hope the boss will back me up on this. I've practically given you the joint. Wait here while I get the okay—if I do."

He left them in the little office and walked into the back shop. Bill Markham was checking out the parts inventory. The strain lines on his face showed as he saw Jerry.

"Did you sell 'em?"

Jerry looked at him, his contempt twisting his lower lip. Sell them, he thought, what's to sell? He gave them a dream in the morning and used it to suck them in when they came back to find it. He picked up the back phone on the parts counter and dialed.

"I got to get them some money," he said to Markham.

The line was busy and he put the phone down, waiting. He was in no hurry.

"Funny thing about a couple like that one," said Markham, walking around the counter to Jerry. "In the old days you'd just roust 'em in back to the cheapy lot, sell 'em some rusty junk for cash. They weren't customers—but they're customers now."

"They were the only walk-ins I had all day," Jerry said. A dead dealership. An old jerk owning it who lived in the days when he'd been a cocky young guy selling Moons or whatever.

"Yes sir, Jerry," Markham said, lighting his cigar. "If there's one big change I've seen in my time, that's it. Used to be that the new things—the fancy, high-priced new stuff—all went to the young married folks with lots of money. Rich families, or young doctors and lawyers, looking for the latest and best."

He chewed the cigar around. "But that's all changed. Do you know who the first people were that bought television sets? The ones who couldn't afford it, like that pair you got out there. Same way with deep-freezers and all the automatic gadgets they've got in houses these days. Poor people bought them first. Today if you haven't got something fancy and expensive that the poor people will buy you're out of business."

The old son-of-a-bitch was out of business himself and didn't know it, Jerry thought.

"Just look at our own lines," Markham continued. "Buick third in sales, even Olds ahead of Plymouth and the other low-priced cars except Chevvies and Ford. I can remember when the automobile business was built on a family paying one-third cash down on the cheapest four-door sedan they could find. Now we sell to poor people who want two-toned convertibles or hardtops with an engine four times bigger than they need."

"You know what?" said Jerry, dialing again. "There aren't any poor people any more. Watch me prove it—"

A girl's voice answered him on the phone. "Garvin Finance."

"Harris there?" asked Jerry. "Harry Harris?"

The girl switched his call and heard Harris answer.

"Harry? I got a fast one here for you. Bartender and his wife—both employed, making better than one-fifty a week take-home. They need three hundred for a down payment. No furniture, couple kids. It's worth twenty-five to me if you okay it—"

Jerry listened to Harris, nodded, said goodbye and hung up. He'd got the cash for the suckers—all they had to do now was go over and get it. Twenty-five dollars in grease to the loan man.

"Fix it up?" asked Markham, smiling wetly around his cigar.

"Sure I fixed it up. What else?" said Jerry, turning and walking away from him.

Old Bill Markham watched the young man as he went toward the front office. Lot of get-up and go to Jerry Flagg, he thought. Live wire. Salesmen didn't have the fun selling cars like they used to before the war. Or even more—back when he'd first started. It was fun, a real game. He could remember that Ford dealer, sweating ice-cubes in 1926 when old Henry just shut down because nobody'd buy his Model T any more, shut down and tooled up for the Model A. There'd been plenty of excitement and rumors about that Model A, all kinds of wild guesses. Pictures on the front pages when it finally came out. Not a bad little car, but not good enough. Henry'd had to go the V-8 mighty soon.

Yeah, Henry and that red-hot V-8. Ford had changed everything twice. Once with the Model T. It hadn't been the working men that had bought the Model Ts, but the farmers. And it sure changed their families; maybe not them so much, but their families were never the same after they could go to town every night. They went to town to see movies and between the two—a car and the movies—they got to be folks.

Then Henry Ford got mad at Chevrolet and put a V-8 hunk of power in his cars. If you wanted to put a finger on where today started, Bill Markham thought, you could put it right on those first V-8s and hitting the road at eighty miles an hour. America had never got over it.

Cars had killed over a million of them—fast cars and people who had nowhere to go going there too damned fast. Maybe twenty million, or maybe fifty million girls had got the hard straight facts of life for the first time in an automobile, Markham thought, feeling an old, lost lechery for the darkness, the mohair upholstery, the edge of the front seat cramping against you. Fifty million, hell! Maybe all of them.

Changed the whole damned world. Taught folks to go over their heads in debt, taught them to be ashamed of a car more than three years old, taught them to be too lazy to shift gears or raise a window or even push down hard on the damned brake or turn the damned wheel without power doing the job for them. Taught them to be restless as hell, and it taught them what a hell of a fine damned big country America was.

Let the poor people buy three-thousand-buck fancy wagons in circus colors with every fancy gadget Rube Goldberg could think up. Let the poor people race by on a damned billion-dollar superhighway, looking for fun at ninety miles an hour, proud as pigeons because they were in a brand-new car and everybody knew they were right up to the minute and doing wonderful. Maybe that young fellow Flagg was right and there weren't any poor people any more.

But why was the fun gone out of the automobile business?

A nice little dealership like this was a fine investment; there were a certain number of people who always bought Hudsons, or Nash, or Studebaker, or Packard, or Grahams and Reos. Now GM and Ford and Chrysler were like monsters, with fifty different kinds of models, and it was pretty hard for the little fellow.

He pulled his shoulders back; the only answer was the same old answer—get out and sell.

Only things seemed to have changed so much. Maybe if he got a franchise for these little foreign cars—folks seemed to be interested in them, you saw them all over the place. But it was kind of late to try a new trick.

Markham thought that he was still glad to be in the car business, only if it was more fun like it used to be, years ago.

Jerry Flagg shook his head as he came into the sales office.

"No dice," he said sitting down. "The boss ate me out good for that deal I was trying to give you. It's no dice."

The Burnetts looked at him with one open mouth, one tightly shut mouth, both dull with disappointment.

"But maybe I've got the answer—" He was smiling, warm and friendly.

This was where he sank the harpoon into them, and he wanted to do it so neat and easy they wouldn't even feel it.

"The main trouble is that trade-in I offered you. The boss won't go for more than seven hundred—"

The woman spoke quickly. "Well, that'll be all right—"

"No, it won't, because we need eleven hundred for the down payment."

"Eleven hundred?" Both Burnetts showed that this was a big figure to them. Big because it was right now.

He came in hard with his question. "How much cash can you add to the down payment?"

They looked at each other. It was the look of doctor bills unpaid, a couple of tabs at the bar in their block, the rent coming up, sixty dollars at the little grocery store, the look of being in the hole and never getting out of it.

Jerry knew the look. He was going to push them a hell of a way farther down that hole.

216

"Well, I've got some good news for you," he said, without waiting for their answer. "I told you I'd make this deal. I told you that you'd drive home today in that beautiful honey of a car, and I'm going to see that you do."

The Burnetts looked as if—after weary, rusting years of dirty days—they had found a truly good man, a friend. They were going to drive home, after all, in that powerhouse of a car, that big-guts car with all the class in the world, that brand-new hardtop convertible.

"I'll make arrangements for you to get three hundred dollars in cash right now. Of course you'll have to pay it off, but you can see that it doesn't cost you a cent—you can see that, can't you?"

"How won't it?" said Burnett.

"We already got one personal loan—" began his wife.

"That's all right. Here's how you don't pay anything really. I'm giving you eight hundred on that Hudson. I'm cutting the company's profit and my commission one hundred dollars to do it. That's because I won't go back on my word." He waited for their look of appreciation and then went on. "That means that you could sell your new car right now and make a profit. You're getting the rock-bottom discount, you're getting more than seven hundred dollars extra cash value for your old car. That's why the loan is just free money to you. You see that, don't you?"

"Why, yeah—"

"Okay, I'll take you right over and we'll get that money now." He picked up the credit forms and walked slowly toward the door.

Twenty minutes later he brought them back, a check from the Garvin Finance Company made out to the Agency for $300 in his pocket. Later today he'd give Harry his cut. Today the finance company loan man would be hungry for the extra loot, tonight he'd sweat because he'd made another bad loan; for the next months he'd hound the Burnetts for each $34.20, making sure they paid Garvin before anybody else. A hell of a way to squeeze twenty-five bucks, thought Jerry.

He gave the endorsed check to Markham first. Now let the

217

Burnetts try to wiggle off the hook when he gave them the bad news.

"Three hundred in cash, okay," he began, once again in the little sales office. "Eight hundred credit on the trade-in. That's eleven hundred. Now the basic price of this car is $3428.26. You want power steering, power brakes?"

"Sure. That's what you said comes with it—"

"Fine. Underseal, a permanent wax job so you won't have to ever wax it yourself, tinted glass windshield, two-tone paint—" as he talked he put down a list of figures. The figures—like the basic price he'd quoted—he made up as he went along. The actual retail price of the car was $2978.26. He had picked up $450 of the trade-in on that alone; now he was after packing the final price another $300. Each item he listed was ten to thirty dollars higher than the actual retail price. He did not total the figures in the sales office, but instead looked down a table of monthly payments.

"Okay, sign the contracts and I'll have the Service Department get your car ready for you to drive away."

"How much does it all come to?" asked the woman.

Jerry smiled, looked serious, patted her on the shoulder. "With that good money you and your husband are making you'll be able to handle the payments easily. Of course I quoted you on a 48-month basis, and because of your kind of work you only qualify for 36-month contracts but that just means it will all be paid off sooner."

Burnett was already signing the papers and his wife followed him.

Flagg looked at the Burnetts with cool anger and contempt. "The payments will be $98.78 a month," he said picking up the signed contracts.

"I thought it was only going to be around sixty—"

"That would be on a longer contract. But you've got a really fine car and you've made a good deal. Without spending a penny out of your pocket you've got an $1100 equity in this car already—"

"Yeah, but we didn't figure on paying so much a month. We owe on that loan payment, you know that you just took

218

out for us, and we've got another personal loan we've got to make payments on, and we just traded in our old TV set and there's payments on that—"

"And on that wrist watch you got me for my birthday—" Mrs. Burnett thrust out a yellowish wrist with a yellowish watch on it. There were diamond chips in the dial of the watch.

"You've made a good deal. Your car will be ready for you by five o'clock." Jerry bent over and shook hands with Burnett. As he felt the hesitancy in the finger pressure of the bartender Jerry wondered if either of them would ever realize that they had committed themselves to pay out a total of $3966 for their new car. And if they tried to sell it tomorrow they'd be lucky to get an offer of $2250 for it.

They'd drive away happy tonight. And somehow they'd scrape up the money to meet the payments. Not on time, always late, always after dunning letters from the bank, after phone calls by collectors, but eventually they'd pay.

And so he'd moved another car for old Markham. The credit clerks at the bank would look over the deal, and it would look good. Before the papers would be taken over Jerry would fix them to show an allowance of only $150 on the old car, the remaining $950 would be shown as a cash down payment. Steady employment and steady residence in a house with their own furniture. Good people.

The kind of people the whole crazy new world was built on, thought Jerry. The designers and engineers in Detroit knocked themselves out trying to please the Burnetts; the ad guys yelled at them on TV, showed them pretty young broads with big knockers and bare legs next to the cars; the mile-long factories squeezed the steel into shape; other jokers poured concrete for the freeways, bulldozing out the orchards and farms to make way for them; the banks finagled with a few billion dollars in credit for the Burnetts.

But they were better off. They'd always been lousy peasants, living bad, sweating plenty, and dying soon. And now they were free to move, this generation of Burnetts. Move, sitting on foam rubber, listening to the car radio, in a bright bubble of steel and tinted glass. It sure was living.

Tonight he'd go over to Jean Martin's house. He'd give her the same go that he'd just given the Burnetts.

Why the hell did he want Jean Martin so bad? Why shouldn't he? It was the basis of the whole deal of living—getting into the sack with the very best there was. What else did you run the whole tough ratrace for?

21

FOR A FEW SECONDS after he was awake David Martin was completely happy. Love with Jean, more than sex, much more, love. There had never been one like this one before, never so complete, with him lover and master, untiring as he had been this time. Nor ever had Jean been so rich and warm, as if her body was dancing with his. The perfect one, the utterly complete one in which each had taken all, given all, each sharing the life shock—bodies vibrating from spine and loins for the climax. Wonderful and perfect.

He'd been dreaming. Morning and living came slowly to him and then he knew he was in a room at the Hollywood-Roosevelt Hotel in Los Angeles, and he was alone.

Dream girl. The Jean Martin of that perfect one was a sleep shadow, a dream. He swung out of bed and knew the clarity of thought that comes sometimes like a shaft of sunlight and is gone, first after wakening. Jean was like that dream Jean; it was there for him, always there, her body rich, warm, strong, eager, wild.

He had been the dream shadow. A David Martin like a young bull, a stallion.

A wish dream.

Standing in the shower, the water cool and stimulating on his body, he remembered last night and Dr. Paul Wood Lesser. It was pretty jumbled, he must have got really stoned last night. Probably had a little hang-over this morning without realizing it. Fantastic to run into Paul Lesser in a little bar off Hollywood Boulevard and get drunk with him.

He had not even looked at his watch, did not know what time it was. Hadn't called Jean last night.

Lots of talking. The Purpose of God. The cold, simple truths of human biology—the little girls playing with dolls today had better not plan on being the mothers of four or five babies of their own when they grew up.

He stepped out of the shower, rubbed himself hard and rough with the towel.

He picked up his watch from the headboard of the bed. Ten minutes to nine. He'd really overslept this morning.

Funny. That dream, that perfect dream, must have come during a time when his body knew that he should be awake, should have been up for an hour.

A good time to call Jean. And then call G. C. Wise at Coast Gas & Power. A quick breakfast and start the big job today.

He picked up the phone and asked the switchboard operator for long distance. Within a minute he heard the phone at Sunrise Hills ringing. He waited another minute before canceling the call.

Jean would be at Betty Kreitzer's for a morning cup of coffee. She liked to do that. Or maybe she'd gone to San Francisco to get a job.

He finished dressing thinking about Jean. It was understandable that she was bored. Even good, because otherwise she might go way out on clothes, her garden, and the furnishing of the house.

She needed a child. Simple and obvious and painful. And since he hadn't put one into her she had to go out and search for some other means of fulfillment.

Every day had sixteen hours or so of living. Jean could not continue in these splendid years of her life with the idiot's game of letting each day fall away without satisfactions.

Saturday night came again to David's thoughts and he didn't want to think about it. Maybe that was why he'd had this morning's dream—because of Saturday night.

No good, Jean getting a job in San Francisco. It wasn't the way of living they'd planned. But what could he say to her? She was right, she couldn't let these years keep sliding into the past, to be remembered only as the year she changed the living room or planted the Shasta daisies or was elected secretary of the local Mental Health Society.

And so she'd remember them as the year she got her San Francisco job, or the year she bought her own big convertible, or the year she took her first vacation—Hawaii?—alone.

A wild factor again. The waiting egg within Jean, frantic

racing sperm—and nothing. The egg unruptured, the sperm swimming until their tiny bursts of energy were gone and they were dead. Why? Because of that series of failures something good and fine between a young man and a young woman in love was endangered.

It wasn't a problem that Paul Lesser had to face. He could recall, more clearly, the conversation last night. Lesser's point had been simple—sexual love and emotional love are intertwined, but the time when such love is coupled to procreation is ending. Must end unless the race finds some other way of slaughtering itself.

Talk to a man—man? practically a god to David—and talk coldly about children, not as if they were human, laughing and friendly, but as they were in truth—biological vectors, components of an impossible curve of population. Talk with the evaluations of scientists: the curve must flatten out, there must—and the word *must* was a word of law, as much a part of God's laws as gravitation—be fewer children born per family until the rate of increase was approximately zero.

Talk like a scientist and then think like a lover; want Jean to find her fulfillment as a woman, find his own soul-deep satisfaction as a father.

The universe was full of wild factors.

He took the elevator to the first floor and had a breakfast of orange juice, ham and eggs, whole wheat toast and coffee.

At a quarter of ten he called G. C. Wise at C.G.&P. and was asked to come over immediately. Wise would meet him at the western branch billing office of Coast.

David took a cab and started thinking about his job during the ride. In its simplest terms his job was to make Wise see that full automation in Coast's billing and auditing departments was inevitable.

If he failed to do that the pilot installation to be set up in the West Los Angeles branch would be inadequate. Some other electronics firm than Verdun Laboratories would get the eventual Coast contract.

Jean was right. This was a point of separation. If he failed with Coast's vice-president David Martin's career at Verdun would level off—a good project man, but keep him in the office. If he succeeded in doing what Bill Verdun, Turner Fry, Sokolik, and Seaman Cowles wanted he could move up into what was supposed to be a wonderful world, the world of important men. Not right away—but he'd be on his way.

Only his ambition looked upward in another direction. Be a man like Paul Lesser. Go forward to the outer frontiers, farther until you were alone, as Lesser had. Know the same exultation that Drake or Magellan or Cook had known, but so much richer than the exploration of a planet, this was the exploration of the universe from meson to galaxy, and exploration of time and the reason for time, and exploration of God.

But he didn't have the mechanism of the mind that God had given—for His own purpose—to Paul Wood Lesser.

To be a Lesser, or any of the other giants of physics, required a brain of special and vast abilities. Without that David Martin would be no new-day Drake or Magellan, but rather a merchant's clerk, sitting in a Bristol countinghouse.

He smiled. Fancy similes for the truth. He wasn't as smart as Lesser and he wished he was because that was the way his ambition went.

Strange that he would use the concept of God so often this morning. A concept like the white-bearded Father, enormous in wrath as in mercy, asking only that His children obey the Law, and worship Him.

Understanding of the Law is the worship of God, thought David. Use any concept or symbol you want, and it came out that way.

The cab double parked, David paid the driver, and went into the functional-design building which was the western Los Angeles billing office of Coast Gas & Power. There was no reception desk, but a girl at the front switchboard told him that Mr. Wise was expecting him and was in the divisional accounting chief's office. She told him the office was at the rear of the billing department.

He walked past the rows of gray steel desks. Heads turned slowly as he went by; probably they knew who he was and why he was there.

Mostly they were girls in their twenties, but there were

stouter, gray-haired women at some of the desks. Along the wall to his right, under the high band of tilted windows, was a row of desks with men. Young men and old men, the ones just starting in the tournament to get to the big jobs, and the men who had lost out.

G. C. Wise was waiting for him at the opened door of the divisional chief's office. He was a big man, broad-shouldered, his face red-veined and rough-skinned.

They shook hands and Wise led him into the office, introduced him to the divisional chief. She was a small, brisk woman who reminded David somewhat of an older, smarter, successful Isbel Flagg.

"So you're the man who is going to turn us all into robots," she said, smiling. Her name was Helen Meary, *Miss Meary* on the desk name-plate.

David felt a flicker of embarrassment. Basically that was exactly what he intended to do. Whatever Miss Meary's job was in supervising billing at this major branch, it was almost certain that there would be no job for her if Verdun put in a full automation setup. Nor jobs for those girls and older women out there, nor jobs for the eager young men and the tired old men. A crew of maintenance technicians—nobody else.

"Well, not exactly," he said, and wished he had not.

Wise made a few minutes of small talk before they got down to business, seated around Miss Meary's desk. Intuitively David recognized the purpose of the small talk about weather and Los Angeles and Verdun and where David lived. It was to put him at ease while Wise sized him up.

David realized that he was at the showdown point right in the beginning. Miss Meary represented the old way, and as the old way was destroyed by his equipment the very basis of her life would go. Wise knew this and was on her side.

It was the side that could not win. Maybe he, Martin, would not be skillful enough or strong enough to convince Wise, but automation would win out, and soon.

One of those girls at a desk out there would process a few hundred bills during a day's work. Her reason for existence—engineering-wise—was solely the processing of those bills. To

225

maintain her at that job required several pounds of food a day, shelter for her at home, clothes for her to wear, some sort of amusement as a kind of dessert for her days, some degree of sexual satisfaction or at least sexual excitement. All of this for the purpose of processing a few hundred gas and light bills.

She would make some errors; she would get sick from time to time; she would get restless, want more satisfactions, less drudgery.

In her place Verdun Labs would put a component of the total automation setup. Some transistors—small wafers of germanium—and some relays, a little geared mechanism, and that was all. The component would process a few thousand bills a day, requiring only a little current. It would not make mistakes.

If your objective was to have light and gas bills processed there wasn't much choice between the girl and the component.

Wise was ready. "I'd like to have you explain this pilot system you are going to install here to Miss Meary," he said, his voice gentle.

It was a time for simple honesty. David began, "It's a straight line automation. Your meter readers will mark standard Hollerith cards with electronic pencils. These cards will feed through a bank here in which the account number and the readings will be taken off the cards by scanners, collated in the memory drums, calculated for billing purposes, and printed on bill forms. The bill forms will be enclosed in envelopes and readied for mailing. There are only three human elements in the process—the meter readers, the technicians who maintain the equipment here, and somebody to take the bills to the post office. It will cost a fraction of your present payroll and will pay off the cost of the equipment within two years. It will be a lot faster and completely accurate—"

Miss Meary interrupted him. "But what will my girls do? What will I have to do with all this machinery?"

David shook his head. He didn't have any words for her. This was another case of the wild factor, and here the wild factor was human beings.

Wise studied the young man. Everything was so simple for young men.

And if anybody should understand all of the ramifications of this special situation, G. C. Wise should. He had known Coast for forty years, from the time electric-light bulbs had little tits for points and plenty of people still used gas for lighting their houses, to now when he was equally familiar with the plans for the new atomic power plants to be built all along the Coast. He knew Coast G. & P., and he knew the people that worked for them; he knew something about the owners of Coast G. & P., too, from iron-bellied and iron-hearted Joe Hunt who owned the old Oakland Illuminating Company and had built the power octopus outward from it by everything from purchase to slugging and blackmail, not to mention subornation of courts and the bribery of whole legislatures, to the remote and competent executives of the insurance companies which now owned the major share of Coast stock. Hell, G. C. Wise knew Coast, and this young man didn't know anything about it.

But neither did he, thought Wise. Not any more. Not this exploding force which was Coast, building plants to get electricity from atomic energy, building the billion-dollar Flaming River project which would change, utterly, a hundred thousand square miles of mountains and high plains country, ever developing new labor-eliminating devices, ever hiring more people, ever searching for more sources of power, ever searching for more needs for power. Coast Gas & Power was beyond understanding.

So this young man was here, and he would talk a little but not much because this boy wasn't a talker. He was one of the engineer type.

Not like the gawky farmboys who used to come out of four years of jerkwater college in leather boots and flannel shirts, not knowing much more than how to wind an armature, like the engineers of forty years ago. Not like those smooth ones of today, who had eyes like surgeons.

He wouldn't talk much, but he'd get the plans ready for the pilot billing automation, and in another year or two Coast

Gas & Power would be even a little less human than it was now.

This boy wouldn't know or care about the long nights ahead in some hotel room arguing with the union representatives, working out some way of keeping them happy while you dumped a couple of thousand of their members. That would have to be hard politics, giving a few of their strong members some kind of a break, trying to hold their seniority while you found jobs for them in some other division. Hard politics, hours of talk, and nothing gained in the end.

Not like the old days in the late 30s when you and the union boys hammered out a better deal for everybody. That was what had killed old man Hunt, turned him purple and popped his heart like a grape. Letting Coast get unionized. Old man Hunt would have put on a blond wig and gone to work in a whorehouse to make a buck, but he didn't much believe in unions.

And you felt like you were really doing something worthwhile when you and the union boys worked out the health and welfare provisions in the new contract. Gave you a good feeling to know that the men and women of Coast had protection so neither they nor their kids would have to go to County if they got sick, or even die because they couldn't afford a doctor, like it was forty years ago. That was good, that month-long session on the health and welfare in the new contract.

This would be different. Arguing and playing hard politics about who and how many would get the ax. The kind of jobs you could get for those you didn't ax. Just a dirty job of letting a couple of thousand people go.

In the old days at Coast you had the same two jobs as today —making and selling electricity. When old iron-belly Hunt was still a buck male, living it up with the assemblymen at parties in Sacramento, furnishing them with drinks and girls and money, most of the current Coast made went for lighting. There weren't many factories west of the Rockies and most of them had their own steam plants, using steam power to turn the belts that ran the machines.

Hunt and Giannini, they were the boys that built the West.

228

Hunt fighting the long-hairs, getting hold of the water rights, building the dams and the hell with anybody that tried to stop him, stretching the power lines—and Lord, the power loss that used to leak off those old time high lines—while Giannini, looking like a picture of Caesar behind his big desk at the Bank of Italy, raised the money to build them.

The days and the fights, the problems that had to be whipped, and World War II coming like a hurricane that changed the West forever. Coast was damn near ready for that war. It was Coast power that made the aluminum, powered the riveting machines on the ship hulls and the plane wings. And now Coast planning for a hundred years ahead, going to trap the Flaming River up north, spend a billion dollars, another billion on the atomic furnaces, getting rid of the human beings that worked for it.

Coast had a life and an intelligence of its own now, thought G. C. Wise. It was putting its own kind into the system, things that thought in ultra-high frequency, and talked to each other in the language of electrons.

In a way it kind of scared the hell out of him.

Helen Meary felt herself becoming tense and angry.

This young man, this good-looking young man, coming into her department so cocksure of himself, coming to change everything.

He didn't know the first thing about utility billing; if personnel hired him and sent him to her department she'd have to break him in like a green kid. She could just see him fumbling, getting account files mixed, making mistakes all over the place, spending more time trying to make the tabulator girls than he did working.

No that wasn't fair. He seemed to be a serious, careful young man. She'd known a couple like him when she'd started for Coast right in the billing department in 1931. One of them was head comptroller now and lived in Bel Air; she hadn't seen him in fifteen years. But he'd been something like this young fellow.

Clean-cut. Probably married. All the young men got married these days. They didn't have a depression to contend with, and she had had a father out of work in those days.

Eighteen dollars a week—that's what Coast paid and she'd supported four people on it for five years. And all these little bitches that were getting fifty-five dollars to start and only forty hours a week and vacations and all the rest of it, and who could go out and find a young fellow with a good job any time they wanted to get married, they snickered at her and called her a dried-up old maid.

What was going to happen now?

She didn't want to listen to him. His face had told her the truth: he was sorry for her. Sorry like a doctor telling a woman she had terminal cancer.

He knew nothing about utility billing, he didn't know how to handle a department of girls and dressed-up young punks and worn-out old men, and score an efficiency record of 98 and 99 month after month, year after year.

They'd had comptometers when she'd started, and there was even a roomful of old men using pen and ink on ledger sheets. Then they'd let all the old men go when they'd changed over to machine records and it was the bottom of the depression. She'd seen one of the old men working on a park road with a lot of other raggedy WPA workers about a year later.

It took a lot of ability to head a department as big as this one, and when they'd offered her a transfer to downtown she turned it down because this was like a little kingdom to her and what she said went. Downtown there'd have been more salary, but there'd have been women bosses over her and she wasn't sure how she could take that.

She couldn't understand why they wanted to change things. Her girls were good. Of course she had a fairly high turnover; they were forever getting themselves caught, usually a year after the office collection for their marriage, and they'd stay on the job until about the fifth or sixth month, and then there'd be a shower for them, and about a month after the baby was born they'd come back to work again.

Not like taking care of four people on eighteen dollars a week—and the girls at Woolworth's were getting only ten, because they were too dumb to handle figures or weren't pretty enough—and going on park dates or walking dates for

230

five years with boys that either didn't have jobs or weren't making enough to get married.

It wasn't so much that she missed having children, but she'd like to have had what these girls had without even thinking about it. A man, and a nice home, and the money you earned could go for nice clothes and nice things and vacations, maybe to Hawaii or Mexico.

She'd worked hard for a good many years and what she had to show for it was an apartment, a nice car, money in the bank, and her department.

Not that she hadn't had men. These wet-pants little chippies who thought she was a dried-up old maid should only know what she knew about men. It was plenty, sister.

But it was like a circle, or a cycle or something. Those dates, back in the depression, all Dutch. Maybe each of them would spend fifty cents, or on Saturday night as much as a dollar, and that meant cutting out lunches—not cutting out buying lunch in a drugstore, but cutting out the peanut-butter-and-jelly sandwich you took to work in a paper bag. Cutting that out so you could save the peanut butter and bread money for Saturday night.

And you knew the feeling of wet grass on your bare behind, too, because there was no place for the two of you to go except the park.

Well, the circle was around again. Not going Dutch exactly, but buying your own drinks at a bar while some fellow sized you up or tried to make time with you, and sometimes loaning a man friend some money for a date which you almost never got back. Not all the time, because there were still plenty of men you could run into that treated you wonderfully, but enough times to worry you a little bit.

At least you never felt cold grass on your bare can any more. Sometimes she wished she could. It had been crazy fun, and just about all the fun she'd had in those days.

You'd think his being comptroller and everything, he'd drop around the branch offices—at least once in fifteen years. But to hell with him, he sure hadn't been the only one.

This young fellow wasn't doing much talking. She'd better

forget about herself and start showing him up. That's why G. C. Wise himself was here, to have Helen Meary pick this new idea to pieces, show why a good billing department needed competent employees who knew what they were doing and not just a lot of machines that didn't.

There was no machine made that would be more efficient than her department.

". . . you won't need additional power lines," said the young fellow, David was his name, a nice name. "The entire system here won't use as much current as the lights you have over the desks now."

Helen Meary broke in. "But who checks for errors?"

David Martin turned to her. "These systems find their own errors, usually in microseconds—that is, the error is located by feedback at the instant it is made, and is corrected at the same time. Of course the word *error* is not quite right. The system doesn't make errors—not like a girl misreading the meter report for example—but it is capable of malfunction. A capacitor may be faulty, for example, or the printing mechanism may get out of order."

"Then you do need girls to check the bills—" Helen Meary broke in. "If you need girls to check them it would seem a lot more efficient to have the girls at our regular billing machines handle the whole operation. My girls are trained so that they can spot an error faster than any machine could—"

"What I'm looking for," said G. C. Wise, vice-president of Coast Gas & Power, thinking of the unions, of the management reports, of severance pay and pension funds, of the attitude of the directors, of public opinion and publicity, "is some happy combination of people and machinery. The trouble with your automation setup, as I understand it, is that it is inflexible."

"A mechanical monster," said Helen Meary.

The Bank of America had put an automation deal in, thought Wise. What did they call it? ERMA? Something like that. They'd handled the publicity end by running big ads bragging about their automation system and how much better their customers would be served. Of course bank employees

232

weren't union members and they still had to have tellers and the men you went to see about loans.

Wise said, "This morning I only wanted you and Miss Meary to become acquainted and to start discussing the problems in this test installation. We can all have lunch together, and then this afternoon I'll have our technical boys in for a practical round table on installation and procedure."

Wise had sized him up and had decided he could push him around, thought David. Wise was going to insist on a bastardization of the pilot system, maybe cutting the billing staff in half, breaking into the straight line flow of the system at intervals for human operations.

That was what Bill Verdun and Sokolik had sent him down to see didn't happen.

If he took too strong a stand against it Wise might decide to postpone the test installation at this branch. That would let Verdun's competitors come back in, after Turner Fry had spent three months selling them. One month on a marlin fishing trip off La Paz, one month at Palm Springs and Las Vegas, one month here in Los Angeles. Sold them a Verdun test installation, and that would lead to a full Coast G. & P. installation. A fourteen-million-dollar order.

But details had been left under the personal direction of G. C. Wise, and Wise was gun-shy of the real high-powered men of Verdun Labs.

He was playing his game very simply. Let Martin talk, then tell Martin he wanted a mixed system—machines and people.

Because he was old. Because he didn't understand that it was as if Coast Gas & Power was an entity in itself, like a great animal. It ate falling water and the streams of natural gas in the giant pipe lines; it ate coal and drank a million barrels of oil a month.

Then it did the work that was required of it. It cooked ten million meals a day, it lit the homes of four million families, it powered the tools and machinery of two million workers. It made aluminum from ore, and hammered and forged steel. It was power.

It was changing, like a tadpole becoming a frog, or more

233

accurately like a collection of power plants and transmission lines becoming an entity of power with its own nervous system.

Money as such meant nothing to Coast—it manufactured wealth. Whatever hundreds of millions of dollars it needed for the realities of its power plants and transmission facilities it paid back over and over again.

Coast was moving toward the time when it would need human beings only as a brain, not as part of its muscles nor of its nervous system. And only human beings who qualified to be cells of the brain of a supergiant which spread its multifold power over a million square miles.

This tiny function of billing customers resolved most efficiently into a straight line full automation system. That was what the entity which was Coast would get. And if human beings stopped it, it would be a kind of illness, an injury to Coast.

In human terms, ordinary terms, this old man was trying to get in the way of the inevitable.

This didn't really matter to David Martin. In projects at Verdun Labs he knew how to solve the problems of this kind of automation system. He knew how to search out the wild factors of electronics circuits, and how to curb them.

As an engineer he knew the vectors of this situation: human beings could not compete with the automation system.

But here he was face to face with people. With this woman, no longer young, who would lose this job, maybe have trouble ever finding another job. With this old man who wanted to keep things as they were.

It would be like what Jean had talked about yesterday. Tricks, pressure, politics, until he put in the system Verdun wanted and Coast must have.

As they talked, almost small-talk again—the evolution of the Coast billing system as described by Helen Meary from her unmentioned twenty-five years of experience, the advantages of a highly flexible system in any department of a growing and changing monster corporation like Coast, as given by G. C. Wise—David set up his plan of attack.

Helen Meary began to talk about her girls, picking out the stories of individuals. She mentioned their payroll savings purchases of government bonds, the office parties they had for weddings and baby showers.

"These machines of yours sound like something out of communism," she said, breaking into her own stories of her girls.

"Do your girls like to sit in an office all day, making out utility bills?" asked David.

Helen Meary nodded. "Some of them do. It keeps them busy, they're around other girls they have something in common with, and they get paid for it. Sure they like it."

"You're going to tell me," said G. C. Wise to David, "that machines have ended drudgery. We used to work a hard sixty hours a week at Coast—and no overtime either. You're going to say that machines have made that forty hours, even thirty hours of pretty easy work. Well, that's true. And for more money.

"But now you want to make it no hours a week, and no pay checks either. That's the part I can't see."

"We can talk about it after lunch," said David.

Helen Meary watched the young man. A nice clean-cut fellow with a heart like a rock. She could tell, she knew men. He'd be kind and polite, he wouldn't even be selfish, he'd make a *Ladies' Home Journal* kind of husband.

But a heart like a rock. When he was through here there wouldn't be the sound of people in this building, or the smell of the girls' perfume, or the gang around the water fountain, or the kids going out on coffee break, chattering and laughing.

There'd just be his cold machines.

He had a heart like a rock.

22

BETTY KREITZER, coming from her kitchen to the living room, saw that Leola Noon was at the window, looking toward her own home. Harmon was in front of the TV set watching "Ding Dong School."

Of course Isbel Flagg had to be told, Betty said to herself. Until something was done about that man no woman in the neighborhood was safe.

Rape was worse than murder. It was the final attack on the center of all living—the family. The purpose of living was to produce a healthy, God-loving and God-knowing family, to guide them into womanhood and manhood. This was the purpose of man on God's earth.

Violation of a woman, of a decent married woman, was the most terrible crime she could imagine. Except for the conscious and willful destruction of a child's faith in his Savior. That was the ultimate sin.

All of Betty Kreitzer's world was shaking today. She realized that she had allowed herself to drift into a world of illusion. Sunrise Hills had done that. The houses of Sunrise Hills, so comfortable, so pleasant, so rich with the satisfactions of the flesh.

Harmon, only four; and instead of tugging at his mother's skirts and following her around the house, or playing outside in the sun, he sat on the floor, his eyes locked to the glowing screen.

Like millions of other little boys and girls all at the same time, not living in the real world around them, not living the real lives of little boys and girls, but as if they had no bodies— only eyes and ears, and a soft plastic brain to record what the TV set told them.

Not that "Ding Dong School" was bad—it was like a TV kindergarten—but a kindergarten of little ghosts sitting in a million living rooms. Not playing and laughing and crying, only watching.

And so they were led away from the truth of life, that we are here by God's will and for His purpose, to worship Him and obey Him and to live by faith. Instead they were led into a lie, that we live for pleasure and bodily satisfactions.

That was Troy Noon, like a savage out of the past. Caring nothing for the laws of God, nor even the laws of man, and destroying a good woman.

The unchurched, the drifters, the Philistines worshiping at their golden calf of pleasure, Egyptians, exactly as Scripture described them.

They knew nothing of Jesus, nor of His teachings. Nothing of humility and gentleness, nor of being humble workers in the vineyard of the Lord.

But they were not far away, in another time, another place. They were here among us, and they came evilly in the night. But how could you raise a child in God's way in these times? They mocked and laughed and told your daughters, "Have big breasts and long legs so that all men will lust after you. If men's eyes are not hungry for your body you are nothing."

It would be hard to raise Sandra and little Harmon in these times. Betty dreaded the years ahead when Sandra would enter the phase of being boy-crazy, of wanting to stay out late at night necking with boys, when Harmon would change from the little boy he was now into something strange, wild, and brooding.

The only protection she could give them, a richness for eternity rather than for the few fleshly years on this earth, would be faith and religion. If they truly loved their Savior they would survive the evils of these times.

But she was alone. Herman's strength of the father was needed to guide the children, and Herman was becoming an unbeliever.

Leola Noon turned from the window, shrugged her small shoulders.

"There's no reason for me just to hang around here," she said. "I might as well go home and pack some things."

Betty nodded. "Do you want me to come over and help—and in case he comes back?"

The girl's lips curled. "He won't harm me none if he comes back. Maybe he wanted to break it up. Maybe it was all my fault."

"Don't even think that, Leola. A man couldn't want a nicer wife than you."

Leola ran her fingers across her face. "He sure must have wanted her more than me. To do what he did—even drunk."

"Leola—you don't go to church, do you?"

"Not much since I was a kid. We used to go to different churches then. Like to the Church of Christ for a while, and then to the Assembly of God, or maybe the Baptists."

"But you don't go yourself now?"

"We didn't even get married in a church."

Betty nodded. What family bonds could there be without religion? Without faith you were merely going through your few years of life like animals in a pasture, with only the appetites of animals to give purpose to life.

Leola looked at Betty, fiddling with her fingers against her coat. "Why did you ask?"

"You're so young. Prayer would be a great source of strength at a time like this."

Pray to a God to strike down Troy Noon, thought Leola, to strike him dead for what he did? And when God's eyes looked at her, seeing into her secrets, what then? Teasing David Martin, showing herself, knowing that men would get excited and itchy. If God punished, He would punish her.

He has, she thought, and the thought was a loud sound in her mind.

The anger she had not felt last night was like a pain within her now. It was not screaming anger, but pain. You try to build a life and you find it's not easy—not easy to keep a house clean and tidy, not easy to make Troy happy and easy with himself, not easy to make the man you love give you the babies you must have. You think maybe it will work out if you show Troy you love him enough, and you make all kinds of plans. Take better care of the house, get a Singer and make

238

some nice clothes for yourself, learn from Jean Martin how to be smart and smooth and cool. Learn from her!

Yes—but sometimes you'd be so damn nervous you could jump out of your skin in that house. People were having fun and excitement in lots of places, there were juke-joints all along the highway.

It would be really crazy just to go out, like when you were a kid and still in school, putting on lipstick, fixing your hair in a pony tail and going with Janey Down or one of the other kids to meet some boys.

Rhythm and blues music—Troy hated it—with a real beat that made your backbone wiggle. Riding on the back of Billy Gallegher's motorcycle, feeling the hard vibration set your thighs to humming like bass strings, letting the beat of the cycle and, in between, the rock music in the juke-joints get to you like if a boy was really doing it to you, only it was safe and fun and crazy.

When she'd met Troy Noon she saw a man. He could make her shiver inside just with those black, fierce eyes. And he treated her the way a man treats a woman, strong and fierce, kind of silent. She'd wanted to marry him from the first time she saw him.

He was lots older of course, but that was okay. And he didn't like the things she did, but she figured he was right, and he'd teach her to be a real woman. They'd had it kind of tough for a while, but then he got promoted and she'd worked on him for so long until he agreed to buy the house in Sunrise Hills.

Sooner or later he'd have got excited sometime and put a baby in her. After he saw the baby he'd love it and her life would be complete. So when she got restless or just plain lonely to hear a bunch of kids laughing and messing around, she'd tease Troy and get him to loving her—but always careful, always that damned preparation—or they'd go to a movie, or take a drive along the ocean on Route One. Life had been pretty good, and she had plans to make it better.

So why had she gone over to that dreamboat, that David Martin, and let him look at her?

That's what had made Troy into a wild man. More than anything else he was fierce and proud; to mock at his pride was throwing a match into gasoline.

No, she couldn't pray to God and have Him look inside her and know it was her weakness and foolishness that had caused it.

When they were kids at church she believed what the preaching said, believed the minister. Hell and damnation, with souls burning forever for their sins. She still believed, way inside of her, but when you started to grow up and got interested in boys you kind of put it into the back of your mind, because there would be plenty of time for church later, when you were old.

She'd always admired Betty for raising a good, religious family, sending them to Sunday school and everything. Maybe if her own folks hadn't wandered from one church to another, getting her and the other kids all mixed up, she would have stayed with it more. But the kids whose folks made them stay with all the church activities had messed around just as much as the juke-joint crowd. They'd be real religious, but that didn't stop them from finding out about messing around.

She felt tired. She didn't understand things.

"I changed my mind," she said to Betty. "I'm not leaving, not right away at least."

"But what about him?"

"I don't know. Maybe I ought to stick with him. Maybe it wasn't all his fault."

Betty went to the television set, turned it off. "Harmon— you go outside and play."

Harmon began to argue, his lower lip bending down in readiness for tears.

"You go outside, right now!"

He marched off, and at the door he turned. "You never let me have any fun!"

Betty put her arm around Leola. "You must be awfully tired. Why don't you lie down for a while and try to sleep?"

"No. I'm going home. I was all shook up last night, but I can't see that I'll make things any better by running off. If there's any trouble he'll need me."

"But a man who'll do something like that—"

"He's been a good man. Moody, sort of, and hard. But he's been a good husband. I've got to stick by him."

"Leola—even if Mrs. Martin doesn't have him arrested we can't let him keep on living here."

"If she doesn't have him arrested it's because it's her fault! Are you going to let her keep on living here?"

"Jean Martin is my best friend now and as long as she's lived here she's never done one single thing—"

"How do you know what she's really like?" In sudden anger Leola went to the door. "I'm sorry. You were wonderful to me last night and I don't know how to thank you. But I've got to be alone for a while—think things out—" She pushed open the door and went out.

"Leola—" Betty began and then shrugged. The girl was right, she needed to be alone for a while. But Troy Noon had to be punished for what he had done.

If men like that were not punished fast and hard no woman would be safe.

She went back to the kitchen where Isbel Flagg was sitting at the table, pouring another cup of coffee, a cigarette burning in the ash tray.

When Isbel had come over this morning she had told her. For Jean's sake she wished it could have been hushed up, and there was no reason it could not be hushed up, pretty much, after Troy Noon had been tended to; but it was only right that every woman living next to the beast should know what he was like.

Isbel had gone back to her house and had popped right back, all big-eyed for more scandal and excitement. And she'd certainly been listening just now.

"She must be crazy," said Isbel. "Sticking up for him!"

"She's just a kid. She doesn't know what to do."

"Maybe there's something to what she said, though," Isbel said, her head forward like a bird's. "Jean knows she's got a luscious figure and she sure shows it off."

"We all dress like that around here," Betty answered, sitting down and pouring coffee for herself.

"I wish I had a husband like yours—never even looks at another woman—"

"Isbel—I've got to go over to Jean. I'm worried just sick about her."

"I'll go with you."

"No—I think it would be better if only one of us went."

"I'm just as good a friend of hers as you are."

"But because Leola came here and I called Jean and everything—I think I'd better just go alone."

Isbel looked at her with open resentment. She wanted to see Jean Martin, see her humbled and ashamed. Dirtied up. She'd always been so smug and proud, showing off those legs, pushing her tits forward, talking about jazzing and loving as if it was the most wonderful, natural thing in the world.

Well, she knew what it was like now. She'd wiggled in front of one man too many and now she knew what it was like from some man that wasn't all love talk and sugar like David. Now she knew what it was like to get it from some man stinking from whiskey, and falling all over himself, and dirtying her up. There wasn't anything all romantic and pretty about that.

And wait until her husband heard about it. She'd like to see David Martin's face when he found out that his lah-de-dah beauty had got hers from a grease monkey like Troy Noon.

She had to talk to her.

"But you've got little Harmon here and Mikey's at school. Jean and I have always been good friends—" Isbel said, getting up from her chair.

This was a woman's job, thought Betty. Like it had always been. Men worked, and fought as soldiers, and built things or tore them down, but it was women who held the world together. Men were the ministers, but it was the women who were the strong fiber of the church.

And it was women who had the deep knowledge, the old mother wisdom, that was needed at a time like this.

There was Jean to be helped and comforted, Jean's marriage to be saved, Leola to be helped and understood.

And Troy Noon to be punished.

Women had seen to it that their men had pride in them, pride in their virtue and modesty, and on that pride their men had erected laws and punishments to protect their women.

But if Herman did not do something about it, she would.

"Look, Isbel," she said. "I'll go over there, and call you here. You watch Harmon and—"

Isbel looked at her with masked bitterness. Always running things, that was Betty Kreitzer.

23

THE SHOPPING CENTER of Sunrise Hills never seemed quite real to Herman Kreitzer. It was nothing like the clutter of glassy store-fronts that had been the business streets of Chicago when he had been a boy and a young man.

This seemed like something built for children, gay and bright, playful, insubstantial. Some of the store-fronts here were not glass but an open, winding garden instead, or the glass might be canted forward, or arranged in strange shapes.

The stores he had known as a young man in Chicago were painted in browns, grays, light-greens. Here the colors were bright pinks, deep yellows, even white-and-black. Light was unexpected, sometimes quiet and pleasant, almost not seen, or sometimes bold and exciting.

Money had less meaning. That is money as Herman had known it, green bills folded carefully into purses and coins counted out one by one. That had been a long time ago, in another age. These people in the shopping center of Sunrise Hills—who once would have been called "ordinary working people" for the most part, as he was himself—used checks or charge plates. In the acre of supermarket they paid for groceries mostly with cash, but with tens and twenties, and a twenty-dollar bill might not cover the cost of a basket of food.

Like a playground for children. Everything was pretty and graceful, amusing and inviting. Yet the gross volume of goods sold, he knew, was more than a half-million dollars a week.

He thought of the short television commercial the Bank of America used, a simple line cartoon of a little man with a belt around his arms, "Are you strapped for money? Go to your nearest Bank of America and ask for it by name, M-O-N-E-Y—"

A playground for happy children, and the toys were frozen dinners or strawberries in January, passion fruit juice, sliced breast of turkey; television sets and twenty-dollar slippers; nylon sports sweaters, dacron shirts, orlon suits; a dozen eggs in a plastic strip, a jar of instant coffee—that was another bank commercial, one about "instant money" spooned out and bubbling.

Herman parked the car at the edge of the ten acre asphalt-paved lot near the store he managed.

There must still be people who didn't shop in a playground like this. People who went into tired little stores, brown and dusty, smelling like a store, not air-conditioned, without bold, exciting lights or flowering plants at the entrance; who bought things they needed with tired paper dollars taken cautiously from worn purses. People who couldn't go to the Bank of America and ask for it by name.

But that was the old way and it would be gone, if everything held together.

If Russia did not turn out to be a Troy Noon, or if—maybe —we weren't a Troy Noon ourselves. If there was a time of guided missiles with hydrogen warheads, the playgrounds would be gone.

He went to the rear door of the store, unlocked it. Jeannie, the cashier, would be getting out of her husband's car in front just now. Jim Kemp would be along in five minutes, and Kennedy, his other salesman, a few minutes later.

Herman flicked on the banks of fluorescents, went to the front door and opened it. Jeannie was sliding out of the car, directly in front of the store.

Jeannie, mother of two small children. Her mother took care of them during the forty-four hours each week which earned Jeannie take-home pay of fifty-seven dollars. That fifty-seven dollars, added to her husband's ninety-two from the machine shop, gave them enough to belong to the class that could have "instant money" from the bank, that could afford three thousand dollars' worth of new car every two years, that could sign checks and use charge plates in pretty playgrounds like this shopping center of Sunrise Hills.

Peasants. They had been peasants like his own family, Herman thought. Twenty years ago—when Jeannie had been a little girl of ten or so—what had they done then in the bitter depression? Who cared now? They weren't peasants any more, and they were far too powerful in their middle-class tens of millions to permit a nonsense of depression again. They had been told for more than twenty years that the government should not and could not help them, that easy money prosperity was an illusion, that high wages and short work weeks would wreck the country, and in a pleasing vague way Jeannie and her husband believed all this, complained about taxes, were sure of waste in the federal government, and voted Republican. But if the endless, expanding flow of easy money credit stopped and—the drying-up process reaching Jeannie and her husband quickly, within weeks—their paychecks were affected, these two would be aware and demanding, linked quickly with sixty million others like them, all aware and demanding. In the 1930s their fathers and mothers had not known where money came from, and dumbly they had accepted relief bread and WPA shovels; Jeannie and her husband knew exactly where the money came from. It came from Washington. If it started getting scarce they would see that the government invented a new supply.

And, thought Herman, as long as there was energy enough —coal and oil and gas and hydropower, and soon now the atomic reactors—the government could always invent new money to use to buy the torrent of wonderful things: cars, houses, boats, appliances, trips, that the energy and the tools produced so easily and abundantly.

Strange and weird: the great clash of the twentieth century was supposed to be between capitalism and communism, and no one seemed to notice the Fifth Columns on each side that made the differences between the philosophies grotesque and misshapen. On the communist side the new tools and the new energy sources to power them were beginning to turn out consumer goods, furniture and clothes and television sets. Ivan and Anna with property became middle-class, talking and thinking much like Jeannie and her husband. The Russians were enjoying a Fifth Column of consumer production, but even more potent in warping and catalyzing Marx was the change brought by the automatic machines. If it was toil or drudgery, an automatic machine could do it cheaper and faster than a human being; therefore toil and drudgery were disappearing from the Soviet Union as they were from the United States. The exploitation of human sweat was ending, not because of Marx, but because human sweat was too expensive and inefficient.

Jeannie came in, smiled at Herman, said something about the weather, and went to her battery of machines, neat and colorful. During the next nine hours the branch store Herman managed would sell about one thousand dollars' worth of goods, and Jeannie's fingers would translate the transactions into punched cards and tabulated records, taking in the money, the checks, and the signatures at the bottom of the contracts, as good as money. In a sense Jeannie was a sensitive nerve-end and a small, hungry mouth, connected neatly with all the other small mouths and nerve-ends of the corporation.

So we had our own Fifth Column, Herman said, almost aloud. The people bought insurance, paid their premiums, and the daily flood of money, adding up to billions of dollars each year, was buying everything in the country. The insurance companies were the majority owners of the utility companies, the railroads, the mines and manufacturing companies. It was a kind of practical communism, an insurance-premium communism: executive decisions were made by managers, men whose ability was in the office functions, not production, not sales, not research, but management. And management was ever more based on the book, as it was in Herman's own branch here. Research and statistics turned out the figures, and policy was decided. Management followed policy.

We had a Fifth Column of commissars, thought Herman, and in the end it was very funny that the world might be destroyed because of the ideological clash between communism and capitalism.

Admittedly the generals could be switched, exchanged between the Red Army and the American Army without any trouble except language, because generals, if they were any good as generals, were all very much alike.

247

But the management men could be switched too. A solid young executive, Republican, Episcopalian, suburban, Stanford, could be exchanged for a young commissar, Komsomol and party member, and their attitudes and semantics would be nearly identical. Both devoted to efficiency of management, increasing the human elements of courtesy and team spirit, reducing the human elements of fatigue, error, and social friction. Both believers in increasing automation, increasing communication, extending communication into the vast nonlanguage areas.

Maybe there wouldn't be a war, Herman thought.

He knew why he'd been playing with this kind of thoughts. Last night he'd made up his mind to do something about Troy Noon. And he didn't know what to do.

Leave it up to Jean Martin? And supposing she didn't do anything about it?

Go to the police? An outsider, interfering?

Beat up Troy, drive him away? That fierce, lean man could smash Herman down and he knew it. He was soft, not the tough-muscled Sergeant Kreitzer of so long ago.

So when you did not know what to do about a real problem, one close to your own life, you thought about abstract things—the way the world was going, the great social implications of the Sunrise Hills shopping center.

He could be frightened, Herman thought of himself. He was frightened when he thought of the thin crust over chaos on which Betty, Harmon and Sandra lived. That was what his thoughts about Troy Noon had led him to face again.

The killers, the torturers, the rapists, the men who smashed the skulls of children, walked with their wives along the pleasant avenue of the Sunrise Hills shopping center, as they walked, masked with faces in repose, everywhere in the world.

He had seen them peeled naked in the war. Boys he had known in the basic training camps, Coke-drinking boys, movie-going boys, writing-letters-to-home boys, carrying-their-girls'-pictures boys—and when the war gave them a chance, because the war did not change them, it did nothing more than allow them to tear off the masks they'd always had to wear, they were cruel, givers of pain and givers of death for the deep pleasure such giving was for them.

Herman had known this from his own boyhood in Chicago. We live together in a security of taut threads, bound by tight threads of what we believe we must do, or should do, or would be punished for doing; but when the threads break, the man who delivers the milk, or drives a bus, or sits behind a desk, or smiles from the other side of a counter is again the man who killed father, mother, son, daughter and baby of a Protestant family on St. Bartholomew's Night—not because they were Protestant, but because the threads were broken that night for the killers if they killed only Protestants; he is again the crazy kid, barely out of the harness of his parachute, spraying bullets at the blank-faced civilians of Pyongyang; he is again the amiable German at Buchenwald, the amiable Englishman putting down rebellion in India, the amiable Russian killing the Hungarian boys in Budapest—not because they were Koreans, Jews, Indians, or Hungarians, but because the threads were broken and the men could inflict pain, could kill.

Troy Noon had not raped for lust or for love. Men seldom did. Somehow the threads which had bound Troy Noon to the ways of life of Sunrise Hills, his service station, his home, his wife, had broken. And when those threads had broken he had raped for cruelty.

Deep within himself Herman Kreitzer was frightened. The urge to cruelty was a part of living and a man walked with his family through the years protected only by his own strength and the strength of those threads of custom, law and hypocrisy that kept men within bounds.

The mob in Cicero which had stormed up the apartment steps and had thrown the Negro family's furniture from the windows, beating the man and his wife, had not really cared that these were Negroes; that they were Negroes had permitted the mob to do what they wanted to do—hurt, destroy.

It was part of the organism of life, pain. God—Betty's God of Old and New Testament, or Herman's God beyond time and space—had put the capacity to feel pain, pain from the annoyance of a bruise to the unendurable torment of cancer, into all living things. The more complex the living thing the greater its capacity for pain, until in the human animal pain was a symphony of hurt—worry, loneliness, envy, remorse, jealousy, all pain of the mind, all self-inflicted cruelty; and the pain of the body might be self-inflicted as well, the punishment for one's certainty of one's own guilt, one destroying one's own lungs or liver or heart or brain in a blind need to resolve guilt in pain.

Strange that the Christians believed one came into the world already stained mortally with guilt, and that Christ had cleansed the world through his own torment and pain. It had had to be pain.

Peru—he had read somewhere of the old aristocratic families on the latifundia high in the Andes slopes, immensely rich, rigidly pious, who had preferred to have their house servants old, sick and ragged so that they could savor the pleasant taste of cruelty merely by looking at them.

Yet people were kind. In this nation, in this United States, the threads were becoming stronger, the urge for cruelty was becoming a shameful thing, diseased. Kindness and sympathy and generosity were social graces. One should not let another human being suffer.

Was it nothing but another kind of palliative to the soul-deep feeling of guilt, this need to ease the pain of others? But soul-deep guilt for what?

Betty would have answered him. The soul-deep guilt of original sin. And in the name of God, what did that mean?

He remembered the Indian warriors, the Sioux, the Cheyenne, the Blackfeet he had read about by a kerosene lantern in a Chicago flat. The warriors brought their captives back to the villages for their women and children to torture.

Being a human being was a strange and wonderful and terrible thing.

Betty was right; a man must have faith. But how to find faith?

Jim Kemp came in and their eyes met.

"Good morning, Jim," he said.

Jim smiled at him, walked past Herman to his locker in the room at the rear of the store.

This was a new day, thought Jim. The third of the new days he had known at this store in Sunrise Hills. Maybe the fourth or fifth new day, depending on how you counted them.

The new day that had been his first day at this place. The colored man coming to his destined appointment with mop and broom, with dustcloth, with his muscles ready to move the heavy cases, his mouth ready to smile and say "yes." New day so old, so weary.

Then the new day when Mr. Kreitzer had encouraged him to fill in on the floor, and he had been like a jungle animal suddenly in a new and dangerous place—the pain of waiting and watching for rejection, insult, or merely surprise in the white faces when they found that a black face was offering to serve them with their television set or refrigerator or vacuum cleaner. New day of pain and excitement, to fade quickly into a better new day of acceptance, of finding the customers were only people, friendly people, mostly. So that when rejections came, and they were rare, he could be objective, knowing that the white face which was cold, hostile, cruel, was so not because it was a white face, but because it was the face of a sick person.

New day when Herman Kreitzer had taken him to the luncheon club. New day to bring home in its shiny wrapping to his wife, to tell her about, sometimes laughing, sometimes quiet and serious, because this meant a better way of life for the children. And that was the important thing.

And this was a new day when he started all over again, still a black man in a white man's world.

He had come home last night and told her.

She had said, "You know, Jim, I haven't been sure in my mind about our moving into a white neighborhood. I'm not an imitation white woman any more than you're an imitation white man."

Kemp stood up. "Maybe I am. Maybe that's what's wrong with me."

251

24

JEAN MARTIN was on the wide highway headed south. The morning was bright and warm, U.S. 101 was a fast, fine road. Driving was release, freedom, solitude.

She had started toward San Francisco, stopped and drunk two cups of coffee at a drive-in, and then—knowing what she wanted to do—she took the Bayshore away from the city, toward the Monterey Peninsula, maybe toward Los Angeles. She wasn't sure of that as yet.

Somewhere, later today, she would call David. Two things to think about as she drove in freedom and solitude: whether to tell David about last night on the phone, or go to Los Angeles and tell him face to face; the other decision was more difficult, not easy to sort out—find the truth and tell him that.

The truth was a tangle of many things. While she sipped the black coffee at the drive-in she had made the first decisions. David had to know everything, no other way was decent.

They had the structure of a good marriage, an easy marriage. Now she was discovering what was hidden from the surface in this marriage. She was learning something of the complexity of being a woman, of the perverse and powerful currents below the surface of good looks, good clothes, a nice home, the right man for a husband.

The violation of her body was not the most important thing. In a way the man's brutal use of her was not important.

If the nearly scalding water, used so late, had been too late, and if she—barren for David—became pregnant by this man, that might be important.

Her fingers were tight on the wheel—if, in two weeks, she had the first sign of pregnancy, what then? David had been with her Saturday night, a child could be David's. But after these barren years?

252

Then there would be the months of waiting and finally the first searching study of the small, wrinkled, red creature, hunting for a tiny replica of David's nose, chin, eyes—

Abortion? Never. Regardless of what man's child.

She put the thought of pregnancy away; it would be something, maybe, for David and her to face when they were together and after the first terrible words.

She thought again, making her fingers relax on the wheel, that the physical contact with the man was not in itself important. Bar thoughts of pregnancy and it was nothing.

Her response? The outward shell of a female can break away in the frenzy, and the response is not that of the woman, Jean Martin, but of gland and muscle and blood and nerve, conditioned and uncontrollable.

Yet her response to that man—had it been more intense than ever with David?

Maybe it had. Tell David of this too?

Break the male pride of her husband? Let him believe that in this final totaling of love, of man and woman, he was the lesser male? What sexual union could they have after that?

Honesty could not be complete. The truth was a tangle of many things. She could not continue her marriage with the man she loved if she tried to conceal last night from him. There would be no point to any succession of days in the cool, empty house in Sunrise Hills.

But if she told him that Troy Noon, in a strange rage, had forced her, brutally and without even the words or gestures of love, must she also tell him what she believed was true: that she had been physically jealous of Leola Noon?

Could she look into David's eyes and find understanding —but not, please, compassion—when she told him of the night hours after it had happened, after the man had left? Of trying to find herself, her motives, her true emotions?

Without truth to David she would have no marriage, and life without marriage and David she could guess at. Other men, because she would have need for other men, and probably another marriage, but with the sure structure of marriage gone. She would move from the splendid class of women, to which she had belonged so securely until last night, the class of women to whom life had a kind of perfection, into the sleek and rootless class of women who had apartments, wonderful jobs, cocktail hours, men, and no hope of any kind of perfection.

But above all this, in these morning hours she had discovered a quality of tenderness in her love for David. And a need for David, the need a wife has for the strength of her husband, akin to the need a daughter has for the strength of her father.

He was four hundred miles away, and distant from her now in a way beyond measurement because she had a burden for him that he did not yet know; but she felt closer to him, as if they shared a single warmth, than she had ever felt before.

So she must give him this burden of truth to continue a marriage with him, but she could not tell him the entire truth or the marriage would be destroyed.

What would he do?

Would he sense, as a woman might, the dark, powerful, unknown currents within her that she would not admit to him?

Would he want to kill Troy Noon? Go to the police? Pretend, by silence and some kind of flight, that it had never happened?

What would it mean to him? Virgin bride, faithful wife—not necessarily a part of the American morals these days; the virginity value was clouded and uncertain, faithfulness was more probable, more important. He'd had both, and in the richness of her own body she'd had not even the need to wonder about him.

Violated wife. This was the man she knew so completely and so well, loving the knowing of him, and she could not guess at what he would do or how he would feel toward her.

And yet the violation—all that he would know about—was so unimportant. A penetration, an orgasm, anger. What should be important to a man would be the other things—the mask

254

of the actress that a lewd wife wears toward her husband, a final contempt, that would be important to a man. Not this.

Faithlessness was in the betrayal of belief; the concealment not only of adulteries but of the need for adulteries, of the hunger or weakness which led to the acceptance of whatever seductions were offered. A wife, promiscuous, sleeping around, could still hold to the core of faithfulness to her husband if she wore no deceit.

Jean shook her head; it wasn't so. The whole business of faithfulness and chastity was not concerned with that stuff; maybe it was an invention of women, a way of building security for themselves, their children.

The mechanisms of sex in the man directed him toward unplanned lusts, restrained by rules, fears and pressures set up by women. She, of all women, should have a clear understanding of the way it worked. Even as a little girl she had seen the rewards and the dangers; she had shaped her girlhood and her womanhood toward the idea of this time, this society. As a woman she was a success, and such success is seldom an accident.

She had known what she wanted; she would not have loved a charming vagrant or a stolid shopkeeper; she was fashioned —largely self-fashioned—so that she could find love only for a man like David. Finding him, finding love, she had moved through these first years in the right direction. Given him a completeness of woman, of body and grooming, of smartness and style, of wantonness and tenderness, of understanding and companionship.

These things she had done, easily and naturally. Then there would be a home and children, with the man earning the prestige and importance which would be necessary to the fullness of their middle years. Far in the future, her sons now men, her daughters now mothers, would be the time of the careful and wise matriarch.

And all the patient planning and working of a hundred generations of women, particularly of European—and later, and more successfully, of American—women. Using the pity of men; building on men's memories of their own mothers; using rich attractions of sex in the young years, the demands of sex in the older years; using the sensual comforts of a home and of food; using religion; all of these stratagems and forces to set up a system of marriage, of importance for women, of overriding importance for children.

Men had to be led to believe in the importance of the chastity of their women to themselves; led to believe that modesty was a natural virtue of women; led to believe in families and the sanctity of the home. The women of the ancient continents, Asia and Africa, and even most of the women of Europe, had never been able to achieve this importance and security for themselves and their children.

And of all the lives of women for a hundred generations and more the final success was in a woman like herself.

She had the freedom to be a wife—if she chose. She had the freedom to be a woman with the prerogatives and rewards of a man, if she chose. Married and in love, she had enormous prestige and security. Single and promiscuous or selective she could still retain prestige and security in her own abilities.

Jean gave a soft sigh. All of that was one side of the coin.

On the other side of the coin: most women tried to conceal from most men a woman's essential self. Sex-centered and sex-driven, twisted and suffering from their own self-imposed restraints, stronger and more brutally realistic than men, as completely female as a bitch in heat, frantic to love and be loved, with a perverse urge to be debased and hurt, wanton and flagrant in display.

Jean thought of the women she knew, particularly of the women who now were her neighbors in Sunrise Hills.

Betty, daughter of the hundred generations. Strong, her life directed only for her family. The forces which led women to work with every means possible for the security and fruitfulness of their families were so powerful in Betty that the other side of the coin had no meaning for her. The dark urges of a woman were locked deep within Betty. Even more than Jean she was the simple survival strain of the female human. She had less total freedom than Jean because many of those freedoms had no value to her.

Isbel. A woman who was losing the battle women wage. She had lost prestige and security, was crippling her little boy, because she did not know how to control her man. And her man, broken away from the pattern that women try to set for men, was lusting openly, lost, without direction. As a male he had charm and excitement, using it half with knowledge gained in the backs of cars and on the beds of motels, half instinctively, toward the dark side of the women he met. So his own woman had turned, defensively, toward her own dark side while trying to remain accepted and belonging to the world of the proud, secure women.

And Leola.

Leola was something of Betty, something of Isbel. Her man was one of the lonely ones whose star was tragic. Tragic for any woman he touched, tragic for himself.

He was not like Jerry Flagg; he probably did not know of the dark side of women, would despise any woman who revealed it to him. Yet he was the solitary, fierce rogue buck that women could scent, and they would invite him, maybe unconsciously, maybe unwillingly, maybe in fear, but always in simple, instinctual lust. For the tired, too consanguine breed might need the sons of such a man.

Not smart, not subtle, he would believe what women told him were the eternal truths, and when women acted in another way he would not distrust what he had been told but he would loathe the women.

That was what had happened to her, and that was what she must tell the man, loved by her bright side—but not tell him all.

She was south of Gilroy where the highway was separate ribbons of concrete, each two lanes wide, winding through low, velvet-like hills.

Drive forever, knowing only the pattern of greens beyond the road, the sky, the clouds, the wind. Be alive only in her eyes, her hands on the wheel, her foot on the pedal.

"David—" maybe on the telephone. And he would say *hello, darling,* and be glad with the first sound of her voice.

"David—something has happened—" He would speak

faster, his voice lower and husky, asking what, if she was all right.

"Last night—a man—" To a man the word "man" would start a deep alarm.

He would wait, then, for her next words.

"David—he forced me—" And then he would ask either if she were hurt or who, and that might make a difference to the rest of the words.

What after that? He would want to come to her. If he didn't, well, that would be the end of a great many things.

But she did not want him to come north. She would go to Los Angeles. It would be easier there, maybe safer if Troy Noon came back to his house in Sunrise Hills.

She did not know whether she would telephone David, or drive all the way to Los Angeles today, or stay tonight on the Monterey Peninsula—peaceful, lovely, different—and search out herself until she knew who she was.

This ripping tear across the fabric of her life might have been only an accident. Noon, psychotic or enraged, doing that to her with no more importance than he might have crashed through a red light and wrecked some stranger's car, desperately injuring some stranger. If Noon and she were strangers, regardless of how near their homes, it was an accident.

An accident can mean pain and injury, dreadful costs in many ways, but it is of the surface of living. Struck by a car, struck by lightning, overwhelmed in a flood, suddenly sickened by some airborne disease. Pain and cost, but with no importance beyond getting well, paying off whatever costs there were.

If this ripping tear across the fabric of her life was no accident, but something invited, perhaps something inevitable, then it was of importance to the whole structure of her life.

To be a person. To be Jean Martin, with a core of living; to be someone known and understood by herself, so that she would know what it was that she wanted, what it was that she would work or suffer or endure to achieve. To know the flaws, the soft spots in her own structure of being a person.

258

To know what she was, to be a person; not something shapeless and changing, murky, not understood by herself, lost.

It had been easier yesterday before he had come to her door. Then she had tried to do nothing more than the easy things: search out the values in her relationship to the man she loved, thinking more of understanding and knowing David than she had of understanding herself.

Strange that the problem had been another facet of this greater problem she faced today—her irrational dislike of that girl, Leola.

How deep was a woman. How violent and strange it was being a woman.

Men would know nothing of these things.

How small their giving, how small their taking. And when a woman opened her being to a man, how great or how small her giving could be.

In the end it was only the blind, eager, striving sperm she took, heritages of an endless bloodline locked in their tailed frenzies as they sought the vast, vulnerable egg. This was all that a woman accepted, in reality, from the man she loved, or allowed, or was indifferent to, or was raped by. The words, the love words, the pompousness, the stroking, the kisses, the tongue, the hands hard or soft, the forcing, rigid lovemaker— all of these, whether wanted by her mind or not, were only the circuits and the machineries to bring the blind strivers to the egg.

Dam them back with the film of latex, kill them with poisons, flood them out and away from the waiting egg with too-hot water, and you knew the emptiness that was the denial of being a woman.

Men could know nothing of the endless storm of being a woman. Nothing of the final strength of a woman, of her toughness, of her unexcusing, unforgiving sense of reality.

But they knew the weakness of women, of their needs for cruelty and for tenderness, of their damning willingness to dream and to believe.

And the weakness of men made liars out of their women.

She had to stop thinking about all this. She had to be just Jean Martin, to whom an unfortunate and rather terrible thing had happened, and who would put it out of her mind for a while.

The road curved ahead and her car rode the gray concrete between the brush hills.

25

Wise looked at David Martin and tapped his yellowish, wrinkled finger on the table. "It's very simple, Mr. Martin. It's people against machines. I'm not going to sacrifice the people."

"There won't be anything for the people to do, Mr. Wise."

"Set the system up so there will be."

"It won't work. You'd only be fooling yourself."

"I'm not going to put several thousand men and women on the streets."

"They'll find jobs." David wanted to be anywhere but here, doing anything but this.

But what had Jean said? There were plenty of technicians, men who would spend the rest of their lives laying out circuits, doing the ordinary work. The kind of man she wanted was the man who won battles over other men, there was no other way of coming up to the top. Her man had to be on his way toward the top.

It was only fair; he had taken the finest woman he knew or could imagine. She did not belong with the mediocre.

"Find jobs?" said Wise, his blue-lipped mouth curling. "Men and women in their forties? They'll break their hearts looking for jobs. I won't put them out."

"There will be no places for them in your billing and accounting departments, Mr. Wise."

"There will be if you set up this damned automation so human skills and human abilities still have a place to function."

"You've seen the schematics. From the time the meter reports are put in process to the mailing of the bills and the tabulation the entire system is fully automatic. I'm sorry, Mr. Wise."

"Mr. Martin—you're human. Can't you see my position?"

The whole afternoon had been designed to show David

the position of Coast's vice-president. He was fighting for time, trying to delay the full automation installation, yet knowing that it was inevitable.

"I can see that eventually we may have to go as your firm plans," Wise continued. "But I want to do it gradually so that we can absorb some of these men and women in other departments; let normal attrition cut down our job load in billing and accounting. It's the only humane way to do this."

"People don't like artificial jobs, Mr. Wise. They have to feel that there is a need for the work they're doing."

"People don't like to be through with life at forty or forty-five, either, Martin," said Wise.

"There's only one right way to set this up. The right way will not permit interruption of the system by unnecessary human operations." David felt cold and impersonal as he said this, but it was showdown. This was what he had been sent to do. His future at Verdun Labs depended upon this job, this coldness.

"You want me to put my people on the street?"

"I want to do this job the way it should be done. You know the cost and efficiency comparisons, Mr. Wise. There's only one answer."

"No. I have another answer. I'm going to my board of directors and recommend postponement. Coast has a duty to its employees as well as its stockholders, and Coast knows the importance of good public relations. That's the way it has to be, Martin."

This was failure, thought David. This was the way failure felt: all the logic was with him, and the decision would be against him.

"You have a duty to Coast, apart from stockholders and employees, Mr. Wise. You won't use inefficient equipment in your power lines. Why use inefficient equipment somewhere else?"

"Human beings are inefficient, Martin?"

There was no point to answering. The old man and the young man looked at each other silently. Wise was trying to protect the gray-haired, bird-eyed women glancing up at him as he had walked through the branch billing department.

Trying to protect several thousand others like them in the scores of Coast offices in the Pacific area.

Wise would take a stand on postponement, knowing that the unions would back him up.

Somehow, David knew, he was almost right. It was kindness, paternalism, softness. The realities were cruel: for most of these people there would be no other jobs. The men would look over the help-wanted ads, seeing the phrase "under 35" until they gave up hope. Maybe something like selling brushes or magazine subscriptions, for most of them there would be nothing better in the rest of their lives.

They were men with children still in high school or college, with homes bought bravely against 90 per cent mortgages, with wives whose faces would gray and tighten when they heard that the jobs at Coast were gone.

The old man started to stand up, one hand on the desk.

"You're going to recommend postponement?" David asked.

"Yes."

"That's cowardice."

Wise sat back into the chair. "Why do you say that?"

"You know the answer."

"I was willing to compromise."

"And that was cowardice, too."

The old eyes searched into David's. "The easy thing would have been to let you just go ahead, get rid of all these people."

"That's the hard way," said David. He felt a new understanding of people, of what Verdun expected from him, of what Jean meant yesterday. When a human being is your obstacle you find the points of weakness, use them. Wise did not want to think of himself as a coward. "You're doing it the easy way—postpone, put it off, pretend it isn't there. Cowardice."

"This is a mighty poor way to try and sell Verdun equipment."

"I'm not a salesman."

"No, you've got the easy job, Martin. Dealing with machines. Machines don't look at you; machines don't have families; machines don't know you for twenty years as a friend. You don't have any problems, Martin."

263

"And you're afraid to face yours."

Wise rubbed across his mouth with his hand. "Maybe I am."

"It won't be any easier on these people a year from now."

"What will the public think if they read in their newspapers that Coast is getting rid of thousands of office people, putting machines in—?"

"The same thing they'll think a year from now, Mr. Wise."

"This automation of yours isn't inevitable."

"Saying that is hiding your head, another kind of cowardice."

Wise nodded heavily. "Yes. I understand your automation system well enough to know that we'll have to go to it sooner or later. You're right, I know that."

"Most of your billing employees are young girls. Losing their jobs at Coast won't hurt them for long. They don't have trouble finding jobs."

"I'm not worried about them. But the middle-aged people—"

"Does Coast hire anyone over 35 now?"

Wise shook his head. "Most departments the top hiring age is 28; in some departments they'll go as high as 35. That's true of most firms. Pensions, group insurance, the difficulty of retraining an older person—it doesn't seem fair, sometimes, but our policy is to start them when they're young."

"All of these older people in billing and accounting have pension credits built up?"

"Yes. They'll all have fair amounts of money coming to them. But a lot less than if they stay through to retirement age."

"You've been a fighter, Mr. Wise. I know that."

The vice-president of Coast pursed out his lips, nodded. "I've had some fights."

"You were fighting for the best not only for Coast but for the people who work for Coast, too."

"That's the way I've tried to play it."

"Then cowardice is no answer now."

"I don't know the answer now."

"Retrain these people. Have your aptitude analysis people in personnel test the middle-aged group in billing and ac-

264

counting. I'll bet half of them are in billing just by accident —they'd like a different kind of work and do it better. Use what you've got instead of hiring young people."

"Retraining would cost quite a bit of money."

David Martin smiled. "But the public could read about that in the newspapers. Coast upgrades its veterans when automation comes in; finds better jobs for them, trains them to do the better job."

"That wouldn't be entirely true, Mr. Martin. I suppose we could fit most of them in, but not necessarily at better jobs—"

"In a way you'll be making them young again, Mr. Wise. Twenty years in a billing department must be pretty monotonous."

"They'd grouse and complain and go to their union—"

"Isn't this a better program than postponement? So they do grouse—some of them. You know how to work with that. The whole thing's a challenge to you. One that you know how to whip."

Wise was far away, thinking. Setting up a program on retraining choices by seniority and aptitude. Maybe some of them would be upgraded; it was damn hard to measure a person's abilities in the repetitive drudgeries of billing.

"Use the west branch not only for Verdun's pilot system, but as a retraining test and experiment," said David.

Wise stood up. "You were right about that cowardice. I don't know if I can whip these other problems, but it's worth trying—now."

His eyes narrowed as he looked over the younger man. Somehow this boy had hit him with the right word. Ostrich head in the sand—that's what any attempt to water down the automation system with people doing unnecessary jobs would have been; that's what postponement would have been.

This way he was facing the real problem: not what to do with automation, but how to do best for people automation replaced.

"Go ahead with your pilot system, David," he said. "Contracting and Engineering will send the forms to the legal department tomorrow. But you've got my verbal go ahead right now."

They shook hands.

"I'm going to be working late tonight, thanks to you," said Wise. "I've got to start the works on a testing and retraining program."

"Don't forget to tell Publicity," said David.

Wise smiled, crinkling his face. "Did you think I would?"

He drove David back to the Roosevelt and there was little conversation on the drive. Wise was busy thinking over the scores of job classifications in Coast, of the percentages of replacements needed, of the practical details involved in retraining. But running through these thoughts was the realization that young Martin had not suggested anything that he had not already considered; it was only that David had forced him to make a choice by calling him a coward.

During the drive David was thinking of what he had learned today. When you were in trouble you fought.

Wise parked long enough in front of the Roosevelt to confirm the details of tomorrow's contracts for the pilot system, shook hands again, and drove away.

There was a message in the key box at the hotel desk: Call long-distance Operator 17 at Monterey. . . .

Monterey? He didn't know anybody at Monterey—unless Jean had driven there for some reason.

For a moment he thought of stopping at the bar and having a drink, brandy maybe, as a simple and brief celebration, but instead he went up to his room and put in a call to Sokolik at Verdun Laboratories. This, and telling Jean, would be celebration enough.

It took only seconds before he heard Soke's voice on the phone.

"David? How's it going?"

"Fine. Coast's legal department will have the contracts ready tomorrow. You can send the crew down right away."

"Full automation? No bastard system?"

"Exactly as you laid it out. Full automation."

"How about that vice-president? The one who doesn't want to fire people?"

"He sees it our way. No trouble."

"You're sure?"

"Soke, the contracts will be ready tomorrow. You can send the boys now."

"I see. Well, thanks, David. I might run down myself."

"Swell."

"Okay, David. Thanks."

Sokolik put the phone down. Martin was careful; if he said there was no chance of trouble in the Coast layout there wouldn't be any. He pushed back his chair and walked out of his office toward Verdun's. Knocking at the private door he heard Bill yell, "Come in."

Seaman Cowles was sitting in the dove-gray leather chair beside Bill Verdun's broad desk.

"David Martin just called me," Sokolik said to Verdun.

"Oh? How's he making out?" Verdun leaned forward, arms on the desk.

"I think he's in trouble. I'll catch a plane and get down there first thing in the morning."

"What kind of trouble, Soke?"

"He wasn't too clear about it."

"Probably Wise is insisting on holding his billing staff and putting in automation."

Seaman Cowles pushed out his cigarette. "How can he justify several million dollars in plant expense for automation and keep the same payroll?"

"He can't." Verdun looked angry. "You're sure Martin's in trouble?"

Sokolik shook his head. "David's a good engineer. This was his first try at this kind of thing."

"I had hopes for that boy," said Verdun. "Did he ask you to come down?"

"Well, yes." Sokolik seemed hesitant.

Verdun slapped the desk with his open hand. "I don't like him yelling for Mama on the first day. He's up against a tough old boy in Wise, but if Martin expects to get someplace at Verdun he's going to have to be able to stand on his own feet."

"I'll go down in the morning," said Sokolik.

"Okay, Soke."

As Sokolik turned he saw Seaman Cowles's eyes, speculative, cynical. Sokolik stopped at the door and said, "I've got a lot of confidence in Martin."

"Well, right now I don't have," said Bill Verdun.

Closing the door behind him Sokolik sighed softly. It was going to work out. He'd fly down tomorrow, call Verdun tomorrow evening, tell him he had the contracts.

He'd be able to keep David Martin like a cow—milking him, not worrying about Martin becoming a rival for his job.

His shoulders slumped as he opened the door to his own office. There'd be others like Martin, and some of them would play hard and dirty to get up another notch on that ladder.

Getting the Coast thing straightened out might make it possible for him to ask for a year's leave to go back to the university. He needed it, he was sliding behind and he knew it.

But he wouldn't be able to sit in with those classes of young men, watching them change from the open respect they'd give him at first—"project vice-president at Verdun Labs"—to the cruel contempt when they had a chance to measure his abilities. He couldn't take that.

David lifted his phone again, asked for Operator 17 at Monterey. The operator had a call for Mr. David Martin at the Hollywood-Roosevelt Hotel, but she could not reach the calling party. She would try again in twenty minutes.

He called his home at Sunrise Hills. There was no answer.

There was a strong sense of frustration in not being able to reach Jean. He wanted to tell her how right she had been about people. There was the taste of success on his tongue, a sense of understanding how Bill Verdun had built the Labs: the knowledge that it was more than transistors and circuits, more than competitive bidding and better equipment. He liked dealing with people—for the first time he actively wanted to be the kind of success that Jean must have.

All because he'd called Wise a coward. The next time it would be a different problem, a different answer, but the rules of the game would be the same. He was going to learn the rules.

His phone rang.

"Hello?"

"Is this Mr. David Martin? San Francisco calling."

"Yes." Jean, maybe. He was expectant for her voice.

"Dave?" He recognized the easy speech of Seaman Cowles.

"Mr. Cowles?"

"Hi, Dave."

"Hello, Seaman." Cowles encouraged informality, but sometimes cracked a slender, almost unfelt whip, with an abrupt use of an employee's surname after minutes of easy first-naming.

"How's it going with Wise?"

"Fine. As I told Soke, everything's set. Contracts ready tomorrow, and the crew can come in right now."

"Full automation?"

"Exactly as the prints set it up."

"Wise on your side now?"

"Completely. He's setting up a program to retrain the employees with seniority."

"I see, Dave. Does Soke know all this yet?"

"I called him a little while ago."

"An hour ago?"

"Less than that."

"You only called him once?"

"That's right."

"Well, now. That's good news, David. Bill will be glad to hear that you won the ball game the first day."

"Wise is a hell of a fine man, Seaman."

"Soke's flying down tomorrow, Dave."

"Fine. Bringing the crew with him?"

"They'll be along later. Anybody you want particularly?"

"That's up to Soke."

"Soke? I'd like your recommendations, Dave. Think about it tonight, and call me tomorrow."

David felt as if he were suddenly in a dark room. "Wouldn't it be more along channels if Soke called you?"

"Maybe not this time, Dave. By any chance do you know where I could reach Wise? Do you have his home phone?"

"I think he's going to be at Coast's offices. You might be able to reach him there."

"I see. Or if not tonight, I can reach him in the morning. Thanks, Dave."

"Sure, Seaman."

"Have Sokolik call Verdun about two tomorrow, will you, Dave?"

"Sure."

"Good night, Dave."

That had been an odd conversation, thought David. It was unusual for Cowles to have called, and difficult—especially with Sokolik coming down—to bypass the projects head in recommending personnel for the layout crew.

Before Cowles had called he had been so damn sure of himself in this human aspect stuff of his job. Now somebody had turned the lights out because important things seemed to be going on at Verdun, concerning him, that he did not understand.

Cowles had always treated Sokolik with an arrogance; Soke was unsure of himself with the younger man, stammering, talking too much.

But his loyalty had to be to Sokolik; Soke was his boss, and the man who had given him this chance with the Coast problem.

He wanted to talk to Jean. He was damn lonely for her.

26

JERRY FLAGG came home. Any night but this it would have been stopping at Pete's and the Gilded Cage and half a dozen other spots, calling Isbel and telling her to hold dinner for him, calling her later and saying he'd have dinner in town.

A big night for a good day. Two things had set him off. That sale this afternoon, and thinking all day about those long legs, about going to her house—Martin away, gone to Los Angeles—and knowing that he was going to get it.

Feeling like a high school kid on a date with some tomato he'd been itching for and getting her to swig the vodka, watch it take hold and the tomato get silly, knowing that he was going to get it. That was the best part, when you were hot and ready, moving in on it like a tiger for the kill. A man could stand hours of that part, talking some jive to the tomato, kidding her, looking at all her goodies, still under wraps and covered up with dresses and slips and bras and panties, but knowing that you were moving in steady and sure. That's the way he'd be with old long-legs tonight.

So that even though today had been a hotshot day, working up to the big move where he kissed off old fuddy-nuts Markham and got in with a fast-moving outfit, he wasn't going to get drunk tonight.

That had been the kicks. Leaving the floor, calling old Lucky Joe, the volume dealer, and hitting him just right when he needed an assistant sales manager.

Nailing the job. Lucky Joe was moving three hundred cars a month, and he didn't care how they were moved as long as the banks took the paper.

Now Jerry Flagg was set. No more hanging on by the teeth from week to week, watching Markham sweat blood over each repossession, listening to Markham fight off the bank, chew at the district manager.

The independents were dead. Let them flop for a while

271

more, like fish in the bottom of a boat. Jerry Flagg was riding with a main line volume dealer, and he'd move his car or two a day.

Sell them like he'd sold those people today. Some guys got their nuts off going fishing—well, this was the same as trout fishing, play the fly over their open, stupid mouths, and then sink the hook into them.

Not a worry in the world and what a wonderful night it would be to stop at every joint along the line and throw a good one. But he didn't want to be drunk when he rang on old long-legs' door.

"Jerry—'" she'd say.

"I had to stop over," he'd say. And she'd look at him to see if he knew about that hillbilly son-of-a-bitch jumping her last night, and his eyes and his smile would let her know he did, but he'd give her the soft jive, all sympathy and being a good neighbor, until she offered him a drink, and he'd size it up to see what was the best move.

Isbel would know of course, but what the hell, Isbel knew that he'd cut anything handy and a lot of stuff that wasn't. Isbel might even get kicks out of knowing that her husband had put the blocks to one of her best friends.

That was what they always said: the easiest make is your wife's best friend, and he had plenty of experience to prove it damn well was true.

Right now he had everything worthwhile in life. He'd nailed a good job with Lucky Joe, and it was the kind of thieving, conniving setup—run plenty smart and cool—that he could really operate with. Old Markham had practically bawled when he'd given him the hard news, offered him all kinds of stuff. What could a busted old fuddy-nuts like Markham offer? A franchise that wasn't worth wiping your can with, a building he couldn't pay the rent on, and a yard full of cars he couldn't move. He could stick the whole works up his keister. Let Markham dream about the old days when he was full of stuff.

Everything worthwhile in life. Not a bad old bag for a wife. Isbel yakked too much and she was always trying to give him a bad time, but she fed him good and ran the house okay and she didn't try to spend all the glue—always yak-king about saving money, and she could go a lot when he got her worked up a little. She could give him a hell of a go when she got hot enough.

Things were wonderful. The kid bawled all the time, but he'd shape up into a good kid after he got some meat on him. It was kind of nice having a kid. When he got older it would give him something to live for. Nothing but the best for the kid when he began to shape up. He wanted that kid to think his old man was the greatest son-of-a-bitch in the world. He'd have his own dealership someday; send the kid off to Har-vard; bring him back as a partner. The kid would always say, "My old man is the greatest guy there is, a real long-tailed son-of-a-bitch, but great." Now naturally the little bastard was a hell of a nuisance, but he'd grow out of it.

Everything fine. He was Jerry Flagg, a fast mover, still plenty young with all the real hot years ahead of him. He had a nice home in Sunrise Hills, a good job, a wife and a kid, and he was going to move into something he'd been leching for since he'd first seen her.

When you were old the only things you had to show for the whole damn ratrace was the number of cute quiff you'd had, and a good kid like Mikey to carry on where the old man left off. Eat good, dress sharp, live in a good pad, ride the good old Martini route—that's what living was.

What a day, what a night, what a life!

He unlocked the door and walked into his house. Michael came running up to him.

He almost tripped over the damned kid but he felt so good that he reached into his pocket and found a half-buck.

"Here, Butch. Get yourself some ice cream tomorrow." Michael's hands were always sticky and the little bastard always seemed to be dripping at the nose.

"Get away from me before you mess me up. G'wan, watch TV, I want to talk to Mama."

Isbel was in the kitchen; she smiled at him.

"You're home early, dear."

"How about mixing me a long, cool one, honey?"

"What are you so happy about?"

273

"Got a new job."

"What happened at Markham's?" The smile was gone, and her mouth was tight and tense.

"Made a good sale and so I called Lucky Joe. I'm his new assistant sales manager. I got a hell of a deal."

She was still uncertain, suspicious. "You're sure it's a good deal? Markham didn't—"

"I quit the son-of-a-bitch cold. You know I was figuring on it. But today I just happened to strike it lucky."

"How much?"

"Five bills certain every month, regular assistant manager's override, thirty per cent of all the special pack." He smiled at her, youthful, with an elfin boyish charm.

She was crazy about him when he looked like this. She always would be. Like a boy, and real cute, with the devil showing out of his eyes.

"Hey, while you're fixing the drinks, tell me what happened."

Isbel glanced at Michael. He was standing beside the rough brick of the fireplace, looking at them.

"Michael, you go watch TV. I mean it. Go on—that's final."

Slowly the little boy retreated, still looking at them. She turned to Jerry.

"Well, it's hard to know what did happen."

"Did that son-of-a-bitch really rape her?"

Isbel took the vodka from the shelf, opened the refrigerator.

"That's what Leola says he told her."

"What about her?"

"Leola?"

"For Christ's sake, no. Jean."

"She went away."

"What?"

"She got in her car and drove off. She hasn't come back."

"Damn."

"What's the matter, honey?" Isbel filled two glasses with ice cubes. "On the rocks all right?"

"Yeah, sure."

"You seem mad all of a sudden."

274

"I'm not mad. Hell, a neighbor gets raped by a guy next door, don't you think I'm interested?"

He reached out for the tall, cool glass, took a long drink, letting the ice slide against his lips. It tasted fine. Damn it to hell, where was she?

"No more than I am," said Isbel, after she'd taken a drink. "But nobody really knows anything."

"Where's Leola?" She wasn't in the same league with Jean Martin, but she was young and kind of pretty. Hell, he was hot to trot tonight and he had to have something. She'd probably be sore enough at her old man to let him just out of meanness. It would be worth trying.

"She decided to go home and wait for her husband. I don't know what's going to happen. I feel so sorry for Jean—"

"Yeah. That David is so damned perfect and correct, what's he going to say when he finds out?"

"They're such a nice couple—"

"She was always showing her stuff off. Shorts—"

"I noticed you were always looking."

"Why not?"

"I bet you envy that Troy Noon."

"Look, we don't even know if he really did it."

"I'm sure he did, and I know you just wish it had been you."

"I don't go that route. A man doesn't have to slug a babe to get it."

"You're disgusting."

"Forget it. Make me another on the rocks. I feel like getting looped tonight."

"When don't you?"

"Don't start yakking at me the minute I get home."

She came up to him, a hand stroking his arm.

"Jerry, honey—"

"Yeah?"

"I had a long talk with Betty Kreitzer today—"

"So?"

"They're such a happy family."

"He doesn't have such a hot job—managing that branch."

"They get by all right. And they're happy together."

"Both a couple of squareheads. Like a couple of cows."

"But they're nice to each other. All the time."

"We get along okay."

"I want us to get along better, honey."

"Like how?"

"Do more things together. Be more of a family."

"What for example?"

"Michael's big enough now so he enjoys going places with us. He really needs it, Jerry."

"He's always a pain in the tail when we take him out. Bawling about something, wanting everything he sees—"

"But you do love him, don't you?"

"Well, sure, but—"

"The Kreitzers went to the zoo yesterday. Michael'd love to have you take him to the zoo."

"Why don't you take him?"

"Why don't we all go together? Maybe next Sunday."

"Maybe."

Her hands still caressed him. "We could have so much more fun together—if we only tried. About all we seem to do is drink and get into arguments."

"What's Betty been feeding you?"

"Nothing, except she seems happy. You're better looking than Herman, and you make as much money—"

"I'll make more now. I've got a real deal—"

"Jerry—"

"Yeah?"

"What do you really want?"

"Why?"

"That's what Betty asked me, when we got to talking."

"What did you tell her?"

"Jerry, I didn't know what to tell her at first."

"Nice house, husband, a kid, nice car, money in the bank, what else?"

"Sometimes it's like you hate me, Jerry."

"Baby, what's got into you?"

"Oh, it was what happened to Jean, I guess. I was all full of hateful thoughts, and I got to talking to Betty and suddenly I realized just how dirty and mean I'd been thinking."

"What kind of dirty thoughts, honey? I'm always interested in dirty thoughts."

"Not like that. Well, maybe that, too. But there was Betty, and little Harmon, a sweet little boy. And I felt so different from her. It was a creepy feeling."

"There's nothing wrong with you, honey. How about another drink?"

"That's what you think—there's nothing wrong with me. I'm all mixed up, so that I almost feel I'm going crazy—"

"You just got excited about what happened. Upset."

"Thinking about her started it. But then Betty was so nice, listening to me. After a while I just poured everything out to her. About you and me, and everything—"

"Look, don't you go telling other people about our private lives—"

"I had to. I had to talk to somebody. To another woman. To some woman who was happy—"

"You're happy enough."

"Jerry, why do you have to chase around? Is it something wrong with me? Is there some way I could change?"

"Don't start on that."

"You don't know how I feel when you come home drunk, smelling of other women—"

"That's the way men are. You know that. If a man's not hunting strange stuff he's either too old or too scared—"

"We don't have a good life together, Jerry, and if we don't have it now, when we're still kind of young, we'll never have it." She buried her head against his jacket. "You know what's wrong with us? We don't believe in anything."

He laughed. "I believe in money. I believe in money and living it up. You show me something better than that."

"I wish I could," she said. "Oh God, I wish I could."

"What's the matter with you, Isbel?" Jerry asked. "Is that Kreitzer woman getting you on a religious kick?"

Isbel pulled away from him. For a while, this afternoon, it had been like a fog lifting for her. Betty made living seem so simple, worthwhile.

"Each day," Betty had said, "like today, it's the only time you'll ever have this day to live. Why let it be a bad day for you? No matter what happens, what troubles you have, live the day so it will be the very best it can for you."

And later Betty had said, "You can't like other people if you don't like yourself. If you hate other people it's a sure sign that you hate yourself."

Betty hadn't talked much about Jesus or her church, but somehow she had realized that Isbel enjoyed the fact that tragedy had come to Jean Martin and Leola Noon.

The realization had not shocked Betty; she knew that people made themselves unhappy and that viciousness—such as Isbel Flagg showed in the curve of her mouth and the tongue wetting her lips as she talked about Jean—was the sign of a sick soul.

She wanted to help Isbel as she would help nurse a neighbor sick with disease.

Utterly lonely, utterly unhappy, Isbel had responded this afternoon. It was as if she could see the mark of disease upon herself, seeing the vicious enjoyment she felt in Jean's tragedy. The whole person Isbel Flagg might have been struggled to live because Betty Kreitzer treated Isbel as a whole person, only temporarily ill.

She had come home, leaving Michael playing with Harmon, planning to change her way of life. If she and Jerry could like each other—simply like each other, enjoy being together.

To do that, each of them would have to like the kind of person they were. She herself was crushed and poisoned by the terrible sense of guilt which made her want to punish herself, consciously and subconsciously, in the perversely enjoyable pain of envy and malice. It was difficult, almost impossible, because of the wrenching hurt in awareness that tightened her stomach and dried her throat, to try to understand herself.

Jerry. She felt that Jerry was even more lost. There was no Jerry Flagg, he had never lived as yet. He was a young red-haired man, glib and charming, sometimes with a cold shrewdness, but in reality he was only appetites—something that walked and looked and acted like a man, but who had no core of self, no true person, only appetites. He lived only for the satisfaction of his appetites for food, for liquor, for women, for vanity, for cruelty.

There had to be a real Jerry Flagg, a person. If they were to save themselves, if Michael was to have parents, she would have to help her husband live as a person.

But she was an unhappy, guilty, twisted woman, and life was bearable to her only when she was punishing herself by envying and hating.

She knew this and she could not bear to think about it for long.

If they could stop all this drinking; go places as a family and have fun; if she could fall asleep just once and say to herself that it had been a good day, a day she had enjoyed living.

If Jerry could find satisfaction in helping someone else be happy.

There would be a chance for them then.

It was all stuff they tried to tell you when you were a kid, and you didn't pay any attention to them.

She smiled at Jerry and he smiled back at her.

Maybe he'd have a chance to try out Leola tonight; she wasn't the living queen that long-legs was, but she was no pig. Young and wide-eyed; he'd give her the "big brother, you're in trouble and tell me all about it" routine until he got her worked up.

He put his arms around Isbel and pulled her to him; might as well soften her up a little for the business of taking off later.

When you got right down to the point, he thought, there was really only one single thing women respected in a man; if he was a direct and open stud. You could look them in the eyes and if they saw right away that you saw them as a hot lay you wanted bad, they were interested in you.

All the rest was game; it was that look that counted. You could be a dwarf, or have a wart on your nose, or anything else, they were still interested.

Michael was watching from the edge of the fireplace. As he saw his daddy holding his mama he climbed up on the pink chair and fell over, the chair toppling with him. They turned at the noise and he began to scream. He'd hurt his arm and bumped his head; he had known that he was going to fall, but he didn't want to be hurt, or maybe hurt a little bit so that Mama would come to him.

When his daddy tried to pick him up he kicked and screamed until Jerry swore at him and handed him into the arms of Isbel. Michael still screamed, "Go away! Go away!" until Isbel took him into his room and curled on his bed beside him.

Jerry poured another drink. Damned kid, always climbing on things and falling off. Clumsy, awkward nuisance. The kid's yelling hurt his ears so that he couldn't stand to be in the house around him.

He wondered when kids outgrew that stuff.

As Michael screamed, Betty Kreitzer had looked across the table to Herman. Her husband shook his head. "Too bad about that little boy," he said.

"Isbel was here off and on all day," Betty said, spooning out salad for Harmon and Sandra.

"All upset about Jean?"

"She's a pretty unhappy girl."

"I think Jerry plays around too much. Heavy drinker, too."

Betty glanced at him. "I'm going to try and get her to go to church. It would help her a lot."

Herman took a bite of roast. It was going to come to a head. Better that he face it soon—maybe this evening—than to keep postponing it.

"What are we going to do about the Noons?" he asked.

Betty shrugged. "What can we do? Jean went away without a word—I'm terribly worried about her but I'm sure she can take care of herself."

"I mean the man."

Betty shook her head, tilting it toward the children. "What man?" asked Sandra.

"A bad man," said Harmon. "A bad man lives in that house."

"See?" said Betty. "They pick up every word."

"I tried to figure out what to do today—"

"There's really nothing for us to do. Unless he comes back."

"How is he a bad man?" asked Sandra.

"Eat your salad."

"I thought of something, but maybe you won't want me to do it."

"We'd better talk about it later."

"This isn't exactly that, Betty. You know that colored fellow who works for me?"

"Jim Kemp? What about him?"

"He wants to move into Sunrise Hills."

Betty put down her fork. "Oh, that's too bad."

"It isn't fair that they don't have a decent place to live."

"Some of the projects are taking colored buyers—only a certain percentage of them. He might try—"

"He works in Sunrise Hills. He'd like to live here."

"Does he want you to help him?"

"He did. He didn't talk about it at all today."

"Oh. Harmon—finish your salad."

"But I was thinking—he could buy the Noon house."

"Next door? A colored family next door? Herman, I don't know. Wouldn't that hurt property values?"

"I don't see why it should."

"But the other people—it might cause trouble, Herman."

"I know. But maybe it wouldn't. Not as soon as people got to know Kemp. He's a real gentleman."

"But when there are projects that do take colored buyers—"

"Betty, would you accept a Negro family as neighbors?"

"They are sons of Ham," said Sandra. "After the Ark landed—"

"Sandra, drink your milk."

"How do you feel about it, Betty?"

"I don't know. I don't understand why the Noon house—"

"Something happened last night. Maybe it wasn't what Leola said, or maybe it was—"

As Betty warned him with her eyes Sandra asked, "What happened, Daddy?"

"It's about a bad man," said Harmon. "Last night the bad man—"

"You children take your milk into the living room and watch TV."

281

"But I think Noon had better sell out and leave. It's a chance for Kemp to buy direct."

"But could he get a GI loan, Herman? Wouldn't they—?"

"If he can qualify otherwise they couldn't stop him just because he's a Negro."

"I don't know, Herman. It seems like just asking for trouble."

"But Betty, you're the one that's always trying to do good Christian acts—helping people. Wouldn't it be Christian to welcome a Negro family?"

"We have our own family to think about, too."

Sandra came back to the table. "Could I have some more milk?"

Betty poured milk into Sandra's glass.

"What happened last night, Mama?"

"Nothing for you to worry about. Go back in the living room."

As the little girl left Betty watched her. "It's terrible to have something like that happen where the children might find out about it."

"That's why the Noons have to leave."

"I told you she said she'd stick by him—if he comes back."

"I wonder what really happened."

"I think it's exactly the way he told Leola last night. And Jean's too proud to go to anybody—"

"I wonder if she'll tell David?"

"They should both go to their minister, Jean and her husband. This is the time when people need guidance. People shouldn't try to face these things alone. The church—"

"Daddy hardly ever goes to church," said Sandra from the corner of the fireplace.

"You go back and watch TV," said Betty sharply. She turned to Herman but she said nothing. He understood her look without words.

"Herman, can't you see what you're doing to the children's faith?" she said after a few seconds.

A man could not dodge moral decisions, thought Herman. What he should do—if anything—about Troy Noon was both a moral and a practical decision.

Jim Kemp's plea to him involved a moral decision.

The most important moral decision was this one. Religion. He did not believe in the dogmas of his wife's church, the church in which he had been raised. The choice was simple and complete: either he must ignore the church, which meant a deep chasm between him and Betty, and which would affect Sandra and Harmon's attitude toward the church, or he must pretend a faith he did not have.

A man lived by the moral decisions he made. At the end of life the good or bad in it rested on the kind of decisions a man had made on moral issues.

If Troy Noon came back he would face him, tell him to go. What Troy had told Leola, regardless of its truth, was sufficient cause to drive the man away. Herman knew that he was no sword of justice to punish Noon; that feeling had been anger, disgust, and a sickening knowledge that rape was a crime all men might be capable of; some of the anger had been at himself, knowing that he was decent only because he kept the threads that bound the animal within him tight and strong, yet feeling a sense of guilt that the animal existed.

It was not for him to punish Troy Noon; those were decisions for Jean and David.

But it was right that he should drive the man away.

With Jim Kemp the moral decision was not so clear. By driving Noon away he might make a place for Kemp and his family. They would be his close neighbors, his total responsibility would be apparent. Yet where was the moral decision? Feeling part of the collective guilt of all American whites for the cold exclusion of dark Americans and for all of the cruelties, was he only trying to ease this sense of guilt by helping Jim Kemp?

And finally, most important because it affected the lives of the three persons who were everything to him, was the moral decision about the church. He could not postpone it any more.

He was a Christian in the broad meaning; he was not ashamed of his ethics, nor of his faithfulness to his code of ethics. He tried to live by truth, he felt a fellowship for all

283

other men. He tried to look into the dark places of his own being, and to be strong.

Was it also necessary to pretend beliefs he did not have? To pretend to pray when he had long since felt that prayer was only a kind of self-consolation, possibly even self-deception? To attend church, shaking hands with a well-meaning minister, when he believed the minister was self-limited to understand less of the immensity of God than he himself did?

Was it right to pretend with his children, letting them think that the orthodoxies they were taught in Sunday school were all utter truths when he believed them to be a tangled web of ancient histories warped and stained by time, of myths and folklore, of expedients determined by theocratic politics, and even of pagan worships accepted and skillfully altered—as the Christmas tree and the Easter egg?

Would he be honest and decent if he joined with the other churchgoers on Sunday, talking pleasantly after the service, letting it seem as if he, too, were a believer?

But if he was honest, tried to be honest, he might have no family. Betty could not forgive him if he destroyed the faith of her children in her church.

If the world in which they lived crumbled, as it might, if the adult dollhouses of Sunrise Hills were deserted by people hunting only food and survival, if millions of soldiers swept over the Americas and our cities burned, if his children had to live through catastrophe—might not the old religion give them courage and comfort?

Could he deny his children the right to believe as generations of their fathers and mothers had believed?

Could he explain to his children that the whole time of man on the Earth had been to the existence of the Earth as only the last hour of the last day of a year? That the history of man, from the clay tablets and the cave drawings, was only as the last minute of that hour?

Could he explain that the erect, two-legged primate, clever with his opposed thumb, forward-seeking eyes, and omnivorous hunger, was only a presently successful life form on one planet of a minor star in a galaxy of billions of other stars, with billions of other life forms, fantastically different, and

284

that this galaxy was only one of uncounted galaxies in a universe beyond comprehension to that wonderfully curious, searching primate?

The simple, good Jesus somehow dying terribly on a cross so that good people would live in Heaven forever was something children could understand.

The universe that Herman, uneducated but eager, was trying to learn about from magazines, from books, and from his own lonely, searching mind, would not give little children faith or hope.

It was a decision he could not put off. If there were sins, and Herman believed both in sin and in immediate, exact and merciless punishment inherent in all sins, the weak inability to make a decision was a sin.

Harmon came slowly around the fireplace. "Daddy," he said, "that bad man will go to Hell, won't he?"

"If he's bad he'll go to Hell," said Herman. For this little boy Hell would be something like being spanked, only worse; and Heaven would be zoo trips every day, and ice cream, and father and mother would just be little children, too.

For Betty they would be much the same; she could imagine more pain and more pleasure than the little boy, and there was only one other difference—her concept of eternal life for the redeemed linked her, unaware, with all of the mystics, all of the great religions of the world: those who lived would achieve a oneness with God.

Herman, too, believed in a continuing life, a oneness with God. But more humble, actually more worshiping of the immensity of God, he had no need to believe in an eternal continuance of the brief arrangement of metabolism and colloid and nervous system which at this point was Herman Kreitzer.

The little boy was only now outgrowing his philosophy of life which had sustained him through most of his third year—that in time he would be big, his mother and father little. Now he was entering into some awareness of death, which presently had the meaning of night and sleep and being put away, but of course every night and every sleep ended in a fine new day, and things put away were always taken out again, still familiar and unchanged.

Sandra understood something of death, but for her it was only a rather scary door to a kind of Disneyland, where everybody was very nice.

Herman had to admit that his children were happier because of their Sunday school. But as adults, peeling off beliefs slowly as he had done, feeling a little guilty and a little lonely as each belief dried and fell away? Or having it come suddenly, as it did to a lot of kids when they hit their teens and swung scoffing far out the other way, without knowing enough or searching enough to achieve his humble understanding that God was greater than man could know?

Or if, like their mother, they held to the dogmas for the rest of their lives? More content, but he thought of it as the contentment of kine in a barn, believing in only the kindness and power of the farmer.

Man and his animals, he thought obliquely as his mind searched out other meanings to his simile of the cattle and the farmer: the cattle lived, by their millions as a continuing species, only because their grown bodies were useful to man; meat, and milk, and hide, and glands. So the race of cattle continued.

The horse, once loved, once almost a centaur joining with man, once the companion, the living mark of nobility—"cavalier" and "caballero"—was now bred for dog food. Ruthless man, useful himself or he would not survive. Useful for how long?

But the question to him was simple: would he go to church with his family?

He looked across the room to Betty scraping the waste from the plates into the garbage disposal's rotating jaws. He could not hurt her.

Love for his wife: such a complete, fulfilling thing. Man and woman, husband and wife, father and mother, companions, partners, lovers.

He had sixty or seventy years of living; forty years or more would be spent with Betty, God willing. Life had been good for them, as it was for most Americans, but they would not change toward each other if it should be bad.

There would be no other women for him; to want any of

these things that Betty gave to him from another woman, or to offer to another woman any of himself, would be to divide himself, make him less than a whole man, no longer one complete person.

He wasn't much. He would achieve none of the great things he could dream about, he did not have enough education nor any training. He was the manager of a branch store which sold washers and television sets. But as far as he could help it, he was one person, as complete as he knew how to be.

He loved and was loved; Betty and he would—as companions and lovers—try to bring their children into able, healthy maturity. He was humble before God, and yet he had a brave little pride in being a man.

What more could he ask?

"Herman," said Betty, from the window. "He's come back. Troy Noon's come back."

27

DAVID MARTIN walked into the Cinegrill bar of the hotel and slid on a stool. There was one other man, young with close-cropped hair, two stools away.

Twice more he had tried to reach the Monterey call, and twice more to reach his home. There was an edge of worry now; he had to believe that Jean, for some reason, had gone to Monterey and he'd talk to her there.

There could not have been an accident, or something else going suddenly wrong, illness; there would have been a message if there had been any trouble.

The call from Seaman Cowles was a little bothering; it was as if Cowles knew something that David should know and didn't.

He ordered a Martini. There probably wasn't ever a drink as good as the first Martini.

"Hi," said the crop-skulled young man.

"Hello," David said, taking the first cool, other-world taste of his drink.

"You know I died today?" asked the man.

Talkative drunk, thought David. Nuisance.

Shaking his head, the man smiled, "Not drunk yet. Going to be."

"How did you die?" Go along with the joke.

"Slowly. Always thought it would be fast. Bam! And no more."

The barman was listening to the young man too, and glancing at him David realized that he was listening with real interest. Apparently the man had been explaining some of his story earlier.

"I was just telling Don—" gesturing toward the barman— "what a funny feeling it is to be dead."

"That makes sense," David agreed.

"Been happening for some time—never realized it until today."

"Mr. McCabe is a test pilot," said Don, the barman.

"Was," said McCabe.

David reached over to shake hands as the young man offered his; closer he could see that McCabe was thirty or better. The short hair had gray in it. "David Martin," he said. "What happened to kill you? Or is it private?"

McCabe laughed, took a long drink. "I never felt less private in my life than I did today."

David waited until McCabe spoke again. "Usually that's the loneliest place in the world. Flying. You talk to the tower, they talk to you, but man—you're alone. I was alone today, but I damn well wasn't private."

He gestured at his body. "They had wires all over me. Little gadgets taped to my skin. Knew my heartbeat, knew my skin temperature at a dozen different places, measured the sweat at a dozen more places—not even sweat, just if a gland got a little dew on it."

McCabe took another long drink, emptied his glass, motioned to Don for another. "There was a gadget on my helmet that analyzed my breath. Hell, if I'd had a hard-on those jokers in the tower would have known it before I did.

"About fifty gadgets measuring Bill McCabe and all of them telemetering the results to moving charts in that tower. Another few dozen gadgets telemetering plane performance back to the tower. They knew more about my ship than I did, and more about McCabe than I did. Whatever else I was, I sure wasn't private."

Martin was familiar with the over-all process. Telemetering was the transmission of measured and coded information from sensing devices to measuring and recording and computing devices at a distance. In this case from the plane to the control tower.

"You know what told me I was dead? The lieutenant. When they lifted me out of that bird, like taking a baby out in a Caesarian, and when I saw the lieutenant, I knew that I was a dodo."

"You have trouble?"

McCabe shook his head. "No, it was a perfect test. But Bill McCabe didn't have anything to do with it. A buggy whip socket."

He saw the expression on Martin and laughed again. "Old story—first motorcars had sockets for buggy whips on the dashboard. Planes like this one have a socket for the pilot. Same thing."

"What he means is he felt useless," said Don.

"Less than two hundred pounds of McCabe in that bird, more than two tons of monster." McCabe nodded. "A monster made out of wires and gadgets. You know what the two hundred pounds of McCabe does? I turn a switch. Then the two tons of monster tells the jets to get ready, decides when and how to take off, what climb to make, and how to fly. If there was a bogie the monster would find the bastard, recognize him, figure out what the bandit was going to do, and nail out a rocket, using theory of games to decide when. Do you know what the two hundred pounds of McCabe does while all this is going on?"

"What?" David nodded at Don for another Martini.

"I go along. Of course today McCabe's body was busy as hell breathing and sweating and pumping so those brainy sons-of-bitches in the tower could look at the squiggling pens on their charts."

"You still control the plane," said David.

"Yeah, that's what it says in the book. Last year's book. This year's book has a new chapter."

"How do you mean?" David was thinking of the billing department at Coast, of the research division of Verdun, of the finger of God marking out the near vertical upsweep of the curve of man's technological progress. The girls in Coast's billing department would know what McCabe was talking about.

"They call it SCAN. It's part of the monster. The real son-of-a-bitching part. Let's say I decide I want the ship to do something. I put my order into the controls. SCAN checks out my order and decides whether it's a good idea or not. If that collection of gimmicks decides I'm goofing it cancels out my orders. The controls just pay attention to SCAN, not to that weak-minded McCabe. But it took the lieutenant to show me I was really dead."

"Tell me about this lieutenant business—"

"This was a major test. It's a ship I can't even get into by myself. Old Bob Klause, when we were flying for FEAF, used to say they'd never build a ship he couldn't walk away from.

"Well, they sure as hell built one I can't walk to or from. I'm in a suit so damn heavy they lift me by a crane and put me into my ship—my ship? hell, the monster's ship—and I plug in the telemeter cable, turn my switch, and ride. When I come back I don't even have to turn off the switch, the monster takes care of that. If I try to, SCAN checks to see if it's a good idea.

"Now, Don," turning toward the barman, "and you, Martin, understand I'm no wheel. I'm just a test guy. But on a major test like this one you kind of get used to seeing a couple of generals, the shots from the plane company like three or four vice-presidents, and a whole lot of other jokers waiting for you to climb out after the test. They shake hands and are all eager to ask you questions.

"For me today there was one courtesy Air Force lieutenant. All the big numbers were still up in the tower. They didn't have to ask me anything—they already knew a hell of a lot more about that plane and that test than I did. Thanks to telemetering. Do you know there's even a kind of damn TV set in that ship that looks at the ground no matter how dark it is? But do you also know I don't get a chance to look at the picture on the screen? There's a gadget that looks at it and checks it against charts. You see McCabe might goof— but the gadget won't.

"One lousy lieutenant. Man, I knew I was dead as a dodo then."

Martin felt a sadness. McCabe was having a gallows joke. There must have been a time when a fighter plane and its pilot were like a horse and its rider, when a good ship must have seemed almost alive, but when the pilot still was a little god riding it. It must have been fun, once.

"But I'm going to leave a legacy," McCabe continued. "You know what I'm going to do? I'm going to hunt till I find one of these metal brain monsters that's female. Then I'm going to screw it until I knock it up.

"There'll be a bastard—it should weigh somewhere between two hundred pounds and two tons—that'll be half-McCabe and half-monster. My legacy to the world."

He stood up, bowed to David, and walked away, head high.

"Real nice guy," said Don. "A little loaded now."

"He's got a problem." David looked at his half-empty Martini glass.

"I read a story by Ward Moore once," said Don, "about the next war. All of these automatic things, intercontinental missiles and all that. They're very successful—they wipe out all the people—but they don't quite win the war for either side. So they just keep going, with everybody dead, all automatic for year after year until they finally wear out. A very depressing story."

"Human beings are too tough," said David. "We're the toughest thing the world's been able to evolve. We'll keep going."

"Yeah, but where?" asked Don.

A woman's voice on the public address system announced a call for Mr. Martin, Mr. David Martin.

David went to the house phone at the end of the bar. The call was from Monterey and it was Jean.

"David?"

"Jean—I was getting worried—"

"I drove down to Monterey."

"Any special reason?"

"I guess not."

"I wish I was there with you. The house just got too big for you?"

"Something like that, David."

"Jean—I did it."

"What, David?"

"I put it over here. Big success. Verdun'll give me champagne and orchids—"

"Oh good, David. Wonderful."

"Your voice sounds a little odd, Jean. Are you all right?"

"I'm driving to Los Angeles tomorrow, Dave."

292

"Fine. Lonely?"

"Yes."

"I'll get us a pool cabana here at the Roosevelt. This is real good news!"

"I'll be in about five, David. Will you be free then?"

"Soke's coming down—but I'll be free. Hell, I'm a success, junior grade, now."

"I love you, David."

"I love you, Jean. Look—"

"Good night, David."

The phone was dead in his hands.

Something was wrong. Something serious. Jean had something to tell him that she would not tell over the phone.

And why Monterey? It was a place they both liked and they had gone there often on little holidays. But if she had wanted to come to Los Angeles it was an easy one-day drive from Sunrise Hills. And why so suddenly to Los Angeles?

He walked away from the phone and back to the stool at the bar. He wanted to call her back, but he didn't know where to reach her. Sometimes they had stayed at a motel on the Carmel Hill, sometimes at a small hotel on Ocean Avenue in Carmel.

It might not be fair to call her back even if he found her. She had not wanted to talk over the phone.

The strangeness between them that had started over that girl, Leola? How important could that be? Jean had talked about getting a job, and instead she was coming to see him here.

Even his news about his job had not brought much response, and yesterday she had been so intent, so forceful in talking about this opportunity.

Something important and serious had happened.

In Monterey, more than three hundred miles north, Jean came out of the phone booth beneath the stairs at the Mission Inn. She and David had never stopped here, but she had known of it as a small, pleasant place in a building of Monterey's historic period, more than a century ago. It was a quiet place, a place to think.

Her decisions were pretty well made.

All women are vulnerable, she thought. All women, sometimes consciously or unconsciously, become more vulnerable to a special man.

He'll always be a wrong man; it might be this wrongness that makes him special.

For her there had been vulnerability for this man. Not that she had wanted him, nor could there have been real communication ever between them.

Some of the guilt was hers, for being vulnerable. But only she would ever know that. The man didn't; however intuitive his action might have been, he knew only that he was using her to be hurt, to show his hatred for her kind of world.

David would know only that it had been like an act of madness, brutal and irrational.

And she would always know more of herself than she had known before.

Much of her life, now, would depend upon what David did when she told him.

She walked past the dining room of the inn and into the small, dim barroom. A couple sat on stools, two young men were talking at one side. The white-shirted bartender was heavy, balding.

"Scotch, not much soda," she said.

Drinking alone at a bar was something she had never done before; there was no occasion to do so. Maybe, in a sense, she had graduated into another class of women, those who sometimes want to be at a bar, alone, and have a slow, quiet drink. She had never understood before quite why a woman would want to do that.

There was another sense of guilt. David. She'd been selfish in her call, wanting to hear his voice, telling him that she would be there tomorrow. Beyond that she had not wanted to talk.

Now he would worry. There had never been a phone call like that between them before. She had given him no explanations, she hadn't even shown excitement to match his over his job, and she had practically hung up on him.

The only good thing about that call had been telling him,

more deeply than she ever had before, that she loved him and hearing him say the words she needed tonight.

"That'll be sixty cents," said the bartender.

She looked at him in surprise, she had forgotten everything except David. He took the dollar she handed him, rang it up on the register, looked for a moment at the register receipt.

"You're lucky," he said. "You got the red star."

"Red star?"

"It entitles you to another drink, free."

"Oh? Thanks."

The other four customers were looking at her, smiling.

"See," said the woman, "you have to be beautiful to get a red star from Smitty."

That was a friendly thing for a woman to say, thought Jean. She smiled back.

Two drinks, that would be enough. Call David once more, soon. But what could she say? That everything was fine, not to worry? And then tell him tomorrow that his wife had been raped?

She could tell him that something important had happened, that they would have to face it tomorrow, but not to worry. Not to worry? That would be worse than it was now.

Jean realized that she was being womanly, motherly, trying to protect David from a bad night. And there was no good way to do it.

The second drink of Scotch seemed to ease her and she knew that she didn't want any more. She could overhear the conversations between the young men—about other people on the local newspaper they both apparently worked on—and the couple—about the work they intended to do on their garden the next weekend—with Smitty joining in both conversations from time to time.

There was nothing she could do to make it easier for David tonight. It was better that in a way he was prepared for tomorrow.

"Thank you for the red star," she said to Smitty, and walked out to the street. There were dark evening clouds over the tall trees on the hills above Monterey, and she could feel the coolness of the bay.

This was better than having gone directly to David; staying alone at Sunrise Hills would have been impossible.

Treat it like a bad accident that had happened to her, nothing more.

Nothing more? And if she were pregnant?

Oh, God, she thought, no wonder women are strong.

Jean walked for more than an hour. To the Wharf, with the big seiners floating, pale against the dark water of the bay; out along the Wharf, between the clutter of buildings over the softly slapping water.

People would glance at her because she was alone but she felt free, among unknown friends, and it was different from Sunrise Hills. This was old, women had faced worse problems than hers in these old houses above the bay, faced them and still found life good, if they were that kind of woman.

For David there had been a solution. The clumsiness of Saturday night was important, more important than he had known, he thought now. Jean had decided not to let a string of days and nights intervene between a bad time and the time they were together again. That was why she was coming to Los Angeles, and that was the explanation for the oddly brief phone call. The meaningful words had been those of their love for each other.

This was a comforting explanation. Jean wanted to be with him. And, disquieting, was the knowing that he faced directly the problem of his body and Jean's. Words would not help much in this.

She was female, rich, giving, demanding. He was the male who failed in both answers to her: he had not given her a baby; he was not the complete, matching physical partner for her. Excuses for these two failures are understood by the woman to be excuses.

Tomorrow night they would be in one of the casual pleasure rooms, so carefully designed to be elegant and comfortable, fronting on the big pool wrapped in the open center of the hotel.

There would be talk and food, maybe a drink or two. And then the fine clothes would come away from her fine body.

And he would be painfully aware of himself trying consciously and thereby badly to be a stallion, always aware of himself at the time she knew only that she was female.

He wanted to be a man with red-blue skin on his jaws, and blue-black hair tight curled on his body, thinking only of his own sure power and strength, or the cruel joy of having the woman.

28

Troy Noon parked his car and went to the door of his house.

If she was home he'd have it out with her. If she wasn't he'd pack a bag and leave.

She had heard the car, and the door opened as he came up to it. He waited for her to speak.

"I'm glad you came back, Troy," she said.

"Where'd you go?"

"To Mrs. Kreitzer's."

He closed the door behind them.

"I've been working on the house, getting it clean."

He looked around. "It looks pretty good."

Both of them were silent and he went to a chair, sat down.

"Anything happen, Leola?"

"She went away. I don't know where."

"Yeah."

"What are we going to do, Troy?"

"What do you want to do?"

"Stick with you."

He wanted to get up, take her in his arms. But he looked away. "Things piled up on me yesterday. I lost my head."

"We can't stay around here, Troy. We'll have to go someplace else."

"I'm not so crazy about this place."

"I liked it real well, Troy."

"If you want to stay, we'll stay. I'm not afraid of anybody."

"Was it—was it her fault, Troy?"

He didn't answer, lit a cigarette, stood up again.

"Or were you—"

"Was I what?"

"Were you mad at me? Is that why?"

"I just lost my head. I don't belong with these kind of people. They live too soft—all rotten sweet."

"Did you work today, Troy?"

"The station had to be run, didn't it? I went there."

Well, he hadn't lost his job, anyway, he thought. The rich bitches had phoned in all right, though. The supervisor told him about it. But his record was too good, they wouldn't fire him because of a phone call.

Fine job. The money was all right but he needed something more—be in the Army again, something like that. But not this droop-drawered peacetime army.

"I don't know what I want to do."

Leola was a good kid; maybe just too young, foolish. But she'd lied to him yesterday; he'd never forget that.

"Yeah, sure."

"Mrs. Kreitzer was awful nice to me."

"I suppose you told her everything?"

Leola began to cry. "I didn't know what to do—"

"So now everybody knows about it."

"I was so scared and upset—"

"I thought you were gone for good."

"I started to go, Troy—"

"Leola, I'm thinking of going back to Tennessee."

"Wherever you want, Troy."

"I don't belong with these people, not in this kind of a house. Nothing solid or real—not the people, not the houses. Nothing."

"They get along pretty good. Mostly they're nice people—"

"Soft, rotten. Raising soft, rotten kids. They just live for more pleasure all the time. They don't know how to work hard, they just want to live fancy. One of these days they're going to find out—"

"Don't hate them, Troy."

"Sure I hate them. You know who else hates them? Hates these soft, rotten, fancy Americans? A couple of billion people in the rest of the world who goddamn well have to work hard for a crust of bread. The Communists are just getting ready, planning and building up, and then they'll hit us hard.

"Somebody hits us hard and these soft, rotten people are going to fold up. Their spoiled kids won't fight, they'll expect somebody else to do their fighting. Automatic rockets, maybe.

"And there aren't enough guys like me left."

"If you want to go to Tennessee—"

"I want to be with real people again. People with hard hands and straight backs. People that live for work and not fancy pleasure."

She looked at him. Poor Troy, she thought. He'd go through his whole life angry because other people weren't the way he wanted them to be.

"Do you want me to start packing, Troy?" She wanted to go away, too. Away from Jean Martin, away from Sunrise Hills.

"All we've got to pack is our clothes. The rest of the stuff doesn't even belong to us. Out here nobody ever really owns anything. The people that owe the most even look down on the folks that don't owe as much."

"When would you want to leave?"

"The sooner the better."

The door chimes sounded and Troy whirled around. He stood tense, arms a little out from his sides, his eyes narrowed, as Leola went to the door.

As she opened it he could see Herman Kreitzer standing outside. Troy walked up to him as Herman entered, and Leola stood at the side of her husband.

"What do you want?" asked Troy.

"I've got a man that wants to buy your house."

"What makes you think I'm selling?"

"You're going to sell."

"Why?"

"What happened last night is none of my business, directly," said Herman. "But you're moving out."

"You fixing to make me?"

"Yes."

Herman wished that he was still the Sergeant Kreitzer of years ago, hard-muscled and confident. If it came to a fight with Noon it would be a rough go, but if it had to come to a fight he'd try it.

"Start trying," said Troy. Leola threw her arms around him and he started to push her away.

300

"We're going. You don't have to come here," she said to Herman.

"Yeah—but he can't make me go. I'd stay here and rot first."

"That's all right," said Herman. "Do you want to work out a deal with this man tomorrow?"

"Why are you sticking your yap in?"

"The man's a friend of mine."

"Who is he?"

"Jim Kemp. He works for me. He's a Negro."

Troy looked at him as if Herman were playing a joke on him.

"A nigger?"

"He's got dark skin."

"You want me to sell out to a nigger?" Troy turned to Leola and then smiled. "Sure I'll sell to him. There's nothing I'd rather do for you folks around here."

Herman looked at him without expression. "I'll call him tonight. You two can work out the deal tomorrow."

Noon shook his head. "I'm not sitting down at a table with a nigger."

Herman wanted to hit the man in the face, knock him down. "If you want to get your money, you'll have to."

"Yeah. And maybe it's worth it to put a nigger next to you people in Sunrise Hills. I'll bet he's a nigger with a college education."

"He's a good man," said Herman. "A real good man."

"Yeah. Bring him around tomorrow morning. We're going to get away from this lousy state tomorrow. Leave it all to the fairies and the phonies and the whores and the nigger-lovers."

Herman didn't answer him. He turned and walked out. Troy watched him go. It was hard to figure. He thought Kreitzer was a pretty good guy, and he'd been kind of ashamed to look him in the eye when he came in—a guy that forces a woman hasn't got much to be proud of—and Kreitzer turned out to be a nigger-lover. Low and dirty enough to bring a nigger family in to live next to his own kids.

Betty was waiting beside the door when Herman came in.

"Was there any trouble?" she asked.

"He was a little bit nasty. But he agreed. I'm going to call Kemp."

"Herman—don't you think you ought to ask the Flaggs, and maybe the Martins, if they come back, before you go ahead with this?"

"You know what Jerry Flagg would say, Betty."

"It'll cause trouble."

"I can't pretend to believe in things and then be afraid to live by them, Betty."

"But why look for trouble, Herman?"

"I hope it's a kind of courage, Betty. By the way—I made up my mind about something else, too."

"More foolish courage?"

"I'm going to church from now on."

Betty's face seemed to glow, and she put her arms around him. "You'll feel a lot better for doing it, Herman. It's the best thing you could ever do."

"Sure, Betty."

"It'll make so much difference to Sandra and Harmon. They've been worried about you. Christ is a very real and wonderful person to them. And He will be to you again, Herman."

It could be honest, thought Herman. The words of Jesus were words that he believed; being part of the church was important to the three people he loved; and as the children grew older they would make their own judgments, find their own fabrics of faith.

But he wondered if some of the violent, cruel hatred the adolescents of these times had for the adult world was because of the series of disillusionments they endured as adolescents, coming—for many of them—to a point where they had no faith in anything, not in law nor custom nor ideals nor of being useful, because growing up had meant finding so much was false, so much was hypocrisy in the adults they had once loved and respected.

"Sunday I'll make friends with the pastor again," said Herman going to the phone. He had Kemp's home number in his pocket notebook.

"Herman—I feel better about your going to church than

anything that could happen. And Herman—about this colored family, I'll do everything I can to make them feel welcome."

She went toward the kitchen. "But remember—it was your idea."

Herman put the call through and heard Jim Kemp's voice. "Jim? This is Herman Kreitzer."

"Yes, Mr. Kreitzer."

"I think maybe you can get a house here in Sunrise Hills."

"Oh." Jim Kemp looked up at his wife, covered the mouthpiece of the phone. "It's Kreitzer. He thinks he can get us a house."

His wife shook her head. "We talked it out last night," she said. "We've made a choice, Jim."

Kemp sighed softly, spoke into the phone. "Thanks, Mr. Kreitzer, but we've been thinking it over. We're proud of being Negro and we've decided we'd rather stay with our own people."

"It's the house next to mine, Jim. A nice place."

"I'm sure it is, Mr. Kreitzer. But my wife and I want our children to be proud of being Negro, too. We might get to feeling too white in Sunrise Hills. My people aren't out of trouble yet—and I'm not deserting them."

"You'd have to make up your mind by tomorrow morning, Jim."

"Thanks, but it's made up, Mr. Kreitzer."

"Okay, Jim. See you in the morning."

"Good night—and thanks anyway, Herm."

"'Night, Jim."

Kemp put the phone down. "He's a real man—that guy," he said.

"But we made the right decision, Jim. What was that?"

There was a crash of glass outside, a shrill scream. Kemp went to the window and looked out.

"Looks like a couple of gangs of kids."

"Must be the Black Princes—they run all the kids in this block. Don't mess with them, Jim, they're mean—"

"They're fooling around next to the car. I'll run them off."

He went to the door and stepped outside. Two girls, about fifteen, were facing each other. Behind each girl was a group of boys and girls, from twelve to seventeen in age. Both girls had naked switch knives, pointing toward each other.

"Dirty, filthy, mother-lovin' whore—" said the one girl in a monotone rhythm.

"I'm goin' cut your fat tits off and feed 'em to my mother-lovin' dog—" screamed the other.

"Hey you," yelled Kemp. "Break it up."

"Ooh, hear the man," said a gangling fourteen-year-old.

"Hear that old daddy-oh—" yelled another.

"Mother-lovin' daddy-oh!"

They were all facing him now.

"Break it up. Get moving," said Kemp, keeping his voice low and hard.

"Fuck you."

"You know who this mother-lover is? He works in a white store. Just goes with white people. Oh, this mother-lover's a real one."

"Got his nose in white man's ass."

"Bring him down—"

Hands reached for Kemp, the hands of children. By the time his wife reached the police and the patrol cars screamed in they had smashed Jim Kemp's face in with bicycle chains, and he had been slashed more than a dozen times by knives.

Later, after the police were gone, they came back and smashed the front windows of Jim Kemp's home.

The police did not take him to a hospital; they gave him first aid and left him at his house. He was in bed when the windows were smashed.

It was hard to talk through his broken face.

"They've got to be like that," he said.

29

TUESDAY WAS BEAUTIFUL in Sunrise Hills. Five thousand roofs warmed under the sun, and dew was bright on the flowers that grew around nearly all the five thousand.

Traffic was heavy, as always, on the Bayshore road. Jerry Flagg drove to his first day at his new job with his usual hang-over beating at his eyes. Last night had been a flop; long-legs gone away, the Leola babe's raping old man back home, Isbel and he had got drunk together, had the usual night. So he felt crumby the usual way. And the kid was pure devil at breakfast.

But it was still a hell of a good world. He had the kind of job he wanted—and he was going to move cars until Lucky Joe's eyes popped out. Markham was in bad trouble, there might be some distress merchandise he could move for a fast buck through Joe after Markham was really hurting.

And as for Jean Martin. He'd get her some day soon. He knew she could be had, and he was just the patient, soft-talking, fast-moving-in son-of-a-bitch that could get her now.

Everything was really wonderful—except for the hang-over.

Going south the Bayshore became a highway again instead of a clogged sewer of cars morning-bound for San Francisco. Far south it became the broad fast road of 101 on the flat-lands of the Salinas valley. There Jean Martin drove, toward her husband.

Sunday night was no longer real to her; it was something that almost could not have happened.

In Los Angeles David Martin finished breakfast at the hotel and called the contract man in the engineering department at Coast.

At the Sunrise Hills shopping center Herman Kreitzer learned that Jim Kemp was ill, his wife phoning. He told her to tell Jim not to worry about a thing.

Leola Noon finished packing while Troy went down and

quit his job, getting the pay due him. Kreitzer had called. The nigger wasn't going to buy the house so Troy was just going to leave it. Let the Sunrise Hills company take the damned thing back, let the furniture and appliance people come and get their crap. He was through. He and his wife were going back to Tennessee. Maybe a cop didn't have to be a college graduate back there.

In a plane out of San Francisco and due in at Los Angeles before ten that morning, Sokolik sat and worried. He was gray-faced, his mouth tight and dry.

He called David Martin at the hotel as soon as his plane landed, and David was waiting for him in the lobby of the hotel when the airport bus reached the Roosevelt forty minutes later.

"Dave," he said, forgetting to shake hands. "Bill Verdun is coming down here this afternoon. I want you to do something for me."

"Sure, Soke. What?"

"Verdun is going to ask you about your phone call yesterday. Cowles got hold of me last night—you know he's never liked me—"

"I don't understand, Soke—"

"I want you to tell Verdun that you called and asked me for help yesterday."

"Asked you for help?"

"It means my job, Dave. You've got to do it."

"Yes, but I don't read you at all, Soke—"

"What I want you to do is tell Verdun this afternoon that when you called me yesterday you told me that you were in trouble and you needed me to come down and straighten it out."

"Is that what you told Verdun?"

"Yes."

"Why?"

And this was the way it went, David thought. The kind of thing Jean had talked about Sunday. Sokolik had tried to pull a fast one—and had been caught. A fast one to make him look bigger, to make Martin look smaller.

Jungle. Different kind of teeth and claws, different way to

306

use poison, but exactly the same purpose as in the jungle. Kill and feed, grow strong on what you killed. Be sly and wary, hiding in the shadows until you could kill safely so you could feed and grow strong.

"Let's say I misunderstood you, Dave."

"It was simple enough. Wise agreed to exactly the pilot plant projects set up for Coast."

"David—I've helped you a lot. Haven't I always helped you?"

And this was true. Sokolik had been a good boss; he had brought David along; he had looked for ability in Martin and when he found it he developed it. A good boss. A friend.

"Yes, Soke, you have."

"Now I need help. I made a mistake—but you can make it right by just saying half a dozen words."

"Cowles called me last night."

"I know. But if you and I both say the same things today— Cowles is no engineer, Dave. He's just a rich boy who married a rich girl. You can still set it right."

"But why did you tell Verdun that, Soke? It's not like you."

Tell this young fellow about the greasy dishes you washed so you could get a degree? Tell him about the ICS courses? Tell him how you knew you were slipping behind, that you were getting out of date, obsolete? That you were getting frightened? You'd make mistakes and they'd look at you, Verdun and Fry and Cowles. How could you tell this kid, just started on the way up, that if you thought Wise would have been that easy you'd never have sent him? That he'd been sent as a whipping boy?

"I don't know why I did it, Dave. But I need you. I need you real bad, Dave. It's my job if you don't stick with me."

He looked into Martin's eyes, put a hand on Martin's arm.

"You've got loyalty, Dave. What I'm asking won't hurt you —and it means everything to me. Remember when you made mistakes sometimes? I took the responsibility for them. You know I did."

This was true, thought David.

"You going to back me up, Dave?" Soke's voice started thin, ending with firmness and confidence.

"No," said David Martin.

Sokolik's fingers tightened on his arm. "You can't mean that."

"I'm going to tell Verdun that I got Wise's approval by myself yesterday."

"You think that'll get you my job? Is that what you think?"

"I don't care about your job."

Sokolik's face seemed to break. "Dave, Dave—I know I was wrong, but you can't turn on me like this—"

He could not help this man, thought David. He would like to help him, put his hand out and tell him that everything could be straightened out. But it wouldn't help, not really, in the end. If David persuaded Bill Verdun and Seaman Cowles that Sokolik had misunderstood, that he was guilty of nothing more than misunderstanding, it would not really help. Sokolik would know the truth, Martin would know the truth, and Sokolik would hate him, must in time try to destroy him.

The best thing he could do for both of them was to stay with the truth now. Help a weak man in his weakness and you earn an enemy.

"I'm sorry," said David.

Sokolik wet his lips, and turned away. David Martin never saw him again.

In the afternoon Bill Verdun came and by then the memorandum on the contracts was ready.

"Let's go into the bar and have something cool, Dave," Verdun said, glancing through the memorandum. "I've got a lot to talk about with you."

He waited until they were half through with a couple of Tom Collinses before he began.

"Sokolik is resigning," he started abruptly. "You know why?"

"I think so. He didn't tell you the Coast deal was in the clear yesterday."

"He lied. Deliberately lied."

David waited.

"Lying would be enough," Verdun continued. "The only reason a person ever lies is because he's afraid of the truth. But this lie showed that Sokolik had lost all confidence in himself. We can't have an executive who's a hollow shell of a man. You're taking over as head of projects."

"Yes."

"If you work out—in a year you can have the vice-presidency that goes with the job. But right now, Martin, you're going to feel like a new boy at school on the first day. Being head of project engineering is a hell of a different job than being a good man in the projects department. A hell of a different job."

"I'll try."

"Stay here for this week, get the Coast pilot rolling. Then I'll help you break in on your new responsibilities." Verdun twisted his tall glass. "You'll start at ten a year. Stick with the job, show you're capable and it'll be twenty with the vice-presidency. Okay?"

"Fine."

Verdun didn't talk about the job or Sokolik again, but he seemed to want to stay. They had another Collins round, and then Verdun had some Jack Daniels while Martin sat with an empty glass.

"There's another thing . . ." Verdun shifted in his chair as if it were uncomfortable. "You're sort of in the family now—and you've got a right to know about the family troubles."

"Troubles?"

"Verdun Labs is my company. I built it and I run it."

"Yes." When Verdun was talking as he did now he wanted a listener, not words.

"Seaman Cowles would like to take over the company."

Martin made no comment.

"He's smooth about it, and he's going about it the smart way. There's no friction between us yet—but someday there'll be a showdown. When that happens—if you're a vice-president, Martin, I want you to stand on my side. That's all for now on that, except to point out that Cowles was out to get Sokolik. The first time Sokolik slipped, Cowles nailed him.

"Sooner or later he's going to find out whether you'd be with him in a showdown against me. If he decides you'd be against him—he'll be out to get you, too. Clear?"

Clear. The jungle. He wondered if Jean had thought of the cost to the man as he fights to be top animal in the jungle.

"I understand," he said.

Verdun stood up, put a bill on the table. "Okay, Dave. Good luck!" They shook hands and Verdun walked away.

Head of projects engineering. David began to think of his department. His friends would change, now, in the way they treated him; he wasn't Dave Martin, he was the boss.

There were a couple of spots in the department that needed working over; he had ideas on the print techniques, too. And there was the whole work flow system—he'd always thought that could be improved. But maybe Sokolik had reasons for doing it this way.

Don't go fast, play it cool—

He really had something to tell Jean now.

He waited in the lobby, reading a copy of *Fortnight*. A few minutes after four he was paged. Answering at a house phone he was given the call—Jean.

"David?" Her voice was different.

"Hi, darling. Where are you?"

"Way out on Ventura. I should be there in half an hour."

"I've got our room—you'll like it. Right on the pool."

"In half an hour, David. I love you."

The phone clicked off. He felt tension; it would be hard to wait the half hour or so. So much to tell her. Only two days ago she had lectured him on success; since then he had called a hundred-thousand-dollar-a-year man a coward, and the man had backed down; he had refused to weaken for Sokolik's pleading, and now he was head of project engineering with a vice-presidency only a year away.

And he had been shown the jungle. Somewhere ahead would be Seaman Cowles, the family money and his wife's money; Seaman's ambition to control Verdun Laboratories.

Trouble in the family, Bill Verdun had called it.

Sometime in the months ahead he would come to the point of decision—align with Bill Verdun and Fry when Seaman Cowles called for a showdown, or maybe find that he would join with Cowles.

A man in the jungle had to make his decisions at the time

for decisions, not before. That was the way to the kind of success his wife wanted. That he wanted, too, having tasted it.

He couldn't remember what he was reading in the magazine, and then—the half hour stretched out and past—she was there, walking toward him from the garage corridor, a bellman carrying her bag behind her.

She ran to him, her arms around him, her face against his coat. For a moment he held her, and she was looking up at him, her eyes wet with tears.

David took her hand, motioned to the bellman to follow them. He led her out, around the edge of the shimmering blue pool to their apartment.

The bellman was gone, the door closed, and she held him, her face buried again in his coat. Then she pulled away, turned and walked to the window. As he came toward her she held up her hand as if to stop him.

"David—"

"I've got terrific news for you, darling."

He saw her eyes and stopped.

There was no need for a question; he waited until she was ready to tell him.

"David—" she began again. It was impossibly difficult to speak.

He put his arms around her and she fought to keep from hiding her face as she wanted to do.

"Troy Noon." She said the two syllables and communication was complete; David knew.

"When?" It was spoken with pain, almost a whisper, and his arms were rigid, like metal arms.

"Sunday." Now she could hide her face.

He took her hand, walked toward the door, bringing her with him. He walked rapidly, holding her hand still, as they went around the pool into the garage.

She said nothing as the car was brought to them, nothing until David was driving at sixty-five on the northbound freeway.

"You're going home, David?"

"I'm going to find him."

She wet her lips, put her hand on his.

He asked his first question. "Did he hurt you?"

"A little. Not much."

They were a hundred miles north before he spoke again. "Why did it happen, Jean?"

"I don't know. He came in. He was angry—it was only a few seconds before—" she tried to find some word to use, found none—"before it happened."

He did not answer.

"You wonder why I didn't call you right away?"

"I guess you didn't know what to do, Jean."

"I didn't know who I was. I've spent two days trying to find out."

"Who are you, Jean?"

"Not much. Not as much as I thought I was."

"I love you, Jean."

"I've found out how much I love you, David. Let me tell you what I know about myself."

He waited, driving steadily at seventy-five, his eyes searching half a mile ahead.

"Selfish. Not even knowing I was selfish. The same kind of selfishness that Jerry Flagg has—I lived for the satisfaction of my appetites."

"Not like Flagg," he said.

"Exactly the same—only smoother, nicer, refined—but I've taken only pleasures, and that's all I've ever really given."

"You are all I ever want."

"A female Jerry Flagg—and I thought I was a smarter, fancier Betty Kreitzer. She gives love, real love, and she gives her complete self to those she loves."

"You, too, Jean. You do that."

"No. I never did. But I thought I did."

They were silent again.

North of Salinas, hours later, he asked the only question that mattered.

"What's ahead for us, Jean?"

"If you want to—you're going to watch a woman grow up, David."

He didn't have to answer, his hand was on hers.

Sunrise Hills was dark when they turned off the Bayshore. David drove through the curving streets at fifty.

"David—" She was going to say that Troy Noon was very strong, and stopped herself in time.

Troy came out of his house seconds after he heard the squeal of the tires in his driveway. As he opened the door he saw David coming toward him. Leola was behind him, her hands pulling at Troy's arms and he broke loose from her, shoving her back with a push from his left hand.

David was at him and Troy came in with both fists low, his upper arms close to his body. The son-of-a-bitch had a right to try—but the muscles over his guts and heart would be soft. Troy put his left in fast, felt the toughness of David's stomach leather-hard against his fist. Troy rolled his head in taking Martin's right lead, and he brought up his knee.

Martin turned his body, his thigh and hip turning Noon's knee away and Troy went for his eyes with both thumbs. The thumbs dug into the corners.

Jean screamed. Troy couldn't see her—he saw only David's face bending back as he tried to hook his thumbs under the eyeballs, and then he was going back, the first eruption of pain coming up from his groin, making his legs and spine soft.

Son-of-a-bitch got me, he thought. Forgot he could knee too. Have to hold on for a moment, pull him down.

David hit Troy in the face, his knuckles breaking the small bones of nose and cheek, bending back and tearing loose Troy's front teeth.

Troy felt rage red from the pain and he put his right fist into Martin's ribs over the heart, felt them give. But he couldn't see, couldn't find Martin. His eyes were dark and thickly wet from blood.

He charged and their bodies hit.

Tough son-of-a-bitch—thought stopped as his head snapped back—and now he was on the ground. He rolled as Martin's heel smashed down, hitting his shoulder but not his face.

Troy pushed himself up with his legs and butted Martin in the face with the top of his head, knocking David back.

313

Now to find those broken ribs, kill the son-of-a-bitch, stomp him to death.

He hit Martin high over the heart, heard him explode air from his lungs through his mouth. Troy used the back of his left hand to rub at the blood in his eyes.

Martin's knee came up, dead on target this time, and Troy bent over, holding himself with his open hands pressing against the torment, not even feeling Martin's hands beating in his face before he fell.

Got to be like this. Right. Okay. Make it right, he thought, and then he felt the hard heel ripping his gut muscles as David Martin stomped him. Somebody was yelling above him and then Leola was bending over him.

He tried to talk to her, tasting the blood bubbles as the words were lost in his broken mouth. "It's all right now." He tried to say that and got to his knees and she helped him get to his feet and he was falling again and she held him. He wouldn't be able to drive tonight, she'd have to. He was lucky to have her.

Herman put his arm around David's shoulder, but David looked at him, tried to smile, and took Jean by her hand. Herman watched them as they crossed toward their home.

Jerry Flagg looked at Herman, then turned away. His palms were wet and cold and he was sick.

God, am I lucky, he thought. He needed a drink, a big one.

At his doorway Herman left them, and David took his wife into their home.